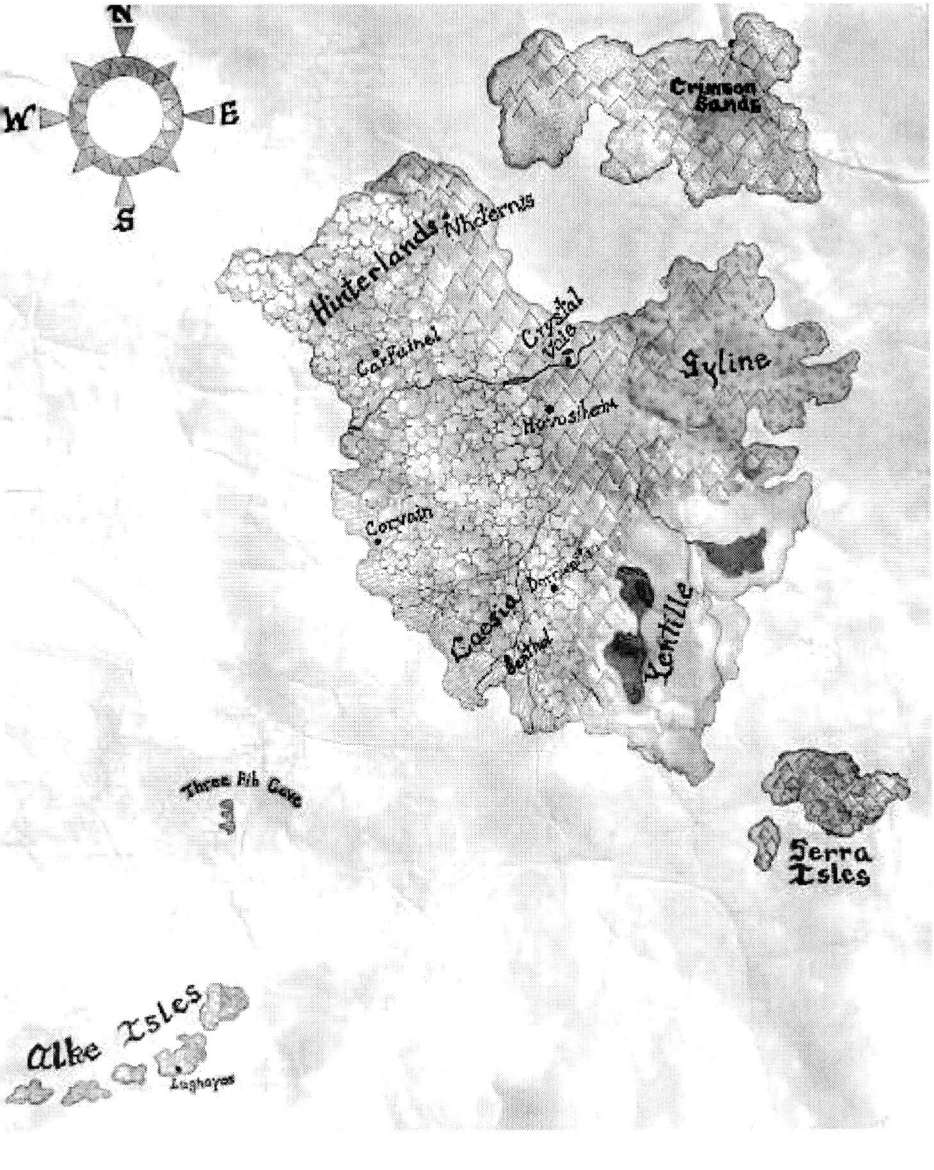
N
W
E
S
Crimson Sands
Hinterlands
Nhdernis
Crystal Vale
Carfainel
Syline
Corvain
Caesia
Kentille
Serra Isles
Alke Isles

Nightingale

Melissa Mickelsen

HADLEY
RILLE
BOOKS

NIGHTINGALE

Cover art © by Baranyai Gábor baranyai.deviantart.com

Map © by Patricia D'Angelo dangelo.elfwood.com

Trade Paperback ISBN-13 978-0-9849670-0-1

Edited by Kim Vandervort

Published by
Hadley Rille Books
Eric T. Reynolds, Editor/Publisher
PO Box 25466
Overland Park, KS 66225
USA
www.hadleyrillebooks.com
contact@hadleyrillebooks.com

To everyone who encouraged, prodded, demanded,
and suggested, this is for you.

Prologue

THE MAN THREW THE SMALL BLOOD-SOAKED CORPSE into the marsh and snarled. He watched the body float in the tea-brown water, bending whipgrass under its slight weight. The air was silent. Behind him, his men were still, voices locked tight within their chests. The birds had vanished and the frogs were hidden in the mud and under loose-packed weeds. The man turned, his leather gloves stained with filth and salt from the brackish waters of the bog.

"Fool," he snapped in rage. "All this time spent hunting and you've killed it!" The man lashed out, catching the closest follower in the face with his fist. The bands of metal on his knuckles broke the flesh on the cowering man's lips and cheek, sending blood spurting red onto the black soil of the bank.

"Sorry, sir!" the fallen man gasped. "It was an accident, I swear." He raised his mud-flecked hands to his face in supplication.

"Do you know," the lord said, "how much effort it takes to find these places? Do you know how many years I've dedicated to this task? Do you how often that worthless General Talros thwarts the raids?" The man brushed the blood from his knuckles, the lines in his face set deep. "An accident," he repeated.

The downed man quavered, well aware of the usual consequences of his master's wrath. The death had been an accident, in truth. The bonds slipped when the small thing fought and the knots pulled too tightly in the waterlogged rope around the creature's neck. In the struggle, the knife had slipped, cutting flesh instead of cord. The great vein in the slender throat had severed and the blood had rushed forth. The heart had stopped in moments.

The broad-shouldered leader lifted his head, clenching his fists in suppressed rage. He looked around him at the endless marsh and the piled, already stinking bodies. The hot sun and the humid air were not pleasant to the deceased. "Burn the bodies," the commander sneered. "That one as well," he continued, pointing at the small, floating corpse in the bog. He strode past the man, ignoring him for the moment, and went to the captives, kneeling and bound, between his captains.

He eyed them, wondering. They were all stiff-necked, the master thought. Too proud for their own good. Two males, black-haired and pale-skinned, eyed him hatefully. No females, never any females. They always died too swiftly. The lord clenched his teeth. His task would be so much easier if he could take a alive. Twice he had succeeded, but the does had killed themselves soon after, not willing to become a part of his great scheme. It was impossible to keep them alive if they did not desire it. Even the captured males would fade too swiftly, refusing to cater to his whims. These wilting people were so eager to cross the Plains, it seemed.

The lord knew of a stone—a myth, in truth—that might bind these creatures to his will, but he had not yet discovered it. His books had yielded little and the library only slightly more. Nothing solid, no real facts. Only stories. Still he studied, even late into the night. One day, he vowed, he would know. He would gain his weapon. He would achieve his dream.

He had obtained maps, and that was a start. He could continue the hunt and find the creature that eluded him. Surely where there was one there were more. The sullen leader turned to glare at the fool who had killed his mark. The hunt would have been over by now if not for him. He snarled, his heart aflame. The commander's head snapped up. To the captains, he said, flicking his fingers at the prisoners, "Kill them swiftly and put them in the flames." The men nodded while the captives spit unrecognizable insults in their lilting language and struggled at the ropes. They were of no use to him. They would refuse the breeding and die anyway. Why delay their fate?

The master turned away. "Varlo," he said, and the kneeling fool shuddered at the sound of his name.

"Yes, sir?" he asked cautiously.

"That was a priceless creature. Perhaps the only one in the world. Did you think of that?"

"No, sir," the man said quietly. "It was a demon, sir."

"A demon I desired, Varlo. And you've killed it."

"An accident," Varlo said again, clenching his scarred fingers in the mud.

The lord shook his head. "One I will not forgive," he said, and flicked his fingers.

The sword fell, taking Varlo's head half off his body before the man fully realized what was happening. Blood spattered from the slashed neck baring bone and wet, red muscle under the hot midsummer sun. The body quivered, twitched, and fell to its side in the moist, dark soil, the fluttering fingers scraping grazes in the dirt. The booted feet drummed before falling still, showing mud on the heels like dark plaster.

"We are done here," the master called to the rest of his men, "as soon as this corpse joins the rest."

"Yes, sir," they cried, scrambling to haul Varlo's body to the dancing flames. The bonfire was massive, vomiting oily black smoke that blanketed the sky. The air smelled of ash, charred meat, and burning hair, a nauseating stench that voided the stomachs of less-hardened men. The steel-bellied leader watched the flames eat the bodies of the anthelai. Behind the pyre sat the ruins of their village, splintered and broken. Its inhabitants were vanquished. Soon, the twisted platforms would be torched so that nothing but charcoal remained. The lord smiled.

Now there was one less place for such creatures to hide.

Chapter 1

PRIESTS TOLD STORIES IN CARFUINEL, by fireside and under moonlight and in the depths of the wood. Colorful, vibrant stories filled with courage, fortitude and deception, darkness, fright and bravery. I cannot recall the tales verbatim anymore; I have spent too many years avoiding memories of my childhood. I do remember, however, that my father told tales to me as I fell asleep at night. My favorite was the legend of Brandin the Thief, an anthela or *cardea*, according to whoever told the tale—turned brigand in the highlands of the northeast. He was said to have a dagger with three interwoven blades of the purest gold. Instead of killing men, the dagger put them into a deep slumber at the merest touch. Brandin, apparently invulnerable to its contact, was then able to pick apart the unfortunate victims' possessions at his leisure. Sometimes he gave the valuables to people who needed them, while other times he left his victims' coffers intact, leaving only his mark as a lesson to those who would venture without fear into his territory.

Brandin was a careful, cautious thief. At seven years of age, I often wondered why he did not merely rush in and tap the travelers with the dagger instead of stalking them for days at a time. My father explained to me time and time again the usual need for stealth. "It is wise to be cautious," he pronounced, "as you may never know if the thing you hunt is stronger, faster or more agile. Would you challenge a bear face to face, little one, or would you keep your distance until it left the berry patch?"

"I would wait," I answered. "A bear would eat me!"

"Indeed, it might," my father answered. "You must always be careful. That is why you must learn to defend yourself. Tomorrow, you will learn to use a dagger."

I remembered pausing for a long moment, feeling my heart pound in my thin chest. I had always wanted to learn to use a weapon. My father excelled with the bow and shortsword, and I idolized him. If he used weapons so skillfully, then I wanted to do that as well. Even my mother, whom I had never seen kill anything, practiced with a dagger occasionally. My young friends in the anthehome, of my size and mentality if not my age, often carried small daggers on their belts. I had wanted one for some time, and now it seemed as if my dream would come true.

Still, haltingly, I said, "Mother has said I am too young for a dagger. She will be angry."

"Do not worry about your mother, *Sa'tiul*. She has given her assent."

"Truly?" I could not keep the smile off my face.

"Yes, truly," my father answered, grinning down at me. He ruffled my hair, and I could see him looking at my ears. An odd look came over his face, one I could not comprehend. All I knew was that it both frightened and saddened me. "It will be good for you to learn to defend yourself and I wanted you to learn as soon as you are able."

"I am able now, *Senou*. I promise!"

"I know you are, little one. I have seen you run through the trees as if you were one of the barking squirrels, and I have seen you tickle fish from the water. You learn swiftly and with little instruction. That is good, indeed."

"Could I learn to use a bow, too? I want to go hunting with you."

My father laughed, a deep chuckle, comforting in its familiarity. "Later, child. That will come later."

He kissed my brow and left me alone in the darkened corner of the *tarsul*. I snuggled deep into my blanket, shielding myself against the chill of that late spring night. I could hear my mother moving just beyond the small divider that separated my sleeping quarters from the larger one that belonged to my parents. Staring through the dimness, I watched the subtle shadows twist and writhe on the wooden wall, touching the myriad of dried leaves I had pinned there before slipping away again. Cicadas, crickets and frogs filled the twilight air with their songs. The noise was unceasing and raucous, but I loved it. It was when the sounds stopped that one should worry, my mother explained once. If the creatures of the forest were frightened, then they usually had good reason.

Nightingale

I turned in my blanket, burying my head under the soft fabric, and yawned. I do not remember falling asleep, but I recall waking the next morning in a flurry of excitement and mingled nervousness. Today I would finally receive my dagger!

The sounds of insects and amphibians in the night had transformed into a cacophony of birdsong by sunrise. It was a normal occurrence for me, and as such, I paid it little heed. I threw off my blankets and rushed into the next room, only to be herded back to my sleeping quarters by my mother. She insisted that I dress properly first before accompanying my father to the practice field, and forcibly combed my hair. I always hated this morning ritual. She pulled too hard at my delicate scalp and pinched at my softly pointed ears, but on this particular morning I gave in to her ministrations with a halfhearted struggle. Even at seven years of age, I realized that the sooner I let my mother have her way, the sooner I would be free.

Dressed in a grey tunic and leggings, I pulled on my tall leather boots and let my mother tie my hair back from my face. She pressed an apple into my hand when she finished, and made me promise I would not forget to eat. I often did that when I was overexcited, and I recollected a time not long before when I managed to forgo eating for a full three days.

It had been late winter. The snows had thawed for the most part, but there were still areas of deep snow that refroze on brisk mornings. A group of hunters were in the deep forests, tracking elk that would undoubtedly be trapped in the lingering snow. My father was among the group, and my mother was worried. I overheard them arguing one night. I tried not to listen, but I could not stop myself. She said that there was no reason for him to go, and that he should think of his safety and ours. I understood that something had happened in their past to make her think this way, but I did not know the reason. When I asked my mother, she refused to tell me, and that made me wonder all the more. For two days I asked after my father and the other hunters that had left. I stopped inquiring when she raised her voice at me.

I had gone to my special tree and huddled on my own private branch high above the ground to pout when the messenger came. I saw him from my perch, and recognized him. He was the older brother of one of my friends, and also a hunter in my father's party.

Without word to anyone, he went straight up the spiral stairs to our *tarsul*.

I could hear hushed voices but could not make out the words. They were swift and distressed, and I understood that something had gone awry. I could only think that someone was hurt, perhaps badly. Mayhap it was my father who was injured.

I slid down the tree in order to hear better what my mother and the messenger said. As I listened to the soft voices through the noise of wind and birdsong, I caught the gist of their conversation. *Cardeai* bandits had attacked the party, swords and knives singing through flesh before the rest of the band had overcome them. Several of my father's party had been injured, some gravely. The messenger, sent out in the height of battle, said he did not know who was severely hurt or if anyone had been killed. He requested aid in the form of horses and healers. My mother granted his petition immediately. The messenger set off without delay to the residence of Carfuinel's talented healers and to the stable filled with small dun ponies.

I followed him. So intent was he on his errand that he did not notice a small, gangly child tagging behind him like a wary dog. I watched as he gathered two healers—older men with streaks of gray in the dark hair that hung over their sharply pointed ears, dressed in the brown and burgundy robes of their office—and swiftly made his way to the stable built into the trunk of a massive tree. I often played around the stable and so I knew the safest niches in which to hide and watch. The stablemaster chose five of the strongest and fastest ponies at the messenger's behest, moving swiftly when the messenger invoked my mother's name.

I watched as he mounted the lead pony. The healers followed suit, taking the halters of the remaining ponies in hand, and begun to move down the slight ramp that led out of the living-wood stable. I bounded down the path. I had wanted to hear mention of my father, but so far there had been none. Heedless of my own safety, I bolted in front of the messenger's pony.

Startled, the sturdy beast reared up, neighing and nearly throwing its rider. However, the messenger was skilled and regained control of his mount. He stared down at me with angry, inquiring eyes.

"My father," I demanded, breathing heavily. "Is he hurt?"

"I know not for certain," the messenger answered, eyes softening just slightly, "but worry not, child. The healers will do their job."

"Indeed," one of the healers added. "If the Lord Cerin is hurt in any way, we will attend to him directly."

"I am coming with you," I said. "I want to see my father."

"Oh," the other healer gasped. "We cannot allow that. Your lady mother will be furious if we were to permit such a thing."

"She will not know until I am gone," I retorted, climbing onto the back of one of the spare ponies before the men could react.

"She will know now," a voice said flatly. My mother rounded the wide path, coming into view beyond the rough, reddish bark of the stable. Her voice was hard, like chips of flint, and there was a glint in her eyes that stalled my protests. "*Sa'tiul*, you waste these men's time with your childish requests. They could have been on their way by now had you not halted them."

My throat closed at her words. I knew she was correct, but her tone caused a puerile distress to well up within me. "Mother—"

"Come with me now," she demanded, holding her hand out to me in a way that brooked no protest.

I slid off the pony, embarrassed and ashamed to the marrow of my bones. I heard the steady, dull clomping of the ponies' hooves as the men moved onward without word. They had witnessed my mother's anger at me. I had delayed treatment for the wounded in my father's party, maybe even of my father himself. My mother's eyes bored into me like awls; I felt them in the pit of my stomach, in the back of my throat. "I am sorry," I whispered, shrinking into myself. In that moment, I was terrified of my mother.

She merely motioned to me, beckoning me to follow her like an errant pup. I slunk up the narrow spiral stairs after her. She glided in front of me, legs hidden behind the waves of pale fabric that made up her dress. My mother was the Lady of Carfuinel, and she dressed the part.

We climbed the spiral stairs higher and higher, moving through the boughs and dancing leaves, moving effortlessly from tree to tree. The thin steps were made of twisted vine and creeper, still living for the most part, with planks of smooth redwood and fir. It seemed they would shatter under our weight; the planks were so thin the light could be seen shining through, faint as the gossamer strands of cobweb and cloud. Miraculously, they bore our weight with surprising ease.

I thought we would go back to our *tarsul* for my inevitable scolding, but to my shock Mother took the left path instead of the right. The left path led up and away from our tree, heading instead to a massive redwood that housed the library and solar. When we reached the substantial *tarsul*, she pushed aside the heavy curtain that served as a door and bid me enter first.

I stood just beyond the doorway, anxious and still. The room was not dark, for a wide balcony took up most of one wall, the railing made of slender twisted branches bleached white by the sun and wind. Shelves of leather-bound tomes, treatises, and omnibuses lined the walls, protected from the elements by a trellised partition. Ivy sprouted from soil-filled pots at its base, twisting upward through the pale slats of wood, a stark contrast against the deep green of the leaves. I looked at the books askance. I had never read any of them, mostly because they were too advanced for me but also because I was not allowed to touch them. I had a tendency to squirrel things away with dirty hands. I thought nothing of it, but apparently other people did not enjoy finding their missing belongings days later stained with little fingerprints.

My mother walked deeper into the room before turning to watch me. I stood still, hunched at the shoulder, with my hands grasping my elbows. Why had she brought me here?

"Sit," she commanded, motioning to one of the cushioned chairs beside a section of especially old tomes. I did, hauling myself into the nearest one. It was too high for me; my feet dangled in the air. I had to struggle not to swing them in an infantile manner.

"Little star," my mother said not unkindly, "do you know who you are?"

I cocked my head, confused. "I know my name, Mother," I said.

"I know that, child, but do you know who you are?"

I paused, wondering. I did not know what she was asking. "I suppose not," I answered.

She sighed, eyes shadowed underneath her dark blonde sweep of hair. "*Sa'tiul*, you are the daughter of the lord of Carfuinel. You are heir to the circlet. Do you understand what that means?"

"That one day I will be the Lady of Carfuinel," I replied. That was something I had been told since I was very young.

"Yes, that's true," Mother answered. "But it also means that you must behave in a manner that befits that title. You cannot force your way into things, child. People will one day look up to you, and they will depend on you. You must learn to control yourself."

"What if I do not want them to?" I sulked.

"You have no choice," she said. "It is something that will happen whether you want it or not." She swept a hand through her hair, exposing the slender silver band across her forehead—the symbol of her office. Turning, my mother pulled a chair close to me and sat. "*Sa'tiul*, I know that you are still a child and I want you to have a childhood, but this is the way things must be. Your father might be hurt, and you did something that directly affected his care. What would he say if he knew?"

"He would be angry," I said, looking between my swinging feet at the wood grain of the floor.

"Yes, he would," she answered. "Now, what is it that you should do?"

"Apologize," I answered.

"And?"

"And make my oath to Lenos that I will keep my word."

"That's right."

I sighed. The wind had picked up, and clouds skimmed across the blue bowl of the sky. Mottled sunlight touched the smooth floor and danced across the waving leaves just beyond the balcony. The cheerful sounds of the birds belied the heaviness of my heart. "I am sorry for what I have done," I murmured. "May Lenos hear me and witness."

"Good." My mother smiled and brushed a hand over my hair. "All is forgiven."

I wanted to believe her. But Lenos was the wolf-god, the steel blade in the night, and Her yellow eyes saw everything. She was merciless, in the manner of hunting beasts, and gave Her prey no quarter. My parents had gifted me to Lenos at my birth and, because of that, I was a god's creature sworn to obey Her will if she made it known. But I had always been stubborn and willful, and Lenos never spoke in a way that I could understand, if She spoke at all.

For the next three days, we waited for word of my father's party and of his condition. I could not shake the feeling that I had caused him trouble, and I obsessed over it. If he was injured, I could not but blame myself. I did not eat. I barely slept. For three days I was as one half-gone. My private branch became a place of refuge, and I rarely left it. My friends could not entice me to play. Indeed, I did not have the heart for it. My mother tried to coddle me, but after that moment in the library her mind was more on the predicament of my father than on me. I did not begrudge her that.

I was not the first one to notice the arrival of the hunting band on the eve of the third day. One of the other children scrambled up to my branch, calling to me that my father was home. I do not recall who told me, or if I asked questions, nor do I recall leaving my branch and sprinting through the anthehome. All I remember of that moment is the sight of my father, safe and hale, upon the back of one of the ponies.

I did not rush up to him, but stood in the crowd, almost lost in the press of bodies. He greeted my mother first, with a kiss. I noticed other people moving forward, eager to see their loved ones and to make certain of their safety. The healers led several injured scouts back to their remedy-filled residence, and the families of the wounded followed. There was no wailing, no lamentations, so I figured that no one had died. A breath of deep relief left me.

Then my father turned and somehow he found me in the throng. Swiftly, he came and swept me up in his arms. I clasped my arms around his neck and hugged him tightly. I thought I would never let go.

"*Sa'tiul*," he said, "do not cry. There is no need for tears!"

"I thought you would not come home," I replied haltingly. "I was afraid."

"I am home now," he answered, squeezing me. "I will always return home to you."

I buried my face in his neck, not listening as he spoke to Mother. I was conscious of movement, of cold air finding a way down the neck of my thick tunic. I remember my father taking me to the *tarsul*, watching me as I ate my first meal in days.

"There are times when hunger is inevitable, *Sa'tiul*," he told me. "Do not go without if it is unnecessary."

19

And now, in the *tarsul*, I remembered that statement still, and so I ate the apple my mother pressed into my hand. I was not hungry—I was too excited—but I ate the flesh, core included, and spit out the seeds into the leaf litter of the forest floor as I dashed to the practice field.

As I ran, my friend Sellien passed me. She was taller and a little older, with gleaming brown tresses and bright eyes. "Where are you going?" she called, turning on her heel to run alongside me.

"The practice field," I replied. "I am getting my dagger today!"

"Oh, good for you!" Sellien exclaimed. "I wondered when it would happen. I almost did not think it would."

"What?" I asked, stung. I planted my heels in the dirt and stared. "Why do you say that?"

My friend hesitated. "Well," she replied faintly. "You are . . . you are different."

"How?" I frowned, my hands clenching at my sides.

"You know how," Sellien answered. "You cannot say you do not. Your ears are shaped strangely; your mother. . . You hear what they call you sometimes." She threw the last words out in defense even as she raised her hands to me in unselfconscious supplication.

I turned away, my shoulders drawn up to those marked ears. "Halfblood," I whispered. "I know."

"I am sorry," Sellien said. "Truly. I did not mean to cause pain."

"I know that, too." Above all, she was my friend and I could forgive her almost anything."Will you come watch?" I asked.

"I was going to help load the trading carts, but I truly would rather come with you," she answered, feet landing lightly on the matted leaves of the ground. She made no noise when she ran, except for the light hiss of her breath. Side by side, we dashed over the arched bridge that spanned the burbling stream and on into the clearing half-shaded by black walnut and horse-chestnut trees.

My father stood there, speaking with a tall, light-haired man. I recognized him after a moment: Rellas Thorntree. He had recently come to Carfuinel from Havosiherim, another anthehome far to the northeast and located deep within the sandstone cliffs and twisted pines and cedar. He often told tales of his former home, but never where the children, myself included, could overhear. Or so I had been told.

He was a weaponsmaster, more skilled at swordplay or archery then even my father. He was older too, with strands of grey weaving through his yellow locks. Wrinkles bunched in the corners of his eyes and at the creases of his mouth. A scar, thick and silvery-white, spiraled down his left forearm, and Rellas often wore his sleeves short to display it as if it were a trophy. I had overheard mention that he had fought in a war, but I knew of no war that had taken place anywhere in my memory.

Rellas was in charge of training younger men in matters of blades and bows. I watched him whenever I could, perching high in the branches above the practice field or sitting in plain view just beyond the undergrowth. I never knew if my attendance was unwelcome or distracting, but I was certain that Rellas always detected my presence and subsequently ignored me. He never included me although I desperately wanted to join. I had the feeling that he did not like me, though I could not say why. He never chased me away or forced me to leave the practice area, so I did my best not to annoy him.

I did not know why I loved to watch weapons practice, but I did. Mother once told me that it might be because I was born under the sign of Lenos, who was the goddess of steel. I knew nothing of the gods, except that there were four. Lenos Nightblade was the only one I felt I understood. She was mine as much as I was Hers. Stars, steel and the creatures of the night. Even my own name, my true one, reflected Her nature. I was Starlit Blade in Caesarn, the *cardea* tongue. Starlit Blade. It was a name I liked immensely, but in my native language of Anilo it rolled more easily off the tongue. The Anilo pronunciation was prettier, my mother said. She rarely used my name however – most did not – as names held a certain kind of power. Names were a means of binding, of conquest and control. Enemies should never learn someone's true name, if it was in one's power to conceal it, I had been told. To give one's true name was an act of intense trust in the nature of the other person.

Rellas was now watching as Sellien and I approached. We had settled into a more sedate pace, though it was a swift walk that did little to hide my excitement. I wished to run, to stretch my legs and sprint as fast as I could, but to do that in my father's presence was unthinkable, even more so when he was granting an audience to another high-ranking member of our community. I was supposed to act the part of a young lady, a child of noble birth, but I did not often achieve it. To be truthful, I could have tried harder – I did attempt when the occasion demanded it – but sometimes I could not reign in my exuberance.

I stopped before Rellas and my father. "Good morning," I bid them both, trying to be poised. Sellien echoed my greeting, drawing her fist across her chest in a gesture of respect.

"Pleasant morn to you both," my father said. Rellas nodded but said nothing as my father faced me. "*Sa'tiul*, today you are old enough to receive your dagger. You may choose the one that fits you best."

I watched as Rellas drew a bundle of wrapped leather from behind him. Kneeling, he unrolled it, exposing three shining knives against the dewy backdrop of the grass. I could hardly breathe, not yet daring to believe that this was happening. I had not known I would get to choose my dagger!

The first knife gleamed in the sun. The hilt was dark, hard mahogany polished to a brilliant shine. The blade was some strange dark stone with subtle reddish tints. There was a small symbol carved into the wood, a curving mark like a falling star. It was a short knife, only the length of my palm. I paused on it for a moment, and then slid my eyes to the next in the procession.

The second knife was longer, though not by much. The hilt curved to better fit the shape of a hand. I could not discern the material for it was wrapped in lengths of taut leather, but I thought it might be an antler. Two tassels of shredded deerskin dangled from the handle, tied off with red cord. The small design on the handle was the silhouette of a bird with outstretched wings, a black impression without detail. The blade was tapped from flint, evidenced by its oily sheen. I could see evidence of use in the chips on the blade, and the sheen of oil on the leather. I looked to the next dagger.

I could not take my eyes off the blade. It was fashioned from some sort of spiraling horn the length of my forearm that had been bisected and set into a hilt. Cream, copper and pinkish hues danced and flashed through the horn like sunrise on clouds. It was the most beautiful blade I had ever seen. The hilt did not do it justice; it was an unadorned fabrication of poured bronze. I picked it up, feeling the cool metal on my fingers. The dagger was much heavier than I had imagined. Tendrils of bronze curled at the base of the blade like writhing fingers.

"What horn is this?" I asked, addressing Rellas instead of my father. Part of Rellas' occupation was to create the daggers used in this tradition. I also thought it might please him if I asked for his expertise.

"Inukern," he answered, no emotion detectable in his deep voice.

Sellien gasped behind me, covering the sound of my own. A dagger made of inukern horn? I had never seen a living forest-horse, but I had seen illustrations in the library. Inukerns were near mythical creatures. Dark brown horse-like bodies were striped with pale grey and cream, while short manes bristled from muscular necks and long tails tufted with silky hair. Their crowning glory was a spiraling horn up to three feet long that sprouted from underneath the forelock. The horn shone like the moon on a dark night, and it was for that horn that the inukern had been hunted to near extinction. *Cardeai* did not know that the horn could be harvested without killing the animal, and neither did the *doshen*, the rock people. It was said that the spiraling projection had magical properties and was consequently used in home remedies – for a heavy price.

I could not believe that Rellas had created a dagger from part of the mythical creature. How had he come across such a valuable item? The dagger's value rose in my eyes. I could not fathom owning this creation. It was much too expensive, much too grand for a child like myself. What if I broke it? The very thought filled me with panic.

I had hoped for a dagger like the thief, Brandin, all shining gold and twisted blades. I never hoped for this pearlescent jewel. I realized then what my choice must be.

I picked up my choice, took one step back, and heard Sellien's faint breath.

"A good choice," my father said proudly.

"You have chosen a weapon that has proven its worth," Rellas stated, "instead of an untried blade. You have passed your first trial of the knife." There was a hint of a smile on his face, and I could not believe it.

"My trial?" I questioned, feeling the tassels of leather hanging from my new dagger brush against my arm.

Sellien smiled broadly and touched me on the arm. "Luck to you!" she laughed before dashing away into the trees.

I stared after her, puzzled, then turned my attention back to Father and Rellas. I could not think of anything now; I could only wait for what might come next. I gripped my new dagger, feeling the leather-wrapped hilt in the palm of my hand. It was a good feeling, and I quite enjoyed it.

"Your second trial," Rellas began, "is to prove that you are capable of using a dagger."

"But. . ." I replied. "I have never held one before now."

"That is no matter," Rellas answered. "If you are meant to use one, I will know it."

I glanced at my father, but discerned nothing in his face. He stood at the tree line, in the shadows, his arms folded before him. He was watching intently, but I had the feeling he would not interfere with this trial.

"Show me a defensive stance," Rellas commanded.

I mimicked a stance I had seen while watching the young men in their practices. I crouched, bending my knees so that my weight balanced on both legs, and stabilized my posture. I twisted my upper body, turning my shoulder toward Rellas, making myself a smaller target. I brought the dagger up in a diagonal position, ready to guard against a blow from an opponent.

"Good," he said. I thought I detected a hint of pleasure in his voice, but could not be certain. Then: "Offensive stance!"

I brought my rearmost foot closer inward, setting it almost directly underneath my body. I leaned forward so that my foremost leg held most of my weight. With both hands on the hilt of the dagger and my right elbow high in the air, I raised it up beside my face, the blade horizontal and facing my imaginary enemy. I appeared ready to lunge forward in a heartbeat, and that was the way I wanted it. That was the way the men looked at practice.

Rellas nodded. "A decent attempt, young one. Not perfect by any means, but decent. I see your intrusions into our practices have not been for naught."

I colored, feeling my cheeks burn, but I would not apologize. I had learned, that much was clear, and I would not be sorry for that.

I looked at Rellas, refusing to break my stance or my silence. He eyed me for a long moment, and then nodded.

"Lord Cerin," he called. "Your daughter will do."

I allowed myself to relax, but tensed again as soon as Rellas returned his attention to me.

"You do not have to watch our practices from afar from now on, if you like," he said, and this time a clear smile was visible on his face. "How would you like to learn true blade-play?"

"Oh, I would like it very much!" I cried, grinning.

"Then if your lord father agrees, we will meet tomorrow," he finished.

I turned to my father, smiling widely although a tinge of worry thrummed within me. Surely he would agree. He wanted me to learn to use a dagger. He had told me that in his own words. I stood, holding my new dagger at my side, waiting.

"Of course I agree," Father answered, grinning.

I hesitated, something just coming to mind. "There is no third trial?" I asked. "In the tales, there are always three."

"Life is not a tale, child," my father answered.

"No one said your trials were over," Rellas stated. "It is tomorrow that they begin."

I knew this day—these trials—had seemed too easy. The next day the true work would begin. I had seen enough of weapons practice to know what was in store for me. It would be hard, filthy work and I could not wait for it to begin. When my father and Rellas dismissed me, I dashed off to tell Sellien the news and to glean any information I could from her. She had already gone through her ordeals and I wanted all the information I could get. I wanted to be ready.

And at this moment, I wanted to flaunt my new dagger.

Once, in his childhood, Astin Talros had glimpsed a captured anthela in the markets. Tied hand and foot, the creature exuded preternatural calm even as it was hounded on all sides. It made no move to dodge the stones or rotten fruit heaved its way, nor did it turn aggressively on the captors that held fast to the ropes and billhooks. No amount of prodding or taunting would break the anthela's eerie motionlessness.

The crowd grew bored with the lack of action and slowly began to drift away. For half an instant, one guardsman turned his back to the creature. That was when the beast struck. Even with its hands bound, the anthela killed four men before it was brought down and dispatched in the market square. The tree-swinger had snapped their necks like half-rotten sticks and had not spilled one drop of blood in the process. Talros remembered the screams of the panicked crowd once they finally realized what was happening. He remembered the flat deadness he had mistaken for calm in the anthela's eyes. The beast had killed indiscriminately and in the coward's way—waiting until the enemy was unaware of the danger. To strike at an unprotected back was unforgivable to Talros. It was something predators did to prey; it was not something to be done to people.

But that did not seem to justify what these men had done.

"Raids are illegal," he stated, one hand on the hilt of his sword. "King Cosian has declared it."

The three men set down their burlap sacks, the contents poking against the rough fabric. They looked at him, but refused to meet Talros' eyes. The general noted their bony frames, unkempt hair, and dirt-crusted skin. Vagabonds or grubbers, selling the spoils of the hunt to seedy merchants or backstreet apothecaries. A merchant doubling as a fence would pay a great deal for anthela-made items; an unscrupulous apothecary would collect the ears or bones for use in so-called medicines that did more harm than good.

Talros frowned. "Dump the contents."

"But, sir. . ." one protested.

"Do it." General Talros crossed his arms, waiting, and was glad for the four Weapons at his back. If these raiders were desperate, then there was no telling what they might do.

The men flipped the sacks over and tipped their contents onto the ground. Four hands, fine-boned and bloodless, and four sharply pointed ears caught Talros' immediate attention. A sundry of other items fell free: a silver-wrought bracelet, two small rings made with beads of obsidian, a green tunic with a white-threaded design.

"How could you know?" asked one of the raiders, his hands clenching and loosening rhythmically at his sides.

"Deer poachers don't wrap their boots in felt to soften their steps," Talros replied, motioning for his soldiers to bind the raiders' hands. That was not the only thing criminals did; they also darkned their faces with soot and mud to hide better in the shadows, wore mail silenced with linen and tar, and carried small bags for trophies instead of meat. The men protested, of course, when the manacles were clasped on their wrists, but Talros did not care. He was tired of chasing raiders and runaways and poachers.

The king's law had been issued many years before. Fears based on myth and legend solved nothing; in fact, they only tended to make problems worse. The large-scale raids had stopped, from what Talros noticed, but the smaller jobs continued. Every so often, he came across a band of men in the forests of Caesia, hunting what they should not. He worried sometimes, in the darkness of his bed, that one day the anthelai might retaliate for all the ones they had lost. Though their numbers had dwindled significantly, the creatures could still claim a threat. It was said they had powers that men did not.

Turning away, Talros mounted his horse and called for the raiders to be put in the wagon. They would be taken to the nearest town gaol for sentencing. While the Weapons were the king's blades, Talros preferred to leave the smaller tasks to the local guards.

The Weapons traveled as King Cosian the Second bid. They captured those who would spy on the kingdom of Caesia; they arrested those who sought to overthrow the crown; they executed those who brought danger and rebellion to the land. These small raiders were brought down before they could become larger threats, but Talros did not seek them out exclusively. These three he had come upon quite by accident.

He and his Weapons had received orders from the king to quell a blood-feud in the northern city of Luella. Traveling from the capitol city of Dernwellen to the northern border of Caesia had its share of challenges: bandits, highwaymen, heavy snowfall, panthers, and raiders. Though anthelai were few and far between, there were sometimes enough to cause fear to spring up in the outlaying villages that perched at the edges of the deep forests. A goat would go missing, a child would die of blight, or a cow would fail to give milk. All these things were blamed on the anthelai. Talros did not see the point of it. If the people thought anthelai demons, let the priests handle them. Instead, men would sweep the forests and often find nothing. When they did, the local guards dealt with them accordingly.

In this case, Talros had happened to be in the right place and the right time to stop a few the guards might have otherwise missed. After dropping the raiders in the gaol in the village of Settler's Ridge, Talros and his Weapons continued north to Luella.

It was not strange that there were problems in the city. Luella had a checkered past. Governed by two guilds and neighboring the kingdom of Yentille, Luella was ripe for disorder. King Cosian II disliked chaos, and so it fell to General Talros to stop the feud before it caught fire.

The Yentiliáne Guild provided the tinder. All the stonemasons and blacksmiths reported to the Guildmaster of Yentiliáne. He paid them wages if they joined his ranks. If they did not, then he made it so that they could not find work. It seemed common guild practice to do so. Other professions also gave their services to the guild first, taking what they could, then set up shop in the market section of the city. Without a guildmaster's approval, a business could not open, a merchant could not erect a stall, a fishmonger could not hawk her wares. The barons and lords did little to change the practice; it had been in place for hundreds of years. Many had belonged to guilds themselves as former masters, earning their riches from the pockets of laymen, so they did not try much to inspire revolution.

Such practices were not Talros' problem, yet. If the king decided change was in order, it would be done, but Talros would not take the initiative. He traveled north to confront Karibik Deomiel, current Guildmaster, and Warren Tarik, a rising contender for the title. Deomiel had not been Guildmaster long, perhaps three years, and it seemed that he was quite disliked by the factions in Luella.

Power meant much. It could build guilds, kill rivals, and gain riches and glory. Two guilds had dissolved and combined to create Yentiliáne. Dissolution meant weakness; it meant infighting and slander and unhappy deeds. Deomeil had taken that vat of bitter soup and created something edible, if not exactly appealing. His method worked, but Warren Tarik did not agree.

As possible instigators of rebellion, it fell to General Talros to stop them, one way or another.

The Weapons arrived in Luella a few days later, in the midst of a drizzling rain that soaked through their uniforms and flicked from their horses' ears. The biting flies had gone, unwilling to wet their wings, and the hot sun retreated behind a thick wall of clouds.

Talros did not waste time. Instead of going to an inn or tavern for respite, he marched to Yentiliáne's front door, followed by his willing men. The guild headquarters were located in a manor in the northern section of town. Hedges, neatly trimmed and uniform, lined the walkway. Clay pots filled with oil sat on the front step; Talros knew at night they would be lit like torches.

He rapped his knuckles on the heavy door and did not have to wait long for a servant to answer. "General Astin Talros of the Weapons," he said to the peering face. "I am here to speak with Guildmaster Deomiel."

"I'll fetch him," the servant said. "One moment."

The man closed the door, leaving Talros out on the front stoop. The general was not accustomed to such treatment but did not let it hinder him. People were often wary of authority, the king's authority especially, and a guildmaster's servant was no different.

The door opened again swiftly and the servant appeared in the open entryway, his face red and worried. "I'm so sorry, General. Please come in. Deomiel has asked to see you right away."

Talros stepped inside, his boots reflected on the shined, stone floor. He followed the servant into a room, Deomiel's study, by the look of it. Thick rugs, red and black and gray, covered the floor. The windows were open on the left wall, letting the gray light trickle in with the hints of a breeze. Talros could smell turned dirt from the gardeners below the windows; he could hear the scrap of shovels on stone.

"General Talros, what a pleasant surprise," Karibik Deomiel said, rising from his seat behind a desk in the rear corner of the room. "I take it King Cosian has gotten wind of the spat brewing in Yentiliane."

"Yes," Talros replied. "I am here to decide what to do with you and Warren Tarik."

"Tarik is the upstart," Deomiel said, his face darkening. "There is no point in deciding otherwise."

"Perhaps." Talros crossed to the windows and looked down, watching the gardeners plant rosebushes in the dark soil. He pulled the glass down, cutting off the sounds from outside. "This situation bodes no good for anyone, including you," he continued. "The king wants any hint of strife stomped out. Immediately."

"I have done nothing wrong." Deomiel set his hands on his desk, glaring. "Threaten all you want, but it doesn't change anything."

"So tell me of Tarik. Why has he suddenly decided that you are not fit to be a guildmaster?"

Deomiel waved a hand. "Who knows? One small reason or another, it all ends up being the same: they think they can do better." He sat back down in his chair. "I took this guild from the ruins and turned it into something greater, something that works. And all Tarik sees is that I got here before him. Well, too damn bad."

"I see," Talros said. His men were viewing the grounds of the manor, looking for anything suspicious. He did not think they would find much, at least not what Talros wanted. Despite Deomiel's history as a hard and unscrupulous man, the general thought, in this instance, that the man was telling the truth. His gut instinct was usually right. "Very well. We will find Tarik and question him. Could you point us in his direction?"

"Like as not, he's drunk. Check the taverns."

"Is he often drunk?" Talros asked, frowning.

"When he hassles my servants on my front step, he is. When he hollers in the streets at night, he's apt to fall on his face. When he's not doing those, I don't know."

"And the blood-feud?"

Deomiel's face went dark. "He killed my best footman on the pathway. I've put a bounty on his head. So far, there have been no takers."

A murderer as well as an instigator, Talros thought, if what the guildmaster said was true. "Murder? How long ago?"

"A month. The priest that took the body can show you the grave if you want details."

"And why has no one made an attempt on Tarik's life?"

"I don't know." Deomiel smiled grimly. "Perhaps they like him better."

"Understood." Talros turned and went to the door. "Thank you for your time. If you have any plans on leaving Luella, I would stay them for the time being."

"Under arrest, am I?" Deomiel inquired, his tone dry and flat.

"No, but we're watching until this situation is resolved. If you run, that only implicates you."

"I understand how this works, General. King Cosian's strife will be stomped out, but I promise I won't be the one under the boot."

"Just remember what I said, Guildmaster," Talros said, leaving the study and closing the door behind him.

He met his men on the pathway between the hedges and explained to them in detail of what he and Deomiel had spoken. They would search the taverns and inns of Luella and nearby villages. If they found him, Tarik would be brought to the Luellan gaol for questioning. If they did not, then they would search harder—house to house, if necessary. The king's desire would not be thwarted.

The Weapons mapped their targets, mounted their horses and separated into groups. Warren Tarik had to be found; either he or Deomiel would pay for disturbing the balance of the kingdom.

Chapter 2

IT WAS AT THE PRIEST'S FUNERAL that I first heard the word. The haunting cries marking his death had lasted for a full day and long into the next. He had died well, they said, and his bier would be lashed with ivy and mistletoe instead of hemp and flax. My mother had been the last one to speak with him and her eyes were red-rimmed and flat as she clutched my small hand in her cold one.

My father spoke the eulogy, as was his duty. "May Lenos Nightblade and Oryn Deepwater take you and keep you well, son of Carfuinel," he said, his voice rising like a winged thing above the forest clearing. To Joilu Brightstar and the Dark God Énas, we did not speak. Joilu did not take the dead, and Énas craved them too strongly.

I peered up at the bier, a pale flimsy-looking construction of the twisted limbs of ash and birch, and saw the form of the priest draped in a loose shroud. His staff lay next to him, and the beads of his office. These tools he would take with him, finished and well-handled, to show that he had been important in life.

As my father stepped down from the head of the bier, his hair a dark rippling shadow in the moonlight, the eerie wailing closed with a trailing whisper. When the lamentation finished, the anthelai filed past the body. Each left a token on the wood—a carved bead, a pretty stone, a feather—and continued down the path back to Carfuinel. My mother stayed still and silent, clutching my hand. I wanted to leave. I did not want to think of the body lying there, almost asleep. I had not liked the priest in life, frightened by his countenance, and in death he seemed otherworldly and strange.

"*Lasbel,*" I whispered, "What happens to him?"

My mother's eyes glanced down at me and I did not like the strange glint in them. "They leave him. In a few months, someone will come and bury him." She grimaced, sharp, even teeth nipping at her bottom lip. "We never did things like this in Stendel."

That was unexpected. "Stendel?" I asked, seizing upon the unfamiliar word. "Where is that?"

"Far away," she answered, her face turning away from mine as if she regretted her words. "You will likely never see it."

"Why not?" I inquired, twisting my fingers against her grasp. I could feel my pulse throbbing in them.

"Because. . ." my mother muttered. Abruptly, she loosened her grip.

"Because it is a *cardea* settlement," my father said, coming to stand beside us. "And we do not go there."

"Why?" I asked again, my curiosity overcoming my fear of the dead man scant feet away. The eventual smell would not reach the anthehome, distant as it was from the graveyard. After several months had passed, the bier-tenders would make the trek back to the cemetery to bury the bones under the shadows of a shaded glen. There would be no fire to devour the bones, only animals and sunlight and the roots of ancient trees.

"You ask too many questions, child," my mother said.

"Dendé," my father, Cerin, said quietly, ignoring me. "He upset you when you spoke?"

We walked back down the narrow pathway to Carfuinel, to food and sleep and warmth. I stayed quiet, feigning disenchantment with my parents' conversation, and danced along the path looking for stones and leaves and insects as my dagger bounced against my narrow hip.

"No, he only reminded me of what we had agreed." She looked at my father with an expression I could not read. "He said nightingales were speaking to him—and I didn't like it."

Why should my mother not like such a thing? I thought. The birds had always, in my knowledge, portended good things to come. They were the voices of the gods. I did not realize then that was something of which to be wary. I went down the path, my parents following behind with their soft voices winding under the low-hanging boughs. I did not listen anymore; my mind was filled with other things.

My mother had once been in Stendel, a place of which I had never heard. She had not always lived in Carfuinel, then. I knew she was not anthela, but I had never known she had actually been to a *cardea* settlement before. They were a different people, according to the tales, and full of hate and hunger. The "deaf ones," the word meant, because those strange people could not hear the whispers of the trees. Why had my mother been in such a place, with such people? *Halfblood*, my heart whispered. My mother *was cardea*, she had told me, and she was not full of anger and violence. What was I to believe?

The next morning, after a night filled with tossing and turning and dreams of dead men, I found Sellien and asked if she knew anything about a place called Stendel. I had asked in secrecy, behind the wall of ivy trellises in my parents' solar. They were meeting with delegates from Nhoternis in one of the lower *tarsuls* so we were in no danger of being overheard.

"No," Sellien answered. "The library might have a history, though."

I made a face, hating the thought of the library. Reading the tomes and scrolls was usually one of my punishments when my mother decided I had been willfully disobedient in one situation or another. Sellien laughed at my grimace and tugged my hand, and together we slipped upward to the wide room.

It was unoccupied, except for two attendants dusting the leather-bound manuscripts and sweeping the leaf-strewn floor. They looked up when we came in, eyes carefully blank when they saw me. "Young mistresses," the attendants greeted. "How shall we be of service to you?"

Sellien took the lead, using the advantage of her age over me. "We would like to see the histories, please."

"Which one?" the older attendant asked, motioning with a hand toward the covered walls.

"Ah, of the *cardea* settlements," I asked.

The two librarians glanced at one another. "I think you want this one," the first said, going to the wall and lifting a thick, well-worn book and setting it on the small table nearest the window. Sellien and I went and perched on the stools, turning the pages with nimble fingers. The attendants retreated to a respectful distance, though I knew they would keep watch on us, being young as we were, I could not expect otherwise.

"What do you see?" I asked when she stopped after flipping halfway through the tome.

She frowned, eyebrows bunching on her delicate brow. "I cannot read it," she answered, turning her head this way and that.

I looked over her arm and read, "The coast is filled with cities of as many as ten-thousand people. Corvain is the largest seaside town, exporting all manner of goods from its port."

Sellien was staring at me, eyes round with surprise. "That is not Anilo!" she said. "What language did you just read?"

I looked down at the page, at the tight, neat script. "My mother taught it to me. Caesarn, I think."

"I think that is a *cardea* language," she said, taking her small hands off the parchment with slow realization.

"Mother is *cardea*," I murmured, understanding swiftly. A halfblood was an anthela and a *cardea* together. I was two things mixed in one body; two things that were supposed to be enemies. I bit my lower lip. "She is not bad," I whispered to myself.

But *cardeai* were supposed to be bad. Did that mean I was not a good person? Did my blood determine that? Sellien did not hear my plaintive musing. Instead, she continued to turn the pages.

"Look, some of it I can read," she said. "The villages around Corvain are farming communities. There are no walls and very few guards, so Etamé Treemoss declares. Livestock is abundant and often free-ranging." She glanced up at me. "I do not understand why this is important."

"You do not see Stendel?" I asked and she shook her head and slid the book to me across the smooth tabletop.

I flipped the pages for longer than I thought possible before giving up. "Nothing," I decided, and sighed.

"Maybe we could look in the genealogies," Sellien suggested. "If your mother came from there, mayhap it would say something."

"Mayhap," I answered and went over to the attendant closest to the table. He was studiously avoiding my eyes. "May I have the genealogy of my family?"

"Of course," he answered and found a scroll in a fastidiously arranged compartment in the wall, but he withdrew his fingers when they accidently touched mine. I bit my tongue, suddenly angry without knowing why. He seemed like he disliked me. I went away without thanking him and clambered back up on my stool, spreading the scroll out for Sellien to view.

Together we pored over it, marking anthehomes in our minds. My mother had no anthehome listed. *Stendel, cardea village* was written below her name. It was not Dendé Teriel listed there. My mother was listed as Dendé Cowell, a *cardea* name. No lines traced behind her, no ancestors, no bloodline, no history. I narrowed my eyes at the parchment and moved my finger forward toward my name, but something stopped me in my tracks.

It was an odd thing indeed to learn that I had once had a brother from the genealogy tome and not from my parents. *Nameless boy-child*, the delicate ink traced on the parchment. *Nine months of age.* I frowned at the single line indicating the deceased son of Cerin and Dendé Teriel, my parents and ruling consorts of Carfuinel. My young eyes could not believe it. He had died before I was born. I had never known I had a brother.

I felt myself becoming engrossed in those small, seemingly insignificant words. Reading tomes and scrolls in the small library of the anthehome was supposed to teach me a lesson in doing what I was told. Never before had I read something of interest, until now.

I had traced my father's line back hundreds of years, ending—or beginning, one might say—at something called the Rift and a man named Lentan Yellosei. Those meant nothing to me except that my father was from old blood whereas my mother had no records in the genealogy tome. Her name was alone except for a small line joining her and my father. *New blood*, my mind supplied, meaning nothing.

"*Lasbel*," I said as my mother entered the library, motes of dust dancing in the beams of light slipping through the open windows as she moved past the corner of my eye. "Why did you not tell me I had a brother?"

"Oh," Dendè said, her brown eyes wide. "Sellien, would you leave us, please?" The two attendants slipped away, almost unnoticed, as my friend rose cautiously from her stool, casting a sympathetic glance at me as she nodded respectfully to the Lady of Carfuinel, and went outside.

I sat in my place, straight-backed and silent, and waited.

My mother bit her lip, a sign of nervousness that I had never before seen from her, and took Sellien's place at the table. "I did not know the time to tell you," she said by way of explanation. "You are very young."

"I am seven," I replied. "Old enough to want to know things about my family."

"Yes, " Dendé sighed. "That you are. Sometimes I forget you are so capable. When I was seven, I thought only of chasing horses and playing in the mud." She smiled at me.

Still, I waited.

"*Sa'tiul*, your father and I did not think we would ever have children. There were many painful years for us. Your brother caught a sickness as a baby and died. It is a hard thing to think of even now. We did not even have time to name him."

"Did he die because he was different?" I asked, feeling my throat close in sudden fear. "Because he was a . . . a halfblood like me?"

"Oh, *Sa'tiul*, no!" my mother cried, coming around the table to wrap me in her arms. "No, he was sick. It had nothing to do with that." She pushed me back to look in my eyes, her hands tight and cold on my shoulders. "There is nothing wrong with what you are, do you hear me? Nothing." She seemed so certain that I was almost convinced.

"The tales say *cardeai* are bad, *lashel*," I whispered. "And if I am half, then I might be bad, too."

"I am *cardea*, dearheart. Am I bad?"

"No," I said. "But you live here now." My knowledge was the conviction of a child. "Maybe you were bad when you lived in Stendel."

"I knew you would catch that name," Dendé said, shaking her head in exasperation even as a small grin creased her lips. "Your father knew me in Stendel and he will tell you I was not bad then, either. There are good and bad people everywhere, child, *cardea* and anthela. It doesn't matter what blood you have."

"*Senou* knew you in Stendel?" I inquired, my fingers mindlessly running along the edge of the scroll until my mother pried it away.

"Yes," she said, remembering. "I saved his life before I even knew his name." She looked at me, brown eyes like polished acorns. "I knew he was an anthela, though, and still I risked my life for him."

"Why?"

"Because I had to. Because something in me demanded it. And if I had not, *Sa'tiul*, then we would not have fallen in love and you would not have been born. And because he loved me, your father brought me here among the people he cared for. We are different, but we are happy. You will be happy, too, despite what other people will say of you."

"I can be happy," I said dubiously, "even though some people are scared of me because I am a halfblood." I thought of the attendant and his curling fingers, of the mothers that would not let their children play with me, of the hunters that would not allow me to watch their practice despite Rellas' demands.

"I know so," my mother stated with determination. "Halfblood is nothing but a word, dearheart. It has nothing to do with who you are."

I thought of the stories of my kind which labeled me a demon, a guardian of the Plains of Centura which was Énas' realm. Mother always told me those were falsehoods, children's fables meant to scare others into obedience. Since there were so few of my kind in the world, no one understood them. It was my duty to prove otherwise, but I did not know if I was up to the task. My face must have betrayed my thoughts for my mother eyed me closely; I felt her gaze in my heart and all the way to my spine.

"Do you believe me, *Sa'tiul*?"

I twisted my shoulders, not wanting to answer. "Father says my life will be hard, even in Carfuinel. He says I need to learn to use my dagger well."

Dendé sighed, a sad, wrenching sound. "It may be true, and I hate that more than anything." She bowed her head, hiding her eyes under a curtain of dark blonde hair, and I was horrified to hear a stifled sob.

Unable to help myself, I sprang from the stool and slipped into my mother's lap, hands grasping around her shoulders as she wrapped her arms about me. "*Lasbel*," I whispered. "I am sorry. Do not cry. Please, please."

"Your father is a good man," Dendé said, "and he wants you to be safe, but sometimes he forgets you are naught but a child. You have years yet to live in peace here. We have years to teach you to defend yourself."

38

And I did, for the most part, live in peace. I had friends, family, teachers, a sturdy home, and miles of wilderness in which to roam. It was a good life; even at seven I recognized that. There were very few who taunted me; the daughter of the rulers of Carfuinel was not an easy target. My parents could be formidable when provoked, like bears protecting a cub, and few dared to risk their wrath.

"I will stay here forever," I told her, pressing my forehead against her collarbone and breathing her familiar scent. "Do not be scared."

She laughed. "Oh, silly child. When you are grown you will be tired of your parents always underfoot. Maybe you will find a handsome man and he will tease you away."

I knew she was jesting with me; I could hear it in the tone of her voice, but I was glad she was no longer crying. "No," I declared. "Never. You and Father would be sad if I left."

"Yes," she admitted, "but we would be happy if you were. That's all that matters."

"I would be happy if you would tell me of Stendel," I coaxed, stilling myself and wondering if she would take the bait.

"Little imp!" my mother cried. "When did you get so sneaky?" But she was smiling and that was good.

And when she spoke, I listened.

"Why should we listen to the guilds?" the man cried. "What do they do for us?"

"Nothing!" some men in the crowd howled back. Other people hesitated, shuffling their feet in the dirt of the square. This was a new way of thinking, one that could cause problems for all cities, all guilds, and all people if it continued. Some were quick to adopt it, while others hesitated, afraid of what it might mean.

"They take our coin, our profit, and our freedom! They give us rules on how to run our businesses. Should we allow this?"

"No!" More in the audience had joined in, the idea spreading. This was dangerous. People would die, guilds would topple. And what of the king? If he embraced the idea, would he be hated or loved? If he cast it aside, what would happen?

Small skirmishes, laymen against guilds. Civil war if it grew, spreading like a weed over rich ground. Death for many, regardless. Change did not come easy. It did not come without a price. Revolution was bought with blood, paid for in lives. This was what the Weapons needed to prevent.

Talros stood in the front window of the boarding house. On the outskirts of Luella, in the middling-size village of Veros, he watched as Warren Tarik set fire to the multitude. In seemed that most of the village's populace had turned out to hear the man speak. This made Talros' task much more difficult. He could not arrest the man now, even though he had clear proof of rebellion. The crowd could turn on him and, Weapon or not, Talros could not defend himself from a horde.

He would have to wait and take the man unawares. Talros did not think of what Warren Tarik said. He did not agree or disagree with the man's assessment of guild-rule and politics. That was neither his place nor his job. Talros did as King Cosian II bid, and that was enough. Being a general was all he had ever aspired to be, and now he had it. He would not chance that title being revoked. Not on rebellion or anything else.

When the crowd dispersed, Talros walked out into the street. Tarik was already leaving, weaving his way through the lanes. His blue tunic, sleeves slashed with green, stood out against the drab wattle homes and the whitewashed fences. Talros followed him, in turn followed by two of his own men. From a distance, they watched as Tarik passed the tavern and entered a private residence.

This was better, Talros thought. He did not relish the idea of confronting the man in a crowded area. A home would be better, provided it was his own. He crossed to the door and knocked, flanked now by the Weapons who had followed him.

Tarik opened the door. "Yes?" he asked, and his voice died in his throat as he saw Talros' badge of office. Though his voice failed, his jaw jutted like a stubborn bulldog and his chin rose in defiance.

"General Talros of the Weapons." Talros walked into the house uninvited, unwilling to arrest the man in plain sight of the street. Tarik stepped back as a Weapon closed the door. "Warren Tarik, you are under arrest for inciting rebellion."

"Rebellion?" Tarik asked, his voice harsh. "We live and die by the guild's word! And you think guild policy doesn't need to change?"

"That's not for me to decide. That's King Cosian's pleasure."

"The king's a lout."

"Add treason to the list." Talros took a rope from his belt and tied Tarik's hands behind his back. "You will await sentencing at Luella's gaol."

"I can't go to Luella. There's a bounty on my head. They'll kill me the moment I set foot on the cobblestone."

"I've been told that no one has tried to claim it," Talros retorted. "You'll be safe enough."

Tarik struggled as Talros pulled the knots tight around the man's wrists. "Speaking is not against the law," he protested.

"It's also said that you've killed a man," Talros replied. "I don't have to take you to gaol at all. I can render justice here if you prefer."

Tarik's shoulders sagged. "Fine," he hissed. "Take me away, but know that I'm just the beginning. Change will come."

"But not from you." Talros motioned to his men and they took Tarik by the upper arms, leading him from the empty house. There were few people in the streets to see; most were preoccupied with evening chores and tavern songs.

Tarik was loaded into a small wagon hitched to two of the Weapon's horses. Talros sat in the bed with him as the other two Weapons climbed into the seat and turned the wagon back toward Luella. It was not a long distance but they would not reach the gaol before nightfall. The thought did not bother Talros; he was accustomed to late nights.

"Karibik told you about the footman, didn't he?" Warren Tarik asked once the trees enclosed the rutted road. The limbs were thick overhead, obscuring the orange-tinted sky. The horses plodded; the wheels found unseen dips in the packed dirt. Talros said nothing, and Tarik continued. "Bigoted, selfish, money-grabbing fool."

"The footman or Deomiel?" Talros said, sliding into a more comfortable position on the planks.

Tarik chuckled. "Oh, funny. Didn't expect humor from you." He flexed his bound arms. "I'll admit I killed the footman, but only because he cheated me at cards. He stole from me so I stole something of his. That makes us even."

"That makes you a murderer." General Talros stared at the man, making certain he heard every word. He knew his men heard as well; they were silent and still, attuned to their surroundings.

"I disagree. That makes me someone who stands up for my rights. I'm tired of being trampled."

"So you kill Deomiel's footman, insult the king, and try to incite riots and rebellion? That seems to be an overzealous attempt to regain a few cheated coins."

"It's not about the coins. It's about honor. Karibik Deomiel is a fool and he's running the Yentiliáne into the ground. I can do better."

"Better?" Talros inquired. "He built the guild up from ashes. Luella is prosperous and growing even more so."

"I could have done just as well, if given the chance," Tarik sneered, his shoulders straining at the bonds. Talros stiffened, ready to move in case things got out of hand.

"Then ask for elections. Keep your sights on Yentiliane. Why go for the kingdom's guilds?"

"Because they are part of the problem!" Tarik cried.

Talros frowned. Warren Tarik sounded like a selfish, arrogant boy. What was the need in taking him to gaol now? He had already confessed to murder. He had been witnessed slandering the king's name and enticing people to riot. King Cosian desired an end to the problems in Luella. With Tarik gone, those problems would end—for a time. Talros did not expect the dilemma to disappear forever, but unrest would take time to build again.

The question now was what to do with Warren Tarik. In gaol, he could speak. Others would still hear his words and spread them. With him dead, his voice, his ideas, would be silenced. The slander against the king was treason; the public call for rebellion was reason enough for execution. The murder was a third mark against the man. King Cosian II would demand Tarik's life; it was undeniable.

"Why are we even doing this? You know as well as I do that my head's for the block," Tarik muttered, watching Talros. His face was pale but firm, and the muscles of his arms bunched with strain against the ropes.

"You're right," Talros acceded. "Stop the wagon."

"Wait—" Tarik burst out as the wagon rolled to a stop.

"Like you said earlier, they'll kill you in Luella as soon as you touch the cobblestone. You will have a manner of calm and quiet this way." Talros jumped down from the bed and went to his horse tethered at the side-rail. Reaching into a saddle-pack, he dug a stoppered bottle from the bottom and brought it out as the two Weapons lowered Tarik to the ground.

"Do you have anyone you want told?" one Weapon asked.

"No," Tarik answered, chin high though his voice wavered. "No one."

"Drink this." Talros pulled the plug from the bottle's mouth. "It's good ale. For courage."

"Thank you. That's . . . that's more than I expected."

Talros tipped the jug to Tarik's mouth and the man drank, chugging most of the ale before coming up for air. Talros let him. It would dull the fear and the pain, neither of which would last for long, but he wanted to give the man a measure of kindness before the end.

The other Weapon held the bottle as Tarik set his lips once more on the bottle. The rebel closed his eyes and drank unsteadily, knowing what was coming. Talros set his dagger against the man's ribs and pushed the blade upward between the bone to puncture the heart.

He moved fast and with skill, and Warren Tarik died with ale still on his lips.

The Weapons took his body to the char-house in Luella, leaving his name with the priest that manned the books. Then they went to the inn where they would rest until the morning, and Talros penned a missive to the king. He told all of what he had witnessed, and of Tarik's end. It would be weeks before King Cosian received his letter, but General Talros already had other tasks to finish and had no reason to await the king's reply, should there be one.

In the morning, the Weapons would begin anew.

Chapter 3

I WAS EIGHT YEARS OLD, almost nine, when my life changed forever.

The day started innocently enough. I awoke before my parents, as usual, and slipped out of my quarters and onto one of the swaying branches high above the earth. The air was cool and the living wood was beaded with morning dew. Soft new leaves brushed against my face, tickling my skin and leaving little trails of moisture on my nose and forehead. I loved morning best and so I smiled at the joy of it. Breathing deeply, I savored the chill of mid-spring and the scent of fresh flowers and turned soil.

I could hear birdsong everywhere, an explosion of raucous calls and chirrups that never seemed to end. Crickets still chirped in the grass below, and in the distance, a lone wolf howled. Almost hidden in the noise were the soft sounds of my parents' slumbering breath. I glanced around, my sharp eyes landing on the twisted, spiraling staircase that wove its way down from our *tarsul*. I was not supposed to leave without first telling my parents where I was going, but I was anxious to be gone. I could already see my friends below, darting and weaving between the massive trunks.

My hand slid down to the dagger I always wore at my waist. It was my favorite accoutrement, and I do not think that it ever left my side except for when I bathed or slept. Dressed in a pale blue tunic and grey breeches, I thought that the darkness of the small knife went rather well with my outfit. Touching the hilt had become a habit. Mother wanted me to say a prayer to Lenos when I touched it, but I often forget. When my mind wandered, I always came back to find my hand perched upon the rounded handle. I did not think much of it, and I did not know if anyone else even noticed. There had not been occasion to use the dagger except for practices with Rellas. I felt I was growing rather skilled with the slender blade, and I was able to keep up in the training bouts with opponents several

44

years older. Merely wearing the dagger gave me a sense of responsibility, of strength and importance. I enjoyed it.

A high-pitched giggling erupted from behind me. My gaze snapped over, passing through the waving leaves and twisting shadows to rest on the girl bounding up the narrow stairs. Sellien laughed up at me.

"You slept late!" she called. "Come play hide-and-search with us!"

I put a finger to my lips, glaring down at her. "Quiet," I hissed. "You will wake Father!"

"It seems it is too late for that," a voice rumbled behind me.

I wheeled around, miraculously managing to keep my balance on the narrow branch. My father stood in the open doorway of the *tarsul*, one hand on the twisted white wood of the low arch. His feet were bare under the long, loose pants of his nightclothes. "I am sorry, Father. We did not mean to be loud."

"You are up early, little one," my father said, trying to smooth his hair into something more presentable for a lord.

I glanced at my friend from the corner of my eye. The dark-haired girl stood silent and waiting, a little nervous at having awakened the Lord of Carfuinel. "Sellien does not think so," I replied impishly. The girl in question widened her eyes at me, waving her hands in negation. I grinned at her, knowing how she hated to be in trouble with anyone, and realizing that my father would not resent her presence.

Father raised an eyebrow at me, then looked over at Sellien. He could not see much of her, I knew, because she was already disappearing from the view of my higher vantage point. I understood that she would retaliate later. I would probably get a thorough dunking in the stream, and shivered involuntarily. The water would be freezing. However, my fear of a push in the stream outweighed my desire to interact with my friends. This would be the last opportunity we would have for at least a month, for the time was coming when traveling would be best. Many families had relatives in other anthehomes and soon they would be on the move. Sellien herself had grandparents and great-grandparents in Aullesnié, a distant settlement on the western cliffs. She and her parents, along with her eldest brother, would be leaving the day after next for a month-long visit.

"Sellien and the others are playing hide-and-search. . ." I finished, giving him my best pleading look.

"Go ask your mother."

"Oh, Cerin, let the girl go. There is too much talk going on this morning," my mother called sleepily from the *tarsul*. She must have been listening. I could barely hear the rustle of the bed sheets beyond the thin wall as she settled into a more comfortable position.

"Thank you, Mother!" I called to her. My father was grinning as I flew down the stairs.

"Take an apple with you!" she called.

It did not take long to swoop back into the *tarsul* for an apple, then dash down the long, spiraling stairs to the ground below. I skirted the central redwood when I lighted on the open floor. My soft leather boots made little noise on the matted litter of the ground, but I knew that I made more sound than did my playmates. They always seemed to be able to hear me before I arrived. In a game like hide-and-search, I had to improvise in order not to be found immediately.

When I reached the stand of hawthorn, apple already eaten, the first game had already ended. Sellien and six other children were gathered around a thick, heavily-leafed conglomeration of gorse and gooseberry. I rolled my eyes when I realized what was happening. Tenar was denying his defeat yet again.

"Found you, Tenar!" Enallá called, glaring through the thick brush. She started to push aside the dark leaves when a voice grumbled from within.

"No, you did not!"

"I did," the pale-haired girl said flatly, crossing her arms over the chest of her brown tunic. "You are in the bush."

There was no answer from Tenar, but he could clearly be seen shifting position inside the tangled leaves. He crouched low, curling into a ball.

"Tenar is a cheater!" the other children, including myself, began to chant. "Tenar is a cheater!"

"I am not!" he cried.

"If you are not, then come out and be the hunter! It is your turn anyway because I found you first!" Enallá griped.

"I do not like being the hunter," the boy grumbled, deciding to emerge from his hiding place. He slid out of the brush like a weasel, shooting Enallá a withering glance as he regained his feet and brushed the dust off his clothes. The girl laughed.

"Well, you should not play then," she answered, looking down her nose at him. She cocked a brow in derision, a move that I had often tried to replicate. It made her look very adult, very standoffish. I wanted to be like that, not like a spindly little girl who was always treated as a child.

Tenar grumbled under his breath as he stalked over to the tree designated as the den, the safe spot. Pressing his forehead against the wood, he let out a breath and closed his eyes. "One, two, three, four, five. . ." he counted, a hint of annoyance in his soft voice.

We scattered, each of us racing to find the best hiding spot. I ran, ducking under low branches and jumping logs. I knew the perfect spot, one that I had found during my many explorations of the area surrounding Carfuinel. It was a small cave, its entrance hidden beneath a huge log and concealed with a thick facade of brush. Tenar would never find me there! The cave had shown no evidence of use, no soot or chips of stone, no stacks of firewood or caches of food or weaponry. It was just a shallow bowl of empty granite some several hundred yards beyond the boundaries of the anthehome practically indistinguishable from the surrounding landscape.

I passed Rellas as I dashed out of Carfuinel. The arched bridge made no noise under his feet as I went by him. "Hah, little one!" he called. "Where do you go so quickly?"

"Tenar is the hunter," I replied, not slowing in the least. "Do not tell him you saw me!" I twisted on my heel, grinning widely and giving my teacher a little wave as I dashed away. I passed under swaying branches and pushed through heavy undergrowth, skittered over loose stone and clambered over boulders. A rabbit sprang away, zigzagging through the brush and disappearing into the tree line. I ignored it, keeping my eyes on my target. The cave was close now. Within a heartbeat, I was there.

I risked a quick glance around; I did not want any of the other children to find *my* spot. Their voices were audible in the distance. So, some of them had had the same idea as me. They were moving beyond the bounds of the anthehome. There were no rules that stated we should not, but most times we all stayed within the city. It seemed today we were all restless and wanting to run. I pressed through the brush concealing the narrow entrance to my little cavern, feeling the rough log scrape against my hair, catching little tendrils and pulling them free. I ignored the feeling, only caring about hiding from Tenar. After crawling into my cave, I pushed the brush back up and arranged it haphazardly, trying to make it look as if nothing had come through. Then I sat and waited.

I hated waiting. Endless minutes passed. Sighing, I sat back and pressed myself against the rear wall of the cave. What was taking the others so long? I could not hear their voices any longer, so I thought they must have gone to the other side of the anthehome. I must have truly chosen a perfect hiding spot, after all. Perhaps too perfect. There was no telling when this game would end. I would not know who was found first or last or even if the game had ended while hidden all the way out here. I shifted on the grainy floor. I should not have come out here. Tenar would never find me; no one would. I could be stuck out here all day, wondering if his turn as hunter had ever come to an end. I reclined in the coolness of the grotto, staring up at the rich colors that twisted and arced across the ceiling. Veins of rich purple and flecks of white moved through the deep grays of the stone. Colors were nice, but I preferred action.

The other anthelai did not seem to have a problem with waiting. They could lie and stare at the stars for hours, or sit endlessly and listen to birdsong and the whisper of the trees. I could hear the voices of the trees, although they were very faint. They did not speak in words, or at least not in any words that I could understand, but somehow I knew what they were saying most of the time. I had never truly stopped to listen to the trees before but, with the awareness of an eight year old, I felt that if the trees had something important to say, then they would say it loud enough for me to hear them clearly. At that moment, I did not hear anything speaking. Bored, I curled up on my side, trailing a finger in the dust of the floor. Eventually, I fell asleep.

A noise in the brush. Heavy footsteps trying to be cautious. My eyes snapped open, but I stayed silent and motionless. Was this a training exercise? Had Rellas and the warriors wandered close?

Pulling myself into a sitting position, I cocked my head like a bird studying the ground for worms, listening intently. These did not sound like any footsteps I had ever heard. Anthelai walked lightly, hardly making a sound. These footsteps sounded like the beats of a drum to my sharp ears. Whispered voices sounded right in front of my cave.

"Remember the plan, Detik. If something goes wrong, it's your head that'll roll. Lord Caspon himself is observing this one."

"Yes, sir. It'll be a routine procedure."

There was an exchange of whispers, but I could not concentrate on the words. My mind spun. Who were these people? The heavy footsteps moved away and the voices dropped into complete silence. What was that? Who were they? What did they want? A thousand questions raced through my mind until I realized I could not hear the footsteps anymore.

I had heard nothing about visitors coming to Carfuinel, and my mother always told me things like that, mostly so I would dress appropriately. She would never have let me play hide-and-search if she knew visitors were coming. Those men did not sound like any delegation I had ever heard. Their voices were odd to me; they did not speak the same. Had an emergency occurred? I stayed in the cave for several more minutes, trying to decide what to do. I needed to tell my father, I realized. He would know what to do. Confused and a little frightened, I crawled through the brush that littered the cave entrance and emerged into the early afternoon sun.

I saw nothing. No people moved through the landscape. The trees waved in the soft breeze, and the lush grass rippled green and silver as the wind caressed it. I looked past the heaped boulders around me, and saw nothing. Something else seemed odd as well and it took me a moment to realize that, for the first time in my life, the world was absolutely silent. No birds filled the air with their songs, no crickets or cicadas buzzed and chirruped in the foliage. The stillness was unnerving. A cold chill raced across my spine.

A shrill scream suddenly rent the silence in twain.

I made a noise and took off at a dead run, sprinting toward the *tarsul* of my parents. I needed my mother and father. The dagger slammed against my thigh as I ran, but the idea of using it never crossed my mind. I had only practiced with the thing, chopping at dead limbs or parrying the blades of my partners. I could not comprehend the thought of spilling blood.

I passed through the field of boulders and the lush meadow. The rabbits that usually nibbled at the crisp field greens had vanished, and along with them had gone the meadowlarks and red-winged blackbirds. There were more screams now, but they were few and far between. Something bad was happening, but I did not know details. I stopped beside a twisted oak, a massive and ancient tree, and looked up at it. "Have you something to say?" I asked, biting my lips. For a heartbeat I waited, and when the tree remained silent I continued on my way.

I rounded the brook downstream from the arched bridge, and stopped dead in my tracks at the sight that greeted me. Rellas and some of his warriors spanned the wooden structure, blades and bows drawn. Several men I did not recognize faced them with their own weapons. Even as I watched in horror, the group clashed in fierce battle.

Rellas and his group were outnumbered. I staggered back. I should do something, I knew, but what? I could only cry out in terror as the bodies fell, splashing down into the water or slumping onto the red-streaked wood. The din of steel on steel coupled with the twang and hiss of the bows echoed in my mind, reverberating through my entire body. The agonized screams and howls of rage breathed further life into the flame of terror and confusion flickering in my gut.

These strange men poured over Carfuinel. They were everywhere in my sight, boiling around the trees and trying to swarm up the terraces and stairs. Archers cut some down, but the defenders were unorganized, fettered by chaos and confusion. Ignoring everything but the man in front of him, Rellas cut down his opponent with a ferocious slash, marking the side of the white ladder in a ragged splash of blood. He staggered a little, breathing heavily, the last survivor on the bridge. Swallowing my fear, I raced over to him.

"Rellas!" I cried, pulling to a sudden halt at his feet. I had made footprints in the blood; crimson spattered my boots. I gagged, but remained in control of myself. "What is happening?"

"Child, you should not be here!" Rellas answered harshly. "We are under attack."

"Where are my parents? Who is attacking us?" I howled. "I want my mother!"

"You should not be here," he repeated, taking me firmly by the arm. "Listen to me!" Rellas shook me roughly, snapping my attention onto his words. "It is not safe here. I want you to hide, now. I will take care of your parents."

"Who—?"

"*Cardeai* from the southland," he replied. "Now go before they notice you!"

He pushed me away, turning with sword in hand before I even had time enough to step backwards. He left me on the bridge and sprinted into the heart of the anthehome to face more of these strange people who had come to do us harm. I could not understand why people were attacking us. I did not want to, and all I wished was for this madness to end.

I pivoted on my heel, slipping on the slickness of the wood, and followed the flowing water upstream. There were people everywhere now. I could not escape them; the crowds on the ground were too thick, all fleeing from the men that had invaded our sanctuary. Thinking rapidly, though probably not coherently, I scaled a nearby oak tree to its highest branches and perched there like a terrified squirrel. Clinging to the slender trunk, feeling the living wood move in the steady wind, I watched the carnage unfold below.

A woman still in her morning dress dodged the chaos, dashing down the spiraling stairs only a few yards away from me. "Tuliá, where are you?" she screamed. "Tuliá!" An arrow cut her off in the middle of her cry, and her voice gurgled like the brook below. I squeezed shut my eyes, feeling cold tears work their way free to slide down my cheeks. I knew Tuliá; she had been one of the girls playing hide-and-search that morning.

The surprise attack had caught the people of Carfuinel entirely off-guard. How it happened I could not say. I could not, and still cannot, understand how a massive number of armed soldiers marched into the heart of the anthehome and cut down the terrified inhabitants. However, my eight-year-old mind was not thinking of that at the moment. I was focused on the sheer sight of the swirling maelstrom below my feet. Horses screamed; hooves pounded like thunder as a contingent of mounted men swept across the floor of Carfuinel, cutting down anyone in their path.

Many people still tried to gather their weapons, tried to refocus their efforts into forming a working army. The invaders were staved off for a short time, held by archers at the bases of the stairs, but the trickle of men that made it up the spiraling staircases became a river of leather and steel. Screams, both shrill and fading, were constant now, overriding even the sounds of clashing steel and frantic ponies. I peeked through the thick leaves of my hiding spot, watching in horror as a new wave of men poured into the anthehome from beyond the river. My friends fled before them, crying and shrieking and stumbling as the men ended the cheerful game of hide-and-search with something much less joyful.

I shrieked as I saw Sellien die. "*No!*" I screamed, my voice rising above of the canopy and plummeting to the blood-soaked ground. "*Sellien, no!*" I cowered against the rough bark of the oak, pressing my face into the wood and shrieking wordlessly at the top of my lungs. The sounds were indistinguishable from the cacophony below. I struggled not to vomit, clenching my teeth into the flesh of my hand to take my mind off the nausea. The soldiers would notice vomit raining from the trees.

I hugged the slender trunk with all my might, not caring that the bark scraped against my face and drew little beads of blood from my nose and forehead. *Make this end, make this end, make this end!* I prayed. I suppose I called to Lenos, the god of wolves and steel and night to whom I had been given at birth, but I did not have a specific deity in mind when I wailed. I called to anyone who would listen, to anyone who would act.

It seemed as if no one listened that day.

I saw things from my perch. I clutched the wood in frozen fingers, my mind awash with blank, jittering terror. The anthelai were falling, left and right. Cut down by blades and bows. I watched, helpless and alone, as they rallied. It was too late. Something had to give. These armored, heavy men had stormed the anthehome, barreling in without warning. It was unfathomable, but speculation was no recourse.

A slender man darted through the trees, and I fought a scream. I knew him. At least, I thought I did. My overwrought mind was burdened by the weight of my fear and I was lost in panic. The man looked like my father, fighting with grace and strength, pivoting on his toes like a dancer and gutting *cardeai* like fish. I could not count the number he slayed. Not enough, as more poured in the fill the ranks of the fallen. The marauders were ants swarming from an overturned mound. My father, Lord Cerin Teriel, shot them with arrows faster than my eye could see before a sword strike broke the bow in half, splintering the wood in his face. I fought a scream, not wanting to distract him as he killed and leapt and twirled.

The sword swept free of his scabbard as he lunged, as he dipped and twisted, parrying the strike of a huge beast of a man, and pushed him backwards. I knew what my father knew. This was the worst time for an attack. In my lessons, such things had I learned. All of the inhabitants of Carfuinel were home, finishing preparations for the oncoming traveling season. There were no visitors in the anthehome, no band of hunters in the forests. If Carfuinel needed aid, it would be weeks before the other anthehomes would know it. If Carfuinel died, there would be no one to carry the tale of the enemy's approach or methods.

My breath came faster; fear clogged my throat. The *cardea*'s feet slipped on the slick forest floor and that momentary lapse granted my father just enough time to thrust his slender blade into the man's unarmored throat. A second sword took him under the arm and it was then that I noticed Rellas' presence. He was breathing hard but not panting, and his clothing and blade were spattered with clots of blood.

"My lord," I heard Rellas say. "Are you hale?"

"I am of no concern, Rellas," my father said. "Have you seen my daughter?"

I wanted to yell, to scream that I was here just above his head. But my mouth locked tight, my breath would not leave my lungs, and my fingers would not relinquish their iron grasp on the tree. I could not be brave, even though I wished it.

"Yes, my lord," Rellas said. "I sent her into hiding before the attack grew too heavy."

"The humans have not seen her?" My father's voice was harsh and worried and I knew why. I was a halfblood and the *cardeai* feared my kind.

"I think not. She is a clever girl, my lord, and will have sense enough to stay hidden."

Oh yes, I had sense enough to do that.

"I want you to find Dendé and protect her, Rellas," Carfuinel's lord said. "I doubt that she will have such sense. If something should happen—"

"Lord Cerin, you must come with me!" the battle-hardened warrior interjected. "Together, we will protect the lady. Is it not your duty to her as your wife?"

"My duty is to all my people, Rellas," my poor father replied. "I cannot change that, even as much as I wish it. I will be of little use above the ground."

"You will be of even less use if you are dead," Rellas responded, using a tone and manner completely inappropriate when addressing his lord. My father ignored his outburst, and I cringed back into the leaves as they moved back amongst the trees to avoid another horse-led charge across the center of the anthehome.

"I gave you an order, Thorntree, and I expect you to obey it," the Lord of Carfuinel said in a tone that brooked no argument. I could barely hear above the cried and neighs and ringing steel, but I strained to make out their words. Rellas looked stubborn, as if he might dispute his orders, but instead dipped his head in submission.

"As you wish, lord," he said, darting away up the closest staircase. He went to my mother and I wanted to chase after, to clutch at the hem of his tunic so that he would carry me with him. But my father stood down below, and I could not leave him.

He watched Rellas go, eyes dark and hot like the flames of the priests' fires. He did not turn immediately to the next attacker. I watched his face with horror, with pain. There was no softness in that face I loved, no gentleness in his eyes or the set of his mouth. He did not seem to think, to feel, as he moved. Instead, my father fought like a beast, like a demon, as he chopped men down like weeds. The iron-salt scent of blood filled the air, along with the screams and moans of the dying and wounded.

I had heard stories from the priests, but I had not believed them until now. The priests said that the *cardeai* had come to other anthehomes, but never as far north as Carfuinel. We were protected by the deep, black forests and the winding river that ate dugouts as owls eat mice. No one had expected the *cardeai* to make the perilous journey, but they had and now it was too late. The priests had called for preparation, more caution, but ears closed to the warnings that appeared as children's tales. Those tales had spoken of one thing: the extermination of anthelai by *cardeai* hordes. And the tales were coming true in the most horrible way.

A look in my father's fire-bright eyes caught me. I had witnessed it in the training ground when the scouts fought too hard. A fearful rage seemed to take hold of him, sinking deep claws into his belly. My vision became a blur of haze and smoke and I lost sight of him for a moment, and another. The anthehome was burning; the trees were screaming for aid in voices that even I could hear and understand.

People were dying all around me. There was a sound as a blade caught in flesh. A scream of agony sounded underneath me. I cried out, then pushed a fist into my open mouth to stifle the sound. *Not my father! Not* Senou!

I clambered up to an open spot. I had to see; I had to know! My father wrenched his sword free of a *cardea's* broken body and swung again. A gasp and heavy thump sounded in my ears, filling my brain to brimming. Another attacker was down. There was blood running into my father's eyes, streaming from his gore-matted hair. A gaping wound stretched across his forehead. I gagged on my terror.

In the single moment it took for him to wipe his sleeve across his eyes, everything ended. A man struck him from behind, one half-hidden in the smoke. A searing, blinding man filled me as I imaged what it had done to *Senou.* I grasped the tree, retching dryly and unable to look away. *Senou's* hands clutched the dirt, his knees dug furrows in ground wet with blood, and his trembling arms threatened to spill his weight.

He gasped, unable to breathe, and I felt his pain as my own. A sharp, biting pain writhed and gnashed in my chest, burning like wildfire around the spear that hung from his ribs. *No, no, no!* He could not see it, but I knew he felt it as a wolf gnawing at his entrails. Slipping, fading, dying. The Lord of Carfuinel collapsed in the compost. I heard him whisper my mother's name.

"Tally's fourteen!" a man cried.

"The young ones don't count, Rhutt!" a thick voice answered mockingly.

I screamed and screamed, but the sound was only in my mind. My lungs had failed. My mind was lost. And I was adrift on an endless river of black smoke and white-hot, utter despair.

My throat was dry and raw. The endless, mindless screaming had faded. I could make little noise now, just a heaving breath every now and then that threatened to dissolve into a sob. A strange smell filled the air, battering at my nostrils. It was a smell that took me a moment to recognize. That unpleasant salty odor, faintly metallic, reminded me of the time when Sellien's older brother killed a deer too near my hiding place during a past game of hide-and-search. I knew that scent. That blood smell.

"Oh," I gurgled, swallowing bile and biting at the wood. I would not vomit. I would not! My heart thudded violently in the cage of my ribs, threatening to escape. Tears trickled from my closed eyes, more slowly than before but still hot and blinding. I did not think they would ever stop.

The voices had stopped, at least. In my mind, that notion was some small comfort. I would not have to hear screaming anymore, but I realized that was because there was no one left to protest. I had heard names cried to the wind and trees. The names of my friends called by their mothers, the names of husbands called by their wives and so on. My name, however, I had not heard once. I did not know what to think of this.

There was a new scent in the air now, and this one was strong. It was becoming overwhelming. Smoke drifted through the trees like a bluish mist. I lifted my head, sniffing at the wind. The air was hot. Crackling flames snapped and roared in my ears. I risked a look down at the periphery of the anthehome and gasped.

Carfuinel was burning.

The flames were close. Too close! The meadow had been set ablaze and the wind pushed the fire toward the *tarsuls*. I gasped. What should I do? Rellas had told me to remain still, to remain unseen and hidden. Growing frantic, I stood on my branch and peered down. The flames raced toward me. They would soon lick at the base of the tree where I clung like a stubborn winter leaf.

Smoke filled the air now, and I choked on it. My eyes were stinging and watery. I could not stay here. I would suffocate before I burned. There was no choice. I was frightened, terrified, and there is one thing an eight-year-old girl wants when she is afraid: her mother.

Unthinking, I pulled myself a short distance into the next tree and then into the next, circling around the anthehome. I tried to stay off the ground, not knowing what manner of creature might still lurk there. I made my way to the *tarsul* shared with my parents, hoping against hope that my mother would still be there waiting for me. I dared not call for her. It could not be deemed *hiding* if I deliberately brought attention to myself. And I would not believe the terrible vision I had seen in tree, of Rellas and my father. Oh, my father! It was not true. It was not!

I should have known where I was heading, but in my terror I had forgotten the obstacles that lay before me. An open space stretched out, cutting off my arboreal journey with startling abruptness. The tree I now crouched in was too slender to hold my weight for long; it was already bending. I cursed myself for a fool, but hesitated. Something had to be done. The fire was still approaching, but it would slow at the edge of the anthehome's borders. The stream might slow it, as would the greenness of the wood. The smoke, however, was the dangerous part.

I knew that smoke rose upward, and so I was in the greatest danger of asphyxiation in the canopy. Looking down at the battle-scarred ground replete with blood and bodies, I quailed at the very thought of venturing down there. I was afraid of the things I would see, afraid that I would recognize the identities of the fallen. Things moved in the brush, looking like faint shadows through the haze. They seemed far away, and unconcerned with my direction. I paused for a moment, clinging to the soft wood. It seemed that they might be moving away, heading deeper into the smoke that billowed towards me. Swallowing thickly, I realized that I had no choice. I could not stay in this tree forever. Something had to be done.

Hoping I was making the correct decision, I crept down the slender trunk and prepared to dash across the clearing to the oaks across from me. The smoky haze drifted ever closer, eddying around the trees like morning fog. I had taken one step into the clearing when the hoof-beats sounded.

Suddenly frightened beyond words, I bolted toward the trees, frantic to reach cover before the horsemen spotted me. The thought that it might be the anthehome's own ponies never crossed my mind.

I was a fool to think I could outrun a horse. The snorting, pounding horses—indescribably large and monstrous—thundered around me like ghostly behemoths out of the smoke. A rider leaned down as he passed and snatched me up by the neck of my tunic. The fabric cut off my breath, digging deeply into my neck. I writhed and gagged, fighting for air.

Another rider came up on the other side and plucked the dagger from my waist. He laughed. "Look at this useless toy," he said in my mother's language, fingering the leather tassels on my knife before tying it to the pommel of his saddle. My heart cried for my dagger as my lungs cried for air.

"I knew the fire would draw the rest out," said the man who held me aloft. I brought up my hands to wrap them around his wrists, trying to pull myself up to draw breath. The *cardaei* did not seem to even notice the frantic kicking of my booted feet.

The other man chortled. "Well, I hope this is the last of 'em. I'm ready to go home and get paid. I hate this dirty work." He wiped his hands on his pants, as if cleansing them of his deeds. A wheezing gasp escaped my tortured throat and the man's eyes snapped to me. "You want to strangle the thing, Ludec, or shall we have a little fun with it first?"

The man shook me, and the movement was just enough to aid my belabored lungs. He turned his head away from me for a moment, looking back behind him. I could feel my eyes bulging, my throat burning and my chest aching. The horse shifted as one of my feet clouted it in the ribs. "You think Lord Caspon would like to see a little sport, then," he said to his companion, twisting in the saddle to peer into the smoky depths beyond. "My lord!" he called. "We've captured a young one. Should I set it off for you?"

"Hold!" a new voice boomed. "I should like to see the creature first." I could not tell from where the voice was coming. It seemed to echo all around me, halfway concealed beneath the pounding of the blood in my head. Spots danced before my eyes, beckoning me to join them. I felt my consciousness slipping away. A black mist encroached on my vision.

The jingling of tack and the clopping of hooves grew louder in my ears as another horse approached. The massive bulk of the animal brushed against my dangling legs. Rough hands blanketed in mail and leather pushed my head to the side. I was powerless to protest this intrusion, and could do nothing as the hands pulled my unkempt hair away from my face.

"I knew it!" Caspon bellowed in triumph, grabbing hold of my ear and shaking me viciously. I abruptly and regretfully swam back into consciousness, sucking in another pitiful breath. "I knew there had to be one somewhere," he continued. "Excellent!"

"One of what, sir, if I may ask?" the man named Ludec asked.

"A halfblood," Caspon answered, exulting in my existence with another celebratory brandish.

The men around me hissed in fear and revulsion. "An abomination! The devilry of Énas! Cast it off!" Ludec acted as if he would drop me, but his fingers would not open. However, even failing as I was, I could feel his arm trembling. A grown man afraid of me? I could not understand it. What was so fearful about me? I did not even have a weapon anymore. My eyes creaked open, and I stared at this man who was so terrified of me that his fingers would not even obey him. The blood drained from his face, turning his flesh to the color of snow. It was a wonder he did not drop dead on the spot.

"It is yet a child," Caspon sneered. "What harm can it do? Look at it, nearly dead." His dark eyes narrowed, glinting dangerously at the pale-faced man. "Have done, fool!"

I was dropped to the ground. The abrupt collision jarred me back to the present, knocked me into consciousness. The pain flowed over me, but centered and grew in my throat and head. The agony scorched my skin and bones. My eyesight blurred with tears that threatened to overflow but never quite succeeded in their efforts. My throat burned like fire, choked up as I breathed the smoke from my burning home. I coughed, harsh and ragged, fighting to breathe air and not the haze that coiled among the trees.

The *cardeai* jumped and looked at me with naked fear in their eyes as I lay on the ground, curled into a ball with my knees tucked up against my chest. Caspon dismounted his horse and came to stand over me. Turning my head, I rolled my eyes to peek askance at him. He was a frightful creature, and all my mother's tales of good and decent *cardeai* died within me. These were not good and decent people. Not by any means.

"Bind it," Caspon said flatly, motioning to one of the nameless men. He watched in triumphant silence as the quaking man nearly fell off his horse, uncoiled a rope from the saddle and came over to me. He leapt back as I moved to sit up, and when he overcame his uncertainty and moved to tie my wrists, I bit him. The man howled and cuffed me reflexively. My ears rang from the impact, and I dared not move as he finished the task he had been given. After my wrists were bound before me, the end of the rope was secured to the saddle of Caspon's mount.

I sat without moving. They could drag me if they wanted, but I was not going anywhere. My mother would come for me and then these men would pay dearly.

"Has an unknown human been found among the dead?" Caspon asked his men. They answered that no, one had not been found. Caspon continued, "Then its human parent must still be alive in the village. Search every tree and every landing until it is found. Such a traitor must be dealt with accordingly." He smiled back at me with an unpleasant light in his muddy eyes. "This little creature will serve as excellent bait."

His horse began to walk, and the rope between us pulled tight. I was jerked to my stomach, grunting at the impact, but I refused to move. I did not care if they dragged me through the anthehome. My mother would kill them before any damage was done.

"Get up," Caspon growled. I put my face in the dirt, refusing to pay him any heed.

"Maybe it doesn't understand Caesarn, sir," someone said.

"No," Caspon negated. "No, I think it does." He dismounted the large black horse and crossed over to me, tugging on the rope as he walked. I stayed silent and still, more angry than afraid. "Come," he said to my back. "You are only making things worse for yourself."

I closed my eyes, feeling soil tickle my nostrils. This made him angry, for he yanked me to my feet by the neck of my tunic, strengthening the smoldering pain around my neck. I moaned through clenched teeth and glared at him from underneath lowered eyelids.

"You will walk," he told me, "or you will feel the back of my hand." He held up said hand in demonstration. I gave no response, but flinched when he brought his hand closer. Caspon smiled grimly. "Good," he said, cuffing me on the side of the head. I wavered a little but kept my feet, hanging my head. I felt a maelstrom of terror and rage swirling within me. Such a strange feeling. I had never felt anything with such intensity before.

Even with these unfamiliar emotions alight within me, I followed the horse at a slow but steady pace. The smoke cleared some as the wind picked up. The horses pranced at the reins and showed the white of their eyes, nervous as the haze wafted around their faces. The men knew better; the fire was crackling away from the center of Carfuinel as the wind picked up and the trees were too green for it to spread quickly. Caspon led the men through the breadth of the anthehome. Still, the horse's walk was a touch too fast for my shorter legs, and I had to trot to keep up. Despite my discomfort, my mind raced unhindered. These men planned on using me as bait, as if I were a worm on a fishing line. They wanted to draw my mother out. They would hurt her, I knew. Why did they want to hurt her? What had my mother done? What had any of us done?

The bluish, acrid haze was not so thick here amongst these trees; the breeze coming from the fire had pushed it upwards through rents in the canopy. I could see now, clearly and without obstruction. Oh, I saw too much! The bodies—so many!—strewn about like refuse on a windy day. The faint moans of the near-dead whispered around me, sinking under the cloying scent reminiscent of rotting honeysuckle. I knew it was not honeysuckle, oh no. Not at all.

The worst were the faces. I averted my eyes, but they were everywhere I looked. I choked back bile, feeling cold sweat all over my body. My stomach churned and my heart ached, but I could not summon the strength to scream. My voice was trapped in my throat, and all that emerged was a weak reedy whistle.

I knew these faces. I recognized them, the ones that were not . . . too badly hurt. The faces with their fair, sun-kissed skin flayed and streaked with crimson, the eyes wide and glassy or shattered and weeping. All were staring sightlessly at me, into the hazy sky, at the trees. Oh, I knew them one and all. My playmates lay there, their small bodies limp and broken. Sellien's older brother was amongst them, and I had to turn my face away from the destruction of his body.

I could not breathe any longer. My mind would not function. I paced methodically behind the massive horse of my captor, staring unseeingly at the ground. My heart beat by instinct alone, forced into movement by the sheer anguish and terror clawing at my bowels. My mind screeched. *Where is Mother? Why does she not come for me?* I could not believe—I utterly refused—the answer niggling at the rear of my skull. I denied it whole-heartedly. It could not be true. I had not lost my mother, too.

I could rein in my terror no longer when this thought made its presence known. Planting my feet into the compost and pulling against the steady walking of the horse, I shrieked at the top of my lungs. "*Lasbel! Heltha amu, tórre! Lasbel!*" Mother! Help me, please! Mother!

Caspon halted his horse and the rest of his men. I continued to scream, but my words trickled away until I was babbling to the sky. Jerking at the rope, I struggled to fight my way free but only managed to entangle myself in the slender hempen cord. My strength vanished, leaving me drained and weeping as I sank to the ground. I sobbed into the bloodstained leaf litter, wishing the nightmare would end and knowing it would not.

A whistling sound cut through my weeping, and I hauled myself to my feet in overwhelming anticipation as Ludec tumbled dead from his mount. A gray-fletched arrow protruding from his chest. One of my father's arrows! But who had found his bow? I resisted the urge to cry out and instead stood tall and silent as the men tumbled from the horses and hid behind the large animals. I expected my father to come raging down the spiral stairs, and was shocked when Rellas emerged instead.

The *cardeai* did not notice him right away, too preoccupied they were with the arrows that streaked from above. All missed their intended targets, blossoming instead in the compost and fallen logs. I began to wonder what the archer was doing, up there in the *tarsul*. Was missing part of his plan? After four arrows struck the ground, the archer stopped. I peered into the trees, looking desperately for a friendly face.

"That is enough," Rellas' voice boomed. He spoke Caesarn, the *cardeai* tongue, in a manner that showed this was clearly a second language for him. The men stilled, looking at each other in bemusement. I think that they did not know anthelai were capable of *cardea* language. "Release the child," he finished, tilting the naked blade in his hand so that the filtered sunlight burnt like a flame down its edge.

"This thing?" Caspon said, tugging on the rope tied to his saddle. He had not dismounted his steed, whether in bravery or stupidity I could not say. I was rocked off-balance and stumbled forward a few steps. Caspon sneered. "You are a fool, tree-climber, to face our numbers alone."

"You may think what you wish," Rellas replied. "I will not leave here without the girl." He moved a hand, and another arrow slashed through the leaves to strike the ground at the hooves of Caspon's horse. The beast screamed and danced back. I skipped out of the way, trying to keep the rope from entangling around its legs. "The next will not miss, I assure you."

Caspon peered into the trees. "One archer?" he mused. "I wonder who it could possibly be." The large man glanced back at me, but I noticed the slight movement in Rellas' face. "You think me a fool, beast?" Caspon asked, twisting a little in the saddle. Beneath him, the massive black horse snorted and pawed at the rotting leaf litter. "I know what manner of creature I have bound behind me. I know there must be a traitor here—a traitor to all mankind." He smiled a little, a horrible, worm-lipped expression on his lined face. "Bring the turncoat out and perhaps we can trade, hmm?"

An arrow, unbidden this time, hissed through the air and sprouted from the black horse's rump, missing Caspon by no less than a foot. The horse screamed in pain and bolted. My breath caught in my throat as the loose coils whipped past me. Within seconds, I was yanked off my feet and airborne. There was not even time to scream. The pain in my throat was nothing compared to what I now felt in my wrists and shoulders.

Within another heartbeat, I was in Rellas' arms, the rope binding my wrists to the horse severed. I had not seen him move. I had not noticed him closing in on me even before the horse started to run. I was breathing too hard to speak.

Caspon was already turning the horse around, coming back to face us. Men were milling and calling, readying their weapons and their mounts. Rellas tossed me unceremoniously over his shoulder and bolted to the winding staircase. Arrows fell all around us, from Caspon's men this time instead of the archer in the tree. Caspon shouted at them to stop, that they would hit me and if that happened then men would die. I gasped, stomach clenching painfully, as something obstructed my vision. Pale wood and feathers almost touched my cheek. Rellas staggered, grunting in pain. One of the arrows from the last barrage had caught him in the back by pure luck alone. The shaft quivered just beside my face. A truly unlucky shot.

The stairs up to the *tarsul* were too many. Rellas' wind was failing and the blood poured down his back. He could not make the trek while carrying my weight. Men swarmed up the stairs like ants. Rellas pulled me off his shoulder and set me before him. There was no time to cut the cord that bound my wrists. "Run," he told me, "to your *tarsul*. Do not look back."

"Rellas—" I began tearfully, but he cut me off.

"I am sorry I could not protect you better," he finished, pushing me up to the next step. When I hesitated, he roared, "Go!" I staggered against the force of this one word and wavered no longer, but raced up the stairs as swiftly as I could.

I did not look back, but I could not close my ears to the sounds of death and pain behind me.

My legs burned as I climbed the stairs. Footfalls were loud behind me, echoing in my ears. Smoke filled the air, growing thicker now as the wind died and I could even feel the heat from the flames as it devoured the *tarsuls*. My eyes watered and my breath was short, but I could not stop.

As I passed the library, a hand darted out and snatched me inside the dimness. I had not the breath to cry out, and the only sound that escaped me was a weak gasp. The figure pulled me against it, holding me tightly and whispering into my hair, and it was then that I recognized my mother.

"*Sa'tiul*," she cried, over and over. "I'm sorry. I'm so sorry!"

"*Lasbel?*" I asked, confused.

She sat back and wiped at her reddened eyes, then swiped the silver circlet from her head and cast it aside. It would be better if the men had no evidence of her as a ruling lady. My father's extra bow and quiver lay next to her knees, and I found myself staring at them as she snatched at the cord wrapped around my wrists. The bindings were too tight to be unraveled by fingers alone and my mother's hands grabbed for an arrow. There was such dark sorrow in her eyes, and resignation.

"Where is your father? Have you seen him?" she demanded, staring at the bow instead of my face. The arrow was in her hand. I could feel the point on my back, pressing against my ribs. It hurt, and the pain cut through the fog in my head.

"I can't, I can't, I can't," she whispered, the arrow trembling on my flesh. I went still. An uncertain tone tainted the resolve of her words.

"*Lasbel*, I. . ." The words stuck in my throat. "He is—a *cardea* with a sword. . ."

My mother's dark blonde hair swung over her shoulders as she pulled me close, the arrow dropping away from my ribs. "Oh, child. Oh, no." Her voice was ragged, broken. "Rellas should have stayed with him."

I shrieked, feeling sudden anguish like cold water dashed over my head. It was true, I knew, the horror under the trees. My father had died and I had watched! I had done nothing to help, like a coward. Rellas had run from my father to help me and my mother and I had made him die.

"Hush!" my mother commanded, slapping a hand over my mouth. "We do not have time to grieve." Tears filled her eyes as she tugged me along with her other hand. "We must hide."

"You're too slow," a voice rumbled from the open doorway.

My mother moved like a woman already dead. Her head lifted; she straightened her shoulders and lifted her eyes. Unshed tears glittered and her face was very pale. "So I am," she whispered, rising to her feet with dignity, gripping my hands with one of her own. We both turned to look at the man in the doorway. Four others stood behind him, each with bared blades in their hands. The arrow, still in my mother's hand, trembled and fell. She sighed, a sob held tight within her chest.

"Are you the last?" the man asked.

"There are none here left alive," she answered. I felt her fingers tremble as she held my bound hands.

"Then it would be better for you to come with us willingly," the man said, glancing down at me. The dark stubble stood out on his pale face, and I saw a twinge of unease in his face as he looked at me. My mother noticed it as well.

"I want one promise first," my mother said. "Please, do not let her see."

"It's not up to me," the man replied, "but I'll ask."

"Thank you," Mother stated, clenching my hand as she moved us past the man and out into the air. The others gave us plenty of room as we crossed the landing and glided down the stairs to the corpse-littered forest floor.

"Pile the bodies. I want them close enough to burn," Caspon was ordering when we arrived. He waved a hand indifferently, encompassing the entirety of Carfuinel with a single motion.

"We've found her, sir. Both of them," the man leading us declared, halting several feet from the large leader of the group.

"What of the male?"

"Dead, my lord. Cut down on the stairs."

"Good. Bring the whore here."

The man turned and placed a hand on my mother's arm. She shook him off with a vicious shrug and glared at him. Then, lifting her chin high, she stalked forward after giving my hands one final squeeze. I watched after her, my heart in my throat and all my blood running cold and sluggish in my veins. I wanted to follow her, violently and desperately, but the calloused hands grasping the fabric of my tunic stayed me.

Mother stood before Caspon with several men ringed around them, boxing her in and preventing any chance of escape. He had dismounted from his horse and now stood tall and arrogant with one hand on the hilt of his sword. One man said something, but I did not hear it. I was too full of fear. However, I did see my mother kneel, putting her beautiful dress into the filthy, blood-crusted ground. Even kneeling, she refused to lower her head, her eyes. She stared Caspon full in the face.

"What is your name?" Caspon sneered.

My mother narrowed her eyes. "I am Dendé Teriel. Would you care to introduce *yourself*, you murderous bastard?"

I could not contain my gasp of shock. I had never heard my mother use such language.

"Address Lord Lorcen Caspon with respect, woman!" a nameless man snapped, readying a fist. Caspon stayed his hand with a simple motion. The man stepped back, grimacing in revulsion.

"Where were you from originally?" Caspon continued, but my mother ignored him.

Instead, she turned to the man who nearly hit her. "I see no one deserving of *respect* here," she said in a voice dripping with venom. I had never heard her sound so cold, so heartless or terrifying. "You have murdered innocent people. May the gods send you all to the lowest pit of the Plains."

"You call these *things* people?" Caspon inquired, ignoring her damnation. "I saw no people here."

"Then what did you call them?" Mother sneered. "Animals?"

"No, of course not. I give animals more admiration than that. Anthelai are demons, Dendé Teriel. Pure and simple. Do you not know the stories? They serve Énas, the Dark God, the one who culls the dead and guards the Plains of Centura."

"Then perhaps you should be kinder, because if the stories are true, then I doubt Énas' servants will treat you well, considering the things you have done here today."

Caspon smirked. "Perhaps. But I will not visiting there anytime soon." He took a few steps, moving around the circle of men. "Answer me this, at least," he asked, clasping his hands behind his back. "The creature back there is your child?"

"*She* is my daughter."

"Then it is a halfblood, I imagine."

"If you must call her that, although I would appreciate it if you did not," my mother snapped. "She is as much a person as any of these men here, and her father was a better person than you can ever hope to be."

"You admit her bloodline freely?" Caspon sounded a little disturbed. "You admit your own actions without restraint? Surely you know the punishment for the crimes you have committed?"

"What crimes?" my mother asked. "The crime of loving a man, of bearing his child? I did not know these were crimes. If they are, then the women of the southland must all be imprisoned or dead. I pity you and your foolish notions."

The man gripping my shoulders whispered to the man beside him, and the latter slunk to his master and whispered into his ear. "I see," Caspon said in answer. He waved the man away and resumed his unhurried pacing. "I will grant you your concession," he said to my mother, "in return for your honesty."

"My honesty," my mother repeated, looking at me. "I will tell you everything and more if you will let my daughter go free."

"What more can you say?" Caspon asked. "I have no more questions."

She closed her eyes. "I can tell you where the other anthehomes are, should you wish it. I can tell you their practices, customs, treaties. Anything. Give my daughter her freedom, her life. Please."

"You say she is a child. You would want us to leave it here alone in this wasteland? No parents, no friends, no company but that of death?"

"She is strong," my mother said.

Caspon shook his head. "I think not."

"Then kill her now!" she cried. I flinched, tears choking me again. How could she say such things? "Please! I will do anything."

"I want nothing from an anthela-tainted woman," Caspon retorted.

"Your people are terrible. You will hurt her. It is better that she die with me than live with you." Those words cut me to the core. They were bad men, terrible men, so terrible that my mother wanted me dead than in their hands. I grew cold and still.

"Your halfblood spawn is the very thing I have hunted for all these years. I will not abandon my quest just when I have nearly finished it," Caspon said.

Her hands clenched at the dirt under the hem of her dress. Her fingers moved; her legs tensed. The world seemed to move so slowly as she sprung to her feet, arrow in hand, and stabbed one of the men that held her. Hot blood sputtered from his neck as he gasped and sagged and fell. She tried for the next, her eyes cold and determined as she cast a glare at Caspon, but the guard smashed her face with his hand.

"You are not even trained to defend yourself," Caspon sneered as Mother was forced to the ground by the three remaining men.

The dead man's glassy eyes watched me. She knelt again, skirts brushing across the dead man's back.

"Lenos preserve us," she sobbed, then bit back her words. Caspon made a motion with his hand.

Mother closed her eyes and bowed her head, just a little. My heart grew frantic behind my ribs. A horrible, terrible feeling washed over me. I could not breathe. I could not think. I could not feel anything but stark terror.

"Dendé Teriel, you have been found guilty of consorting with those known as anthelai and the punishment is death. Turn the halfblood around."

The man holding me turned me forcibly in the other direction. I was breathing too fast now. The tears streamed down my face. I could feel the pounding blood in my fingers, my toes, under the sternum and in my temples. I thought I would burst apart, and hoped I would. I started to scream, but the man clamped a gloved hand over my mouth. Frantic, I tried to bite him, but could not get through the leather. My hands were useless for clawing; I could not get them up high enough. Wriggling like a fish, I fought for freedom, but it was denied me.

I heard clearly the sound of a sword clearing its sheath, the sounds of movement in the litter. Oh, I could hear it over the crackle of the flames licking at the corpses of all I had known and loved. For the first time in my life, I heard the true voices of the trees. They cried in pain, in anguish, but even their wordless voices could not cover the wet, dull sound behind me. My bones refused to hold me any longer and I slumped in the man's grasp. My mind went black and silent. I felt nothing, heard nothing, saw nothing. It was as if I were one of the dead.

I do not know how much time passed between the moment my mother died and when I was tied again to the saddle of Caspon's mount. I sat this time, instead of being forced to trot behind, with my arms and legs bound, back to back with Caspon. I slumped, facing the forest and hearing steady hooves all around me. I refused to look at anything but the black tail of the horse swatting at flies.

Images chased themselves through my tormented mind. I could not stop them. My gut churned in grief and sickness, but I had nothing to purge. Gooseflesh danced across my arms, but it was not from the chill in the air.

They had thrown my mother on the pile along with the rest of Carfuinel, and had led the fire with tinder to the staircases and the beautiful arched bridge. Carfuinel had been in flames when the men finished their work and led the horses out of the anthehome, taking me with them. I no longer had the strength or the wherewithal to fight. I could do nothing, and so that is what I did as the band traveled south to a city called Benthol, where Caspon's word was law.

Chapter 4

"**T**ELL ME YOUR NAME."

I looked away, refusing to meet his eyes. My bound wrists chafed and stung. I shifted them behind my back, trying to lessen the pressure of the rope. In the strange room, I was numb. I felt dead. Fear and sorrow had burnt my heart to ash and there was nothing left for this horrible man to sunder.

"It heard me, did it not, Bennic?" Caspon asked, tapping his fingers on the wood of the desk. The oil lamp on the smooth top gave off a murky light that cast shadows on his face.

Bennic twitched again, fussing with the lace hems of his sleeves. His gray eyes, which I had once seen shrewd and narrowed, were now wide and darting under a large forehead and shaggy mane of light-and-dark hair. The nose that protruded from his face was bulbous and mottled red, like a mistreated tuber, and his annoying habit of glancing back and forth as he spoke made him appear frightened, as if he expected an ambush to explode from the shadows at any moment.

"Yes, I believe it did," he answered.

"So, girl-thing," Caspon said, "speak. Tell me tales of the anthelai."

He tried to converse. A flicker of anger flared within me and died. What did he want? He had destroyed everything I knew, everything I had ever had, and then had the audacity to speak to me as if we knew each other. I would not give him what he wanted. I tried to hate him but could not summon the energy. I would save that for later.

"Lord Caspon, perhaps it does not understand," Bennic ventured.

Caspon showed his teeth. "Of course it does. You think its mother would have let it go through life without learning the language of both parents? I certainly do not. It's simple human vanity." His eyes slid to me again. "So. Tell me your name."

Names were power and I would not allow this monster to own it. Such temerity after what he had done. I stared at the stone floor without seeing it.

"Tell me your name!" he bellowed, and I tried to stand my ground against the force of his anger. I bit my tongue but barely felt the pain.

"Your name, bitch!" Caspon roared, slamming his hands on the desk. It shuddered beneath the power of his fists. I ducked my head, only a little, but he saw. It was a weakness, my fear, and he exploited it.

He came around the desk, bristling with rage, and I could not help but cower.

"Tell me your name!" he screamed, spittle flecking his lips. His eyes were wide and red. I cringed as he snatched me up by the front of my dirty tunic, shaking me so hard my head whipped back against the wall.

The hard knock rattled my thoughts, shocked me into awareness. He dropped me at his feet and I fell, landing hard on my side. The fear came back, rushing in to fill the void of my heart.

"You murderous bastard," I snarled in Anilo, using my mother's words.

Caspon stood over me. I turned my head to stare at his ugly face, to sneer my words upward to his ears. I was terrified, grieving, and hurt, but I refused him with everything I had. He would not have what he wanted from me.

I cursed him in Anilo, exclamations flying from my cracked lips. The vehemence of my declarations startled me but I would not stop. I flung every insult I knew, and invented new ones when my supply ran out. My father would have been horrified to find I was capable of such language, and I surprised even myself, but the dam of my lips would not hold anything back. I insulted Caspon horrifically, to his face, and the look of confusion and incredulity on his face was sufficient payment.

When the curses failed me, I stopped. The silence was a deafening thing.

After many heartbeats, Caspon began to laugh. "How perfect!" he exclaimed.

"Lord?" Bennic asked, his voice soft and wary.

"Not a word of Caesarn, but it knows. I know it knows. The thing curses me with everything it has, you saw. I could see its rage and its hatred. Have you heard the tree-climbers' tongue before, Bennic?"

"No, sir. I haven't," the other man replied.

"It sounds too much like birdsong, according to some. It's not worth learning, being nonsense, but the sound intrigues me." He snapped his fingers, turning his back on me and returning the desk. "I have it, a name for the creature. Given my plans, it fits well."

I tracked him with my eyes, wary and spent. My head hurt, and my heart, but I would fight if he came back. My mother had said these were dangerous men and I believed her. My father had died while trying to keep me safe, and I would try to live. But I did not know what else to do but watch.

"I will call it after a certain bird, a harbinger of doom."

"Oh, indubitably fitting, Lord Caspon," Bennic agreed.

Then they both turned away, ignoring me, and talked as if I was not there. I sighed and closed my eyes, fighting back tears.

"There is nothing quite like an extermination raid to raise one's popularity, am I right?"

"Certainly, my lord, but please, I must advise caution."

Lorcen Caspon folded his hands before him as he stared at the nervous, fidgeting advisor, meeting the man's eyes with such intensity that he had to look away.

"Lord Caspon, I fear to ask, but how can you hope to control such a creature? The very Plains of Centura could not hold them." It was obvious that the man feared his employer, his master, but he refused to quit this task. Advising and questioning seemed to be his livelihood, and I saw he meant to do them well. However, it would not do to make Caspon angry. I had seen firsthand evidence of that.

Bennic's master did not speak immediately, but instead leaned back into his leather-covered chair and stared up at the wooden planks of the ceiling. He twirled a feathered quill in his fingers, around and around. His smile had faded, and his eyes dimmed under lowered brows. Bennic watched and said nothing, as did I, knowing it was unwise to speak when Caspon appeared deep in thought. I had learned, in any case, that silence was better. After several long, painful moments, the guildmaster voiced his ruminations.

Caspon glanced at me in an offhand manner, a strange light in his eyes. "The mercenaries that went on the extermination raid, where are they now?"

"The lower foyer, sir. Awaiting the rewards you promised them."

"Yes, of course they want their rewards." He waved a hand in dismissal. "Have them all killed. Tonight and quietly. I want no word of my new prize leaking out."

Bennic's voice stopped in his throat. I considered this from my place on the floor. If he knew his lord, then he should not have been surprised, truly. The blood drained from his face as he openly and obviously considered this command. Thirty men—I had counted—had survived the brutal raid, and now they were to die as all my family had died though they had done nothing but what their lord had commanded. All this bloodshed. Was there any sense to it?

"Is there a problem, Bennic Davlov?" rumbled Caspon.

"Sir," Bennic began, the tips of his fingers trembling, "each and every one of those men have sworn to secrecy. Surely you can allow some leeway—"

"Oaths can be broken, Bennic. I will take no chances." Caspon's voice was cold, his manner threatening. "You would be wise to do the same."

"Yes, sir," Bennic stammered, sketching a swift bow before turning to depart the room. He halted just as swiftly when Caspon called his name.

"I will require the knowledge of certain men. Send Aylan Tavoli, Servor d'Anco and Nichil Boswain to me at once. No, wait. Send them separately, a half-hour apart. That should be sufficient. I would not want them getting any ideas of grandeur or companionship. Also, take this beast to its cage. I don't want it looking at me."

The smile spread back over Caspon's narrow face as he tapped the quill on the gleaming wood of the desk. Then, without another word, he turned his attention to the four piles of paperwork set on the oaken surface, each stacked in an even row before him.

*   *   *

The small, stone room was dank and smelled of musty hay. A cobweb belled downward in an upper corner, a thick gray mass that sent a shiver down my spine. Sunlight trickled in from a small, barred window high on the wall. It was much too high to reach, though I had tried leaping and climbing for the better part of an hour before giving up my efforts to escape. Myriad dust motes danced in the stream of light, teasing me with their carefree actions. I pushed myself back into a corner, far away from the cobweb and opposite from the refuse pail, and crossed my arms over bent knees. With a soft sigh, I rested my chin on my crossed wrists, staring at the few bits of broken straw strewn across the flagstone floor.

I had not yet cried. My eyes were dry, my heart empty, and the knowledge of these facts oozed into my consciousness like a festering sore. I remembered sitting lifelessly on the back of the horse, feeling the uneven plodding of its hooves throughout the uncounted days. At night, I was tethered to a tree like a dugout canoe. I did not recall eating or drinking, nor glimpsing any scenery, any hint of my surroundings. I should have died; I should have starved and withered as a fern denied water.

Lenos must have taken a hand with me, I thought. In the heartbeat it took to remember the god of my parents, the recollection of all that I had lost welled within me, crashing through my feeble defenses like a rain-swollen river. Grief bubbled and pulsed through my body like a spring. Curling into a ball, I pressed my face against scabbed knees and felt the tears start. The knowledge of all I had lost—family, friends, home, freedom—was too much to bear. I had not even been given a chance to say goodbye, and now it was too late.

"*Lasbel*!" I sobbed, the hiccupping cries ripping from my throat with terrific force. "*Senou. . .*" Why? I wanted to scream. Why did you leave me? I could not catch my breath, the sobs choked off the remainder of my words. All I could do was weep as I pressed my eyes against my knees, feeling helpless, alone and terrified.

It was the fault of that man, Caspon. The narrow-faced man, the one I hated most. I grimaced through the tears. He was the cause of all my pain. Slowly, very slowly, hatred and anger replaced my sorrow. Caspon would die, even if it took my last breath. I had sworn it in my mind, in my heart, and now I would swear it aloud.

He would regret the day he came to Carfuinel and took me from my home.

You will die by my own hand. May the stars of Lenos hear me and witness, I cursed bitterly in Anilo. The words were not my own. I had lifted them directly from a story my father used to read to me at night before bed. It was a story of courage and honor and revenge. I thought Lenos would not mind if I reused someone else's expression. The sentiment was my own.

There came a noise outside the thick, iron-banded door. Thinking it was one of the mercenaries, I scrambled to my feet and scrubbed the tears from my eyes. The men were afraid of me. They spoke of me, of halfbloods, in hushed and fearful whispers, saying we were evil creatures. I was feared because of my parentage, and they regarded me as an animal that would attack without reason or warning. Well, I could give them what they seemed so much to desire. I had always been a hard child, but I knew I would have to become stronger. Once more, I swiped a hand across my face, making certain that the last hint of wetness was vanquished. I would not let them see me cry. They would not break me.

The guards had not entered. They had not even stopped as I thought they would. Perhaps they did not even know I was here. I had no real memory of how I had come to be in this room, nor for how long I had been captive. The days bled together, staining the surface of my thoughts.

I had not been fed in quite a while, that I knew, for my stomach was protesting loudly. Rummaging though the musty hay, I managed to find a stale heel of bread covered with a coat of hairy, blue mold. It stank vaguely of fish. The very thought of tasting it caused the bile to rise in my throat, and so I tossed it into the refuse pail, sickened and dismayed.

I needed to keep up my strength if I wanted to keep my oath. Caspon would come for me sooner or later. I might get one chance. But how could I kill—even wound—a grown man so much larger and stronger than myself? There were a few small tricks that Rellas had taught me, but nothing that would aid me here.

I bit my lips to keep from crying out. Hot tears needled again at the backs of my eyes. Oh, Rellas. He was dead now, just like everyone else. The moan that rose from my throat became a savage growl. My fingers clenched hard at the flagstone floor, threatening to peel the nails from their beds. If Caspon thought he could get away with what he had done, he was sorely mistaken. It was my duty to avenge Carfuinel. I was heir to the circlet. There was no other choice. No one else could do it.

A steady noise came to my ears, the sound of booted footsteps in the corridor. I rose to my feet, thinking that perhaps this time someone would enter. I could not appear afraid. That would make me seem weak, cowardly. I could not act like I had been across the Plains and back. Still, my pulse throbbed in the pit of my stomach. My fingers and toes were chill and numb. I had time to swallow once before the heavy door creaked open on rusted hinges.

Caspon strode in, smirking and unafraid. His clothes were immaculate. The leather of his boots and belt was polished and shining, while the dark brown of his trousers was untouched by even the faintest hint of dust or lint. His perfectly-fitted cream tunic was unstained and crisp, matching the impeccable brushing of his hair. He was flaunting his appearance over my own soiled exterior. In my heart, a vile disgust took hold of me. I wanted to dump the refuse pail over his head, or at least scrub a handful of filthy straw across that infuriating tunic. The fingers of my right hand twitched.

"I know you can understand me," Caspon said dryly. "I think I will get right to the heart of the matter."

I said nothing, but continued to stare at him with narrowed eyes.

"You are a halfblood," he continued. "Do you know what that means? It means you are one of the most feared creatures ever thought to exist. Most people do not even believe your kind is real. Little creature, you are the stuff of legend, of myth, of a child's nightmare or cruel bedtime story.

"I see the hatred in your eyes, but understand that the things I say are utter truth. Should you leave, every person you should come across would kill you on sight – if they first did not attribute your appearance to a trick of the imagination. So, you are safer here, even if you do not believe it.

"I have even done you a favor. The mercenaries who helped bring you here have been killed to keep you a secret. If they knew you were here, they would murder you. They would start a riot in the streets, burn the manor to ashes, or send the priests in to sacrifice you. Halfbloods are demons in Caesia. They are monsters. The mercenaries would have killed you because they felt they must. It would have been their duty and their small, simple minds could have not imagined otherwise. However, I am now one of only two people to know of your existence, and I could choose at any moment to scrub it out. No one would miss you; no one would grieve your passing.

"However, halfblood, I am a generous man. I will not kill you unless you do something to deserve it. I realize the feelings that must lay hidden in your heart. The hate, the rage, and the fear. I know that you must want revenge."

I could not stop myself from trembling. These were horrible things that he said, chilling my blood and threatening to stop the breath in my lungs. My mind was a flurry of half-formed thoughts and emotions. There was nothing I could do, nothing I could say. I stood, rooted to the floor like a tree, feeling the cold flood through me.

"I will help you in your endeavor," Caspon said, shocking me to the marrow of my bones. "I have given orders to have you trained by a weaponsmaster, an alchemist, and a spy. They are not to know that you have more than one teacher here. If they begin to guess, mislead them. I want you to grow strong, to become skilled and masterful in these pursuits." He clicked his tongue disparagingly. "You do not believe me, I see. Truly, you will have to learn to better mask your emotions. Your face is like a scroll unrolled for all to see."

I could not stop myself. "I hate you," I hissed, filling my voice with all the loathing I could muster. Oh, if my dagger had been in my hands I would have plunged it into his chest in that instant. I missed it intensely; the desire for it filled my blood like fire.

Caspon smirked. "You want to exact your revenge on me, I suspect. Well, in order to do that you must train and strengthen yourself. In your present condition, you stand not a chance." He drew a length of fabric from a pouch on his belt and tossed it at my feet. "If you want to survive that long, you must hide your identity. Never show your ears. Speak only Caesarn. One word of your tree-swinger trilling could spell your fate.

"The guards beyond have no notion of what you are. After I leave, they have orders to remove you to a more hospitable room, complete with daily rations. Remember, little Nightingale, have a care with your identity if you have a care for your life."

He stepped back, moving toward the door. I could not follow, so shocking were his words. Caspon regarded me with one last glance, and smiled wolfishly. Then, he was gone. The door closed with a loud thump behind him.

Woodenly, I knelt to pick up the scrap of linen from the floor. My ears? A fist closed around my throat. There was no choice but to tie the headband on under my hair, carefully disguising the top half of my ears. Would this be enough to conceal me? Was I that terrifying a creature?

He had called me the Nightingale. The name had dark connotations. If I was to be named after the bird, was I also a portent of sadness, an omen of some dark fate, like *cardeai* believed? A sound escaped me. I would be *Caspon's* fate. He did not know just how poorly he had chosen when he took me, but he would.

I would be a nightingale for him.

Chapter 5

RUE TO HIS WORD, Caspon had me removed from the dank, stone-walled cell. I was taken by the fidgety man with lace cuffs and a squashed nose to a brighter room in one of the upper levels of the manor. This place was so unlike my home in Carfuinel that I almost forgot to be afraid, so enraptured was I by my surroundings.

The halls were completely enclosed. I could hardly believe it, having seen only the airy walkways of the trees and open air. The gleaming wood of the walls was illuminated by lanterns set every few feet, with fat, white candles tucked sturdily within the shining brass. The floor was carpeted with thick-woven rugs. The patterns drew my eyes like moths to a flame. Colorful and vibrant, there was a sense of motion within the wool. I resisted the urge to reach down and dig my fingers into the pile and instead lifted my eyes to the low ceiling. My gaze danced over the brass, coffered luxury above me.

Even without having any knowledge of such things before coming here, I was smart enough to know that I was observing a display of wealth. He was parading it before me as surely as he had flaunted his appearance earlier. He could only be doing it to impress me, or was I reading where there was nothing to be read?

Soon, the man called Bennic stopped at a door. This one was not barred with iron, and had a handle instead of a lock. I paused, thinking something seemed wrong. Caspon trusted me enough to give me a *real* room? I had just told him I hated him. I had promised in my heart to kill him. I swallowed my voice, and resolved to watch instead. I would just have to be careful. I would have to learn everything I could about this place, and about the man who had brought me here.

I stood silent and still as Bennic pushed the latch and opened the door. It swung inward with a slight creaking of the hinges.

"Go on," he said tremulously, motioning to the room with a wave of the hand.

I turned my head, trying to look into his darting eyes. Finally, after too many heartbeats, he met my gaze, widening his eyes as if he thought I would attempt to devour him. I said politely, "Could I possibly have something to eat? I am rather hungry."

The man took a step back. "I-I. . . Yes, of course. Something will be sent up r-right away."

"Thank you," I replied, then walked inside the room and closed the door behind me.

Once inside and alone, the turmoil within me overwhelmed its constraints. I searched the room for an escape route. I wanted to be outside, in the open air and under the trees. I felt trapped and cornered in this endless maze of a building that seemed to have no access to the outside world. Dashing to the window, I clawed aside the gauzy green curtains and slammed a fist on the opaque glass. It was thick and roughly cut, so I could not even see through it clearly. All I managed to perceive was a vague blurring of colors. Stifling a moan, I fought the glass but only succeeded in hurting my hands.

My mind raced. What else was there? The walls were stone again, I was more than dismayed to notice. A massive wardrobe stood like a soldier in the far corner, and a niche in another held a large washbasin and a chamber pot. A small bed covered with a flowered quilt and two plump pillows stretched against another wall, with a square blue rug beside it. Other than that, the room contained nothing.

I sighed in despair. This room was just a second cell, albeit a cleaner one. Absently, I toyed with the tattered hem of my tunic. It was then I recalled my filthiness. Within a few moments, I had rifled through the wardrobe and was surprised to find it filled with clothes. There were tunics and breeches of all colors and fabrics, along with smallclothes, stockings, lengths of cloth I took to be headbands, a handful of dresses and three pairs of boots. Most seemed to be close to my size, although some were much too large, and I could not help but be a little awed. I had never had this many articles of clothing in my life. It took me several minutes to decide on what to wear in place of my disheveled and filthy garments and, when I had, I crammed my old clothes into a back corner of the armoire, hidden behind the boots. They were still my clothes and, even though they were dirty, I wanted to keep them.

Dressed in a new linen tunic and breeches, I went and reclined on the bed. What else was there to do? Fingering a portion of the headband wrapped under my hair, I contemplated my predicament.

I must have fallen asleep. I dreamt a horrible dream, one filled with darkness and blood. In my nightmare, the sky lit up with a flash of white-hot fire that streaked from a vortex of roiling black clouds. The ground was soaked with blood and covered with the convulsing bodies of the dying, their hideous shrieks clawing from ravaged throats with all the force of a breeze winding through naked branches. I could see myself darting across this landscape, out of my mind with terror. I cried for my parents, but they did not come to my aid. They left me alone as I screamed in agony, as I collapsed to my knees in horrified paralysis. Two shadowed figures wavered at the edge of my vision, fading in and out of the black forest, but they vanished like a mist under the rising sun as I snapped awake.

Tears wet my cheeks. A deep biting pain in my chest told me that I had been crying out as I slept. I did not care if anyone had heard me, for it was they who had done this. I sat up and saw the uneven rectangle of moonlight that pushed though the curtains to accompany the rug on the floor. I had slept a long time, longer than I wanted.

I will be strong, I told myself. *No one else will do it for me. No one else will help me.* For some reason, I felt betrayed. I wanted nothing more than to flee this place and sit under the sheltering boughs of the trees outside. Maybe one would speak in something other than faint, voiceless whispers. I wanted to feel rough bark under bare feet and soft leaves against my face. But I had to resolve myself to the fact that my desire might never come true.

So I did the next best thing. I climbed atop the walnut wardrobe, curled into a ball with my back against the wall, and fell into a blissfully dreamless slumber.

The next morning, my new life truly began. After wolfing down the plate of cold ham and honeyed biscuits I discovered in my room, Bennic came to fetch me from my quarters. I gulped down a cup of cold water, ignoring the breakfast he brought, and followed him through the manor hallways to a large room.

I expected to enter immediately, but Bennic paused. I could not believe it when he explained that inside I would meet the first of my trainers, a man named Servor d'Anco, and I was expected to call him *master*. I bit my tongue, knowing that complaints would get me nowhere. If I wanted to kill Caspon, I had to learn certain—and that meant unsavory—methods.

Bennic knocked thrice, opened the dark door, and led me through. At first, I thought the eerie room deserted. Glass contraptions littered the tabletops, cages of mice, birds and various other creatures were strewn about, and myriad plants hung from drying racks all over the room. The stink was strong and bitter, and the sounds emanating from the dark room clawed deep wounds in my brain.

Out of the hazy darkness, a bent old man crept forward. "This is the child?" he croaked, eyeing me.

"Yes, Servor. Remember, you get two days, then she must leave. I'll be back for her," Bennic said firmly. "Two days."

"I know how many days I get," the old man snapped, rapping his wooden staff on the flagstone floor. "I'm not a fool." The man snatched me by the arm and dragged me closer. I could smell his fetid breath and feel the tickle of his beard. "Come, child. Let's see what you know."

Behind me, I heard the faint click of the latch snapping shut. Bennic had left me here alone with this strange old man. Even though I did not like Bennic, I still felt a stirring of unease deep in my belly.

Servor shook me once, and then dropped my arm. I eyed him surreptitiously. His grey robe was tattered and stained, and was cinched at the waist with a wide, black horsehair belt. The toes of battered black boots peeped out from under the hem of his robe. Dark, rheumy eyes stared out from under craggy brows, and his narrow mouth was pinched in a constant state of disapproval. I instantly disliked him.

"What education have you in the administration of plants for medicinal purposes?" he asked impassively, taking up a long pin and twirling the pointed end in a flickering flame that burned underneath a fat, vase-like container. The liquid inside it bubbled and burped, sending out intermittent puffs of acrid blue smoke. Beside the vase, a black rat huddled in the corner of a cramped and filthy cage.

"I, ah . . . I know. . ." My voice failed me as Servor took the glowing pin and poked at the rat through the narrow bars of its cage. The creature squeaked in agitation and pain as it dashed back and forth in its best efforts to escape, but it did not have much chance.

"Speak. Or are you dumb?" the old man grumbled, turning his eyes—and the pin—in my direction.

I tore my eyes away from the tormented creature, but could not find my voice. Servor set the pin aside, seemingly bored with my taciturnity and the squeals of his plaything. I was relieved that he did not appear interested in continuing that trick on a larger specimen. He turned to a rack beside the table and plucked a limp, dark-green leaf from the array.

"Can you name this?" he asked, holding the leaf before my eyes.

"Comfrey," I answered, knowing I was correct.

I registered movement, but was not fast enough to duck as he swung a withered hand at my face. My head rocked back; spots danced in my vision. A red heat blossomed in my head, sprouting from my cheek and spreading roots through my brain.

"You are to call me 'Master' or 'Master Servor,' little idiot. Should you forget you will feel my hand again. Now—can you name this?" There was no rancor in his voice, no anger, only justification. However, I quailed inside. I had never been hit so callously before, never for so paltry a reason. My eyes burned, but no tears emerged. I felt the pain in my face and the tremors in my heart. My despair and hatred grew.

"Comfrey, Master Servor," I answered softly, slowly, painfully.

"Good. What are its uses?"

"I know not. Master Servor."

The old man sighed. "What am I to do with you if you can't even tell me about comfrey? Caspon sent me a little fool. And two days a week? What am I to do with *that*?

I said nothing, thinking. If Servor thought me useless, then he might not train me, and then I would not be able to defeat Caspon. I needed him to teach me, although I already hated him intensely.

Carefully, I eyed the plants on the rack as Servor ranted to himself about my stupidity. Shreds of willow bark hung there, and those I knew. My mother had often used those for various home remedies.

"Master Servor," I began, not knowing whether the very issuance of my voice warranted another slap. "I see willow bark as well. It can be used as a painkiller."

The wizened man halted his pacing and turned to look at me. "Perhaps you are not completely a fool. However, everyone knows willow bark. How is willow bark taken?"

"As a tea, Master Servor. Strips of bark can also be chewed."

Servor mumbled to himself. "Perhaps you are teachable after all." He stamped the end of his staff on the flagstone floor. I watched as he placed the comfrey back onto the drying rack and selected another piece of crisp, dry vegetation.

"This one is cranesbill. The leaves are serrated and the flower is reddish-purple with five petals. The leaves, dried and crushed into powder, will help stop bleeding and heal wounds when sprinkled over the injured area. Repeat that to me."

I did so, and he nodded afterward, clearly pleased. He replaced the cranesbill and chose another plant from the countless others. "This is marigold," he told me, holding it close to my face. "An infusion made from the orange flowers—no others—will fight infection. Repeat."

We went on this way for many hours, until my mind spun and I thought I would perish from hunger. Eventually, Servor grew tired and huddled down on a little stool he had stashed in some dark corner. "We will do this every day," he announced, "until you can name every plant on my drying racks and their properties."

I could feel my face grow cold—except for the handprint on my cheek. The drying racks must have contained hundreds of plants. They stretched across the room, over the walls, under tables, and hidden in corners. I tried not to let my dismay show on my face.

Next, Servor showed me how to prepare infusions, teas, poultices, tisanes, antidotes and all matter of preparations. Hours and hours passed in tedium, for we went back to naming herbs soon afterward.

When Servor was not discussing herbs and infusions, he murmured to himself. I learned much through listening when I pretended to focus on mixing dosages. Servor d'Anco, I learned, spoke biasedly of himself. He muttered that he was eccentric, wizened, but an utterly brilliant alchemist with a penchant for herbal lore. He had come to Lorcen Caspon and offered his services of his own accord. He had not told Caspon what land or city he was from, but the man had not cared. It was loyalty that mattered and Servor was at his master's beck and call from the first day he had arrived on the guild steps.

A girl had come into Caspon's service, he wheezed at the beginning of the second day. I was parched and weak, wishing for water, food, and sleep, but at his words I stilled, then snapped back to attention, fingers working the mortar and pestle, when he struck at me. A young girl whose parents could not afford to pay their debts, he coughed, shredding bark for me to grind. I realized he meant me. Caspon had lied about what I was and from where I had come. Of course, Servor could not know I was a halfblood. I shuddered to think of the experiments he might try to perform. Trained two days a week and to return immediately to her lodgings after each session. He was to ask no questions and make no demands unless they strictly related to her training.

"Caspon is testing you out, girl," Servor said to me. "He wishes to see if you are good at something. So far, I suppose I could tell him that perhaps you have some limited potential. But you won't stay here long if you don't show some promise."

I frowned; I would have to try harder if I meant to succeed in my efforts to exact revenge on Caspon.

Thus passed my first two days of training.

Bennic finally came to fetch me, expecting that Servor would forget that I was his for only two days. And for those two days, he refused to let me eat or rest. It was all training. Hours upon endless hours of training. I retired to my room in anticipation. After two sleepless days, I was more than ready for bed and food. Bennic had left a small meal on a new bedside table and I quickly gulped it down without even tasting it. After eating, I fell asleep instantly.

Thoughts of plants and remedies haunted my dreams.

The next morning, I was slated to work with Aylan Tavoli, the weaponsmaster. Despite my situation, this session appealed to me.

Bennic and I met with Aylan in the hallway outside the armory. I was expecting a man much like Rellas and, truth be told, I was not far off the mark.

"What is this?" the swordmaster grunted. "You bring me a sack of bones." He was tall and hard with muscle, with dark, cropped hair and a long, narrow nose. I felt small next to him. Puny and weak, like a sapling next to the ancient oak.

"For you to turn into something else," Bennic said. He stepped away from me, still reluctant to touch me or even look in my immediate direction. "Do I need to remind you of your schedule?"

"I remember it, Davlov," Aylan replied. He turned to me and crooked a finger. "Come; let's see if there are any muscles to speak of on you."

Resigned, I walked closer. I knew I was slender and bony, not muscled enough to wield a sword or pull a bow. Not strong enough to kill Caspon. Aylan lifted my arms, prodding the skin. He poked hard at my ribs and my shoulders. I could feel blossoms of pain where he poked. There was no padding beneath my skin, no soft barrier of fat or firm fullness of flesh. If he thought me too weak, would he still teach me? He must; he was Caspon's man and commanded.

"Too thin," he pronounced. "Bennic, are you certain Lord Caspon wants this one to learn blade-play?"

"Yes," Bennic answered. "Do what you will. I'll fetch her when you're done."

He left us in the hallway before the locked arms-storage room as Aylan shook his head in bemusement.

"How old are you?" he asked.

"I am just now nine years, Master Aylan," I answered.

"Nine. A good age for learning, I suppose. I would rather you be younger still, though. The younger one is, the deeper the knowledge sets later."

"I will learn. I promise I will do my best," I declared. "Master."

"You will," Aylan replied. "I will not allow otherwise, regardless of your thoughts on the matter."

Strengthening exercises were ordered. I had to lift weights and run laps, haul buckets of water from one cask to another and stack stones. Even so, I received more rest with Aylan than I had under Servor's tutelage. I did not begrudge these tasks as much as memorizing herbaceous remedies. I thought I would find physical activities much more beneficial.

Those positive feelings came and went.

I grew tired and irritable, but swift reprimands taught me not to shirk my tasks. I was not beaten, as with Servor. Instead, I could not eat until my exercises were completed. It was agony to lift stones and haul water while the stomach gnawed and complained. My muscles turned rubbery and weak as I fought to prove myself, and I learned that I was not as strong as I thought.

Aylan was a touch kinder than Servor, in that I could ask questions and he would answer. I asked about him once, and he told me that he hailed from the far eastern regions beyond the mountains, from a massive city called Lekiot built of shining marble and gleaming bronze. I asked of his skills, and he said that he had once culled a deer from the herd at two hundred paces in a hard wind. I was impressed. He was an expert in his field and it showed. He had not looked like much at first, but he was swifter than a snake and his sword could bite just as fatally. The bow, too, was an instrument at which he excelled.

Aylan seemed like a decent man, unlike Servor, and I wondered how Caspon had come to claim him. Was he a captive? Had he been hired? About that Aylan would not speak. I did not ask a second time.

"Do you know Servor d'Anco?" I asked once, sweating and weak. It was my chance to breathe, to rest from hauling water and running and trying not to spill a drop.

"Girl, you should not know that name. He is not a good man. If you see him, stay away." Aylan frowned, his brow creasing. "He hurts for fun. Stay away from him."

"Yes, I will," I said, wondering. Aylan did not know I was studying with Servor. His words would have been different, had he known. *Strange*, I thought. *Why would Caspon not want them to know of each other? Training would be easier if they did.* I kept that thought in the back of my mind to study later.

Agility exercises were easier. Living in the treetops for nearly nine years was bound to teach one balance and dexterity. Even Aylan was impressed with my nimbleness, and said that quick feet make for quick bouts.

The second day, after a quick nap that did not leave me refreshed, Aylan pressed a small dagger into my hands. The blade was dulled and scratched, and the hilt was not much more than a piece of worn wood. It fit well for a hand my size, however, and I understood that it must have come from a previous student near my age.

"Let's see what I can teach you," he said, resigned. "Can you take a defensive stance?"

It was like my choosing all over again, with my father and Rellas and Sellien watching. My throat burned with the sobs I forced down. My head felt heavy with grief and unshed tears. But I went into a defensive stance, bending my knees and shielding my body with an arm and my dagger as I turned my shoulder to Aylan.

His eyebrow went up. "Good. I did not expect that. Someone has taught you. Who?"

I remembered Servor's mutterings. I was a girl, sold to erase her family's debt. No one of importance. "My brother," I lied, "before he went away."

"Ah," Aylan said. "Can you do offensive?"

I raised my arm, elbow high, and held the dagger with the blade pointed at Aylan. My weight settled on my right foot, which was placed in front of the other.

"Strange," my mentor stated. "That is an odd stance. Your brother doesn't teach popular methods, it seems. Where did he learn that?"

"I do not know, Master Aylan," I murmured.

"We will have to undo it. I'm sure it might be a useable stance but it leaves you too open." With savage speed, he rushed forward and smacked his fists against my ribs. My breath rushed from my lungs as I staggered, dropping the dagger to clutch at my smarting flesh.

"You see?" he asked. "Too open."

"Yes, Master Aylan," I gasped. "I see."

"Hmm," he muttered, eyeing me. "Those glancing blows hurt you? We will have to build more muscle to cover those bones. Take up the pails."

I closed my eyes, weary and aching and hungry, before hurrying to gather the pails. Another trip to the well, and another to the trough, hauling more water than I ever wanted to see again.

After working with Aylan, I was sent to Nichil the spy. He was not as I expected. In my mind, I pictured an older man, full of scars and darkness. Nichil was young, as *cardeai* went. Not much more than twice my age, I was certain. There was a softness on his face that I did not anticipate, and when Bennic and I came close to him in the hallway leading to the stables, he handed me a sweetroll wrapped in thin, damp paper.

I had never tasted a sweetroll before. I had never touched one. The guards ate them sometimes, dropping crumbs for mice to find, and I smelled the sugar on the air afterwards. It had always made my mouth water, though we had had no sweets in Carfuinel. The first timid bite was bliss.

"Good?" Nichil asked. I nodded once and he smiled the first real smile I had seen since arriving in Benthol. I wanted to like him but my heart was wary. Nichil could twist from the man he appeared to be. He could change. I would withhold my judgment until I had more information.

"You remember the schedule?" Bennic asked. I was so tired of hearing that phrase from his lips.

"I do," the spy answered. "Don't worry about losing Lord Caspon's first new charge. She is in good hands."

"She had better be, Nichil," he replied, twisting the lace at his cuffs with uncertain fingers. Then he left, leaving the spy and me alone in the long hallway in the servants' quarters.

"So," he said as we started walking to the doorway at the end of the corridor, "you must have questions."

I hesitated. "No, Master Nichil. I am here to learn."

He frowned. "That's no good. You will be a worthless spy indeed if you can't think of questions to ask. Creativity, curiosity. Those are necessary. If you are not curious about your target, if you don't seek to learn all you can about them, then the stone with your answers will lie yet unturned."

"Yes, Master Nichil." He seemed helpful, almost friendly. He had bought me, I realized, with a sweet treat.

"So ask your questions."

After a moment, I did. "How did you come to be hired by Lord Caspon?"

"I was in the Serra Isles to the southwest of Caesia, far in the midst of the sea. The governor of the main island was under threat and I was in his employ. It was my task to discover the assassins and alert the guards before they could close in. I managed it quite well, and killed two of the men myself before the guards took down the rest in the courtyard.

"Lord Caspon read about this attempt on the governor's life in whatever missives cross his desk on any given day. He realized a spy was behind the thwarting of the assassins. He sent his men to the Isles to find and recruit me, and Lord Caspon's proffered salary per quarter was more than the governor gave me in a year. Needless to say, I accepted his offer."

"I pictured a darker man," I said. "Someone old and scarred."

Nichil shook his head. "A spy, a thief, an assassin—they can't appear like the visions in the public's head. That's the surest way to be found out. You would make a good spy. No one would expect a young girl."

"So, I will learn to be a spy?" I asked, feeling almost relieved. A spy might need to fight, if captured, and healing herbs, if injured. A spy could learn things, maybe enough to sneak up on a man in the dark and plant a knife in his throat for Carfuinel.

"That is what I have been tasked with," Nichil replied.

"How will we start?"

"See, there are questions in that head. You must ask them. I will not resent answering."

"Yes, Master Nichil," I said.

"But to answer, you will learn some history first. Then the markets."

I read the tomes Nichil set on the table before me. The lathe and lay of Benthol and the kingdom of Caesia were interesting, but I did not like sitting still when I could be learning to sneak and slip and slide through the streets like a wraith. I wanted to learn to hunt Caspon.

But I studied the histories. King Cosian Ilandros the Second, the current king in the capital city of Dernwellen, left his castle rarely. His father, Cosian I, had led raids on the anthelai as a prince. He had continued the practice after the coronation and until his death. Cosian II did not follow in his father's footsteps. He preferred to study, learning the structure of businesses and cities and people. He was a good king, mostly, and kept his kingdom in line with the help of his Weapons. Through his Weapons, the king maintained the peace by overturning the ambitious plots of rivaling merchants, warring guild leaders, and aspiring nobility. King Cosian Ilandros II demanded peace and he would go through any means to obtain it. His Weapons caught assassins and spies regularly, executing them with swiftness.

The Weapons had been to south Benthol once, a long time ago, to respond to a charge against Caspon. There was little information; many lines in this volume had been marked out with ink and I could not read them.

"Nichil," I began, because he had told me to ask questions. "Why are some lines marked through?"

"Lord Caspon has ordered it. He wants no slander against his name. Be it true or false. Read more. When you are done, we'll move on."

Later that evening, we went into the northern half of the city. It was busier than south Benthol, cleaner and neater and filled with stalls and market carts. Boys followed behind the carriages, sweeping droppings from the streets. Pigeons flitted around the squares, hunting insects and crumbs amongst the grass and visitors. Fragrant trees overhung the pathways through the residential quarter, and my heart was glad to see them as we rounded the causeway.

"Ardal Evoll is Guildmaster of this half of the city," Nichil explained as we walked through the streets, "but he will not last forever. He grows old and decrepit. There is reason to believe that his son, Hanlon, will take on leadership in the next few years. What does that tell you?"

I had read in Nichil's ledgers that Caspon ruled the south of Benthol, located within the *cardeai* kingdom of Caesia, with an iron fist. Businesses and residents both acquiesced to his demands. He never allowed his townspeople to relocate to Evoll's jurisdiction, and it was likewise with the northern guildmaster, but that was the least of the hardships the people endured under his reign. Some unmarked tomes Nichil uncovered had explained, in kinder words, that Caspon was above nothing, including extortion, murder, blackmail. His guild gave him power. Without it, he was nothing more than a small man hungry for influence and control.

"That his rival will be stepping down from power," I said.

"Yes," Nichil agreed. "And what opportunity does that present?"

"Lord Caspon could try to take the north, if he pleased," I answered, tasting bile as I spoke the man's horrid name. As daughter of the Lord of Carfuinel and next in line, I had learned some things about power.

"True, if he wished it. They have been rivals since Lord Caspon came to power. When Ardal Evoll snubbed him by not attending my lord's inauguration, that's when the hatred began."

We headed around the city, taking a path that would lead us through a grove near the wall on the way back to the south. "Why did Evoll snub him?" I asked.

"Lord Caspon sought to steal Evoll's daughter away to his manor, and ended up killing her instead."

"He killed her on accident?"

He cast me a dark glance. "Think, girl. Use that brain in your head if you can."

"Oh. She would not come, so he punished her."

"Right."

"But Lord Caspon was not arrested. The king did not issue a warrant." I knew this from the tomes, missives, and papers I had scoured. Bits and flecks of information permeated my mind, floating like flotsam or waiting for the proper circumstances to dredge them from the depths.

"My lord is wary," Nichil explained, "and Bennic is there to deflect whatever sludge is tossed his way." It was not much of an answer but it was all I would get.

We walked a while longer, until the sun was sinking. Nichil pointed out people shabbily dressed but hiding fat purses, guards in disguise around the Evoll manor, and the Weapons.

Hailing from the kingdom's capitol city, Dernwellen, the Weapons were the central guardian force of the realm. Led by General Astin Talros, as told by the tomes, they traveled to city, town, and hovel in search of criminals that eluded the native guards' abilities. Nichil glanced at them as we passed.

"What are they doing?" I asked, looking upward through my lashes at the tall men. The dark-haired one must be Astin Talros. He acted like a man in command. In the street, he spoke to the watching crowd, one hand resting on the silver hilt of his sword as he strode back and forth before them.

Nichil touched my shoulder, guiding me away from the throng mesmerized by the king's Weapons as they stood in plain sight in the street.

"I think we shall see what they want," he whispered. "And this is a good test for you. I'll bet a sweetroll on it."

"Yes, Master Nichil," I answered.

"Tell me, girl, how would you steal the badge of office from one of them?" He spoke so that his words barely reached my covered ears. The crowd would not hear us over the sound of Talros' voice.

I thought hard. "I would trip one and take it from him as he fell."

He thumped me on the ear and sent a spike of pain shooting through my head. I bit my lip, refusing to cry out.

"No, fool. Then they would know you by face. You must sneak, hide, and cajole the badge from their chests. So tell me how you would do that."

I was silent for several minutes. The press of bodies made me nervous. I resisted the urge to touch my headband and make sure it was still there. Of course it was. I checked every available moment, so scared that someone would discover what I was and kill me. If that happened, I could not avenge Carfuinel. And I lived my life for that alone.

I watched the Weapons carefully, searching for clues. I would not assume to steal Talros' badge; he looked quick and sharp-witted, and proved the latter as he spoke to the crowd and his men. The badges were small circles of silver on their breasts, marked with a shield and a sword. Noting the location of the badge, I continued to watch. The Weapons were hunting a woman from Laléontessa who had run away from her betrothed. There was nothing exciting about this except that she was rumored to tamper with magic.

I waited until the Weapons finished briefing the citizens and slipped ahead of them as they tramped up the causeway to the markets. One of the Weapons seemed young, barely out of boyhood. He might work.

"I would run ahead and pretend to fall before one of them. If he stopped to help me up, I would slip off the badge and hide it in my pocket. Then I would thank him and leave before he noticed."

Nichil quirked his lips. "That is much better. Hoodlums and gutter-rats have done it before, but dressed in clean, neat clothes, the Weapons would be less apt to suspect you of such."

"Thank you, Master Nichil." I felt a twinge of pride. I could do this. I was capable of learning these strange, new ways.

"So, girl, do it."

"Master?" I asked, feeling my heart thump. He could not mean it, not on my first day.

"Follow your plan. Bring me a badge."

I opened my mouth, then closed it. What could I say? "Master—" I began.

He thumped me again. "When I tell you to do something, do it."

"Yes, Master Nichil." I whispered. The Weapons were walking away. I would have to hurry. My palms sweated as I loped far enough ahead, using the trees and homes as cover so they could not see me. Then I turned so I faced back down the path. They would catch me, I feared. They would take me away to Dernwellen. They would find out I was a halfblood. The terror was strong, but I could not refuse. I needed to learn this to defeat Caspon. Breathing deep and leaving no time for thought, I ran, feet light on the cobblestones. Passing Talros and his lead men, I waited until the young one was close. I looked back, as if someone was chasing me, then pretended to trip. My body sprawled on the stones, lungs heaving.

As I thought, the young Weapon stooped to help me up. His hands were on my arms, lifting me, and I had a heartbeat in which to act.

"Are you hurt?" he asked. "Do you need aid?"

"No," I gasped. "Thank you."

He set me on my feet and I disappeared into the mass still mulling behind the Weapons. I hoped in a few minutes he would not remember me, perhaps not even after he realized his badge was missing. I could feel the badge in the pocket of my breeches like an ember. I had stolen, and I had done it well. The breath seeped from my lungs and the rush left my bones trembling in its wake.

"Very good," Nichil said when I returned to his side. "Come. We'll stop at the vendor at the square."

At the vendor's cart, Nichil bought a sweetroll and we walked to a grove outside the southern city wall. Once in the shadows of the trees, we traded items: the Weapon's mark for the confection. As I ate, Nichil perched on his haunches in the dirt, using the badge to dig a furrow in the ground.

"Is there anything of interest here?" he asked.

Always, always testing. It was very tiring. "I do not see anything."

"Of course not," Nichil rumbled, "but that doesn't mean nothing is here."

With the emblem, he scraped away the dirt. "You see this?" he asked.

I saw a piece of wood, damp and filthy. "Yes, Master Nichil."

"What do you think it is?"

Even though I looked and thought and studied, I could not tell. "I do not know."

He dug a little more, uncovering a bar of iron, free from rust despite the damp, and a few nail-heads punched deep. "What about now?"

"I think," I said, leaning close. My fingers touched the bar, following the path it took under the shallow covering of debris and decay. "I think it is a door."

"Right," Nichil said. "But not one for us."

"Whose is it," I asked, "if it is not ours?"

He looked at me, face shadowed under the fading light of the sun. "Perhaps you know, at that."

I frowned. "Lord Caspon?"

"Yes, one safe place of many."

"But this is almost the north," I protested. "He is not welcome here."

"And well does he know that," Nichil replied. "I am trying to help you learn." He sighed. "Tell me about hiding holes."

My brow furrowed. "Animals have them, too," I offered.

"A good start. What more?"

"There is usually more than one entrance."

"Yes," Nichil said, smiling. "So where do you think another entrance might be located?"

"Why can we not use this one?" I asked, feeling bold. This was information I could use. One of Caspon's safe places. I could catch him here unawares. I felt feral and daring, a wolf hungry for blood, and it scared me only a little.

"It locks from the inside and is impossible to open," he answered. I did not know if I believed him. "But answer my question."

"I do not know, Master Nichil. In the manor?"

"That is your task," he stated. "Discover the second door. I will give you one hint: bears eat apples in the area."

"The forest?"

"No, do not answer now. Look around when you have the chance. Hunt when you can. When you can tell me without guessing, then we will speak of it. For now, we're done. Come," he said, standing and brushing off the knees of his breeches. "It is time you were back at your quarters."

"Yes, Master Nichil," I said.

So different my masters were, and though I hated the thought of calling them by the word, it was how my mind designated them. I learned to deal with the fluctuations in my teachers as best I could, and with their unyielding commitment to my education. Servor would teach me herbs and healing, potions and tinctures and concoctions. Aylan would build my strength and polish my skills with knives and bows and fists. Nichil would teach me thievery and lies and skulking.

Thus passed the next six years of my new life.

Chapter 6

IT WAS THE BOW, NOT THE BLADE, which I mastered.

At fifteen years of age, I was tolerable with a blade, but could never be considered a swordmaster. Aylan said my build was not hefty enough, my arms too slender and my wrists too frail. Long knives and the slenderest of short swords were the only true blades I would ever wield. I acquiesced sullenly, wanting to be strong enough to swing the greatsword that hung omnipresent on my master's back but knowing that day would likely never come.

Aylan taught me what he could of blade-work, and I strove to learn, to force all the information he was willing to share into my brain. He taught me to always keep a dagger in my boot, as a safety measure in case my blade was out of reach. Nichil had already taught me that, but I was wise enough to make no mention of it. Not one of my trainers knew I was a pupil of another in the manor. It was safer that way, I had realized. Then they could not guess anything about me. They could not guess that I was learning blades, healing and poisonous herbs, and sneaking. If they asked where I went on my off-days, I told them that I apprenticed with the herb-peddlers or the fishwives at the market. Nichil could have learned, spy that he was, if Caspon was not always sending him out on missions where I was not allowed to follow.

I was always careful, constantly on my guard. It was a hard way to live, but I realized that my choices were few. I watched everything, noticed minute, useless details in the world around me and stored them for later use. I wondered if maybe this was part of Caspon's plan for me, to learn to sneak silently and conceal myself effortlessly, but alert as a stalking cat all the while.

I did that now, as Aylan chatted with the monk who had wandered to our practice field from the low road. Still and silent, I willed myself to fade away into the mottled shadows of the trees. I eyed the monk, noticing his graying hair around his ears and the way his woolen robe draped over his ample frame. Nichil would have me see the color of his eyes, which foot he rested his weight upon, which hand appeared the dominant. And so I looked for these things.

The monk's feet were wrapped in leather sandals despite the slight chill in the air, and his tonsured head was bare. A silver ring glittered on the smallest finger of his left hand, set with a round red stone that looked like a drop of blood. He spoke to Aylan in a friendly manner, the skin around his eyes wrinkling as he smiled. There was friendliness in that smile, but something else as well. Condescension, pity, or something else—I could not tell. I was not skilled enough to read his face completely.

My fingers were cold on the hilt of the long knife I held, but I dared not move them for fear of bringing attention to myself. I could stand immobile for hours if need be, ignoring physical discomfort and distractions. It was a useful skill sometimes, and one of the first things I had been forced to learn.

"Your master was most generous to our humble monastery this year, swordsman. The followers of Oryn Deepwater are grateful for his patronage. Is the Lord Caspon at home, perchance? I must thank him for his donation."

Aylan cleared his throat. "He should be," he answered, then turned his head and spat on the ground. My eyes widened at the gesture, and I glimpsed the brief look of consternation on the monk's face. In a breath it was gone and his features had reassembled into neutrality once more. I wanted to frown, but held it back until the monk turned around and headed back down the low road to the manor.

"If Caspon's given a coin to a monastery," Aylan growled to himself, "then I'll name *myself* Oryn Deepwater. Tightfisted bastard."

I said nothing, knowing it the wisest and least painful course of action. Instead, I stood quietly until Aylan caught sight of me. I was scant feet from him, but he started as if I had leapt at him from the shadows.

"Gods, girl! Quit fooling around."

I flinched, expecting a blow, but Aylan let out a gusty breath and motioned to me. "Put up your knife. I want to test your bow today."

I almost smiled, putting the priest from my mind. The bow made me happiest. I could let all my anxieties and thoughts flow out of me, almost as if they sped away with the arrows that sliced so quickly through the air. It did not hurt matters that Aylan seemed impressed with me, for once, when I hit a bull's-eye at half the length of the field. The years of watching my father practice paid off nicely. My mother had never liked the bow, for some reason I never understood. There was nothing to be done for it now, however. It was my favored weapon.

I took up my bow and the hip-quiver and went to the small rise that marked my standing point. Aylan watched and gave advice with each shot, until all my arrows were spent and stuck in the hay bale halfway down the field. Eight of ten were inside the blue-painted circle of the narrow end and, of those, six were inside the bull's-eye.

Aylan said I could do better, and I knew it to be true.

I retrieved the arrows and tried again and again until they were all inside the blue marker, almost touching the eye-sized spot of red set in its center. On my best round, all ten hit the centermost target. I kept my ecstasy buried deep. Aylan would disapprove of any extraneous display of pride.

That did not stop me from feeling, however.

In a rare gesture, Aylan patted my shoulder. "You did well. Take the rest of the day for yourself."

My mouth gaped. "Thank you, Master Aylan!" I said when I recovered. Never in my six years under Caspon's roof had I ever had even half a day to myself. Now I did, and I found I had no idea what to do.

Aylan waved me away, and I had no choice but to go. I had to place my bow, quiver and long knife back in the armory first, but that scarcely took ten minutes. The silent, stone-faced guard there took my effects without question and I darted away as he turned his back to place them upon my shelf.

I went first to the small grove of maple. There was always so little time for me to sit and relax under the shade of the canopy. I clamored into the high branches, reveling in the feel of bark and leaves and sunlight on my skin. I was reminded of something I had once heard someone in the market say as he tugged a snarling dog from an alley. "You can take the dog from the fight, but you can't take the fight from the dog." I supposed it was like that with me, only with trees.

I stayed in the trees for at least two hours, just lounging in the branches and watching people pass along the dusty road at the base of the hill. I missed my knife, the one I had chosen in Carfuinel. I had not thought it of it much; I had been occupied with learning to survive in Caspon's manor. And it was gone, lost, and there was no point in thinking about it anymore. Taken as plunder and sold, most likely, and I would never see it again.

A faint whispering seemed to surround me, full of life and wisdom. I could not understand the words, but the intent was clear. I glanced around, but saw no one close enough. *The trees?* It must be, I thought. I heard them once before as clearly, like real voices and not imaginings, on the day my childhood had been ripped from me.

I laid a hand against the cool bark. *You speak to me?* The whisperings continued, and although I could no discern words, I felt a lightness come over me. The maples spoke, in their way, and I took heart from it.

So caught up in their voices was I that I almost missed when the portly priest passed across the road. I saw him from the corner of my eye and, within an instant, decided to follow him. He had seemed odd to me when he spoke to Aylan. Something in his manner, or perhaps the look on his face. Was a priest supposed to be stocky, to wear jewelry? I did not know. In Carfuinel, they were frail. It was said they took their strength from the gods. Lenos' priests were always were usually blind; their eyes did them little good in the dark of night when her followers came calling. In tales, priests were thin, kind, poor men. Life, I supposed, was a different beast.

I slid down the tree like a squirrel and made every effort to be cautious as I trailed the man in the gray robes. He moved in a straight line, with purpose, down to the inner city. The dirt road became cobblestone and the trees gave way to high walls as I followed. I had never been so far from the manor alone before, and I felt a sudden thrill course through me. The causeway grew more crowded; there was little chance that the priest would glimpse me, and even less chance that he would know who I was if he did. In the city, I was just another wandering child. I was "girl" or "it" to most people around the manor, and the Nightingale only to Caspon. I could be anything here in the press of the city.

To my surprise, the priest did not head toward the temple area and bypassed the market square. He headed in a direction I had not traveled before, down into the commons where the poorer class lived and worked.

The crowd thinned somewhat as we moved down the winding trails that were once more made of packed soil. Voices roared in the distance. Jeers, shrieks, and applause roiled all around me. I flinched, confused. What was going on?

My question was soon answered as I trailed the priest around a bend. The wooden ramshackle houses here were dark and empty, much more dilapidated than others we had passed. I surmised that this part of the city was close to abandoned. Clearly no one lived in these houses. I frowned. Why do this in a deserted section of Benthol? My only answer was that this spectacle must be illegal. General Talros and his Weapons were in the city; that made this spectacle even more precarious. Hiding away in the rundown bones of the abandoned sector, they hoped that Talros and his men would have no reason to venture this far.

In an open section of ground, ringed with wooden benches, three men in gaudy dress juggled knives and dishes while two women dressed much the same danced between and around the flying objects, fearless and quite enjoying themselves. Carts and wagons draped with red and gold fabric made a semicircle behind the performers. Some were uncovered, revealing iron cages containing pacing creatures of all types. I stood in awe, never having seen anything like this before.

A woman dressed in a swatch of gauzy red fabric and little else swayed through the throng of spectators with a bowl in her hand. "Donations!" she called, smiling brilliantly. "If you like what you see, give us a reason to return!"

Mummers! I realized in excitement. I had heard about them, but never had I seen them before. In the shadowed house where I now crouched, I stared eagerly through the broken shutters at the cavorting, tumbling mummers and their pretty tricks.

One man blew fire from his mouth while another swallowed swords. A woman did flips on the back of a prancing horse while a tiny dog behind her did the same. Later, long after the woman in red had collected a bowlful of coin and moved on, a shirtless man with intricate tattoos took her place. I watched him as he wove through the cacophony of the throng, and noted each purse he cut. Every now and then, a child dressed in brown and grey would dart to him, weaving through the spectators swiftly and invisibly as wind. The man would discreetly pass the purse to the child who would then disappear as swiftly as he or she had arrived. No one seemed to notice them except for myself and the tattooed man. I wondered if I could snatch a purse from him, if I could be one of those children.

I sat, and I wondered. The priest was still down there, amongst all those people. It did not seem to me as a place where a priest should go. The women were half-dressed and the drink flowed freely. Fear washed over me as I looked over the crowd. So many people were there. So many *cardeai*. They could not be trusted, and were dangerous. There were so many reasons why I should leave. The terror within me was a constant thing these days. I never lived without it anymore, since that day I was taken from Carfuinel. My hate made a hard film over it, encasing my heart until it was a cold thing in the hollow of my chest.

My nails bit into the calloused flesh of my palms. I put the thought of the cutpurse from my mind. I dared not try it, not yet. Instead, I refocused my attention on the priest. He watched the tumblers on the cleared stage, taking a pull from a dark mug every once and again. Then he spoke to the man next to him.

I froze, not even daring to breathe. It was Bennic sitting there and speaking with the priest. Caspon's shadow; his dog. What would be done to me if I was discovered here? I shrank deeper into the derelict house, mind working. Dashing back to the manor was what I *should* do, but no, not on this one day of freedom. I resolved to take my chances.

I have never claimed to be incredibly intelligent. My curiosity screamed at me, demanding to know of what they spoke. Refusing to ask myself what I was doing, I left the house and slunk to the edge of the crowd. The noise was louder here, almost causing my ears to burst. I put my hands up to make certain that the headband was firmly in place.

My bones were trembling as I moved through the packed bodies. *Stupid, stupid!* my mind screamed, and I could not help but agree. Everywhere I turned, there were *cardeai*. All around me like flies on a corpse. They ignored me for the most part and I, in turn, strove to ignore them. I angled toward the priest and Bennic. They were some feet from any other folk, a veritable island in a sea of people. I stopped several feet behind them at the base of a stunted, twisted hemlock. The tree at my back made me feel a little easier.

"Another drink!" the priest called, holding his mug aloft.

"When you've the coin for it, priest!" a green-garbed woman called back from the middle of the crowd.

With a grunt, the priest lowered his drink. "Damn," he sighed. "Spot me one, would you, Bennic?"

"No, you've had enough. More than enough. I was a fool to meet you here."

"Oh? You'd rather chat in that garish manor-house than enjoy this pleasant atmosphere?"

"There'll be no *chatting*, Valew. This is business." Bennic cast a concerned and judgmental eye upon the man. "A priest, truly? You'll have to leave off that one. It is entirely unconvincing."

"There are plenty of priests that like a bit of absinthe and mead now and then. Rum, whiskey and ale, too, if they can get it. And I can spout theology with the best of them. I'd say I can get by in this getup for a while longer yet." Valew, the false priest, shifted on the bench. "Since there's no more drink coming, let's finish business, shall we?"

"Fine," Bennic grunted. He patted his pouched sleeve and removed a small bag and scroll. He passed both discreetly to the robed man, who then hid them within the folds of his clothing without even glancing at the objects.

"Caspon's out then, is he?" Valew asked. "He wouldn't grant me an audience this morning."

"Business in the market quarter," Bennic answered. "The guilds are putting pressure on both him and Evoll."

"Ah, something has to give, then. Sooner rather than later, by the sounds of it."

"What have you heard?"

"Evoll's hold on his middle quarter is failing. People are sneaking out, and businesses grow weaker as time passes. They're leaving Benthol entirely, from what I hear. Lassolern is taking them in, and by that I mean enticing them away."

Bennic grunted at that last bit of information, but apparently set it aside to mull over later. "Yes, shops are closing here as well. The southern section of the market square is all but deserted. Caspon demands action. He fears Evoll is luring the merchants away." Bennic shook his head, the one time I had ever witnessed him in disagreement with his master. "He is working on a solution, but it may be a year or so away yet. Evoll first, then Caesia he says. Lofty ideas, both."

"Let's hope Benthol can last the year," Valew answered, clinking his empty mug against the stone bench.

Bennic lifted his own empty glass in salute, then stood and set it in his vacated seat on the bench. "I must be off. Don't drink yourself to death."

"That would be the way I'd go," Valew replied good-naturedly.

Cringing backward into the leaves, I watched unseen as they both went their separate ways. I was gratified to learn that the priest was something other than he seemed. I had known he was odd, and was proud of myself for catching that. I thought over their words. Caspon was having trouble with his city. The guilds were pressuring him. But what intrigued me was the mention of Evoll, the man Nichil had said was Caspon's enemy. If Evoll was failing and his people leaving, what did that mean? Was he stealing business away, as Caspon believed? I did not know. This was something for Nichil, a tidbit that might win me a sweetroll or a strip of patterned fabric for a new headband.

I did not know much about the guilds of other cities, or where Caspon fit into them. I knew about Benthol. The city had two masters: the North, run by Ardal Evoll, and the South, led by Lorcen Caspon. Evoll kept his people in agriculture. He wanted them reliant on farms, groves, and orchards. Fruits, grains, and greens packed the market stalls, accentuated by fish, game, and fowl.

Caspon fought to keep his sector's businesses producing all manner of metal and woodworks. Plows, scythes, wagons, barrels, and more. It was strange to me, since the guildmasters seemed to dislike one another so intensely, that they would stifle their productivity so that they had to rely on each other to survive. Perhaps they had not thought it through. Perhaps they had, but it was too late to change their ways. I vowed to find out.

What was Caspon's solution to the situation? I did not think like him, so I could not say. Would he crush his people under higher taxes? Would he burn them from their homes if they whispered of leaving? I would not put such things past him. And what did Bennic mean when he mentioned a situation a year or so in the making? I frowned, thinking hard. If Caspon was having such trouble, what did that mean for me? He would not release me, I was certain. This training was for a purpose—and not my purpose, but his. What did he want?

Something niggled in the back of my mind. Was he training me to fight someone? To fight Evoll? *An old man*, I thought, aghast. I would not fight an old man. I would fight no one but Caspon.

I set aside the conversation in my mind. I would go over it again later, after I had given the pertinent bits to Nichil. Right now, there was no reason to worry overmuch. Learning was still my main priority, along with satisfying my curiosity about the mummers.

After Valew and Bennic left, a small glitter of metal at the base of the bench caught my eye. Someone had dropped a coin in the dirt. I eyed it, thinking. A bronze glint, it had been. I could buy two sweetrolls with that.

I crept forward and, when no one was watching, snatched the coin from the ground and pocketed it.

To the immediate left of the staging area, an underfed grizzly was being chained to a thick juniper. The heavy links of iron clanked to the ground, allowing the massive bear but a short leash no longer than seven feet. The creature's massive head drooped and wavered from side to side as its wet black nose snuffled the air. The shaggy fur was brindled black and tan, and rippled with golden and red streaks in the sunlight. I glanced at the bear, noticing thick yellow teeth in the blackness of its jaw and dark claws churning in the dust. Both had been dulled almost to the point of nonexistence, but the bear's massive snout was loosely muzzled with thick straps of leather. The men on the front row of the audience cowered back and laughed nervously as the chained beast grunted its displeasure. One young man even screamed shrilly, much to the delight of his companions.

A man in red and blue stood nearby with a club and whip in his hands. "Who is man enough to fight a bear from the northern wastes?" he called, teeth shining in his tanned face. "A silver to try your luck! Beat the bear and you win yours back plus one!"

The audience roared to life, and eventually one man pushed through the crowd, doffing his jacket and hat as he went. "I'll try it!" he crowed, his face red with drink.

The man in red grinned and took the proffered coin, then stepped back to allow the combatants room.

The bout did not take long. Though the bear lacked its formidable fangs and claws, its brute strength had not been vanquished quite yet. The man took a swipe to the chest that sent him careening back into the crowd after less than a minute. He stumbled down beside a bench, breathing hard.

"Another try, sir?" the man in red called. "Only another silver."

"Too much to drink," the failed contender blurted, then groaned and hung his head between his knees. I imagined the spreading pain that must have coursed over his ribs, and frowned in displeasure. These city folk were none too intelligent, it seemed.

I did not see the next round, as something else had caught my interest. Three of the children that had aided the cutpurse had come up behind me.

"That copper's ours," the tallest boy said to me.

I looked at them, saying nothing. They were dressed in brown and grey, unlike the flamboyant entertainers who graced the arena. One had a bloodied nose and the tallest boy's knuckles were scratched. I thought the girl might be my age, though the two boys looked a little older. All were taller than me, though not by much.

"Did you hear me?" the tallest boy snapped, taking a step closer. "I said that coin's ours." His hand clenched at his waist.

I stared at him, knowing that it made people uncomfortable. The boy flinched away from my gaze, but that did not stop his harassment.

"Give it here," he growled, snatching at me. I sidestepped him easily.

"I found it," I told him. "It is mine."

"Like the Plains it is!" the second boy said. "Everything here is ours. Go dig in the dirt somewhere else."

Behind me the bear snarled, a thick wet sound that caused the hair on the back to my neck to stand straight. I heard the creak of living wood. The juniper tree.

"You should mind the bear," I said to the girl, because she had said nothing to me.

She frowned, shifting the scattering of freckles on her cheeks and forehead, and glanced at the tallest boy.

The audience was uproarious. I could not understand the words they cried. It was not a frantic upwelling of sound, just a large group of people enjoying themselves. The bear made as much noise as the people. Underneath rolled the clanking thunder of the iron chain.

The tallest boy's clenched fist whisked past my face. Instinctively, I struck back. His lip busted underneath my knuckles. A howl escaped him, drowned amidst the cacophony of the crowd. The girl gasped and her mouth fell open.

"You hit Timas!" she cried.

I rolled my eyes. *Obviously*, I thought, *or else he would not be bleeding.* "It is my coin," I reiterated. "I found it."

"In our area," the boy with the bloodied nose answered. "That makes it ours."

"His busted lip says otherwise," I retorted, still trying to stare them down. I did not want to fight if I could avoid it. The tallest boy, however, had other ideas, and when he leapt at me the others followed.

I skittered back, leaping backward over the stone bench without looking. The bear bellowed again, and a hideous crack rent the air as the iron chain snapped in half.

My attackers were lost in the wave of panicked people as the audience broke and fled. I used the crowd to my advantage, dipping and ducking amongst the taller adults until I vanished into the jumble of derelict houses higher up on the hill. I slipped into one, crouching beneath a pile of broken slats and moth-eaten linens in one of the rooms.

I could hardly hear the bear over the rush, and peeked out from the narrow window to appraise the situation. I was surprised to see the bear still in the arena, stretching and yawning. As I watched, it sat in the dust and sniffed the air. The muzzle hung free from a strap around its neck.

The man in red tossed an apple, which the bear caught in its long jaws. The creature then plodded over to the wagons and proceeded to climb into the nearest one.

Where the bear eats an apple! I thought explosively, remembering Nichil's words. The second entrance to Caspon's lair was near here. It had to be. For six years, I had scoured south Benthol and found nothing. When the mummers left, I would look. I had to find out if I was right.

The children that had accosted me now picked through the dirt, looking for anything the audience members had forgotten in their haste. By the looks of things, they found quite a bit.

Heartbeats passed. The noise of the crowd still rang in my ears. Voices cried out, loud with authority. I ducked my head, hiding under the sill, and peeked through a crack in the wall.

The black and gray uniforms of the Weapons swarmed over the arena. The children scattered like mice. At the wagons, the mummers rushed to pack their things, but it was too late. The general strode to meet them, followed by two of his companions. The rest of his soldiers circled the area, searching. I watched, barely breathing, as they came close to my hideout. They stood, listening for a moment, then returned to the circle of dirt where the bear-baiters had tried their luck.

"Fine of fifty gold pieces," I heard Talros say to the head mummer.

"This, we cannot pay," the man answered, anger darkening his face. "We are leaving. We will not return."

"No, you won't return," the general replied. "You'll pay the fine and you'll have all your names stricken from the admittance sheet in the guild's office. If you return after that, I'll see you all in gaol." He motioned to one of his men. "Confiscate their earnings."

The soldier went from mummer to mummer, taking their pouches when they offered them or removing them bodily when they did not. The children were caught as well, their grubby hands emptied of everything they carried.

"This is an illegal gathering with dangerous and lascivious activities taking place," the general decreed. "If you obtain a license, remove the bear-baiting and the whoring, you might be able to return."

"Oh, whoring. No, we do not do that," said the mummer, the insolence in his tone barely hidden . From the look on Talros' face, it was obvious he did not believe the man.

Talros counted the coin, plucking a handful of gold from the bags and placing them in his belt-pouch. The other earnings he tossed back at the feet of the mummer. "I'll take these fifty gold as your fine, this time," Talros said. "If I catch you here again, or in any other city in Caesia, and see that you haven't cleaned up your act, then there will be no leniency. Do you understand?"

"Yes, m'lord. We understand." His voice was almost a growl. Resentment boiled on his face, in the way his eyes narrowed and his lips pinched.

"And these children should be in school, not learning trades like this. Buy them some new clothes and shoes."

"Yes, m'lord."

I watched as the Weapons made one more round of the arena and left. Benthol seemed rife with opportunity for them to intervene. Why did Talros get involved with these petty crimes when murders and abductions and real crimes were taking place in other cities? He either enjoyed his job or felt it was his duty to solve every crime he came across. He was famous, after all. Perhaps his notoriety and intervention in small crimes made larger criminals wary. It would make anyone nervous to think that General Talros would suddenly appear in their midst during even the smallest of wrongdoings. The general made his rounds from city to city, changing it up each circuit so no one knew when next he would appear. I had heard there were other generals with their own circuits, but they were smaller and less significant. Astin Talros was famous for his cunning and his unwavering dedication. When he hunted a man, undoubtedly the criminal was found, captured, and sentenced. Barons and other nobles had offered thousands of gold pieces for his services, but the general went only where the king bid.

I wondered when the Weapons would move on to another city, when they would finish their rounds here. I felt nervous with Talros' blade hanging in the air. He was King Cosian the Second's man and it seemed prudent to be wary. People in power could take and do what they wanted with little thought of the consequences. Caspon had proved that. Astin Talros might verify the claim.

Though I could not solve the problem of Astin Talros, I had satisfied my curiosity about the mummers. Still, the day was young and there was more to see. I pocketed the copper I had found, intending to buy two sweetrolls from the cart in the market square when I had finished my business in these rundown buildings. I hunted through the floors of the broken homes, searching for anything that might resemble a door. Several loose boards grabbed my attention, and then several more after that. I found nothing underneath them but dirt, worms, or stones. No door, no tunnel, no hole. But I knew it was here, somewhere. I just had to find it.

Where the bear eats an apple. I assumed the mummers would come back as they had today, once Talros and his men were away in another city on their circuit. They had made good money while it lasted, and they would likely do it again. But even without the mummers, I would be back, again and again and again, for as long as it took to find the entrance to Caspon's lair.

Chapter 7

FOR ONCE IN YEARS, Talros was not visiting a town to hunt criminals or fugitives. Corvain, on the shores of the western sea, was a place of refuge. It was home. He had been born there and he wished to die there when he was old and frail and gray. The seabirds flew overhead, floating on the brisk wind. The smell of salt filled his nose. Seated in the sand, with his head and arms bare in the sun, he watched the water and felt peace.

Under a cloudless sky, blue as a robin's egg, he cleared his head of worries and strife and a kingdom's problems. For one week he could do this freely, then he must return to the Weapons. There was no doubt that he would. King Cosian knew Talros' ilk and gave his leash some slack at times.

Talros closed his eyes and let the sun's heat bake his bones. It was a good feeling, one that came all too infrequently.

"General?" a voice asked from behind, hesitant and low.

He checked a sigh and rose to his feet, brushing sand from his breeches as he turned. "Yes?"

A priest, dressed in gray linen tied at the waist with twine, met his gaze. His head was shaved, the hair under the skin like a shadow on his crown. His fingers were tucked into the sleeves of his robe, but Talros could see them fidget. "General, might I ask aid of you?"

"Of course. What can I do for you?"

"It has come to the Speaker's attention that a man in the city has been . . . conversing with the pirates that sometimes appear in the harbor." The priest looked over the water as if searching for the beings of which he spoke. "Oryn's Speaker has heard it said that the man has been buying people from the pirates."

"Buying people? You mean as slaves?" Talros asked.

"That's something we don't know," the priest answered. "We thought this was a task you would be more suited to discovering."

"How often do these pirates come into the harbor?"

"Perhaps once every two or three months. We have never seen them dock or set dingies into the water, but they must come here for a reason. The guard ships are too small against their bulk, but they block the quay in any case.

"The prison ship from the Serra Isles also comes here. The man has been seen on the shore at that time, too. Its appearance and that of the pirates never coincide."

"A prison ship docks in Corvain? Why?" Talros asked.

"We have room. The Isles don't. So the gaols take the prisoners in for a fee, which covers food and boarding for the term of the man's sentence."

"You are quite knowledgeable for a priest," Talros determined. He bent down to take his sword belt up from the sand and reattach it around his waist.

"It is my duty to know these things. I am a keeper of knowledge."

"So why has nothing been done about the pirates? Why has Corvain not asked for aid against them?"

"They don't hurt anyone," the priest explained, shielding his eyes from the sun with the flat of one hand. "They cause no real problems, strangely enough. They sit in the water and then they leave."

"But they come for a reason. They must," Talros insisted.

"Then they do it out of Corvain's sight."

"I see. So you ask me to investigate this man who is said to buy people, and that's all?"

"Yes, please."

"And would you happen to know of any reason at all why a man might buy criminals and gutterscum?"

"Bodyguards, fighting pits, or the ruins," the priest answered. He looked away, down at the sand, and then back to Talros. The sign of Oryn, a cupped hand, pressed against his chest and fell.

"The ruins?" Talros' curiosity grew. Slaves were illegal, but the fighting pits were not. If a man volunteered, he could fight and win or die. It was a way to win coin to feed a starving family, to settle debts or disputes. But being forced into it was a horrifying prospect.

"Near the marshland. It was once drustan land, it's said. All the ruins are underground except for some broken pillars that rise from the sinking land."

"It must be flooded, being so close to the marsh."

The priest shook his head. "Parts, perhaps, but not all of it. Scavengers come up every so often with bits of gleaming stone or a broken blade. There are creatures there, twisted from the dark closeness of it."

Talros disregarded the ruins for the moment. That was not his concern. "Tell me of the man I'm to find."

"He is older, with straight white hair that falls to his shoulders, and is slim and tall, with clothes well-tailored. I think he must have money, perhaps a large home in the area. He always knows when the ships will arrive."

"And when does the next one come in?"

"Tomorrow near sunrise. A prison ship. Those seem to be his favorite targets."

"Thank you, priest. I will be here tomorrow."

"Gods grant you strength, General. Thank you for your aid."

The priest made Oryn's sign again and left, leaving sandal-marks in the deep sand of the beach. Talros stayed for a few minutes longer, but his good mood was ruined. He walked out from the sand onto the tabby-crusted lane, brushed off his boots and shirt, and made his way to the inn. He had a room booked for two more days but did not know if he would be staying that long. If necessary, he would have to send for other Weapons to help him in this endeavour. The local guards would do in a pinch, but Talros preferred his own men at his back.

He slept well that night, dreamless and deep. In the morning, before the sun peeked over the horizon, he traveled to the seafront markets. Oyster-barkers and crab-sellers were setting up shop. Lobsters sprawled in saltwater barrels, eels swam in sloshing buckets, and sea-bird eggs lay dormant and fragile on mats of woven grass padded with wool.

Talros watched the crowd grow as the sun rose, tinting the sky with pink. The first buyers on the quay got the best items, and the slave-buying man was no different. He appeared at the edge of the market soon after the sellers opened their shops. He looked exactly as the priest had described.

While pretending to browse the various wares, Talros observed the man. The latter made a cursory effort to examine the wares in the stalls, but his gaze kept flicking back to the sea. The ship was late, it seemed, and the man grew impatient. He shifted his weight, crossed his arms, strode the length of the quay. When the sky turned blue instead of pink and orange, and still the prison ship had not arrived, the man turned on his heel and left.

The general followed at a distance. It was obvious the man had not been there for the seafood, ropes, lures, or nets. He had been waiting for the ship, that much was clear; but that was not illegal. The man went up a narrow lane in the central portion of Corvain, into a tall, two-storied home built of tabby and cedar wood. An iron gate barred walk to the front door, but the man unlocked it and slipped through. As Talros thought of his next move, he noticed a metal plate, stamped with the man's name, inset into the left support of the gateway.

Domnic Stark: Purveyor of Strange Objects

Strange objects, Talros thought, wondering what exactly that entailed. Deciding that he needed to know, Talros opened the gate, which the man had left unlocked, and went up the front steps to the door and knocked.

A servant woman opened the door. "Yes, sir. How can I help you?"

"I am here to speak with Domnic Stark."

"Are you a customer, sir?" The woman eyed Talros' badge of office, confused. "We don't get many of the king's men here."

"Yes," Talros answered. "I am off-duty today."

"Oh, please come in." She opened the door wider and stood out of the way so he could walk past.

Talros noticed the opulent red rug under his feet, the sculptures in the niches in the walls. Tapestries and paintings hung in even rows down the corridor and in off-shooting rooms. Unfamiliar items lined tables, each with small wooden tags attached with twine and inked with a price.

"Do many people come here?" he asked the woman.

"Yes," she explained, leading him down the hallway, "mostly nobles and guildmasters. The strangest things sell quite fast. Most are one of a kind."

"Where do these items come from?"

She shrugged. "Here and there. I can't really say." They approached a door at the end of the hall. It was ajar. Lantern light flickered and the smell of incense was strong in the air. The woman knocked loudly. "Master Stark, a customer is here to see you," she called, then moved aside. "You may go in," she said to Talros before leaving.

Talros walked through the door. The white-haired man sat in a plush chair, flipping through a book of plants. A wooden tag hung from the spine, inked with a number that seemed much too high. "Domnic Stark?"

"Yes," the man said, rising to his feet and setting the book into the seat of the chair. "How can I help you today?"

"I believe I saw you at the docks this morning," Talros said, looking at the items in the room. "Do you buy these things from ships?"

"Some," Stark answered, moving behind his table. "Does anything interest you?"

"I've heard you buy men." His tone was disaffected, casual.

Stark's lips flattened. "Who would say such things?" He glanced at Talros' badge. "A Weapon? Your kind doesn't often travel this far."

"I am General Talros of the Weapons, yes. I wish to know more about your business and the rumor I've heard of you buying men."

"I do not buy men. I hire them. Sometimes I'll pay their gaoling fees and have them freed if they agree to work for me. That's not illegal," Stark replied, his face closed.

"It's not," Talros agreed, studying a niche in the wall. A sculpture twisted upward: a woman dancing, dress flowing around her ankles, arms outstretched to cup a bird in her hands, her ears long and sharply pointed. "What do you have them do?"

"They scavenge in the ruins if they seem suited to the task. If they don't wish to do that, they can agree to fight in the pits for bets or travel to one of the small outer islands to dive for pearls. If none of those, they return to gaol and I get back my fee." He tented his fingers on the table after taking a seat. "I do not own slaves, General Talros. I give them a chance to make something of themselves."

"Commendable. And all these items come from those ships and ruins?"

"Yes," Stark answered, and Talros knew he was lying.

"These look like anthela-craft. The ruins are drustan. The two cannot coexist."

. "Perhaps the drustan traded with them once," Stark speculated.

"If you send men into those ruins, eventually you'll pick it clean. You can't continue to find artifacts in such perfect shape for years upon years. And anthelai are not island creatures— not enough forest—so you can't get these from ships bound from those lands. No, I think you get them from raiders." Talros turned, holding the sculpture in his hands. "How many men have died to fetch these for you?"

"Men don't die in my service, General. That is presumptious and, frankly, rude. We have barely met and yet you twist my words against me." Stark set his hands flat on the table and glared. "I was willing to treat with you and perhaps show you some pieces that I have recently acquired. Being of northern folk, I thought they might interest you."

Talros set the figurine back into its place. "I apologize, but you must understand my concern. Caesia will not tolerate slavery or raids on the anthelai."

"I practice neither. Search all you want. Nothing here will prove otherwise." Stark moved his hands to his lap. "Now, General, that that is out of the way perhaps you would like to peruse the wares? I have a new sculpture in from the northern city of Taneis. Human-made, I assure you."

Stark stood and crossed to the sidetable. He stooped, unlocked a door in the wood, and lifted out and small, sandstone sculpture of a bird. The bird had its beak open, presumably caught in song. It perched on a thorned branch, wings flared as it balanced. Below, on the base, were three real, black feathers.

"This was created from an anthela legend but with human hands," Stark explained. "Nightingales are sacred in anthela culture. They believe that the birds portray good things. The black feathers are supposed to bring luck. They are said to wear feathers in their hair, on their clothes, and attached to their arrows and weapons for strength and cunning. How strange that our own beliefs are entirely different."

Yes, very different, Talros thought. Nightingales were ill omens and their feathers were marks of death. No one would touch them with bare hands. To own the feathers was unheard of. People did not do such things; they would even chase the birds from their gardens in hopes of scaring the malevolence away.

"I think I'll not buy anything today," he said. "I will see myself out."

Domnic Stark's smile did not reach his eyes. "Too bad," he said. "My shop will be here if you change your mind or have other inquiries."

"Thank you for your time." Talros walked through the door and down the hallway, then emerged into the bright sunlight of the morning.

He had gotten enough answers. Stark was strange, that was certain, but Talros did not think him enough of a threat to deal with at the moment. When he returned to Dernwellen, he would send other Weapons to Corvain to keep an eye on the man. They would watch and report, and act if necessary. Corvain was out of his district, but he had opened a path for another Weapon to follow. General Talros could not take the entire world onto his shoulders.

"Name this one and its properties."

"Foxglove. In very small doses, it can help steady an irregular heartbeat. However, it is extremely toxic and should be used with the utmost caution. Foxglove, also called dead man's bells or digitalis, can be easily confused with comfrey. Drying does not weaken its toxicity, and the entire plant is poisonous. Even nibbling the leaves can be enough to cause death. Symptoms of foxglove poisoning include. . ." I rattled off a list long enough to suit Servor, who sat still and mostly silent on the small three-legged stool across the table.

The old man nodded as I finished. "Good, good." Gripping his cane, Servor levered himself up from the stool and made his way to one of the low, long tables pressed against the walls. "Come here, girl."

I did, somewhat warily. I could never tell if Servor would whirl on me with something. After the last incident with a rather hot cup of mallow-root tea, I kept a healthy distance from the old man. By now I could name every plant on the racks, what they did and how to best prepare each one. I knew helpful plants as well as poisonous ones. However, I had never put any of this knowledge into practice. In spite of this, with the confidence of a fifteen-year-old, I felt I was prepared to use my learned skills should the need arise.

"Have you heard of firedust?" Servor asked in his wavering voice.

"No, Master Servor. I have not."

"It is a rare thing, very expensive. Not many have heard of it, let alone know how to manufacture such a thing. Fetch the box of saltpeter."

I repressed a shudder. Saltpeter smelled disgusting, and knowing how it was produced made it even less appealing. But I did as I was told. I watched as he took the shallow box with gnarled fingers and set it carefully on the table.

With a spoon, Servor scooped a few grains from the box and dropped them onto a piece of parchment. Setting the spoon aside, he took up a delicate pair of tongs and reached for a thick beaker filled with jagged yellow crystals. "This is sulfur," he told me. "Also called brimstone or cinnabar. Notice the smell."

I sniffed at the beaker held aloft for me, and then cringed away from the rotten stench. Like eggs, it was, all putrid and repulsive. Servor handled the beaker without fear of either contents or odor. He retrieved one diminutive crystal with the tongs and ground it into dust with the mortar and pestle. Then he tipped the mortar and swept the granules together with the saltpeter. "Do you see what I did there?"

"Yes, Master Servor."

"In such tiny amounts as this, there is still danger. The slightest touch of heat, even a careless touch, could set it off. Separately, these ingredients are not so dangerous, but put together they can fell walls. This here is enough to remove a hand from an incautious arm."

I inched away, eyeing the gray-yellow powder. It was naught but a pinch of dust. I could hardly believe it was enough to remove a hand, but my opinion changed when Servor demonstrated the effects of it. He set the end of a slender dowel aflame and, holding the rod by the end of its four-foot length, touched the light to the powder.

The loud *crack* and the acrid smoke that followed were enough to engrave this lesson forever into my memory.

"What else can saltpeter and sulfur do, girl?" he asked, waving a hand before his nose in an effort to dissipate the smoke still rising from the charred circle on the table.

I told him some medicinal uses of saltpeter and sulfur, of which there were few. While I paused to think, Servor related the dangers of these elements, remonstrating what should or should not be added to produce desired or dangerous effects.

I had started out learning medicinal plants and their uses from the alchemist, but the passing of years demonstrated the need for other brands of knowledge. There were only so many plants to learn, only so many healing properties of each. Herbaceous remedies were not endless, and so Servor, in order to remain a diligent teacher, began to educate me in other methods. He had so much knowledge stored in that white-haired head, and I think he was somewhat relieved to have someone willing to learn.

I resolved to learn all the information he would give me. I did not think that I would need it, but I latched onto anything I felt might be important. I was already making plans for Caspon's demise, and Servor's information was a step in helping me succeed in case my other tactics failed.

We spoke a while longer, of nightshade and monkshood and hemlock and several lesser-known poisonous plants. I was grateful when Servor ceased speaking and bid me clean the room. Straightening the drying racks, wiping countertops and making cordage from which to hang the new floral specimens gave my tired mind a welcome reprieve. I fed the caged anoles their allotment of crickets, gave the mice their seed and changed their water, and dropped one mouse in the snake cage for the sluggish reptile. After that, I swept the floor with the ragged broom and pushed the dust and debris through the grate in the corner.

Finally, Servor let me leave. No longer did Bennic have to come fetch me when the old man forgot. I was capable of reminding him when our two days had passed, though I did not do it often. I was still wary of him, of his dark temper and swift cane.

Thus, I abandoned the old alchemist to mutter and fidget in his study.

I did not go to my room, although I was tired. Nichil had given me a task the last day I had studied with him. Somehow I was to bring him the ring from Bennic's finger. I did not see a possible way to do it, since I had never seen Bennic without it. A wide band of gold, it was, set with a square emerald and etched with the runes of his family name. I had followed Bennic around the manor for days, after my studies were done, and not once had I observed an opportunity to snatch the bauble.

Bennic had not even known I was trailing him. I once stalked him all the way to his apartments and he had been none the wiser. Today, I was going to try and venture inside his rooms, to see what was there and if it might be of any use. I would have to take a roundabout route, of course. I could not be seen traipsing up to his rooms like I owned them. Word would undoubtedly get back to him then, and Bennic was afraid of me. There would be consequences, likely from Caspon himself.

I started in the kitchens, eager to snatch a bite to eat before my hunt began. The kitchens were always busy. The cook and her potboys and maids pounded great wads of dough into loaves of oat-crusted breads and mixed vats of meaty stews and peeled vegetables. It was easy enough to palm a handful of berries and a crust of bread out from under their distracted eyes.

I never ate much, just enough to stave off the hunger pangs, and so I remained waiflike even as I grew wiry with necessary muscle. I looked younger than fifteen, due to my small stature. Easier it was to slip through crevices and remain undetected when one was smaller and childlike, I was told. Also, I was taught that there were times when food was unavailable. Learning to do without was a necessity. Sleep was another luxury I rarely allowed myself. I was always terrified that someone would discover that I was a halfblood. Letting my guard down was a critical liability. Should someone happen upon me unawares, there was every chance I could be found out. Thus, I learned to sleep very lightly. Even the smallest noises, changes in air pressure or the quality of light awoke me. These were traits that I did not know how to unlearn. They became a greater part of me with every passing day.

Slinking out through the rear door of the kitchen, I went lower into a maze of servant's tunnels, taking a set of stairs down into a basement area where I had never before dared to go. Nichil had made me learn the manor like the back of my hand, the servants' schedules, the lamp-lit hallways, and the creaking of the floors. But this place, this area, was off-limits. Nichil often went into the basement, but I was not allowed to follow. Caspon gave him secret assignments down here, somewhere. Bennic's lowly office must reside here as well, for he was never very far from his master's side. If someone discovered me down here, there was no way to defend my actions. There was no reason for me to be here. I must not be found.

I padded through the stone corridors, my eyes narrowed against the flickering patches of light thrown by the low-burning peat torches. The echo of distant footsteps reached my ears, and I stepped off into an adjacent pathway. A guard passed, bearing a sheathed shortsword, and then vanished behind a bend in the hall. Stepping back into the corridor, I went on my way.

Occasionally, a thick oaken door barred an exit to an adjoining hallway or room. I had never been through those doors, and had no idea as to what lay behind them. Certainly they were rooms off-limits to visitors and perhaps servants as well. Caspon's own private sanctuaries. The thought intrigued me, and though I was a cautious creature, Nichil had taught me to be curious as well.

When I came across the doors, I pressed a cloth-covered ear against the wood, listening for sounds that might or might not be familiar. Usually, there was nothing to signify any kind of occupancy. Once, I heard the faint meow of a cat lost somewhere behind the granite and oak, but ignored it. Cats were of no concern to me.

Several corridors and nine doors later, however, there came a noise, a voice speaking of coins and cost in breathy tones, that caught my immediate attention and held it in an iron grasp. Instantly, all thoughts of Bennic and his ring were vanquished, tossed aside to be whisked away by a swirling torrent of overwhelming terror and hatred.

I stopped dead still and silent, straining against the tide of my emotions. I struggled to contain myself. My time had come. I could not—*would not*—waste this opportunity. I slid closer to the oaken door, willing myself to disappear, and pressed an ear against the wood.

Faint breathing; the clink of metal; a soft mumble in a voice I knew and abhorred. Suppressing the snarl that clawed upward through my throat, I studied the door, illuminated by the faint light of a dying lamp on the wall. The shadows danced, beckoning my eyes to follow. I almost did not see the faint glimmer of a latch. It was smaller than my thumb, set amid the dark slats of wood. I thumbed it cautiously, my sharp ears catching the faint *snick* as the bolt slid back.

I paused, my breath settling like lead in the bottom of my lungs. Was I ready for this? Could I succeed? *This is foolhardy*, I thought. *It is idiotic.* But I could not make myself leave. My mind raged against the thought even as my heart wavered in indecision. *I must try. I owe it to Carfuinel. When will this chance ever arise again?* I thrust my heart downward, willing my anxieties to silence, and carefully, slowly, opened the door.

At first, I pried it back just enough to peek inside. I needed to be certain.

When my first feelings were confirmed, the old fire flared to life. My heart slammed against my breastbone so hard I thought it would break. My breath died a strangled death in the back of my throat.

Caspon sat there with his back to the door.

He sat at a plain pine table, in a plain pine chair, hunched over the glittering hoard scattered atop it. Gemstones, pile upon shining pile of gemstones, were strewn across the flat surface. There were so many, too many to count, glistening like captured rainbows in the light of the two candles on the tabletop. I could not even begin to imagine the wealth that small area of space contained. It was beyond me.

There were other things on that table as well. Not just gemstones, but also an assortment of jewelry, various medallions like the kind warriors and heroes wore, gauntlets edged in silver, a bronze candelabrum with leaves and birds etched into the metal, and scabbards and sheaths touched with gold and cabochon stones. These latter fixtures were not empty. A dagger was partly removed from its emerald and silver sheath, the hilt glistening with garnet fire. Beside it, a dark leather sheath paled in comparison to the wealth and the brilliant colors.

I bit my tongue to keep from screaming.

It was my dagger there on that table, the one I had chosen from Rellas' selection. The one my father had given me leave to use.

A terrible heat burned within me, turning everything inside me to ash. I do not know what crossed my mind after seeing my dagger. All I know was that suddenly I was in that room with the door closed behind me.

Caspon was still unaware of my presence. I moved so silently that he had not even heard the door open and close behind him. Clenching my hands into fists, feeling the nails bite into my palms, I willed myself to silence. Caspon was so close I could feel the warmth emanating from him; I could smell what he had eaten for supper on his breath.

My fingers had just started creeping toward the dagger on the tableside when he glimpsed me.

He gaped like a dying fish as I snatched my dagger. He exploded up from his chair, sending it flying into the wall in an effort to get away from me. I spun around, swinging my arm to bring the dagger into his chest.

He was quicker than I had thought, for all his size. Caspon ducked to the side, flashing out a calloused hand to smash me in the face. A cry escaped me and I staggered, glaring at him through hate-filled eyes. I gritted my teeth and lashed out again, feeling the blade pass through the thick fabric of his breeches, but it did not touch the skin below. Caspon leapt back, throwing the heavy candelabrum at me with a vicious arc of his arm.

I dodged it easily, believing that his desire to educate me in swordplay had backfired on him. I snarled, feeling much older than my years should have allowed. A slow trickle of confidence threaded through my heart. Caspon was afraid, and fear would let me destroy him. He slid away, and like a dog, I gave chase.

He blocked my next blow with a thick tome snatched from a shelf on the wall. The dark blade bit deep into the vellum pages, parting the leather cover like silk. A good blade, this. Caspon wrenched the book away and it parted company with the blade with a shredding of pale lambskin. My fingers tingled from the rough twisting of the knife, but I refused to relinquish my hold. My stomach was a churning mass of triumph and disbelief. I tried to choke the feelings down, to focus, but could not.

I was young and overconfident, drunk on the flood of power in my veins. Caspon, however, was larger and much too strong. I underestimated him, to my despair. A painting whipped through the air toward me, hissing past my temple and scraping a furrow across my brow in a line of fire. I flinched. The frame had struck entirely too close to my eyes.

Instinctively, I reached a hand toward the wound, losing my concentration for one moment too many. In that short and crucial expanse of time, Caspon managed to grasp the heavy chair and heave it at me with all the strength he could muster.

It caught me full in the chest, sending me sprawling across the flagstone floor and fighting for breath. My head knocked against the stone, sending a shower of haloed stars spinning across my vision.

I was down, and that gave Caspon a good excuse to kick me. He swept the objects off the table. Gemstones rained against my body like hailstones. One hit me in the forehead with a ferocious thud, and the sudden red pain was blinding. Two gauntlets struck me in the torso, bouncing off to lie like severed hands on the floor, turned upward in supplication.

I tried to haul myself off the floor, but my arms refused to move. My breath stuck in my gorge like a chunk of meat. Was I broken? Cold sweat beaded on my skin despite the chill in the air. My bones *felt* intact, though I ached abysmally. My heart grew cold in the hollow of my chest, and the blood pounded in my ears. Terror washed through my veins. *What is wrong with me?* I silently wailed.

Caspon stood beside the table, his chest heaving in an effort to keep breathing. "What's the matter?" he panted with sneer. "Too tired to finish the job?"

A pang of rage surged through me, and I struggled with all my might to rise from the cold stone floor. It was useless. My arms and legs would not budge. I could barely wiggle my fingers. My rage subsided swiftly, replaced by a cold numbness. What had happened to me? I lay on my back, glaring at Caspon. It was all I could do.

A strange, incomprehensible look passed over Caspon's face like a shadow. "What are you plotting, halfblood?"

I could not open my mouth to answer, but my fingers twitched on the hilt of my dagger. Somehow, I had managed to retain my grip on it.

Caspon's eyes snapped to the knife. "Release that at once," he demanded, and my fingers had no choice but to respond. Against my will, the knife slipped from my nerveless hand, sliding from my loosened fingers.

A look of victory passed over Caspon's face. "Coward," he sneered. "Just like your mother and father before you." His face was a grimace, but he stepped back as he spoke, as if expecting me to leap up and tear out his throat. I would have gladly obliged, if I had been able.

"You do not move?" he inquired. "Why do you not attack again? Why do you not speak?"

I fought the sudden and disgusting urge to answer him.

"Answer!" he demanded, clenching his fists at his sides.

Now my tongue loosened, and I could speak again. This time I could not refuse. "I cannot. . ." I whispered, rendered unable to deceive him. I had wanted to let him think this was a scheme, a devilish plot, but my traitor tongue renounced me.

"Repeat that," Caspon requested, a sliver of disbelief creeping into his voice.

"I cannot move!" my voice cried, alien to my ears. "I know not why!" Hot tears prickled behind my eyes, fighting for release, but I held them back as best I could. Caspon stared at me.

"You lie," he growled.

"No," I whispered, wanting to sink through the floor. "I do not." I could not, and now I was finished. I had failed so horribly and so thoroughly that I could not even imagine an outcome for the situation.

Caspon seemed to steel himself. His eyes narrowed in his flushed and sweaty face. He stalked over and knelt beside me. I tried to struggle, but my muscles were frozen in place. Cold fear washed over me. Carefully, Caspon took the dagger and replaced it in my palm. My fingers would not close themselves over the hilt, though I fought for it.

I could not move to attack him, although my heart and mind demanded it.

Caspon's face was thoughtful as he regarded me. Almost gently, he touched one of the gemstones scattered on and around me. Then, one by one, he flicked them away, regarding me like a tethered dog proven vicious all the while. When I still ceased to move after each removal, he grew braver, mocking me as he worked, and finally there was one stone left. Just one small green beryl nestled at the base of my throat. And still I could not move.

"I wonder," Caspon murmured, gazing at the stone.

I lay on the cold stone floor for two full days, unmoving and silent as a corpse, while he researched. To my dismay, I was still very much alive. My discomfort grew by the hour, but physical ailments were nothing compared to the sense of utter failure that loomed overhead. The one task I had set for myself, the one thing I had dedicated my life to completing—and I could not have been any less successful at it.

So sorry, I thought pitifully. *I tried, but I was not good enough.* A single tear escaped my closed eyes, trekking down my face, and I could not even wipe it away. *So, so sorry.*

The door creaked open and shut behind me. Booted footsteps were loud on the flagstone floor, approaching without caution or fear. The presence stood over me, and I could feel his eyes boring holes into my flesh. My eyes shuddered open, and I saw Caspon hovering there, hungry and victorious.

"You are mine," he said, a predatory light in his eyes. "That stone is your chain, Nightingale. You cannot break it."

His face was so cold, but his eyes were alive and dancing in conquest. I let out my breath in a silent sigh, and let my own eyes slide shut once more.

Caspon had won.

Chapter 8

H E BROUGHT THE STRIP OF LEATHER CLOSE. I cringed away
as much as I could. My joints were stiff and aching. My
stomach snarled with hunger; my parched throat burned.
Those were minor pains. Fear gnawed at my entrails like rat. For
two days, I had lain on the floor, holding back bitter tears of failure.
The stone had ended everything.

The leather came close, held tight by Bennic's hands.

"Slide it under first," Caspon said. "Do not dislodge the
stone."

"Yes, lord," Bennic answered, his voice wavering. He had
always been afraid of me, afraid of coming too close or touching me
accidently. I was too worried to feel angry.

The leather slipped under my neck, rasping against the stone
floor, then came up around my throat. I tensed, trembling, and tried
to reach my arms up to scratch and claw and fight. But the stone on
my throat weighed me down. It was as if a tree had fallen and
crushed me into the ground.

"Tie it," Caspon ordered. "Not that tight! I want it able to
breathe, fool."

"Yes, my lord," Bennic said, knotting the strip of leather at the
side of my neck.

I felt trapped. I was strangling. The panic rushed up; my breath
came fast. My hands scratched at the floor, nails scraping a staccato
on the stone. When Caspon saw that was all I did, despite their
closeness, he knelt beside me.

He did something to the leather so it sat over my windpipe. I
heard the click on metal against the ring of office he wore. "Bennic,
hold her down. This must be quick."

I bit my lips as Bennic used his knees to pin my arms to the
floor. I could not get enough air, though my lungs fought for it.
Caspon took the stone from my neck and the blood rushed into me

like a flame. I could move! I could think! I thrashed, snarling and kicking. I wrenched my body, trying to throw Bennic, but my arms were pinned underneath his weight.

Caspon dabbed something on the leather and then pushed the beryl to the strap. For a moment, I choked on the pressure, but he released his hand and the now familiar lack came flooding back. My urge to fight lessened, my panic drained. I stilled on the floor, limbs slack, though my mind raced.

He had attached the beryl to a leather strip now tied around my neck.

"Off, Bennic," Caspon demanded.

The weight disappeared as Bennic rose and stepped away. Caspon moved to stand at my elbow, staring down at me. His face was triumphant.

"Stand up," he said.

I did, bones creaking and pained, but not because Caspon had commanded it. My body felt compelled, but I could resist it if I concentrated. My fingers flexed at my sides. He took a step forward, within arm reach, and I struck.

I leapt at him, clawing for his eyes. I got in one good swipe before Bennic smashed me to the floor. Again, I was pinned under his weight, this time with my chest and face crushed against the stone. Caspon was snarling. A few drops of blood patterned the flagstone beside my face and a sudden, sharp kick to my ribs knocked the breath from my lungs.

"Beast!" Caspon cursed. "You stupid, feral whore!" He kicked again and I could not help but whimper.

"Hold it up, Bennic," Caspon snarled. "I want the stone."

I was snatched up by the arms, feet swinging, and held upward in a painful grip. Bennic was making sure I would not attack again, that I would not escape. I knew his thoughts, his fears. I was a dog that had bitten its master and I was dangerous. Rabid and hungry and wild. I did not have the energy or the will to assure him of his claim. I did not even know if I was right. I had failed once to kill my greatest enemy. Would there be another chance?

Caspon stepped close, sneering. Blood dripped from three lacerations across his cheek, made by my short, ragged nails. I glared, lips curling over bared teeth.

He set his finger to the stone.

"You will cease your senseless attacks on me," he said, and I felt the will to fight flow from my veins. The desire was still there, burning, but it sank beneath his words.

Bennic set me down. My shoulders drooped as he released his painful grip.

"I have read," Caspon said, "that these stones, these beryls, will control your kind. They are magic."

Magic. I had thought it foolish, distant. A child's story. But it was real and it had me trapped in its tendrils.

"So, Nightingale," he said, teeth bared in a vicious smile, "here are your orders."

Just few days ago, I had been freer than I had realized. I could have run, hid, slipped into the forest and disappeared. Now it was too late.

"Nightingale, your first mission is to kill Martinus Fell." His finger was on the beryl as he spoke and a fire flashed through me. I gritted my teeth.

"No," I rasped. "I will not."

His face creased in rage. "You will!" he cried, grabbing the collar and wrenching my head side to side. He slapped his hand against the stone. "You will kill him as I command."

I tried to suppress the urge to accept. I did not want to kill someone else, only Caspon. I would not do it. I would not! The beryl flared at my throat and I cried in pain. Heat pulsed at my flesh, too hot to bear. I could not win.

"Yes," I whispered. "I will do as you command."

This mission proved my defining moment, when the path onto which I had been set could either continue on or vanish. I fought and raged, but chose in the end to keep my life. Cowardly perhaps, but I have never claimed to be brave. Still, I could not feel any remorse for my choice, twisted as I was by the beryl. I was relieved that my father and mother were vanishing from my mind, the images of their faces and the sounds of their laughter dim and fading by the day. It was better that way, I thought. Now they could not see what I was made to do. A child I still was in body, fifteen years of age, but inside I was withered and old.

I was dead inside. A stone. My hatred and despair were fading memories, clutching feeble fingers into the crevices of my heart, fighting for purchase and life. I clung to these memories as tightly as I could. They were the only things left to me, and I refused to relinquish them. But they *were* fading, slowly and surely. In a year, maybe even less, I would be lost. A dead heart to match a dead body. A puppet, a marionette – just as Caspon desired.

The beryl had done something to me, something dreadful and terrifying and humiliating. I could not act with Caspon's express word. I could not feel sadness or happiness or anything in between. I could still experience physical sensations, but emotions were lost to me. I was his slave, without doubt.

I was a person no longer, not even in my own mind. I was a possession, pure and simple. Yet to Caspon I was still more valuable than a piece of shoddy metalwork or an ill-trained courser. I knew my true purpose in his household now. I had realized what being the Nightingale entailed.

It was the collar that made me valuable. Without it, I was a wayward child with reaching ambitions and growing skills. More a liability and a danger than useful. I choked back a snarl as I thought of the strip of leather around my throat, not tight enough to cut off my breath but snug enough to be incommodious. The beryl, that small and innocuous stone now attached to the leather collar, nestled at the base of my throat. Its presence never left my senses. Constantly, the beryl emitted an unpleasant warmth that reminded me of a coal on the end of a red-hot poker. Normally, it did not burn, but the possibility was there. It was a traumatizing experience.

Caspon had only to set a finger to the stone and give his orders. With the beryl thus addressed, I could not stray from the path once it was laid before me. Martinus Fell had to die, but Caspon had phrased the command in such a way that I had some freedom of movement. "Kill him" gave many options for self-expression and leeway. I was useless if I could not think fast on my feet. Though this modicum of autonomy was acceptable, the beryl was issued one very expedient contingency plan. Somehow, the stone understood if I strayed too far from Caspon's path, or if I meant to, the results were painful, to say the least. The fiery agony was instantaneous and unbearable. It was a nightmare. The very thought of the pain sent sweat trickling down my spine.

And so, in truth, I had no choice but to obey the man who had ruined my life.

I was not told what the boy—Martinus Fell—had done to deserve his death, if anything, and I did not ask. It was better not to know. Instead, I set forth from the manor with my bow and quiver of black-fletched arrows and a dagger in my boot. The dagger had been a gift from Nichil on my last day of training, the bow from Aylan. Servor had given me nothing but a grudging nod. I did not know what to feel at these dismissals, and so felt nothing. I never saw my trainers again. Caspon had something to do with that, I believe.

I made my way out of town, following the dirt road as it wound through the thick forests and rolling hills. I stayed off the main path, and instead worked my way through the high branches, following the curves of the road so as not to lose my way. It was safer this way, for I would encounter much less resistance here than on the road. Brigands and highwaymen were thick in this area, and caravan guards were apt to attack first and ask questions later. A young, gangly creature such as myself was not immune from attack; in fact, my appearance made me all the more vulnerable.

The village of Weyen was close to Benthol, and I arrived just after nightfall. It was as Caspon's man Emio Valew – the false priest – had described. Two handfuls of whitewashed mud-and-wattle cottages with thatched roofs stood out starkly in the clearing amidst the dark forest. Sheep and small, hairy cattle grazed on the lush grass under the darkening sky. A dog barked somewhere down below, ignored by the people coming in from the fields to the soft, warm beds that awaited them.

I peered though the leaves, sure and steady on the narrow limb. I knew not to which home Martinus belonged, but I did know that he was a shepherd. Some flocks were still in the fields, and I hoped that the boy had not yet taken his back to the fold. I swallowed a sigh, feeling the beryl grow hot at my throat. *Do not think*, I told myself, fearing the stone. *Thinking leads to trouble.*

I crept down the slick trunk and through the underbrush, leaving my bow and quiver safe in the branches of the elm. Caspon's orders were to use only the dagger. I must get close enough to see the boy's face, to hear his final cry and repeat it back to my master when my mission was complete. I clasped my hatred of Caspon close, and it seared away all other emotions before they had the chance to be recalled.

Circling the village, I came to one of the fields dotted with fat white sheep. Most were sleeping, but a few grazed still, and every once and again a wavering bleat would echo through the evening gloom. It was a sound that grated on my delicate ears. I much preferred the chirping of crickets and night birds to the sounds of a *cardea* settlement. Peering through the undergrowth, I soon spotted the shepherd with relatively little effort. The moon was out already, round and brilliant as a startled eye.

This shepherd was sleeping, it seemed, or perhaps just resting on the grassy knoll. He looked too old to by my target, but I needed to be certain. I wanted until the moon changed position in the sky. Still he lounged, crook resting against his shoulder, and I grew impatient. An idea struck me. A rather clever one, I thought. Cupping my hands around my mouth, I gave a howl that sounded somewhat like a hoarse coyote. The shepherd's heard jerked up and was bathed in moonlight as he peered anxiously around. My instinct had been correct. This was not Martinus Fell.

I slid back into the shadowed brush, leaving the shepherd to his worry. Moving onward, I passed near a second area housing a smaller flock of thinner sheep. I spotted this shepherd much more slowly.

He was out moving amongst the animals, nudging them with his crook if they wandered too far. I was certain this boy was my target. Tall, dark-haired, a twisted left arm. Yes, he matched perfectly.

The beryl burned at my throat as I hesitated, but it was a warning touch. Nothing compared with what could come later. My mind raced as I formulated a plan, but my body was cold and sluggish. I hated Caspon for making me do this. I hated the beryl, the guild, and Benthol. I hated my parents for dying and leaving me alone, and I even hated Martinus for being alive. If he was not alive then I could not kill him. It was a child's logic, I realized, but that did not stop me from heaving up the fragments of hatred left in my memory and compiling them.

Swiftly, to stifle the beryl's warnings, I took my dagger and slit a gash in the belly of my tunic, then rubbed my face and clothes with dirt. A few strategic leaves and twigs could only add to the illusion, so I did not hesitate to include them in my disguise. I would make it appear as if I had been attacked and separated from my family. *Good enough*, I thought, and slipped the dagger under my wide leather belt, hiding it from view and within easy reach. Then I stepped free of the brush.

I made sure to stagger, to look dazed and lost. "Help," I cried hoarsely, making certain my voice was just loud enough for Martinus to hear. "Mama!"

Things happened so slowly. The images branded themselves into my recollection, terrible and constant. Martinus jerked in surprise. Confusion and concern emerged as he saw the state I was in, and he dashed over the aid me. "Girl, are you hurt?" he asked, fear in his voice. His concern touched me, but the beryl stifled any kind feelings I might once have had. The heat at my throat increased as I hesitated, making my eyes water.

My knees buckled, and I collapsed to the ground, panting. Martinus dropped his crook and crouched too close beside me. "What happened? Shall I fetch the healer?"

I glanced up at him, seeing his dark hair haloed by the moonlight and his hooded eyes wide in distress. My heart seized as as if a hand had clamped down upon it. How could I do this thing? How, and remain sane?

"Brigands," I managed to whisper through dry lips. I shook off the invisible fist. I felt sick, and clenched my fingers to keep them from trembling. "My mama's carriage . . . I think she. . ." A broken sob, feigned in voice though not in heart, escaped me.

Martinus swore under his breath. "So close," he growled. "Come," he said to me, taking my arm in hand. "I'll take you to the Elder's house. He'll send some men for your mother." He leaned against me, levering his arm to help me to my feet.

The moment his arm went around me, I struck.

My dagger caught him high, just under the sternum. Skin was harder to penetrate than I had thought, and clothing made the task no easier. I squeezed shut my eyes to avoid seeing his face, but I could not close my ears. Quickly, to silence him, I wrenched the knife free and passed it through his throat. The gurgling, choking, whimpering sounds were horrendous. Frantically, I disengaged myself from his twitching arms and backed away in horror, spattered in hot blood that seemed to burn the skin from my bones. I turned and retched into the grass, heedless of the milling sheep unnerved by the smell of death.

There was a call from the adjacent field. The older shepherd called for Martinus to count his sheep, to lead them back to the inner fields. He had heard things moving about in the brush. I choked back a new flood of bile and wiped my knife several times on the grass, cleaning it as best I could. Then I fled back into the forest, silent as a shadow.

When I returned to Caspon for briefing, I repeated the shepherd's last words, as I had been told. "Your mother, eh?" Caspon mocked, and laughed. I masked my rage, shoving it back and away. Now was not the time for anger. I remained inanimate, blank, frozen. My tormentor seemed to enjoy that.

"If I may ask, master, what did he do to deserve his death?" I felt I should know. If he had been a bad person, it might be easier to live with myself. Caspon lifted his eyes at the sound of my voice, and then went back to scraping his quill on the curling parchment on his desk.

"Martinus?" he said. "Nothing but ill luck. Merely a name on a census." He looked up then, his eyes resting upon my wilted form, and smiled grimly. "How suits the taste of unspoiled blood?"

I said nothing and did not ask again what my victims had done to deserve their deaths. It was not worth the pain.

I killed more within months, all by Caspon's command. It was a hard thing and I hated it. I felt cursed by the blood on my hands.

Almost two years later, after I had turned seventeen years of age, I was ready for something more than shepherds. I perched halfway up a cliff face, hidden in the shadow of a twisted pine. The chiming, clanking bells tore me from my mind's wanderings and back to the task at hand. I focused my attention once more, the beryl hotly reminding me of its presence.

The parade made its way down the center of the outer road, passing through the verdant squares and underneath my hiding spot. A large celebration, this. Horses came two by two down the pathway, tack gleaming under the sun. I counted twenty, at least, before turning my eyes away. There were also trumpeters riding flat carts, ladies tossing red and white flowers to the throng on the street, and soldiers in black and silver, their lances flashing on their shoulders.

I watched, reminded faintly of the mummer's show I had once seen. Spectacles, both. This was the first noble I was supposed to kill, the first person with power and fame and fortune on their side. If I was caught here, the Weapons would certainly take me. First, a cell, then torture. I might expose Caspon if the beryl allowed me to speak of him but King Cosian II would have me executed either way.

Then, in the middle, came my target.

I had to be careful. The Weapons in their dark uniforms stood out starkly from the gaily-dressed crowd. Talros was down there, striding along the street and keeping pace with the carriage. He was everywhere and I did not like it. His intuition, his sense of forethought, was known to me now. There were stories of him appearing where he had not right to be and halting a crime in its tracks. I wondered what he felt about me. I wondered if he knew I was here, waiting, high above his head. Well, he would soon.

The procession did not slow as the young lord passed by in his horse-drawn carriage. I knew it was him by his thick blond hair, the circlet on his brow and the white rose embroidered on his livery. The brown-haired woman seated next to him was of little consequence.

I shifted my bow higher and drew the dark-fletched arrow, my trademark, to my jaw. I was known now, across the lower half of Caesia, for my deeds. The black feathers were my calling cards, present at every death to be found by the authorities who were certainly hunting me. I was meant to inspire fear in the populace, and those pursing me had little chance of relieving it anytime soon.

I was a wraith in the night, vanishing as soon as the deed was done. The Ghost, the soldiers called me. Others knew me as the Nightingale, for the songbird's feathers that I used as fletching and brand. My anthela blood aided in my escapes but I saw running as cowardice. I hated to flee like a fox before hounds, but that was my only choice if I wanted to keep my life and, despite everything, I did. I knew what awaited me if I was caught. I had heard it told often enough. Pain, torture, agony. True, all of it, especially with the additional sin of halfblood heritage.

I swallowed, feeling my throat constrict as the beryl pulsed with an otherworldly heat. My fingers twitched against the bowstring, ready for release. Fire danced in my chest, moving along with my blood.

Sorry, I thought, and the dark arrow cut through the air like a diving falcon.

I had taken the wind into account, as well as the plodding movement of the carriage. A prettier shot could not have been made. The arrow dropped, swift as lightning, and struck the lordling through the ribs just under the armpit, biting deep. My target staggered in the middle of his wave, eyes going wide in shock and confusion. The crowd, momentarily stunned into silence, erupted in shrieks of terror and disbelief.

The young lord tumbled from the open door of the carriage, landing on the stone and dirt and celebratory flowers in the street. He choked and writhed, his movements slight and juxtaposed with the cacophony surrounding him. The young man's back arched in a spasm as pink, frothy blood cascaded over his lips, indicating a lung shot that would prove fatal. There was nothing that could be done for him now. His inevitable fate would take him much sooner than he no doubt anticipated.

The woman beside him shrieked, futilely grasping the front of his doublet in some kind of effort to aid him. I turned away from the sight, though my mind recounted his image over and over again. The lordling mewed and writhed on the road, growing ever weaker as his life-blood and breath spilled out, turning the stone and flowers slick and crimson.

Talros reacted with astonishing speed. Calling for his men, he raced for the cliff.

I swallowed the bile that rose in my throat and scaled the rock face behind me, the brown of my clothes matching the stone, and hated myself for what I had become.

I could hear them running across the gravel at the base of the ledge. The leather of their boots creaked and scuffed as they moved. The Weapons could not see me from below, not with the scrub brush and the jutting stone, and I scraped and slithered upward until the peak flattened out into a plateau filled with squat, knotted pines. A town was not far, but the Weapons would catch me in a footrace. Already they were climbing. I could hear the clink of sheathed swords and the heavy, cursing voice of Talros.

I swallowed my fear and ran, hoping to reach the town before they lessened the distance between us. The bow bounced on my back as I ran; the quiver slapped at my thigh. I heard them in the trees, forcing their way through the sap-sticky limbs and pricking needles. I was smaller, more agile, and slipped through the pines like a squirrel.

In the minutes before they reached me, I slipped behind a woodshed on the outskirts of town and put the last portion of my plan into place.

Once inside the town, it was easy enough to escape the notice of the Weapons. After all, no one expected the Nightingale to be a girl of seventeen, made diminutive by anthela blood and lack of food. My bow was unstrung and used as a walking stick. The quiver with the dark-fletched arrows turned into a basket where flowers and ferns covered the telltale shafts. My excuse, if the Weapons sought to question me, was that I was out collecting forage for my aunt, a crofter in the village. If I thought that would not work, if it appeared that Talros knew someone here, I would feign muteness, vapidity or dullness.

I had to be careful to hide my ears. That portion of my disguise could never change, not with Talros on the hunt.

Other than disguising myself, my other options of elusion were either hiding or flight. I was swifter than the Weapons if they were dressed in armor, but in leathers and linens they would outdistance me. They could not pursue me in the trees or over rooftops. I wanted no hint of my real identity to surface, not even the fact that I was a young girl. If someone gave chase, then someone had seen me, and that I could not allow. Talros and his Weapons had seen the effects of my arrow, the angle of its flight, but I was certain that they had not seen *me*. If I ran or acted strange, that would give them cause to detain me. That would be my death—and left hiding as my only viable option.

With my disguise in place, I ambled through the street of the town, watching as the Weapons barreled in and started questioning the people.

"Have you seen anyone suspicious come through here?" a Weapon asked.

"No," said an old man, his gnarled hands trembling on his walking stick. "No one."

I thought I was rather good at hiding. Though I was frightened, my confidence did not waver. The Weapons filled the streets, hunting me. One came close, brushed against me so hard the quiver nearly fell from my hands.

"I apologize," he said, and I realized it was Talros that spoke.

"No need, sir," I murmured, clutching my walking stick and basket close.

"Tell me," General Talros said. "Have you seen anyone suspicious enter the town today?"

"No, sir," I answered.

"No one has," Talros grumbled, his hand perched on the hilt of his sheathed sword as he stalked away.

A long breath escaped me and I began to walk toward the other side of the village, to the trees beyond.

I had been lucky today. No one had glimpsed a girl-child on the cliff above the crowds. I wove between the trees as I headed back to the manor. It would be a long walk, nearly three days. Two, if I did not stop to rest.

But I was in no hurry to return to Caspon's guild. He had issued no specific time frame for my arrival, so the beryl was lenient. I released all thoughts as I ambled through the thick forest. Despite everything, including the beryl, I could still feel something like peace in a place like this. It was soothing, somehow. The air was cool, the birds were noisy, the soft litter under my feet smelled of soil and compost. I breathed deep, savoring the smells, and felt lighter than I had in months. Eventually, I fell asleep.

A cracking of twigs snapped me awake. My eyes instantly sought the source of the sound. Within a heartbeat's time, I was in the branches of a tree, staring down at an enormous gray wolf that looked up at me with great golden eyes.

It was strange to see a wolf alone. Usually, they traveled in packs. They had been commonplace around Carfuinel. Wolves were representations of Lenos, the god of stars and steel and night. I had been given to Lenos at birth, dedicated by my parents in a ceremony that, to them, assured my good health and safety. I had not prayed to Lenos since my vow in the dingy chamber on that first day in Caspon's manor. She had not answered; She had not cared. But I belonged to Her, or so my parents would say, but I did not know if I believed it.

Even my birth name, after being translated into Caesarn, gave utterance to Lenos and Her power: Starlit Blade. Once, a lifetime ago, I had liked it. Now, it seemed too much like something Caspon would have given me.

I watched the animal, wondering how I had not known of its presence before its approach. The beast was large, as large as I, with a thick coat of gray. Looking closer, I noticed that the fur was not gray, but also white, brown and touched with silver. The guard hairs glinted like steel in the filtered sunlight. The eyes, clear and vibrant, regarded me with an eerie, almost knowing, *cardea* gaze. It was unnerving, the way the creature would not look away.

Something in its eyes seemed almost sorrowful. Pitying. I decided I was stupid. Wolves would not feel pity for people, no matter the circumstances. It probably wanted to eat me, and I was fool enough to misinterpret what I saw.

"*Ayai*," I said, feeling uncomfortable and naked in the wolf's eyes. Away, it meant. And to my utter astonishment, the wolf turned and left, walking into the trees until it vanished completely.

I was certain it had understood me. But again, that was only my foolishness speaking.

Chapter 9

O N THE FRONT STEPS OF THE DEAD LORD'S HOUSE, Talros was accosted by a member of the local guard. Not just any soldier, but the captain himself. A tall man with receding hair and a lined, worried face, the captain grasped a roll of parchment in his gloved hand.

"General, sir. This is urgent," the captain said to gain Talros' attention.

"Captain Riles. What news have you?" The general turned away from the Weapon to whom he had been speaking. The discussion of the latest events paused, the air thick with unease and worry. Murder had occurred right under the Weapons' noses.

In answer, Captain Riles held out the parchment. "You should read it. I think it will interest you."

Talros took the parchment, untied the ribbon, and read the short but meaningful missive. It had come from a guardsman in an outlying village, dated three weeks ago. As he read, Talros felt his stomach drop. This was something he had been dreading.

"Another death?" he asked, gripping the parchment in his clenched fist. The sheet bunched under his fingers. "It's not possible."

"I assure you, it is, General Talros," said the Captain of the Guard. "The victim was found next to the well with a black feather resting on her chest. The same black feathers as those on the arrow that killed Lord Tyban. That's what we were told to look for and we've found it. The village where the feather was found is not far from where Tyban was killed."

Talros frowned. Those damned black feathers had been found on or near eight corpses in various corners of the kingdom. It all pointed to one conclusion: an assassin was working in Caesia. Never before had there been such a prolific killer, not since he had joined the Weapons, not since he could remember. It was a terrible realization. The people lived in fear as rumors spread like wildfire. Ghost, wraith, nightingale. No one had seen the killer, no one knew anything other than the fact that black feathers were left at the scene.

Talros knew it was his duty to apprehend the assassin, to learn his motives, and to stop the deaths. They were taking place in his district, his circuit. The assassin was his responsibility. And he would hunt unto the ends of the land to stop him.

Days later, I had found my way back to Benthol, to the guild-manor owned by Caspon. I had not been followed, and had had ample time to hunt and eat and rest on the return journey. I did not feel rested, however, nor full. I was wary and tense, my muscles aching in the back of my legs and across my shoulders. A deep-rooted feeling that I could only describe as *no* grew in my belly and flowered up into my chest.

I dragged my feet as I passed down the wooded hill to the manor. I looked, but Aylan no longer practiced in the arena. I had not seen him in a very long while. I think I missed him. He had been a hard man, but fair. I had not hated him, and now I wondered where he was. I knew I would not see him again. Nichil, too, was gone. I would have bet my life on this being the doing of Caspon. My one almost-friend, Nichil had been. The trinkets and sweets he brought would be mourned.

I went into the back entrance, my hidden skulking-way, and slunk to Caspon's inner offices. No place was denied to me now, enslaved as I was by the beryl. Caspon did not fear me, not even minutely. I was a panther without claws, a snake without fangs. The only way I could be freed was to remove the beryl from my touch, but I could not be the one to do it. Someone else had to do it for me. A simple task, it should have been, but no one would touch me. I was Caspon's dog. Even though no one but he and Bennic knew of my nature, I was still an outcast among the inhabitants of the manor grounds. Caspon's cur was a filthy thing, indeed, tainted by its master's foulness.

The door to his innermost office swung open as I went in and shut behind me. I would not look in his eyes, but stared at the same spot on the floor as I did at every debriefing. The knot in the cedar-planked floor was like a black eye gazing at me, winking up from between my boots.

"Well done," Caspon said from his customary place at his desk. His voice was low and victorious. I had only heard two tones from him. He was either quietly sly and cunning or deep-voiced with triumph. "Lassolern will be speaking of this incident for years. Your renown has grown great indeed, little ghost." He chuckled. "I've heard what people say, that you're a shadow or a wraith. Little do they know that a Nightingale hunts amongst them. The bird of portent, an omen." Caspon smiled at me then, a quick flutter of his lips. "Soon they will. They'll all know."

I stared at the plank flooring, unable to speak. This was no emotion that choked me, that rendered me mute. This was the work of the beryl. Caspon had touched the smooth stone with a thick forefinger and uttered the words that made me a slave. He had spoken a command to the stone, saying that I must obey him for the remainder of my life. Caspon completed his humiliation of me by adding that if I ever tried to remove the collar, I would die a violent and painful death instigated by that small, unremarkable stone. As Lenos's creature, as a being of night and steel and fangs, I should have fought. I should have protested violently at Caspon's treatment of me. But the beryl made me more dog than wolf, and so I obeyed.

"I have another task for you, my darkling bird. This one has been sent by Countess Irys of Astione herself. A tall order, but I have utter confidence in you." The grin he sent my way seemed painted on and tinged with contempt. I stared at a spot on the wall just behind his left ear, close enough to seem alert but still beyond reach of his eyes. I heard the crinkle of parchment as he smoothed the stiff missive on the table, rubbing his meaty hands over the edges, and then the muted clink of bagged coins against the oak.

It was but half the payment, I knew. Caspon's envoy, Emio Valew, had brought it. Potential employers did not contact Caspon directly; they did not even know of me, save that an assassin existed. Valew's purpose was to ferret out jobs and collect payment. Slyly and stealthily, he made his rounds through the cities, dropping hints as he went. There were always a few ready to gather them up.

"She wants the eldest daughter of Baroness Barbary d'Iseult dead. Spill no blood. This death must look as natural as possible, and our good countess dislikes the thought of blood on her hands."

No blood on her hands, but blood on mine.

I cast a glance at my calloused palms. I could not see the blood on them, but it was there, just beneath the surface. So many people. I had not killed all my victims, but that did not stop the guilt. Some were only meant to be poisoned until they thought they were dying. A miscarriage or two were caused with a careful application of herbs; a stair was greased to break legs and backs. I did not always deal in death, but agony was a constant companion. I could not sigh, not here in front of this man, so I curled my hands into tight fists at my sides until I could not feel them any longer.

Caspon came around the desk and touched the stone at my throat with his forefinger and gave his commands.

And so the path was laid before me.

Chapter 10

ENERAL ASTIN TALROS HELD UP A HAND to the barmaid. "Another round," he called. He and four of his men sat at the corner table in the tavern, breathing smoke and listening to the bard strum his gittern near the bar. The remains of meat pies and trenches sat on thin plates before them, almost empty except for crumbs and streaks of gravy and grease.

Talros sighed, patting his full belly, and tipped the barmaid a coin when she brought the tray of heavy steins. The smell of honey filled his head as the mead sloshed over his lips when he drank. "So," he said, "we need information to send to the king. What do we have?"

His men looked at him. One shifted in his seat. "Sir, we are off-duty. Can't we have at least a few hours without thinking of those damned murders?"

"One hour," Talros acquiesced. "Then we must work."

"Good enough," the Weapon replied, lifting the mug to his mouth.

They drank and talked until late in the night. After a while, the bard packed his instrument and headed out. The barmaid began to sweep the floor and close the shutters, indicating that the tavern was no longer serving drinks and food. The fat priest in the corner began grumbling.

Talros looked. He had seen the priest before. The sight of a holy man enjoying his drink was uncommon, but not nonexistent. What he did on his own time was his business, as long as he kept out of trouble. However, General Talros soon realized that the priest had too much ale in his belly.

The robed man hauled himself to his feet and tottered over to the Weapon's table. "Ha," he slurred. "What say you men challenge me to a game?"

"I didn't think priests gambled," a Weapon said, raising an eyebrow.

"Well, I want to and I've got coin aplenty," the priest cajoled.

"Valew, go sit down. You've lost your head," Talros said.

"Nah, I won't until one of you plays me a game."

"Fine," sighed the Weapon on the corner seat. "I'll play, though I hate the thought of taking the gods' coin."

"Yah, that's what you think," Valew laughed. He took an empty chair at the table, pushing the plates and steins aside with his arm. The other Weapons looked on, shaking their heads, and Talros stared as Valew brought a pair of dice out of a pocket in his robe.

"The game is three-step," Valew said. "First to twenty wins. Whoever rolls closest to six takes the first turn. The bet is ten bronze."

"If I must," the Weapon said, taking the dice in his hand. He tossed them on the table. The bones bounced around the plates and clattered to a halt. Three black dots showed on one, two on the other.

"Five, oh!" Valew hooted. "Very nice." He took the yellowed dice and cast them. "Three," he sneered. "Your turn."

They played in silence. The Weapon did not seem to care if he won or lost. Talros knew the amount of coin in the man's purse. Ten pieces would not make much of a dent in it, and they would be paid as soon as they returned to Dernwellen.

The last cast. The priest's dice showed a single dot on the upward side. His face went pale. His hands clenched on the table, trembling against the wood. "You cheater!" he hissed, whirling. "You cheat a man of the gods?"

A fist flashed out and struck the Weapon in the face. The man's nose burst, blood spurting across the priest's knuckles. The other men sprang from their seats, subduing Valew as he yelled and cursed at the broken Weapon.

Talros checked first on his wounded subordinate. "Broken" he said, peering down at the man's nose. "Don't touch it. Can I get a cloth here?" he called. The barmaid left her broom and rushed to the counter to grab a rag.

He went next to the priest. "That's enough, Emio Valew. Man of the gods or not, you're under arrest."

"Arrest? You can't arrest me!" Valew cried. "You can't!"

"I can and I will." He turned to his men. "Take him and have the guards put him in an empty cell. I know they have one. We'll search him as usual."

"Yes, sir," they said. Two took Valew by the arms while the last went ahead, and they walked the priest down the lane to the gaol.

"Can you stand?" Talros asked the other.

"Yes, sir. I'm hale enough." The Weapon stood, pressing the rag to his face.

"Come, we'll find a physician to set it."

"Thank you, sir."

Talros left the barmaid a generous tip on the table, apologized for the disturbance, and went out. The other Weapon walked at his side. They met the gaol's physician at the door and he scurried away to fetch his tools, bidding the Weapon to follow him. Talros left them alone, focusing his attention on the drunken priest in the last cell in the corridor.

Just another drunk, Talros thought. It was strange that this one was a priest, but that did not matter. He had injured another man, unprovoked, and thus was subject to the laws of the realm.

Talros gathered his men and went into the cell. The priest sat on the bench, sullen and silent, but cooperated when Talros ordered him to remove his robes. Valew dropped the brown garments on the floor and returned to the bench, sitting in nothing but his thin linen underclothes.

His men went through the robes, checking pockets and seams, and found nothing of any interest. Even the dice had been lost, left behind on the table in the tavern.

"He's clean, General Talros," said a Weapon.

"As I thought," Talros said. "Check his shoes and undergarments."

"Yes, sir," his men answered.

They found nothing in Valew's shoes, but in a hidden pocket in his worn smallclothes, they dislodged a small pouch of silver. Normally, this would not have fazed Talros. Some people wore their money close to their skin in order to protect it from pickpockets. However, when he dug through the pouch, he uncovered a slip of parchment.

"What is this?" he asked the priest.

Valew swallowed. "Nothing."

"It is obviously something," Talros prodded, "else you would not look so worried."

The priest looked down at the flagstones. Talros twisted the paper in his hands, turning it over to stare at the strange runes. It was some kind of code language, he was certain.

"If you tell me, things will go easier for you," Talros coaxed. "If you don't, we'll unravel it in any case. It is just a matter of time before we learn what this means."

Emio Valew closed his eyes.

"Fine. Erlic," Talros called, "work on decoding this."

"Yes, sir," the Weapon Erlic answered, coming forward and taking the parchment from the general's hand.

For three days, Erlic and the Weapons worked on decoding the scrap of parchment found in Valew's pouch. It was cunningly done. Erlic managed to crack only two words: *Lassolern* and *payment*. Even partially decoded, the message was enough to set Talros' heart ablaze. It was sufficient evidence to keep Emio Valew for questioning.

Chances were that he had some connection to the assassin, and Talros was determined to follow all leads to their end.

The first few days I spent in the trees, traveling through the branches above the ground. It was faster that way, most of the time, until the limbs thinned and shrank until there was nothing to hold my weight.

When the forest changed to field, I walked. It was long and tiring business, but I did not have to fear brigands as much in the open. They were just as wary of the wide spaces. Near midday, I heard wagons behind me. For a moment, I quailed, then realized there was little to fear. Bandits did not often travel in loud, creaking wagons. They preferred swift and silent horses.

I stood by the roadside, bow and quiver packed away so they would not be seen. I was just a girl, dressed in breeches, tunic, and tall boots. Not conventional dress for a female, but not unknown. Whoever was approaching the wagon would see me as flouting tradition, and that would get me nowhere with priests or old folks. I hoped the drivers would be someone else.

To my luck, it was mummers. The lead wagon paused on the road, the tired mules hanging their heads. The woman tilted her head at me. Children in the covered bed peeked through the curtain. Behind them, two more wagons rolled to a halt.

"Hello," I said. "I am looking for a ride." Hitching rides was dangerous. I could trust no one. But I was tired and I had Caspon's gold. He had given me enough for food and the river ferry. Traveling with mummers, those "grubbing, thieving creatures," as he called them, would make him unhappy—which was reason alone for me to do it.

"I can pay," I added.

The woman, her face puckered by a vicious burn scar on the side of her face, seemed to consider. "Where are you going?"

"The same direction you are," I replied.

She held out a hand and I pressed a small bit of silver into it. "Sit in the second. We will take you as far as the village of Tione."

"Thank you." I went to the second wagon and climbed into the bed. Three young men and two old women watched me. "Hello," I said, setting my pack down in the rear corner and leaning back against it. I was tired.

The wagons moved, bumping and jostling over the dirt road. I rested in relative quiet. The mummers ignored me, speaking amongst themselves in a language that I did not understand. They were *cardeai* but did not speak Caesarn, unless it was some dialect that I had not studied. Mummer language, I knew, was something that Caspon did not care if I learned or not.

It was not long before they turned to me.

"What news?" the oldest woman said. She had a mole on her cheek that moved as she spoke.

"News?" I asked, confused.

"Bah, she knows nothing," said the other woman.

I realized my mistake. Mummers had a ready ear for gossip. All news in Caesia seemed to pass first through them. I could learn if there was anything to watch for in the baroness' estate. But how could I phrase it without raising suspicion?

So I listened to what the mummers said, without interrupting. I learned of unrest and jealousy and love, in simple homes and villages alike. Nothing I could use, at least not at the moment. They spoke in Caesarn to include me, in case I had anything to add.

"The General is coming to the baron next week," whispered the young man perched on an iron-banded box.

"The General? Talros, you mean, the dark one?"

"Yes, I heard it from Avi Desalindao."

"Avi! That pig's ass!" shrieked the woman with the mole. "He spits lies."

"No, he swears! He heard it from Old Teoz that the General is coming to ask d'Iseult for money."

"Money, ai! So greedy."

Damn and damn! Curse Talros and his constant presence. This would make the infiltration and action so much harder. I would have to be careful and quick. He must not have the slightest idea that the Nightingale had been there until I was far away.

The conversation evolved throughout the course of the ride, changing from Talros to horseracing to where the next festival would be held. I rode with them until we reached the village late in the night. The trees had thickened some and I would have cover until the next clearing. I would catch another ride if necessary. There was much I had learned from this one.

I pressed a second silver into the palm of the burned woman. "Thank you again for your kindness," I told her.

"You are safe?" she asked, her voice soft. "So young you are. There is danger in the wood."

"I will be fine," I replied, touched by her concern. "Keep well."

I stayed in the village long enough to eat a trencher of meat and greens from a vendor in the street, and then disappeared into the trees.

I had infiltrated the manor of Iseult. It was a fair ways from Benthol, on the edge of the river Dernan at the gateway to the vast plains. The broom closet where I now hid was narrow and dark, and obviously had not been kept in order for a month, at least. Already, a fat spider had spun its web high in the back corner. I shivered away, not wanting the threads to touch me. The smell of cedar and dust was thick, along with the musk of unwashed winter coats. The dress I managed to find in the servants' quarters was too large in the chest and slightly too long, and itched in the neck and armpits. It would have to do, however. I hoped I would only need it for a day or so. Less, if I was lucky.

I listened at the door, pressing my ear against the wood. The sounds were slightly muffled through the fabric of my headband, but I could still understand what was going on just outside. The corridor was empty. No footsteps sounded on the stone, no voices echoed from afar. Slowly, I pulled open the door, risked a glance, and then hurried out. I made certain the door closed behind me before straightening my frock and brushing away the dust. A glimpse of the map I had studied arose in my mind, and I headed toward the stairs at the southern end of the hallway.

I had made it to the lower foyer when two large, older women brushed past me, chattering quietly. One slowed for a moment, peering at me with narrowed eyes before shaking her head minutely and moving on. I figured she had been trying to place me, trying to remember my face or name. Sometimes the older ones were like that, too curious for their own good.

The shorter one in the red kerchief had not even paused in her speech. "That General what's-his-name is coming tonight, I heard."

"Talros, I think," said the other, lowering her voice. I walked, pretending not to listen, but paused within hearing range to study a stain in the hem of the itchy dress.

"Yes, yes, the dark one. He must be wanting funds, I suppose."

"Bah! He'll get more words than coin from the baron, if you ask me."

They passed onward, bustling down the hallway until their words were lost in the echo of their footfalls. Talros had not arrived yet. That was good, that gave me a little time in which to work. Not much, but hopefully enough. I did not know how much longer I could stay without someone noticing an unfamiliar face.

I moved swiftly, making my way down to the kitchens by following the map imprinted in my memory. The smells that wafted toward me were mouth-watering. The aromas of fresh bread, ripe fruit, and honey-glazed meats floated around me. There was nothing in that moment that could have turned me from my path just then. I was ravenous.

"Hurry, please, Missus Feirn. Lady Miarthe will be getting impatient," a girl's voice whined over the flurry of kitchen sounds. Clattering pots and muttering voices made a careless backdrop to her worried tone. Suddenly, there came the sound of dishes breaking and a woman shrieked with pain.

"Dentea, you little fool! Look what you did! Broth everywhere, all over my counters. And my pastries, they're ruined. Get out this instant or I'll tan that hide of yours!" a voice thick with phlegm and age bellowed. Even I was startled at its vehemence.

"I'm sorry, I didn't mean—"

"Out!"

I darted aside as the kitchen door crashed open and a young girl stumbled out, holding a tray overflowing with an enormous variety of foods. Her dark hair swung over her reddened eyes and I could hear her sniffling, trying not to cry. She looked a year or two younger than myself, perhaps more. She had not seen me yet, evidenced by the way she leaned back against the stone wall, sniffling even louder.

I stepped forward, readying myself to swallow the traces of my anthehome accent. Only the flatlander tones of the prairies would do here. "Dentea?" I inquired hesitantly. "Is something wrong?"

The girl jumped as if stung by a wasp, her red eyes widening in confusion as her head jerked up. She looked at me, sniffing. I would have to prod her along.

"Did Missus Feirn yell again? She has a nasty temper, that one," I continued, putting on my best sympathetic face.

"Yes," Dentea said in a small voice. "She's very mean." She looked at the floor for a moment before her eyes flicked back up to mine. "Um, I'm sorry. I don't think I know you."

"My name is Lathien. We spoke briefly at the festival last week." Thank the gods for eavesdropping, I thought. The kitchen staff would have been overwhelmed by the preparation for the city-wide Candlelight Festival held in the square beyond the d'Iseult estate, cooks and runners alike. The girl had never spoken to me before but she would pretend to remember, maybe even talk herself into the belief that she had forgotten. Minds were easy to manipulate, if one understood how.

"Oh, I-I'm sorry I don't recall," Dentea apologized, clearly ashamed with her forgetfulness. My eyes caught a line on her throat and I glimpsed a little wolf figurine strung on a cord around her neck. A follower of Lenos, for all she did not look or act like one.

I feigned a sigh, but kept the fake smile on my lips. "Do not worry. It seems most people have a problem remembering my name. Now, why did Feirn yell at you?"

"I bumped her . . . again," Dentea answered, shamefaced, but opened up quickly. "It was an accident. I can't help it that she takes up so much room! I needed to get the tray and she was in the way and now it's—oh no! I'm late again! She'll pull my hair," the girl wailed, cringing so that the laden tray threatened to spill to the floor.

I could hear Missus Feirn griping from behind the door, apparently mustering the energy to come and bash in Dentea's head with some form of heavy kitchen utensil.

"Here, Dentea. I will take the tray. You need a break from this for a day. Go down to the fountain or the gardens for a bit. Surely that would be better than dealing with Lady Miarthe today."

"You would do that?" the girl whispered, eyes going wide once again. "Oh, thank you!" I took the tray, as it seemed she would drop it at any given moment. "Do you know where her room is?" she continued.

"Third floor, second staircase, fifth door on the left?" I asked, already knowing I was correct. I smiled at her awed look. "I make it a point never to get lost," I explained, setting most of the weight of the tray on my hip but still grasping it with both hands.

"Well, thank you again," Dentea said, grinning at me. "I never have time to see the gardens!" She gave me a sloppy curtsey before traipsing away down the hall. For a brief moment, I regretted my decision to involve her. It was possible she would be blamed for my actions. *I am sorry*, I thought after her. *You were in the wrong place at the wrong time.* She had also been the easiest mark to follow.

I left the kitchen hall then and moved up the floors with incautious ease. The tray was astonishingly heavy, and the amount of food upon it boggled my mind. Who could eat so much in one sitting? Surely not a sixteen year old girl! It was waste, pure and simple.

One the second floor, I paused in an alcove. This hallway was empty and I was starving. Miarthe would never be able to eat all this. She would not miss a plate or two. After setting the tray on a nearby side-table, I broke open a meat pie with my bare hands, juggling it as the hot juice dripped over my skin. I ate it with relish, savoring the spices inside, and followed the pie with a handful of crisp vegetables. The only drink available was a corked glass bottle, full with dark liquid. I pondered for a moment. The corkscrew would leave a visible hole if I tried to open it. I did not know how observant Miarthe might be, so I resolved to do without for the time being.

I peeked out of the alcove again, wiping my fingers on the hem of my stolen dress, making certain I was alone. I was, and so I set the next part of my mission into place. From under my dress, I drew out the little pouch I kept with me at all times. I slipped the little bag open, withdrew a vial of powder, and sprinkled it generously over the main courses. It was a concoction of my own cunning and I had designed it to work swiftly.

I returned the vial to my pouch and then removed a single black feather. It was my calling-card—I held it flush underneath the tray with my fingers as I left the alcove and continued up to Miarthe's quarters.

The last hallway was lined with windows and the light that streamed in illuminated the dust motes that danced in the air. Small side tables supporting potted flowers and ornate decorations sat between every three. I passed people here, but no one of the upper class deigned to notice the serving girl.

At the fifth door on the left, I balanced the heavy tray on my hip and knocked.

"Enter!" a high-pitched voice called. I nudged the door open with my foot, needing both hands to steady the tray as I moved. The girl's back was to me as I came in. She was seated in a cushioned chair before the massive window, the ruffles of her pink dress threatening to swallow her whole. The sunlight pouring in the window revealed a dirty and disorderly room, clothes strewn across the floor and hanging off the armoire in the corner. A gray cat lounged in the only clear area of floor, just underneath Miarthe's swinging feet. It blinked large green eyes at me before yawning, showing a pink tongue and bared fangs, and then sat up and curled its tail over its paws, staring at the tray in my hands.

"Finally, Dentea! You lazy cow, I'm starv—" the older girl stopped short as she looked at me. "You're not Dentea," Miarthe said as she turned in her chair. "Who are you?"

"Lathien, my lady," I answered, giving my voice the proper amount of fear and curtseying as low as I dared without tumbling the food from the tray.

"Where's Dentea?"

"There was an accident in the kitchen, my lady. She could not come, so I was sent in her stead. I apologize if this inconveniences you."

Her eyes narrowed. "I don't know you."

"I am new, my lady. Just hired last week."

Miarthe sniffed and made a dismissive noise. "Put the tray on my vanity. Tell Feirn I don't want you delivering my tray again. I don't like the look of you."

I bit hard on the inside of my lip to reign in my flash of anger. It died, but embers tended to smolder. "Of course, my lady. I apologize." Wading through the mess on the floor, I tried to settle the tray on the cluttered vanity without it spilling. I let the feather fall to the desk underneath as I released the tray, stepping back just as the cat leapt up amidst the clutter, sniffing.

"No, Bingsley, that's mine!" Miarthe scolded, moving faster than I expected as she knocked the cat aside with a brusque sweep of her arm. The cat twisted in the air to land on its feet, and then dashed underneath the bed, yowling. "Why are you still here?" she snapped, whirling on me.

"So sorry, my lady," I apologized, curtseying even as I stepped backwards to leave the room. I wanted nothing more than to be gone from that place. Retreating, I risked a glance over my shoulder as the door swung closed behind me. Miarthe was cutting a generous slice of roast—one of the main courses. She laid a piece aside for the cat before taking a bite herself. I did not linger any longer and slipped from the room.

I snuck from the estate, taking the back routes to avoid the guards posted at the gates. Once outside, I ducked into the small copse of trees on the outskirts of the grounds and changed from the dress into my tunic and breeches. It was time to return to Benthol, to Caspon and the guild, and I wanted to be far away before General Talros and his retinue arrived.

Chapter 11

"I ASSURE YOU, BARON D'ISEULT, everything in my power is being done to bring these assassinations to a halt." General Astin Talros leaned forward in his chair, fingers clasped on the table before him. He was still relatively young for a general, although threads of gray had already crept into the thick black hair he kept tied back in an immaculate queue. The sharp amber eyes rested on the rotund baron like those of a hawk, giving the impression that the slightest move would be seen and deciphered. In the light of the table-lanterns, the silver edgework of the general's black woolen uniform gleamed.

Despite his deep frustration, Talros did not let his emotions show. He kept his face flat and void. "I am working closely with the other members of court," he continued. "However, our supplies are growing thin. It is a tiring task, keeping men employed and fed as they toil to protect the populace."

Baron d'Iseult's mouth drooped. "I have but little. As you must know, I am funding new roadways throughout my estates. What little I have left in my coffers is open to you, General, but I must ask how long you think your men must work. Days? Weeks? Is there any end in sight? Lassolern was the seventh assassination in the past three months and yet I have heard no evidence, no description at all of this elusive terror." The baron sighed and settled back in his plush chair. "This beast is like a handful of water, slipping through no matter how tightly one grasps. Have you heard of a motive, at least?"

Talros shook his head. "No, Baron d'Iseult."

The baron grunted, scratching his chin as he thought. "Have you no leads at all? Surely you have uncovered something."

"I will send a messenger when I have proof. Undetermined leads must be contained, or else the innocent may suffer for having some likeness."

"I see. I do not like not knowing the details, but I understand your point." The man frowned at the whorls in the wood of the table. "I shall write you a note to take to my accountant. He will see you have the necessary funds. I will have to ask you to wait in the foyer, please, General Talros."

"Of course, my lord."

Talros rose from his chair, stretching out his long legs as he did so. Gathering his papers together, he readied to leave the inner chambers and retire to the foyer, forming the vague hope of a glass of wine or mead.

There was a knock on the thick door, and the servant entered just as the count began to answer. The small, liveried man hurriedly bent a knee and set a fist over his chest. "My lord," he said. The general noticed a trace of frantic worry in the man's voice. He stopped shuffling his papers and instead watched as the servant spoke.

"Speak," the baron demanded from his seat.

"It's the Lady Miarthe, my lord. She won't answer her door, nor has she rung the bell for her tray removal. It is unusual, sir."

"You bother me with this? She must be sleeping. Simply open the door and go in."

The servant licked his lips in nervousness, clearly afraid of displeasing the baron. "We've tried that, my lord. The door—it's unlocked, but still won't open. There must be something blocking it."

Baron d'Iseult sighed in frustration. Talros decided it was time to intercede. "Baron d'Iseult, perhaps you wouldn't mind if I went to inquire of your daughter's well-being?"

"Do you believe something is amiss?" the baron asked. "My daughter is often asleep, and her room. . ." He sighed. "I'm afraid the maids do not keep it as clean as they ought. However, if you insist, my man here will accompany you."

Talros sketched a bow much shallower than the servant's differential one. The baron remained seated as they left the room, and Talros hoped that he was penning the missive to the accountant. Four estates had given their dues so far, but that did not count the others in General Ferra and General Ionan's circuits. He hoped it would be enough for newer weapons and armor, not to mention rations and travel expenses. With the drought and tighter restrictions by the guilds, prices were rising steadily with no end in sight. Something drastic was bound to happen, Talros thought. This situation had the makings of a revolution.

Passing the rows of windows in the corridor, General Talros wondered if the assassin was out there somewhere right now, perhaps even looking at him as he strode down the hallway. The thought filled him with a sense of anger and unease. Of all the night-stalkers and rebels that he had crossed, this one had eluded him the longest. It was infuriating.

"General, sir. We've arrived."

Talros lifted himself from his thoughts. "You said it's unlocked?"

"Yes, sir," the servant answered.

Talros tried the handle, and indeed the door was unlocked. He tried to push it open, but it was more difficult than he imagined. "Lady Miarthe," he called. "This is General Talros. Please come to the door!" He waited for an answer but none came. A trickle of anxiety made itself known, deep in the pit of his stomach. Something was not right here.

"You are certain she's in there?" he asked the servant.

"She never leaves, sir," the man said, eyes wide in his pale face. It occurred to Talros that he should have sent the man away before attempting this. Gossip traveled all too quickly. He soon decided it did not matter; servants almost always knew things before their masters anyway.

"I'm coming in," Talros called to the silent room, hoping for a reply that did not come. He set his shoulder to the door and pushed. The heavy door opened slowly, driving piles of clothes and tangled linens before it. An overturned stool caught against the door and halted its progress, so Talros had the servant reach in as far as he could and detach it.

Once the stool was moved the door slid open much easier and gave Talros his first glimpse at the destruction within the large room. There were piles of linen everywhere, a second overturned stool, scattered bits of food and cutlery, and one dead cat.

Talros froze. "Stay there," he instructed the servant, motioning for him to stand just outside the open doorway. The man nodded and stepped back, confused and afraid. Talros slipped inside, padding toward the cat.

It was most certainly deceased, and not long gone by the looks of things. It was cool and stiff. He touched it, making certain that his eyes did not deceive him. This could not bode well for Miarthe, he thought.

Straightening, Talros looked more thoroughly around the chaotic room. It was abominable, a pigsty, unfit for nobility in every sense. Did the maids never clean here?

There was a discomfiting lump under the quilt in the far corner. The gorge rose in Talros' throat as he moved toward it. He crouched next to the red-checked blanket and pulled back the corner.

Miarthe's pale face stared lifelessly up at him.

"Fetch your lord!" Talros called to the servant, his voice cracking like a whip. "Now!" An explosion of footfalls answered him as the man sped away.

Miarthe was in more appalling condition than her cat. Her mouth gaped in a semblance of a pained wail, and her eyes were wide and bloodshot with vast pupils. She was pale, bloodless in appearance, but her lips were tinged blue as if from a lack of air. Her hair and the floor around her were spattered with vomit. Talros rose and let the quilt fall back over her face, and now he saw that she had somehow tangled herself up in it, probably as she struggled for air and against the obvious pain.

"General Talros!" cried the baron from the doorway. "What has happened?"

Talros turned to face him, feeling his heart slide down his throat and into the pit of his stomach. "Your daughter, my lord, is dead."

The lord's hands clutched his hair, face pale. His eyes were wide and disbelieving. Other than that, he was absolutely still. When he spoke, the words burst forth in a bellow of fear. "What? No! How could this be?"

"I'm sorry, Baron d'Iseult." Talros walked to the stunned man in the doorway. "Call your guards."

"My heir!" the baron moaned. His shoulders were stiff under the folds of his cape. "Guards," he bellowed. "Guards!" To the cringing servant at his side, he yelled, "Bring my wife here immediately."

The baron then pushed his way into his daughter's room. "Where is she?" he demanded, and Talros directed him to the quilt in the corner.

As the baron grieved, Talros noticed the tray of half-eaten food perched on the table. Something dark protruded from under one edge. The sight of it was like a physical blow. *It cannot be.* But it was. The slightly ruffled feather lay flat and triumphant on the table, taunting him with its very presence.

The assassin!

The guards were already crowding through the doorway, the Captain of the Guard stopping short at the sight of the grieving baron. He looked around helplessly until his gaze lighted on Talros. "Your instructions, General?"

"Search the grounds. I want anyone unfamiliar brought to me immediately, as well as the kitchen servants and the maids. If you notice anything—and I mean anything—out of place, notify me at once."

"Yes, sir," the captain said, and swept from the room, his men following without question or hesitation.

Talros turned and eyed the black feather. It was the Nightingale's signature; it was unmistakable. He could not understand how the assassin had gained entrance into Miarthe's chamber. The servants surely would have noticed anything strange; Talros doubted the assassin was a servant on the estate. A new face would be remembered.

Another thing confused the general, and that was the question of how the assassin had gotten the poison—which, unquestionably, had been what killed Miarthe—into the food. The assassin could not have brought up the food himself, as the baron's daughter had special servants for that. He would have had to infiltrate the kitchens, but that would have been almost an impossible task. The kitchens were crowded and bustling. Why had the assassin simply not shot through the open windows? It would have been easier. Talros did not know, and could not answer. The very hint of a thought feinted and dodged along the edge of his mind, but for the life of him he could not catch it.

*　　*　　*

Talros paced in front of the seated figures, hands laced behind the small of his back. He was an intimidating sight in his black garb, with chain mail visible at his sleeves and the hem of his tunic. The short sword, peace-tied but still deadly, slapped against his thigh as he walked. The baron and baroness watched with interest, their faces drawn and pale and a dark light in their eyes. It was obvious to Talros that they very much wished for vengeance, preferably slow and bloody and quite painful. He did not think they would find it amongst the inhabitants of this estate. He was quite positive the assassin had already fled, but any lead would be followed unto exhaustion.

Sixteen servants and maids sat in the dining room as Talros paced at the head of the table. Three haggard-looking men had been brought in as well, though they claimed they were just gardeners. Talros noted the dirt under their nails. They would be questioned as witnesses, but nothing further. All those brought in sat with darting eyes, glancing at the guards that lined the walls, their halberds glinting in the lantern-light.

"I gave the tray to the child, like always. What she does with it after is no concern of mine," the rotund woman with graying red hair said. She went by the name of Feirn. Margrete Feirn, more precisely. "I cook and run the kitchens. She takes the food where it's s'posed to go."

"Do you cook Lady Miarthe's food separately from the rest?" Talros asked.

"No," Feirn stated. "I cook it all the same, unless there's a special request for something. Not one this time. Too many people here to cook all in separate pots. I'd need a kitchen the size of this castle to do that."

"Who usually takes Lady Miarthe's tray?"

"That'd be Dentea there, 'less she spills it first," Feirn drawled, casting a scathing look at the young girl at the end of the table. The child cowered in her chair as Talros turned toward her.

"You are Dentea?" he asked, not wanting to scare her into silence. She was a child, after all.

"Yes, sir," the girl answered, more steadily than Talros had expected.

"Can you tell me what you did this morning when it was time to take the tray to Lady Miarthe?"

161

Dentea looked at him with solemn eyes. "I was taking a nap before Siltev woke me and told me to get my lazy behind down to the kitchens." She cast her eyes to the side and stuck out her bottom lip in angry recollection. "Anyway, I went down to the kitchens and Missus Feirn yelled at me that I was late. She was real angry and I got upset and accidentally bumped her against the soup pot because she was in the way and I couldn't get past her." Dentea shot a sheepish, pained look at the glowering kitchen tyrant. "I'm so sorry about the pastries, Missus Feirn. It was an accident!"

"Continue, please," Talros said, ushering the girl's story back onto its proper course.

"Oh, sorry. Well, the tray was very heavy and I was having trouble carrying it because . . . well, I was trying not to cry and I was scared Lady Miarthe would pull my hair like she sometimes does. Did, I mean. Then this girl comes from somewhere, and she talks to me like she knows me but I didn't remember her at all." Dentea looked up at Talros with wide eyes. "She said I should let her take the tray to Lady Miarthe while I went to the fountain in the gardens and took a nap."

General Talros felt his heart leap. Could this girl work in conjunction with the assassin? "Did she say her name? What did she look like?"

"She told me her name was Lathien. I don't remember seeing her before but she told me I had. She looked to be my age, with dark blonde hair and blue eyes. Like ice, they were. Cutting eyes. She spoke very proper, though."

Someone cleared a throat, and Talros pivoted on his heel. An older woman waved a frail hand toward him, while her other hand tugged at the red kerchief tied around her head. "Lord General!" she called, waving him over. Talros nodded his thanks to Dentea and moved toward the woman.

"You have something to tell me?" he asked.

"I remember seeing this girl, General, in the hallway before noon. It was the hall near the kitchens, with the three large paintings. I thought she was someone's daughter or a new hire but, thinking on it, she didn't look right. The dress didn't fit her quite right, and she just didn't look like the type to work as a maid. This girl looked like she would be a lady someday, not a scullery maid."

Talros glanced about the room, gauging the reactions of the others. They whispered amongst themselves, No one else had seen a girl in the castle with a similar description. It was settled then. Talros turned and approached the count and countess.

"You have come to a conclusion then, General Talros?" the baron asked in a voice raspy with grief and anger.

"I believe so, my lord. This girl is important. I think she is the key to finding the assassin."

The baron grunted, thinking over Talros' words. "Then my coffers are open to you, General Talros. You have leave to take whatever you need to bring my daughter's murderer to justice. I want this assassin dead, and soon."

"He will be, Baron d'Iseult. On my honor, I swear it."

"We have deciphered the message, Valew," Talros announced three weeks later, staring hard at the ragged man seated on the stone bench of the cell. The man's defiant glare wavered, and Talros wondered if it was from the lack of drink or this new bit of knowledge. Valew was a tough man to read, and no one had been able to extract any information from him in Talros' absence. Lieutenant Darsin said it seemed the man was going mad, but he did not know why. Talros rather thought it was just the lack of ale.

Talros had not completely lied. In fact, one of the younger members of the Weapons had been able to partially interpret the message. What had been found definitively tied Emio Valew to the assassin, but the note revealed no names, neither of customers nor anyone else of importance. Talros had a strong feeling that Valew was not the instigator of the attacks, but rather someone for whom he worked. But who was it? It could be anyone, either in Caesia or the neighboring kingdom of Syline, any merchant or guildmaster or member of the nobility. There were simply too many people who could be involved. And motives were nearly endless as well. Did they order the assassinations for profit, for revenge, for spite? Could there be another reason he had not thought of yet? Talros narrowed his eyes. There were so many paths this plot could take. Any one of them could be true.

"Name the assassin and your fate will be less painful, I assure you," Talros told Valew.

"Less painful?" Valew croaked. He was dirty and tattered, wearing the same clothes in which he had been arrested. The priest's robe was torn in places, and the man inside was bruised and sore. The sight that unnerved Talros, however, was the fevered light in the man's eyes, one that bespoke of roiling turmoil under the calm façade. "Perhaps," Valew continued, "but pain is not the worst of punishments."

"You can leave here a free man," Talros pressed, "if you say that one name."

"You would think that, General, but names won't help you here." Valew's voice was hoarse. "You already know that name: Nightingale. There is no other." He broke off into a flurry of phlegm-filled coughs. When his eyes met Talros' again, the fevered light was clear and vibrant. The man smiled brokenly. "If you cross him, she will kill you."

"Who is *she*?"

"I've never seen her, never met her. Shadow in the night, panther in the high grass. Always hunting, always prowling. I'll die if I leave here, most certainly with a dark blade in the heart."

"Do you know her name?" Talros tried to remain calm, but his mind raced. The assassin was a woman, not the man he had previously thought. But not the girl from the castle; she had been too young. A child.

"She has no name, only the whisper of dark wings on the air. Is she here now?" Valew straightened on his bench and spread his arms wide, waiting for something. After a moment, he smiled and closed his eyes, letting his arms fall back to his sides. "It will come soon enough," he sighed.

"For whom does she work? What is the name of her employer?"

Valew laughed, though the sound was more like a gurgle caught in his throat. "The eyes will come now," he said breathlessly. "Those cutting eyes."

Cutting eyes. Had he not heard those words somewhere before? Before him, Valew's head jerked backward against the wall, slamming into it with a sickening thud. The man choked and gasped, his eyes rolling back into his head.

"Call the healer!" Talros roared. The lieutenant at the wall sped away.

"Too late," Valew stated. "Nightingale's too late." He scratched at his throat, and the welts that rose underneath his fingers were vivid in juxtaposition with the pale bloodlessness of his skin. "You cannot stop her," he moaned. "The shadows fly."

"Who does she serve?" Talros asked again, gripping the man's shoulders with iron hands. He must know. He had to know. This was going somewhere and, by the gods, Talros wanted to follow it to its end. He shook the man, willing him to stay conscious. "You are already dying," he said, not unkindly. "It cannot be helped now."

Valew's eyes rolled up to look into Talros' face. "True," he gasped, and a bubble of blood burst on his lips. He seemed to consider Talros' position, and then retched. The healer burst into the room. "Guildmaster," Valew groaned before slumping to the floor. The healer caught him, staggering under the weight. Valew was lowered to the floor, but it was too late to aid him. The healer felt for a pulse, and then shook his head at Talros. The old drunkard was dead.

Talros motioned to the returned lieutenant. "Locate every guild in each circuit. I want names and locations and what they produce or control."

"Yes, sir," the lieutenant answered, snapping a salute and before leaving the cell.

Talros left the healer to what was left of his work. As he paced the halls, a single phrase echoed in his mind: *you cannot stop her.*

Chapter 12

I WAS EXHAUSTED. The journey back to Benthol had been long and strenuous, as I had been forced into hiding to avoid passing horsemen and hunters, never knowing if they were part of a search party sent out by the general I had heard so much about. I had been forced to take great care in concealing myself and any signs of my passing; no campfires at night—which meant cold, dry trail food of which I was not fond—and also no warmth in the path of the oncoming winter. It was dusk on the day when I made my way to the South Guild and I had slunk off to my chambers to slip into a grateful slumber. To my dismay, I was intercepted by Caspon's spineless advisor, Bennic, and herded off to my master's office.

"It seems your training has come to an end. I believe you are now sufficiently skilled to take on your final task," Caspon said, mud-colored eyes frosty and gleaming with a dull, eerie light that flickered in their depths. They were the eyes of a hunter, focused and sharp. I had seen that same look in the eyes of a cat once, right before it pounced on a hapless rat and snapped its fragile neck.

I was quick to make the connection to his words. Those assassinations I had been forced to perform, the destruction of those innocent lives, was only training. Target practice. I felt the hot sting of bile rising in my throat, but I swallowed it down. I could not- *would not*- show weakness before Caspon. *No more!* I wanted to scream. *I am so tired of death and pain. I want no more of it!* If it had not been for the collar, I could have my revenge on Caspon and vanish from this wasteland of *cardea* filth and corruption. I longed to be with anthelai again, to breathe the cool fresh air without smelling the omnipresent stench of sewage and livestock. I wanted to hear the whispers of the trees without a rock wall between us. I wanted to be able to walk at night beneath the stars in safety, without

166

always having to look over my shoulder. I wanted to be rid of this gods-cursed headband.

I wanted to be free.

But I somehow managed to keep my thoughts from showing. I had become masterful at hiding my emotions behind a sullen, silent façade, though inside my mind raced. *I am not a mindless beast, a hound that cringes from its master's hand in fear, and then flees to do his bidding. Even the hound is capable of turning and biting the hand that feeds it.* I wondered if Caspon realized that. He was certain that I had been cowed into submission, that the collar had purged all thoughts of disobedience from my mind. I held my place and my tongue; I would be his hound for a time—until my opportunity arose.

"You are ready for your final task. This will require great skill, but must be accomplished in a short amount of time." Caspon grinned in the dancing light of the torches that lined the study. "I will give you a bit of incentive, Nightingale, to accomplish this last task as best you can."

Though I know you need none, I added for him in my mind, *for you wear the collar.*

"If you complete the job to my satisfaction, I will remove the collar." He smiled smugly, thinking he had hooked me like a fish.

I am young but I am not stupid, I thought. I knew Caspon had no intention of removing the collar, ever. He would have me be his slave for life. I was too valuable a commodity for him, one that would be too difficult to replace. His words repeated themselves in my mind. Final. Last. They were sinister and terrifying to me. Why would this be my last assignment? What was different about this one?

"You must watch for one of Cosian's Weapons," he said. "General Astin Talros."

I had seen the man, but Caspon did not know that.

"He has dark-hair threaded with white, and is around forty years of age. Tall, fit, and a stickler for the king's law. If he scents you, he will hunt you like a dog. I've heard that he is searching for you. Remember your training."

Caspon laid out the plans for the assassination, giving me specific details about how to go about my task. It would be a risky job, both for him and especially for me, despite the target being an old, crippled man. And then I realized why he had thrown me the bait. He did not want instincts of self-preservation to get in the way of the task. I could—it was quite likely, in fact—be killed. He wanted the best performance I could give, both for show and to keep my life so I could continue to serve him. He was trying to override my survival instincts that could impede the assassination. *Does he really believe I will fall for that ruse?* I thought incredulously. Then I looked at his face and saw that he did. He believed me to be truly broken, submissive and subservient to his whims. I wanted to laugh. I might have been a dog—the beryl would not permit otherwise—but I saw wolf-eyes and heard the howling of the wolf-god in my dreams.

I may be young, but I am stronger than that, Caspon. One day you will see.

Talros' lieutenant had found guilds in almost every city within the kingdom of Caesia. There were others, of course, in the neighboring kingdoms of Yentille and Syline, but Talros left those for later. He had learned that the enemy was more often than not the close companion rather than the unfamiliar neighbor. The lieutenant's information contained the name and location of each guild within the kingdom, as per Talros' request, and also business transactions, leaders, guild hierarchy and a calendar of recent past and future events that were important enough to have been recorded by city officials.

According to the research, the city of Astione was home to three guilds, the first of which was the Carvers Guild, located in the northwest portion of the city. This guild appropriated all the woodwork that the city and neighboring townships required, both internally and for exportation. Its current leader was Evian Wainwright, with elections held amongst its members every five years.

The second guild was a Steelers Guild, responsible for the city's metalwork, and was situated in the southwest. Its hierarchy was similar to the Carvers Guild, with Bollan Hardner as acting Guildmaster. And the third guild, similar in character, was the Farmers Guild in the west. Nyatil Armers was its leader.

Talros thumbed the corner of the parchment, absently flattening the curled edge. There was no further information of importance on any of those three guilds. Their dealings were rather dull, in fact. The general laid the parchment aside and took up the second.

The northern city of Luella had two guilds, these more colorfully named than any in Astione. Luella lay on the kingdom's border and was populated by a number of neighboring Yentillese citizens. The Yentiliáne Guild was made of many different professions, though namely stonemasons and blacksmiths. It was located in the southern portion of the city and professed a troubled history. It had previously been two separate guilds, but competition and feuding had forced the two to combine six years prior, with much disagreement and mistrust. Karibik Deomeil had proclaimed himself guildmaster and was many times challenged by younger members seeking to overthrow his reign. Talros had already dealt with one such upstart.

The northeastern guild was much more tranquil, a guild of weavers and seamstresses called Láleontessa, which was the only guild in any city run by a woman. Her name was Nyssa Spallae. To this one, Talros did not pay much attention, except to remember that once he had had the pleasure to meet Nyssa and thought her quite pretty.

Talros pondered this report for a moment. A troubled guild like Yentiliáne would have to be investigated in this matter. Talros took his quill and drew a mark next to Deomeil's name. He would come back to this entry later.

Setting that page aside, Talros plucked the last report from his table.

Benthol, a small city with activity in abundance, was the one and only heading on the page. The two guilds in Benthol—North and South—ruled everything in their respective locations—a primitive practice no longer used by the other guilds as it begat corruption and dishonesty.

The North Guild was led by Ardal Evoll, an elderly man intent on keeping his people beneath his thumb and entrenched in the agricultural way of life. He was not a cruel man, but strong-willed, and his people believed that wisdom came with age. Ardal neared eighty—an age almost unheard of—and planned to hand the keys to his portion of the city to his son, Hanlon, in the very near future. But Hanlon was not as clear-headed and strong-willed as his father;

much less so, in fact. The man cowered in the face of his father's advisors—who were soon to be his own—and would not make a decision without their approval, endorsement and guidance.

The South Guild had the opposite streak of mercantilism, producing metal and woodworks. Though the two areas had to trade goods with one another to survive, they did so without any sense of friendship or camaraderie. There was open hostility, in fact, between the Evolls and South Guildmaster Lorcen Caspon. There had been slight skirmishes between their loyalists—but those had thankfully been few and far between.

General Talros drummed his fingers on the table, the steady noise doing nothing to drown out the currents of his thoughts. He placed the parchment on top of Deomeil's listing. These guilds would also be kept. He scanned the rest of the report, searching for any pieces of useful evidence. After several long minutes, he looked again at the piles on his desk. The stack of unremarkable guilds was taller than the listing of those with evident problems. Talros had thought as much. He sat back in his chair and ran a hand through his hair in exasperation, letting out a heavy sigh of fatigue.

Luella's Yentiliáne or either one in Benthol have some kind of discord, he thought. *But does any of it warrant the use of an assassin?* He frowned, thinking hard and knowing that the puzzle needed to be solved as soon as possible.

He was almost certain that Deomiel would have attached a known name to the assassin. The guildmaster was a man who wanted his enemies to know who struck them down. This assassin, however, did not hold any clues of ownership. So the employer could be Deomiel, but possibly someone else; the situation did not have the subtle stink of Yentiliáne upon it.

That left the guild-leaders of Benthol. Talros leaned back in his chair, rubbing his chin. He did not have the knowledge of these men as he did of Deomiel. Their natures were a mystery to him, but his lieutenant had written down information enough to hazard a guess.

There was no discernable motive for the seemingly random deaths and assaults save profit. Each action had little impact on an individual guild, and there was no epicenter for the assassin's actions. The motive of sheer monetary gain, however, did not satisfy Talros' gut instinct. Deomeil and Caspon both had riches enough; they were the wealthiest guild-leaders in the Caesian kingdom. Did their riches make them feel invincible? Powerful? Careless? Someone with either boldness or stupidity had employed Valew as an intermediary, as the coded note had proven, because the priest had been a sot and a gambler.

Who had the temerity—or foolishness—and the motive?

Talros rose to his feet and crossed to the window. Outside, the stars glittered in the dark sky. For nearly a week he had been closeted in an inn of Tione, a small town between the Baron d'Iseult's estates and Benthol. Time was wasting, draining as quickly as blood from an open wound. Talros' instincts told him that something was coming to a head, and that someone else would die unless he solved this mystery swiftly. The snake was growing hungry and would soon strike again. He was certain.

Talros read again the description of the guildmasters, looking for any trace of meaning hidden between the words. He did not think he had any strange intuition, as the rumors of him claimed. Let others think that, he mused. If it made him more formidable, all the better.

His line of thought trailed away, and Talros found himself staring at the silver blades of grass outside his window. The dew droplets glistened like beads of glass, mirroring the stars above. Talros' eyes flicked upward to where the constellations hung in full view: the Thief's Knife, the Owl, the Wolf and the Lady. He was reminded of a time long ago when he was just a young boy, listening to his father tell tales under the stars of battles and heroes, of Vilwing the Treacherous and Belan the Brave, and of anthelai. In his father's stories, the anthelai had always been skulking creatures hiding in the shadows, stealing babes from their cradles by night and waylaying travelers by day. Talros had been enthralled, but had always wondered at the extent of the truthfulness of those tales. Why would a people so free and hidden always try to usurp power and steal and frighten? He had vowed at the tender age of ten to learn the reliability of these tales for himself, and had yet to do so.

Wait, his gut whispered. *Think again.* The sudden notion clung to the edge of his mind, scrambling for a handhold. Usurp, steal and frighten, the tales said. The same could hold here. He focused on the windowpane, sending all his thoughts inward. With so many deaths and assaults—and so many dark feathers—the assassin's reputation was growing in strides. With sudden clarity, Talros remembered the scene in Domnic Stark's store: the bird statue with black feathers. As a piece of anthela culture, it had symbolized strength, fortitude, and worthy pursuits. They placed black feathers on their weapons. The assassin had black feathers on her arrows.

It was not certain, but it was plausible. Fear-mongering was Caspon's art and Deomiel's joy, based on what he had read in the lieutenant's notes.

But what was the reason for hiring an assassin and, if this killer was a girl, going through the trouble of training one? What manner of sickness was it that used children in such a way?

Caspon wanted a reputation, surely, and a harsh one at that. His jurisdiction already feared him, but that was not enough. Perhaps he wanted all of Benthol to fear him. Deomiel, too, could claim the same. Perhaps he wanted to give his new position a fortification that one would fear to attack. An anthela assassin could be a formidable weapon, and a terrifying defense. But why would Deomiel send the assassin out into the world instead of keeping her close to home for protection? Something here did not make sense.

Talros flipped again through the listing, reading every line with determination and sharp eyes. Deomiel had no recent events, nor happenings of any seeming consequence in the near future. In Benthol, however, a new guildmaster would arise. And to General Astin Talros, that seemed to be a key that opened the unnoticed lock in his mind. Caspon might assassinate Evoll. It made a certain kind of sense, now that the pieces were fitting into place. The general scanned through his papers, hunting for the one dedicated to Evoll's guild and leadership. He read it, eyes flying over the ragged lines. Evoll's resignation and Hanlon's subsequent arrival into office would happen soon, and Talros worried that would be the day Caspon might strike. He penned a message to his king and called for the post-boy.

Talros had little less than a week to stop the attack—if he was correct. If not, then Deomiel would be the next person to confront. In his heart, a voice whispered that he was not wrong, and Talros wanted desperately to believe it. Benthol was close; it would hopefully take a short amount of time to search and guard, if he was correct. If not, then Deomiel would be the next person to confront. In his heart, a voice whispered that he was not wrong, and Talros wanted desperately to believe it. His mind and heart had flipped a coin and the pathway led now to Benthol and Caspon. Deomiel and Yentiliáne rested facedown in the dirt. On another day, with another toss, they might have come up instead. Talros would have to ride his horse into the ground to reach North Benthol on time, but he would do it. He swore he would succeed. The assassin could not be allowed to win. If his intuition was wrong, if Caspon was not the aggressor, then Talros would ride as if the fanged, gaping maw of Énas snapped behind him, hungering to devour him on the breadth of the Plains.

Chapter 13

I PREPARED MYSELF. Trained my muscles and my mind, packed my pouch full of vials and packets, and checked my weapons, leathers and headband thrice.

Five days later, Caspon told me I was ready.

It was too dangerous for me to travel above ground now. Caspon had mentioned that General Talros was on the hunt, so I was reduced to crawling through tunnels like a rat. I crept north, keeping closer than I liked to the dripping, curving stone walls. The rock all around me was covered in moisture that trickled through the cracks to puddle in greasy slicks in the pathway. The moss coating on the walls was matted with it and stunk of dead things. I tried to breathe through my mouth, but even then the stench overwhelmed me. I spit every few steps, hoping to get the taste of it out of my mouth. It did not work. Occasionally, my boots skidded across a slick patch of slime and I was forced to grasp the wall or slide into the flowing watercourse on my right.

This was either some sort of sewer, I surmised, or an aqueduct that had been abandoned and appropriated for some other purpose. I was tremendously grateful for the rare air duct that led to the outside world, for it assured me that I would not be overwhelmed by the noxious fumes and perish in this dank tomb. However, the ducts did not let in any light—the angle was wrong—and my flickering torch did little to illuminate the narrow space. In a way I was glad of it, for it meant I could not see the things that must be floating in the watercourse or squished so nastily under my feet.

I could not count the hours I had been here, nor did I try. Already it felt like days had passed. The northern portion of Benthol was close, though. I could almost sense it like a change in the air. Slinking along, I let my mind travel as it would, and it pored over my task—the one mission Caspon had in mind for me when he took me from Carfuinel. The thought fanned the embers of the rage that burned deep within me, imbuing them with new life.

My mind whispered things to me as I slunk through the darkness. Without Dentea as a witness, I would never have been identified. Her testimony alone was enough to set Talros on the path of a young girl. Things would have been easier for me if I had killed her in the manor, but I refused to entertain the notion. Despite everything I had done, despite my own self-loathing, I could not have killed the girl. She had not been Caspon's target; she had not threatened my life in an immediate sense, so I could never have taken her life. I wanted to think myself incapable of such a thing, but my mind whispered that I could be in the sunlight now if it had not been for her. My mistake was in keeping her alive and I was being punished for it. These thoughts would not cease no matter how much I tried to think of other things. I hated them, and myself, for I was the demon that halfbloods were thought to be. There was no escaping it.

I snarled and smashed a hand against the slick stone. "Stop!" I barked, hearing the fading echoes repeat down the tunnel. Sucking in a shaky breath, I swiped a hand across my face and was startled to find my eyes were wet. "Just stop," I whispered to myself. *Think of the mission. That and nothing else. Do not even think of what might come after.* There was no question of what would come after, I figured. I was as good as dead. If Talros did not kill me, then Caspon would. I would do everything in my limited power to thwart him, and there could only be one outcome from that.

Still, I tried to formulate a plan. Talros and his men would be scattered throughout the northern section of Benthol, watching out for someone who matched my description. If I was captured and not killed outright, then I was doomed to a rough end. I had heard plenty of horror stories about tortured anthelai to keep my mind alight for nights on end.

I continued onward for an indeterminate amount of time, my boots making soft sucking noises on the slick ledge. The torch was small, illuminating a small area around me. I could not see more than a few feet before my feet, and I hoped I was still traveling in the right direction. There had been no map, although I knew Caspon had hundreds of them. He had just told me what to do, and the beryl listened.

The torch flickered. My heart leapt in my chest, hammered in my throat, and then crawled back into place when I felt a draft of cool air brush my face. I sighed in relief and lifted the small torch aloft. The area I had entered was an offshoot of the tunnel. In the dark, the ledge must have split and I had followed the wrong one. My fingers clenched on the torch as I tried to stop them from shaking. I hated this dark, dank place. I hated the way the fear filled my veins. I did not want to be lost here. The thought filled me with terror. If I could not escape, the beryl could kill me, thinking that I had deserted Caspon's plan. That was if I did not drown or perish of starvation first. I bit my tongue before I could cry out, before I could panic.

Lost or not, keep moving, I thought, *or else die in the dark.* There was nothing else do to but walk.

I took a step into the alcove, wishing the torch was brighter. Wandering, I probed the area. Stone pillars built against the walls rose gracefully from the floor and soared to indiscernible heights. It was too dark above to see where they ended. There were brackets in the walls also, some holding the sooty remnants of long-burnt torches. The dank, chill air smelled of ancient rot and the echoes of smoke. There was something darker too, but I could not name it no matter how deeply I breathed.

A stone table was centered in the small alcove, marbled with what had once been different colors but had since faded to a more or less uniform gray. One particular swatch of color had coated the center of the table and dripped in runnels to the floor beneath, pooling between the stones. The sight made me uneasy, for this looked too much like an altar. I had seen sacrificial altars before, on the rare occasion when I had, for one reason or another, entered a temple.

My teeth clenched together, almost clipping the tip of my tongue, as I took several hurried steps back. I scanned the room again, quickly, and noticed a dark spot that turned out to be another, much smaller alcove containing an iron ladder. My fear was already draining away, forced down by the beryl, and my mind cleared. Regardless of where it led, I needed to climb the ladder: retracing my steps would get me nowhere. However, I could not climb while holding the torch.

I hated the dark, but I hated the sewer just as much. Gritting my teeth, I placed my little torch into one of the brackets and set my hands carefully on the ladder. I could not think about what might happen if the rungs broke.

The light grew dimmer and dimmer as I scaled the rusty ladder. Flecks of ochre soon coated my hands and dusted my arms and knees. I moved as quickly as I could, determined to reach the top before the ladder had a chance to crack and throw me. Before long, the torch burnt out below me. I crept along now, moving up the rungs by feel alone. It seemed the ground and the ceiling now were both nonentities; I was alone in the dark.

Still, I forced myself onward. There could be no stopping now, not until I reached my goal or until the ladder broke beneath me.

I would not deny that I breathed a heavy sigh of relief when a cool draft brushed wisps of hair against my face. Reaching one hand upward, I felt a smooth expanse of stone stretched out over my head. There were no bolts or hinges that I could feel, but the square outline of a door was clearly delineated. Holding onto the ladder, I touched the door with one hand, gauging its weight. I pushed carefully, struggling not to fall backward, and was able to force the door open. After lifting it just a crack, I raised up to peek out through the fissure I had created.

My vision was blocked by straw. Odd, I thought, straining my ears for any type of sound, any hint of movement. All I picked up were the soft sounds of horses chomping at the feedboxes or stamping hooves on hard-packed earth. I could smell nothing but the wild scent of large animals. I edged up the trapdoor and slunk out on my belly, crawling like a weasel.

I was in a rear stall, back in the corner of a rather large stable. This stall was empty except for a massive pile of hay, and pieces of tack hung on hooks. My hunting eyes soon noted the rafters above and the cleanly swept aisle beyond the closed stall-door. Silently and carefully, I lowered the trapdoor down into its recess and swept a few handfuls of hay over it so it would stay hidden.

I peeked over the door, but could not sense any stable boys or other *cardeai* occupants. Still, this place was not safe. I pulled myself onto the door, shying away as the horse in the opposite box eyed me reproachfully, and then onto the uneven wall. There was enough of a foothold there for me to vault into the rafters. The ladder near the entrance of the loft would have been easier but I would take no chances of a passing stablehand catching a glimpse of me.

Once in the rafters, it was easy to sneak along to the hayloft and creep into the far corner. I had rested before leaving Caspon's manor, but the trek through the duct had drained my energy and my willpower. Taking the small flask of water from my belt, I sipped half of it, not caring that it was warm and tasted stale.

I burrowed deep into the hay, making certain I was hidden, before curling up into a tight ball. If someone climbed the ladder, I was certain I would hear it. The horses might make some noise in any case. With the confidence born of youth and substantiated by the beryl, I dropped into a grateful and much needed slumber.

I would start the hunt when I awoke.

Chapter 14

"MASTER EVOLL, IT IS FOR YOUR PROTECTION." In the main foyer of the Evoll's manor, Talros placed his boots on the plush carpet and argued his position once more. It seemed futile and Talros grew angry. Why did this man not have a care for his life? It did not make sense.

"I don't see the need for it, General Talros, and nor does my father. I will not have the kingdom's watchdogs marring my ceremony." The man flapped his hands in anger, reminding Talros of a woman shaking filth from a rug. The curved ceiling echoed Evoll's words. The entire room was bright and sunny, lit from the numerous windows. In them, Talros saw entry points for an enemy.

"There is a dangerous and clever assassin working in Caesia and you'd rather not have the Weapons at your rising? I daresay I do not understand your logic, Master Evoll." The general stood stiff, hands clasped behind his back, and watched the man he had sworn to protect.

"What fool would dare attack me while I am under the eyes of my people? The crowd will be too thick, Lord General." Hanlon's face flickered with triumph. He seemed so certain of victory. Talros wanted to sigh, but reined it back.

"Have you forgotten Lassolern so quickly? The young Lord Tyban was cut down in the midst of a parade! You think you have some protection due to the crowds, but I assure you that is not the case. The crowds will simply serve to hide the assassin further."

"That is because you have failed your duty to your kingdom, General. If you had caught this assassin as you were supposed to then this fiasco could never have occurred. If you think placing me under guard during this *very* important ceremony will make up for your blatant misdeeds then you are welcome to it, I suppose. Just keep your men out of my way. I do dislike lackeys in my presence."

179

With a snide wave, Hanlon Evoll turned on his heel and went down the long carpeted hallway into one of the nearby rooms.

"Very good, Master Evoll," Talros all but snarled as the younger man strode away. Talros thought Hanlon Evoll a fool, and bemoaned North Benthol's inevitable fate after it was ushered into his clammy hands. Nonetheless, it was Talros' duty to protect him, and protect him he would, for all that the upcoming guildmaster was a prancing, hypocritical worm of a man.

Talros straightened his swordbelt and stalked through the corridor, down the stairs and out the front entrance of the North Guild's largest building. His lieutenant was waiting by the fountain, hand on his sword and his eyes alert and shifting.

"The ceremony will take place in the front courtyard where the citizenry will be able to watch," Talros told him. "Have three men on every corner and set up a patrol around the perimeter starting tonight. Also, I have been told Evoll has a surprise in store to help usher in the people's support for his oncoming governance. I suspect a commotion to follow." Exasperated, he resisted the rather strong urge to massage his temples.

"Yes, General. I understand." The man sketched a crisp bow and hurried away to do Talros' bidding.

General Astin Talros allowed himself to sigh, breathing road-dust from his lungs. The ceremony was to take place tomorrow afternoon, and he was certain that *something* would happen. He and his men would be ready. The assassin would not escape again, Talros vowed.

He could not allow it.

I awoke early on the morning of what was certain to be my last day of life. The predawn air was cool, raising gooseflesh on my arms as I crawled out of my warm cocoon in the hay. I moved carefully, ears and eyes hunting for any type of *cardea* movement in the stables. I could detect nothing other than the motions of horses in the dark, so it seemed as if the stablehands had not yet made their rounds. Slipping from the hay as silently as possible, I gathered my few possessions, crept from the hayloft, and slipped out a narrow window.

There was light enough from the fading stars and waxing moon to see by, augmented by a few small lanterns hanging from scattered storefronts. I stayed in the shadows, shifting the unstrung bow and leather quiver into better positions on my back and making certain my pouch was secured to my belt. This entire venture would be for naught if I happened to lose either one.

The buildings crowded me on all sides, towering edifices of stone and wood and covered in creeping ivy. They grew more infrequent as I neared the richer districts, but became much more ornate, with flared eaves and pointed arches and rich latticework over the windows.

I saw three guardsmen then, half-hidden under the porch of an inn. I halted, knowing they were likely there for me. They were not facing my direction at the moment, so I took the chance to sink further into the shadows of the eaves, slip around the rear of the building, and pull myself onto the roof.

I cursed as I glanced over the streets. There were more guards posted than I had thought. That would make my task much harder. Glancing up, I eyed the outer wall that towered above me. The wall ringed the northern section of Benthol and was interspersed with a series of watchtowers. The watchtowers were not built into the wall, but set right against the stone. If they did not have Talros' soldiers in them now, then they certainly would in a matter of hours.

I frowned as I crouched in the lee of a brickwork chimney. The courtyard was to the northeast of my position. Soldiers would be on the wall, and soldiers would be in the streets. I would have to move quickly and as ghostlike as possible. Moving across the roofs might be my safest bet, I thought.

I took a deep breath. I had made it this far, and I would not be stopped now. At my throat, the beryl whispered its promises. Straining my eyes, I could just see the courtyard, or at least the tops of the buildings that edged it. The courtyard was the largest open place in North Benthol; there was no question that the ceremony would take place there. From my perusing of Caspon's maps, I recalled the buildings around the courtyard being the homes of wealthier citizens, followed by a few temples and affluent businesses. The Evoll manor was there as well, although set far back from the other structures.

The courtyard doubled as a marketplace for four weeks of the year, when merchants from around the kingdom were invited to sale their wares in the center of Benthol's commercial district. It did wonders for Evoll's coffers, to be sure. From the terrace on the front of the Evoll manor, the guildmaster could watch the goings-on in relative safety. The manor was secure, and far enough from the activity to likely be without any real threat. The alleyways created by these buildings were like the spokes of a wheel. I noted those in the back of my mind, just in case.

Moving across the wood-shingled rooftops, I stayed as close to the wall as possible. The guards atop it would have to lean over and look down to catch sight of me. At least, that was what I hoped. I went carefully but swiftly, as I needed to be out of sight by the time the sun arose. Fortunately, the roofs were close enough so that I could leap between them after checking that there were no guards in the immediate vicinity to spot my obligatory acrobatics.

Soon, the watchtower nearest the courtyard loomed over me. I ducked behind a squat chimney, eyeing the arrow-slits in the circular structure. I would have to cross the ground to reach it, but if I could make it inside and to the top, then it might have the makings of a decent hiding place. It overlooked the courtyard, which was excellent, and was stationed close enough to the wall so that a leap of faith from the tower's top might not be fatal if the situation called for a quick escape.

Grasping my dagger, I slipped wraithlike down the side of the house and landed on the cobblestone. Peering around me, I made certain of the locations of the patrolling guards. The sun was crawling upwards now, its rays just touching the eastern sky with pink and orange. I had very little time left.

A rooster announced the oncoming morn with an unhurried staccato crow, and I fled through the open space between the building and the tower before it had finished. The guards near the door had their backs to me, and the entrance was unlatched. I took a heartbeat to peer through the open door into the lowest level to see if there were any soldiers within, and sensed nothing, and so I slid in through the entryway that I had cracked open just wide enough to admit me.

Closing the door behind me, with my dagger loose and ready in my hand, I made my way up the spiraling staircase. The second, third and fourth levels were equally empty, and I began to breath easier. Still, I could not let my guard down for an instant, for an instant would be all it would take to undo me.

The fifth floor was the highest level in the watchtower. From the arrow-slits I could see almost the entire city laid out before me. I could also see over the stone wall on the opposite side of the tower that encircled the northern half of the city. Until now, all the floors and roofs of each level had been strong, thick timber with iron supports. This floor was the same but the roof consisted of oak boards that looked decidedly weatherworn. Perhaps the conical outer roof leaked, I thought offhanded. I wondered if anyone had noticed the rotting edges of the boards closest to the arrow-slits. The oaken timbers would probably fall before too long.

Forcing the useless thoughts from my mind, I peeked through the slits in the stone. I would have a decent shot from here, at this height and angle. I worried about the soldiers, though, and their inevitable proximity. This was what Caspon had expected: my entrapment and subsequent demise. I ground my teeth bitterly. This was the one place close enough and concealed enough to offer a chance at Evoll, but it was also a corner in which I would be trapped.

There was no other option; the beryl would not allow me to leave now. Caspon had spoken his demands, and I was finished.

Below me, I heard the door on the ground floor open and shut. Footsteps sounded, heavy and unstoppable as floodwaters. My mouth went dry as the beryl gave me a warning sting that made my eyes water. I turned, hunting for a safer place to hide—and saw none. The room contained a simple table and two low stools, with a small pile of empty grain sacks flung on the right side of an arch. I would have to make a stand and hope the disappearance of the soldiers would not lead the others to investigate. I steadied the dagger in my sweat-slick palm. Once the first man fell, the advantage of an ambush would be lost. I sucked in a deep breath, readying myself for failure.

The soldiers were coming up the stairs, pausing on each landing. I pictured them in my mind, swords in hand and dressed in mail, checking each floor methodically. I wondered if I would be killed on sight or captured. I was young yet; perhaps that was a card I could play to my benefit.

They would soon be at the top floor, and I recognized that I had not planned as best I could. I moved toward the empty sacks—my only chance—and that was when I heard the cat.

I let out a breath I did not know I had been holding, and relaxed my tensed muscles. I barely managed to scramble under the sacks and rearrange them to hide me before the two soldiers came up the stairs. I was sure they would find me, hidden under the grain sacks like a frightened rat. What grain sacks were doing on the top floor of a watchtower I did not know, but I did not question my fortune overmuch. The cat, huddled over her nest of mewling kittens, eyed me warily but made no move against me as I slid close.

My breathing seemed too loud as the men approached. I was certain they would hear it and find me. Laying my head flat on the wooden floor, I stared at the cat as if it was the only thing left in the world. I had heard it told that my father could communicate with animals if he chose. Could I not do the same?

The cat stared at me with fey eyes—there was a sharpness in them that made me think of Lenos' yellow god-eyes—and I willed it to listen, to heed me, and spoke in a soft voice almost inaudible to my own sharp ears. Then I sank back, hoping, praying, that my message was received. The cat blinked, stretched, and looked upwards. I swallowed the bitter bile that rose burning in my throat and closed my eyes, the fingers of my right hand kneading the hilt of the dagger.

Through a small space between sacks, I watched. Two men approached, hands on the hilts of their swords. The taller of the two moved in first, moving through the archway and into the empty room.

"Nothing here," he said. "Are you *certain* you saw something?"

"Yes, Jergan," the other man answered. "I could have sworn. . ." He moved into the room, peering at the table and empty sacks. "I suppose it could've been a trick of the shadows."

Jergan ambled over to the sacks and gave them a kick with a booted foot. "May as well check," he grumbled, almost to himself, and lifted a handful of cloth off the floor.

Beside me, the cat's hair raised like a ridge on its spine. The ears lay back on its narrow skull while its tail lashed. When the man touched the cloth, the cat exploded from the pile, hissing like a snake, and shot to the entryway like an arrow from a bow. Jergan

184

staggered back, clutching his bleeding fingers. The small beast, my savior, rushed back at him, a blur of bristling, yowling fur, and leapt at his face. The soldier swung his head aside, swearing vehemently, and missed the cat's unsheathed claws by less than a hair. The cat struck the floor, turned, and vanished down the stairwell.

"Damn it by all the gods!" Jergan blasphemed, sticking his bleeding fingers into his mouth.

His companion, wide-eyed, barked a short, almost uneasy laugh. "Well, I did see *something*, I said. Damned if I knew it was a cat, though."

"You dragged me up here for a cat, you idiot! And now look at my fingers!" Jergan held his wet, shredded fingers out for his companion's assessment.

"I said I didn't know it was a cat! When's the last time a cat left a door unlatched?"

"My dog could do it, back when I was a boy. I daresay a cat could do it, too." Jergan squeezed his oozing fingers in the crook of his elbow, hoping to stifle the bleeding before they went back downstairs.

His companion grinned. "Wait until the others hear how you screamed, just like a girl."

"You dratted clot-headed fool, I'll beat your brains in for that!"

"Damn it, I hate getting patrol duty with you. No fun at all," the other man said.

"So tell the captain, why don't you, Gareth? Let's see how he enjoys your clever little jests. I'll bet you put that cat there yourself, knowing something like this would happen!"

"Idiot," Gareth grumbled. "Why would I go through the trouble?" He sighed heavily. "Never mind, don't answer that. Let's just go. Patrols won't finish themselves."

"Don't think I'll forget this, Gareth."

"I won't," he replied. "You never do." The two men went back down the stairs, silent and sullen, with their heavy boots and sword belts marring the otherwise still morning.

I had gone as still as a corpse as they spoke, hardly daring to breathe, but finally, slowly, the men clomped back down the stairs, and I allowed myself to live again. Scrambling from the pile without disturbing the kittens, I gathered my things and panted as I gazed around me. I knew now why Caspon had taunted me with freedom.

There was not one decent hiding space in the entirety of northern Benthol. The stables were too far away; the tunnel there would have been a blessing. The homes would be too crowded, and the storefronts packed. I needed a high vantage point with an escape route, and this watchtower was the closest thing.

I paced the circumference of the room, peering again through the arrow-slits. Through them, I could see the top of the perimeter wall, and the hazy shadows of the trees beyond. I leaned back, thinking hard, until my eyes rested again on the small section of rotten ceiling timbers.

There, my mind said, and I listened. Dragging the table underneath the planks, I vaulted upon it and stretched upward, pushing with all my might on the dark wood. The soldiers would return, of that I was certain.

After several heartbeats' time, the rotting wood moved. I heaved upward, grunting with effort, as the nails pulled loose, squealing. I was sweating by the time there was a hole large enough to admit me. Standing on the tips of my toes, I hauled myself upward, arms protesting, and vanished into the dark recess inside the roof. A cone of shingles that made up the outer roof shielded me from view. Dust motes danced in the miniscule rays of light that had managed to creep through the worn roof above and tight, planked rafters below.

I tamped the board back into place to remove any trace of my presence. When it was done I breathed a heavy sigh of relief. This was as close as I could come to safety in this place. I turned my attention back to the shingles, and loosened one so I could see the outside. It was not hard, as many of the shingles were as rotted as the boards below. I would have to tread carefully, but did not doubt that the boards would hold my weight for the short time I would be here.

The sun had risen while I had hidden in the sacks. It just peeked over the treetops, but its light washed over the city like a flood. And in the trees beyond the wall, a nightingale finished its song.

The citizenry of North Benthol seemed excited about the new leader stepping forward that afternoon and, although they were somewhat apprehensive about the large number of soldiers stationed around the city, they moved about freely and without restraint. They were dressed in their finest attire while still manning market stalls, leading horse-drawn carts laden with goods, or stumbling drunkenly in the street singing bawdy songs at the top of their lungs. I thought it was too early in the morning to be drinking, but apparently the group of men on the street below did not agree. One of them now was chugging a tankard of strong, brown ale while the others cheered him on until he doubled over in a coughing fit, gagging and retching there in the middle of the lane.

I had found my hiding place to be satisfactory, having discovered an entire section of rotting shingles on the left area of the conical roof, and two others on the side above the board I had removed to enter the roof. These two shingles I removed completely, allowing a little more sunlight to enter but still concealing me from view. The hole they left was no larger then the palm of my hand, just big enough for an arrow and an eye.

I had tried to formulate a plan during the past few hours, but it was foolhardy at best. I shook my head, trying to throw off the coils of fear that threatened to cloud my mind. I could not allow myself to think too deeply now, or permit my mind to run unconstrained. The fear would settle into my bones if either happened, and I needed to stay alert.

I tried to think of anything but the oncoming hours that would likely be my last.

I forced myself to think of things that I had once enjoyed in Carfuinel. I had reveled on the way the morning light shone on the dew-wet grass, the beads of water sparkling like so many diamonds. I thought of walking next to a river, under trees patchy with lichen and moss, moist soil underfoot, with birdsong filling my ears. I ruminated on the way the air there was crisp and moist, and the sound of roaring water as one rounded a bend in the trail and saw the rushing torrent's majesty for the first time, glimpsing the rainbow as sunlight met mist, almost close enough to touch. The simple beauty of an autumn leaf spinning to the ground, catching the sunlight and shining brilliant gold and crimson, like a precious jewel falling from the sky; the feel of rough bark underfoot as I raced through the branches, heedless of the world underneath; the feel of the wind in my hair as I faced a gorgeous sunrise that turned

the world to rosy pinks and oranges as varying as the hues of a field of marigolds; the smell of a newly opened flower, fresh and sweet. .
.

I blinked, coming back to myself. Something had startled me from my reverie. For a moment, I was puzzled, wondering what was different. Then I heard it, a steady pounding from below. I peered through the small hole I had made, and swallowed hard.

Men were building gallows in the courtyard.

"This is your surprise, Master Evoll? A hanging?"

"Of course, General. Why else would I order a gibbet assembled in my courtyard on this very special day?"

Talros ignored the man's sarcastic tone. "I was not aware that the execution of criminals was commonplace at a guildmaster ceremony."

"It's not!" Hanlon Evoll grinned. "I thought of it, and I assure you that my brilliance will be spoken of for years."

Talros gritted his teeth, hardly daring to open his mouth lest his fist decide to do the talking. He was silent as he and Hanlon Evoll watched the gallows rise up from the center of the courtyard. An uneasy feeling stirred up in his gut. This new addition to the rising had the potential to go either very well or very poorly. Talros did not like such absolutes. He wished that Evoll had thought to discuss such matters with him beforehand, but of course, Hanlon Evoll acted before thinking.

"I will tell you something, General Talros, which I hope will wipe that disapproving look from your face. Please try to pay attention."

Talros glared at the man, trying to smother the furious dislike that threatened to rush up and overwhelm him. No one ever said he had to like the man, just protect his life. It was a task that grew harder by the minute. Evoll rested his pale hands on the balustrade and spoke.

"These people," he said, sweeping a hand toward the already bustling crowds, "look up to my father. They do not know me as a leader, but they will. Today, I will show them something that will let them know that *I* am Guildmaster now. I will be the one who protects them. They will see it and love me for it. Do you understand?"

"I understand that you do not want to stay in your father's shadow," Talros said.

Evoll nodded. "Shadow. . . Yes, an apt description." He cleared his throat. "Well, good day to you, General. I have many things to finish before the evening comes." The man turned and swept past Talros, returning indoors and away from the eyes of the crowd. Talros turned to follow, not willing to let the man out of his sight with the assassin still at large.

Boots sounded on the staircase, and a man dressed in the Weapon's livery appeared in Talros' peripheral vision.

"General Talros, sir," the captain said, snapping a crisp salute.

Talros acknowledged him as he passed, not slowing his step. "Follow me, Captain Laguen. Tell me your news as we walk."

The two Weapons fell into step behind Evoll, keeping their voices pitched low.

"Genera, Lorcen Caspon has abandoned his manor in southern Benthol. I've issued orders for several key servants to be questioned, but none have the slightest clue of his whereabouts. It seems he has vanished."

"People do not *vanish*, captain. He is hidden somewhere, probably right underneath our very eyes. Take your men and return to his manor estates. Investigate *anything* that might be a potential lead."

"Yes, sir," Captain Laguen said, sketching a quick bow and leaving Talros' side as quickly as he had come.

Talros thought hard as he followed Evoll's steps. In his mind, his hunch was verified, and he breathed a deep, silent sign of relief. Caspon was almost certainly behind the Nightingale's assassinations. Deomiel and Yentiliáne were pushed into the rear of his mind, leaving Lorcen Caspon in the forefront, fair dripping with mistrust. The man, to come so far in life as Guildmaster, could not have been have been stupid. Leaving his manor now, before Evoll's rising, would appear highly suspicious, yet Caspon had done so. It was as good as a spoken admission of guilt in Talros' mind. It was proof enough for arrest, but the assassin—the girl—would need to be questioned, if possible. Talros desperately wanted to speak with her. She was an enigma in every way, and Astin Talros hated enigmas.

The hours rolled onward and every wolf howl I thought I heard made me think of gods and stars and steel. The gallows stood like winter-killed trees and the townsfolk were restless and milling around the merchants' stalls that had been hastily arranged in the off-shooting alleyways. The Weapons and city guards patrolled vigilantly. There were a few in the bottom level of my hiding place. I could not tell how many, but it was enough to cut off that mode of escape. I could hear their raucous laughter rise through the floor, faint but boisterous. They obviously thought that nothing would happen today. I smiled. They were wrong.

I swallowed the last bit of dry bread. It was flat and stale from being stowed away in my leather pouch, but I ate it nonetheless. It would be better to have something in my stomach, regardless of my lack of appetite. I realized there might not be another chance to eat in the future, and remembered my mother's admonitions to eat with a pang of loss.

The sunlight indicated late afternoon when I stood to watch from my makeshift arrow-slit. The crowd was growing louder, more restless, a cacophony of a thousand voices striving to make themselves heard. It was like rolling thunder in the roaring torrents of a hard rain. I peered downward, gazing across the horde in the streets. A long line of soldiers was all that kept them clear of the courtyard.

The people started to call, chanting as one. Their voices grew higher and louder, spiraling upward to hammer against my ears. It was unceasing, inescapable, a constant assault on my senses. Just when I thought I would go mad, the noise stopped.

The door to the Evoll manor stood open and old Ardal himself crept forward with the unsteady gait of the elderly, using a gnarled staff to help support him. Two Weapons flanked him on either side, silent and unobtrusive as shadows. Hanlon walked six paces behind, four Weapons around him, led by none other than Talros himself. He matched Caspon's description to the letter.

Ardal Evoll, current guildmaster, stepped to the railing of the balcony that extended forward into the center of the courtyard. The crowd was silent, waiting as the old man made his way across the smooth expanse of stone. Reaching his destination after several long minutes, he lifted his wizened arms to the populace of northern Benthol. I watched, taking the already strung bow and waiting for a perfect moment in which to strike.

"My good people," he said, raising his voice so the people could hear. He spoke more steadily than I expected, given his age. There was none of the wavering another man his age might have had. "For sixty years, I have been privileged to be called Guildmaster of northern Benthol. What a glorious time it has been! The economy of our small township is to be commended, the reputation of our goods is unsurpassed, and our population continues to grow. Indeed, northern Benthol has become a place of good standing in Caesia over the past sixty years, but the years are long, good people. The inevitable end has come, and I greet it gladly! It is time for new blood to take the reins, for new minds to bring an even more glorious future to our great township. Might I present my son—and your new Guildmaster—Hanlon Evoll!"

The applause and cheers that followed rose to a thunderous roar that drowned out the very courageous few who dared to voice their dissent. The muffled drone continued until Hanlon stepped forward to take his father's place, greeting the old man with a broad smile. The Evoll family's advisors stood off to the side as Ardal Evoll removed a great ruby ring from the forefinger of his right hand and made a great display of handing it over to Hanlon.

"This signet ring bestows upon you the responsibility and honor of the title of Guildmaster," Ardal intoned. "May you never abuse your power, and always use it for the sake of the people of this town, always acting in the best interest of others. Should you ever abuse your power, the people retain their right to overthrow you, and seek a new leader from one among their number. It is your duty to protect this town from those who would seek to do it harm, from those who would engage in theft or murder. Do you hear and understand?"

Hanlon answered in a voice that clearly showed he had practiced his lines. "I hear and understand. I will never abuse my power. I will always act for the good of the town and protect the people from those that would do them harm. I know the rights and duty of the people should I overstep my bounds. I thank you." He then slid the signet ring over his right forefinger and a wild cheer went up from the crowd.

It was done, and Hanlon Evoll was Guildmaster of North Benthol.

The beryl at my throat burned, stopping the breath in my throat. I had been watching in fascination with the black-fletched arrow drawn to my ear, but in my curiosity had failed to release it. There was still time. Hanlon had yet to give his speech. The fire lessened but did not die. It was there, biding its time, sending an apprehensive heat through my veins.

Ardal Evoll stepped back, and Hanlon turned to face the multitude. "Good citizens of northern Benthol, I thank you for your generous welcome. What I have said in the vows is true. I will not abuse my newly given power in any way, and I will act in your best interest. This town will continue to be as prosperous as it was during my father's time, and hopefully will grow even more so, and my first act as Guildmaster will be to protect you, good people, for there is an evil among us!"

A confused and anxious muttering grew like the buzzing of cicadas until Hanlon motioned with his hand. It then exploded into torrential cacophony as two burly men in black and leather walked to the gibbet, dragging a thin figure between them. The prisoner appeared to be a boy, around fifteen or sixteen years old. A dark blindfold was wrapped around his face, leaving the top of his head and his mouth and chin exposed. His hands were tied behind his back. I pushed forward until my face was pressed against the shingles, watching, my heart throbbing in the cage of my ribs.

The two men hauled the figure up the gallows stairs, to the center of the platform. One took a rope—no, a noose—from the bag at his belt and tossed it over the arm. It was not a thick rope, that much I could tell. Not a regular noose, I thought. But why the difference? Probably to snap his head from his shoulders, a part of my mind whispered.

"This creature before you, good people, is no mere boy," Hanlon explained as his father and the Weapons looked on with little expression. From the look on his face, Talros seemed to be the only one who thought that this was odd.

"This is a creature escaped from the Plains of Centura," the new Guildmaster continued, eliciting cries of shock from the masses. "It is a demon in every sense of the word." That seemed to be a cue, for one of the black-clad men stripped the prisoner of his blindfold, exposing a young, terrified face, unevenly cropped hair, and slightly pointed ears. My heart withered in that instant without the slightest sign of protest. "This is a halfblood!" Hanlon cried, pointing with his entire arm. The throng before him wailed. A woman shrieked in terror, and children were gathered close. Someone fainted. "This demon was found here, in this very town! It stole livestock and crops, broke goods and salted fields! Should we allow this, my people?"

"*No!*" the people screamed. "*Kill it! Hang it! Kill!*"

"Do it," Hanlon said, and one man placed the slender noose around the petrified boy's dirty neck.

Cold fingers slithered down my spine. There was another halfblood in the world, and he was here? The beryl sang against the skin of my throat. *Do it,* it hissed tenderly. *Kill or die.* I could not choose, not yet. The breath caught in a painful lump behind my breastbone. *I* could be the one on the gallows, all but for a difference in circumstance. My mouth was dry, my throat thick.

They were going to hang him then and there, directly in front of me, just because of his uncontrollable lineage. The crowd—mothers and fathers, grandparents, aunts and uncles—cried for the young boy's blood.

It made me furious; the embers in my heart flared into sudden and terrible life. I had heard the stories Caspon had drilled into my head, over and over again, about the horrors and atrocities that ignorant and fearful men inflicted on halfbloods unlucky enough to be captured. I had never seen those horrors take place, had never *truly* seen the fear and hatred men held for my kind until today. The multitude's bloodthirsty cries grated my ears, and I gritted my teeth against them, struggling to ignore the screams of fearful women and the savage cries of the men.

The noose was on his neck, the knot under his left ear. Hanlon Evoll raised an arm skyward. As soon as he brought it down, the trapdoor under the boy's feet would drop. One of two things would happen then: he would mercifully break his neck and die instantly as the rope jerked to a halt, or he would strangle slowly and painfully to the delight of a malicious audience.

Hanlon's arm arced downward, and I reacted without thinking.

As the trapdoor dropped out from under the boy, I released the arrow I had been so long in holding. It cut through the air as a knife through warm butter and severed the rope just before it snapped to a halt. The yard-long length of ash quivered in the arm of the gibbet, the black fletching painfully obvious against the blond wood. On my next heartbeat, I had another arrow to the string, pulled back and released.

The crowd was still crying out, not yet realizing that its will had been thwarted. General Talros was the only one who reacted. With a flash of silver and a hiss of steel, he knocked Hanlon Evoll to the ground. The arrow meant for the Guildmaster's heart chipped a stone column and shattered. I cursed the general's inhuman speed, but grinned absurdly. Who would he choose to pursue: the halfblood boy or the Nightingale? I thought I knew the answer.

"The tower! Top level! There!" Talros roared, pointing his sword toward my location. The crowd was still wailing, but in confusion instead of bloodlust, as his men charged through them to find me. Hanlon Evoll stood in shock, hardly able to breathe, white-faced and slick with sweat. As the general bounded over the balustrade, Evoll fainted. It was luck that the Weapon behind him caught him under the arms.

The beryl burned me fiercely for my failure. I was surprised it had not crippled me yet to leave me at the mercy of Talros' approaching men. However, there was not much time to dwell on the mysteries of the stone. The window of my second chance was closing.

I risked a swift glance down into the boiling throng but could not see the halfblood boy. He had disappeared somewhere in the chaotic confusion below. I could not linger any longer to contemplate his fate; there was a surge of heavy footsteps and angry voices rushing up the stairwell. Even if I stayed in my hidden alcove, I was sure that they would find me. So I did the one thing I could, the one thing I had been able to come up with as an escape route. As I turned, I lashed out with my foot, taking down an entire portion of rotted shingles, and leapt out into the air five stories above the ground.

I landed on the perimeter wall, the wind rushing from my lungs as I gasped in pain. Twin bands of fire shot through my legs from ankles to knees, burning my shins as I fought to stay standing.

A soldier leaning between the battlements turned at the sound of my exit and gaped in frozen disbelief when he saw me. I imagined he did not see young girls armed with bows and daggers atop the wall very often.

I sprinted toward him, smashing the hilt of my dagger into his groin before he could react to my presence. He collapsed, holding himself in agony, eyes rolling and mouth gaping like a landed fish.

An arrow hit the stone merlon just behind me and I whirled like a mummer as it ricocheted. Talros' soldiers were at the arrow-slits of my former hiding spot, but the arrows were flying now from more places than that tower alone.

I bolted, fleeing for all I was worth to the bend in the wall. I had to reach the trees of the other side. I could see them, so close! My breath was fire in my lungs, my legs moving of their own accord. The guard at the corner saw me approaching and drew his sword. I kept going, reaching into the pouch at my waist. He readied to swing, and I leapt, throwing the powder meant for pain, not poison, into his face.

He shrieked and clawed his eyes as the dust did its work. The sword clattered to the stone, spinning under my feet. I rushed past him, dodging arrows, flew between the ramparts and flung myself into space, groping wildly for the tree that seemed too far away.

Chapter 15

A N ARROW WHIZZED PAST ME, slicing through my tunic and leaving a line of blood in its wake. I did not even feel it; fear coursed through me, flooding my veins. My breath came fast. I was falling, struggling blindly for a grasp as the tree limbs flew past. They whipped past my face, some scratching and drawing blood. I squinted, trying to protect my eyes, just as a branch whipped past my ear and caught in the loop of fabric I always wore wrapped around my head. That slowed me and I managed to get a tentative grasp on a limb before the headband unraveled and fell away, leaving me with a tremendous headache and a neck that felt it had snapped in half.

"*Halfblood! The girl's a halfblood!*" a soldier shrieked from the wall. He had seen my ears. The hail of arrows increased, now punctuated by curses against my kind and prayers offered to any divine beings who would deliver the soldiers from my demonic hands, although I believed it was I who needed to offer prayers at the moment. I curled my fingers around the slender branch and swung upwards, making my way through the tangles of twigs and masses of clumped leaves. I rounded the massive trunk and pressed my back against the cool wood, trying to slow my racing heart.

I was at home in the trees. I had been born in one and most of my life had been spent among the branches high above the ground. Should the soldiers choose to pursue me outside the walls, I was confident I could elude them without ever touching the ground— but outside the walls I could not stay for long. The collar stung me, reminding me I still had a job to do. I growled as the arrows cut through the leaves around me, but the trunk of my massive hideout blocked any from finding flesh. I knew I had to return to northern Benthol and dispatch Hanlon Evoll if I could, or die in the process.

I peeked around the trunk, looking towards the wall, although it was nearly impossible to see anything through the dense leaves.

The thick rain of arrows had stopped, but the soldiers were still there, waiting for me to make a move that would give away my position. Then I spied a fallen limb that had become entangled in its brothers and freed it. It was hefty and thick, a good combination for the only plan I had.

"Weapons, forward!" Talros roared, taking the stairs two at a time. The archers fired incessantly, and Talros cried for them to stop. He wanted the assassin alive, if possible. He could get not get the answers he wanted so desperately from a corpse. The wall-guards had raced after the girl but she had avoided them all. The assassin was quick, he would grant her that, but she was either incredibly brave or extraordinarily foolhardy to attempt such a leap from the watchtower roof. He knew of no one else that would have even thought to attempt such a feat. However, that leap was nothing compared to when she had flung herself from the ramparts and into the trees. It was then that General Talros had been astounded. How was it possible that she could have made such a bound? She was smart, though. That jump had been her only chance of survival. Staying on the wall would have meant her death.

He paused to cast a quick glance behind him, reassuring himself that Evoll had been left well-guarded. Talros could catch no glimpse of the man, but the sight of his Weapons stationed outside the door bolstered his confidence.

The soldier's voice came like thunder to his ears. "*Halfblood! The girl's a halfblood!*" If the shock of seeing a gangly girl leap from the tower roof had not been enough to chill his blood, those words certainly succeeded in the task. Talros' gut twisted against the base of his ribs. He was floored at the declaration. A halfblood—it was too much to believe! An anthela was one thing, but a halfblood was a monstrous discovery.

He bounded up the remainder of the stairs and thundered across the top of the wall toward the bend where the Nightingale had vaulted. In his mind, those simple words explained so much. That was why the assassin had been so difficult to capture; halfbloods were notorious for their wraithlike qualities. Lorcen Caspon was a fool, Talros thought, trying to control such a demon from the Plains of Centura, one of the Enas' own. The Dark God would not take kindly to such abuses of his underlings. Caspon could not possibly understand the nature of his assassin. Even Talros, who had been an avid scholar in his younger days, could not fathom the true nature of such a beast. In the scrolls, halfbloods were said to combine the worst traits of man and anthela. If what the soldier screamed was true, then everything had changed.

The Nightingale was too dangerous to let live.

"Hold fire!" Talros called over the frightened din. "Hold, I said! Who called out? Who saw?"

"General, it was me," said a man from the front lines. "I saw her!"

Talros strode forward. The men parted to let him pass, feeling braver now that the decorated general was in their presence.

"You are beyond doubt of what you claim to have seen?"

"No mistaking it, General. I swear on the names of the gods." The archer's trembling hand closed into a fist and touched his collarbone as he spoke, a gesture for divine protection. Talros touched his shoulder in reassurance as he strode to the edge of wall to peer between the ramparts.

He eyed the forest, scanning the dense foliage for any sign of movement or color other than the mottled green and brown spreading before him. The soldiers behind him were still and silent, watching the general in fearful admiration. The Nightingale was not the only one with a heavy reputation. General Astin Talros had one, as well. Talros turned his head, feeling the slight movement of a swift breeze against his face. The wind ran soft fingers over the canopy, the leaves and hair of the men on the wall undulating as it went. A raucous flurry of birds exploded from the treetops and winged away in a chaotic mass, their wings beating loudly over the rush of startled caws and squawks.

"Loose!" Talros cried, pointing at the spot from where the birds had broken. Two handfuls of arrows followed his cry, slicing through the canopy. The general felt a twinge of regret. He had wanted the Nightingale alive, but it seemed like that dream was no longer possible. It was too dangerous to capture the assassin to satisfy his own rampant curiosity.

She could not possibly still be alive, he thought. Not with the sheer number of arrows that had swept down into the forest like a pack of wolves after a hare. Still, he was not satisfied.

"You five," he said, choosing two archers and three swordsmen from the jumble on the wall, "come with me. I want twelve archers and twelve soldiers on the wall, on this particular section, against the trees. The rest of you are to return to the city and resume your patrols. Be vigilant! You have orders to kill on sight only if you are absolutely certain of your target. I will have no mishaps." His voice was stone and the soldiers felt the ring of his words in their bones. Talros' eyes roved the throng. "Whose duty was it to patrol that tower?"

"Mine, General," said a low voice.

"Mine, as well, sir," answered a second, loud but hesitant.

"Very well," Talros said flatly. "The both of you are to come with me. There will be repercussions for your inattention."

I fled through the branches. The soldiers had fallen for my ruse. Throwing the branch toward the perched starlings had been the one thing I could think of. The startled birds had taken wing and burst upward into the sky. Talros must have thought it was I who panicked the birds into flight as I tried for escape. He was right, in a way, but not in the manner he thought. I darted in the opposite direction from the flock of starlings, moving through the twisted limbs of the mostly deciduous forest. There was one place I thought I could go, one place that might be even remotely safe, and when night came I would go there as swiftly as I could. Recuperation and planning were necessary. Hanlon Evoll was still doomed to die, but that task would be more difficult with the soldiers of northern Benthol scouring the streets for me.

I crouched in a crack of a dead oak, squeezing my body in as deeply as I could, and waited. It was late afternoon. Twilight was approaching, and so were the soldiers. I could hear them in the forest below, boots snapping twigs even though they moved with stealth. Silent as they tried to be, they could not match my sharp ears. I pulled my hair back behind me, hiding the blondeness in the shadows of the crevice, and watched the leaf-carpeted floor. I could see six men skulking through the mottled light that filtered downward through the canopy. I wondered for a moment if I should shoot them down, but abandoned the idea. I could not pull a bow here in the trunk of a dead oak; there was no room for the movement required, and moving out onto a branch, even slightly, carried too great a risk of being seen. So I waited until they passed underneath, with their arrows nocked and swords drawn. They did not speak, but fanned out as they moved through the trees that were feathered with the slender, white-fletched arrows which had so nearly cut me down.

Lenos take you, Talros.

They peered upward as well, hunting me with dogged determination. If I stayed, they would find me. There was no doubt of that in my mind. A dead tree, especially as large as this one, was conspicuous. In time, one of them would make the connection. I assumed it would be General Talros. I knew him instantly, though I could not see his face. His bearing gave him away, the way he moved with quiet assurance and stoic dignity. Something about him made me uneasy, and it was not just the fact that he sought my head. I had heard tales of him, of course, but they came through Caspon and were thus tainted. The man told me lies and truths so mixed that there was no hope of unraveling them.

The day grew darker and the forest shadows stretched long fingers that would grasp and hold until dawn. I wondered how long the soldiers would search in the darkness. They had no torches. I strained to hear, closing my eyes and focusing hard. The footsteps were there, but distant. I had to take this chance while I could.

Hauling myself from the oak, I sprang away, lighting on the branches of a neighboring tree again and again until I was once more near the wall. I slipped upward into the highest boughs of a thick cedar, using the crawling vines and cracked bark as leverage when the branches proved too far apart. From my perch, I could look down upon the perimeter wall. Soldiers patrolled there, as I had known they would, and they would continue until I had been captured and properly disciplined. I gritted my teeth, biting the side of my tongue in the process. I hissed at the pain, but it cleared my head. I could not give in to fear. Later perhaps, but not now. Not while there was work left to do.

Hawk-like, I watched the soldiers' movements, memorizing their paths. I had to time this endeavor precisely. After several long minutes, I lowered myself to a convenient level, moved outward onto a thick branch and breathed deep. Jumping from the wall to the trees had been easier, in comparison. The trees had lower handholds; the wall was smooth stone except for the very top. I waited for the perfect moment. Two soldiers passed along the wall, paused, glanced around, and then continued onward. The procedure was repeated every fifteen feet or so. The sun touched the horizon, and the interspersed torches on the wall burned brightly. When the soldiers turned their backs to my perch, I moved.

I dashed along the limb and flung myself across the space at the last second. The sky was open and I was excruciatingly exposed. The trees fell back as the wall towered over me, moving ever closer—but not quite close enough. For a moment, I thought I had miscalculated, but then my nails caught the chinks in the stone. I clambered upward like a spider, twisted between the battlements, and darted between the soldiers as quickly and silently as possible. Like a shadow, I went over the far side of the wall. The stones in this particular area were slick with moss, and I could not keep a firm grip on the slippery, weather-smoothed rock. Maneuvering as deftly as I could while sliding down the wall, I managed to land in a compact ball behind a small, thatched-roof dwelling. This was the lower-class section of town, I knew, and I breathed a silent sigh of relief. I was just where I wanted to be.

My lungs burned, and I realized that I had forgotten to breathe since leaving the branch. Unbidden, my lungs drew in a painful amount of air at the thought and I exhaled slowly. I had made it back into the city, but my work was not over yet. I pressed my bleeding fingertips, abraded from grabbing hold of the wall, into the hem of my tunic, feeling sharp stabs of pain as the loose nails rubbed against raw flesh. There was no time to treat my wounds. Time was flowing onward and the beryl made its impatience known.

I steered well clear of the soldiers that patrolled the lanes and alleys of northern Benthol, making my way as silently and stealthily as I could ever hope to be. I used the shadows to my advantage, skulking like a wraith under the low eaves of the houses and cheap stores.

I had nearly reached the stable without incident when the soldiers stepped into my path. My heart leapt into my throat, choking off my breath. It was my luck, I thought. The two men were dressed in dark outfits, so dark as to be almost indistinguishable from the shadows; only the silver flash of swords and buckles gave them away. My aching muscles cried in agony as I tensed. Weapons.

One stepped forward, his face turned away to peer down an adjacent alley, while the other moved slightly to the side and blocked the path. His eyes glinted in the pale moonlight like those of an animal. A single scar ran down the left side of his face from forehead to chin, barely missing the corner of his mouth. His face was stony as he looked at me.

"You," he hissed, and at the sound of his voice his companion turned, catching sight of me and stiffening as if he had been jabbed with a red-hot poker.

"The halfblood assassin," the unscarred man said. "She is but a child."

In years, that assessment was not quite true, though I knew I looked younger due to lack of food and my delicate anthela-bred frame. I was seventeen years of age, having spent eight years inside Caspon's terrible manor, to which I had arrived two days before my ninth birthday. In mind, I was nothing like a child. My growing-up had been almost instantaneous after the fall of Carfuinel. No, I was not a child. Not at all.

"Coward," the shorter, scarred man hissed. "Slinking in the shadows. Neither gods nor men will have much mercy on you, demon." His sword came up, pointed toward me, but he made no move to lunge quite yet. His taller companion made a covert gesture of protection with his hand, the other steadying his blade.

I would not allow myself to show my fear, though I wondered if they could see the pulse that hummed in my throat. Two men with swords, and what did I have? My boot-knife, a bow that would be useless in such close quarters, a handful of arrows, and the slender short-sword at my hip.

I drew my short blade—a long knife, truly—from the scabbard, never taking my eyes from the Weapons. They both had the advantages of extended reach and strength, along with greater numbers. I hoped I proved faster and more agile, but wishes were useless.

"Nothing to say, coward, before you die?" the scarred man snarled.

I lunged toward him with my blade as soon as the last word left his mouth. *That* was the answer to his question, and I was gratified to see that I had startled him and his companion both.

Swinging the blade upward, I tried to slide my sword underneath his ribcage, but the scarred man managed to dodge and parry the slender blade. I was not much of a swordfighter, but Aylan had taught me enough to hold out for a time—as long as I was swift and paid attention to my surroundings. The scarred man was quick and focused; his companion was slow and ponderous both. The latter was powerful, and swung his sword in ways that would have cut me in twain if the blows had landed. I focused on him, hoping to even the odds.

I dodged his first thrust, feeling the heady wind of its passing, blocked a swing from his companion, feeling the nerves in my arms like hot needles under the skin, danced back, and then darted forward once more. I was enveloped in a whirlwind of frantic motion that was eerie in its silence. Blades kissed and parted, cloth sighed as it split, and I thought of nothing but survival. Time lost all meaning; thought washed away to puddle uselessly in the dark corners of my mind. I kept my distance, darting in when the chance came, like a weasel hounding a snake.

I chopped my blade at the slow one's knees, falling to my own to duck under a horizontal swipe of his sword. He stepped back, ankle twisting as a cobblestone turned underfoot. I leapt, darted close, twisted away as he grabbed at me, and plunged my boot-knife into his throat.

There was no time to think about what I had done. The beryl suppressed everything but the rising tide of my rage. The tall man gurgled and fell, slowly, like a massive oak toppled over by the breath of storm-borne winds. I whipped away, facing the scarred man with my blade in one hand and a dripping dagger in the other. I was spattered with blood, both my own and that of the Weapons.

The scarred Weapon gazed at me. "You *are* a demon," he whispered, so quietly that I knew he was speaking for his ears alone. I tried not to pant, to show my bone-weary fatigue. I knew the façade I needed to maintain, but it was a difficult task. I watched him as he gazed at me. We had clashed blades more than once already, although I could not recall those instances. My mind was still lost in a filmy haze and I could not think straight. The Weapon had a deep cut on his left forearm, steadily leaking blood, and several rents in the fabric of his uniform. In the moonlight, a dark stain showed at his right shoulder. I could smell the blood in the air, a hot, metal scent like iron and salt. A gash on my forehead stung my eyes and matted tendrils of my hair into wet strings. There were also a few injuries that would have been mortal wounds had I been slower to react, most on my abdomen, and one fire-laced line across my back. I was so tired, my muscles felt so weak, and I did not know how much longer I could last.

Give me strength, I demanded, but was not sure if I commanded it of myself or the gods.

I wanted the soldier to flee, but in the same heartbeat knew it would be worse for me if he did. He would bring others to my last known location, which was too close to where I wanted to rest. There would be no peace for me if he lived. It was too late to run. Stealth had been my refuge and that was lost to me now. The exhaustion I felt, both mental and physical, was almost overwhelming; running would end in disaster.

I rushed him with all the speed I could muster. My blade screamed against his, and I sidestepped as he backpedaled, keeping him close but always with my right side facing my opponent. He reacted by sheer reflex, sweeping his sword down in a flashing arc. I jumped back, pivoting away, but he swept a foot behind my ankles, pulling my legs out from under me. I hit the ground rolling, twisting away like a snake, and brought my sword up to block him. His blade came from an unexpected direction, swinging upward from his knees. I tensed, dropping my blade forward and down by instinct alone. I was slower than him, I realized to my horror, as the tip of his sword skimmed my throat from collarbone to chin. My fortuitous repositioning of the blade had kept him from penetrating too deeply; any further and my throat would have been split like an apple. The beryl stung once, violently, and fell silent. The leather slipped on my blood-slick skin.

The pain set me writhing on the ground, biting my lips to keep my agonized howls at bay. Through a thin film of tortured tears, I saw my opportunity. The Weapon's arm was extended above me, ready to plunge down and spit me under the ribs. In that moment, he was unprotected. With the speed born of determined practice and gifted by my blood, I rolled to my knees and sank the point of my long knife upward into his stomach, punching through felt and mail and flesh.

The scarred man looked down at me in utter disbelief. His limbs slackened, but the sword would not fall from his grasp. It still hovered above me, deadly and cold. I pushed the knife deeper, throwing my weight into the thrust, watching until the sword wavered and sank to the cobblestones. It was then that my eyes met those of the Weapon; it was then that my ears heard the rasping, wet sounds of his dying. His eyes were wide and dark, fathomless. I drowned in them, and felt regret. His mouth opened as if to speak but only blood came out. A thick tendril of blood, black in the starlight, dripped off his chin, fell onto the knife still embedded in his flesh. I pulled my blade free, almost gently. The Weapon's eyes rolled and he fell sideways onto the stone, slumped onto his back, and stared sightlessly at the night sky. His breath hissed once, twice, and then stopped.

Rising to my feet, I wiped my long knife clean on his trousers and sheathed it. A soft, ragged sigh escaped me. My hand strayed upward to assess the damage to my throat. It was wet with blood and strangely warm. My fingers slipped against the skin, searching for what seemed different. I paused, suddenly uneasy, and probed again. And then, with sudden heart-stopping shock, I realized the collar was gone.

Oh gods, oh gods! I thought madly, giddy and terrified. *That stroke must have severed the leather.*

Gooseflesh rose on my arms and I thought I would vomit from the sheer overwhelming astonishment. Looking around wildly, even under the bodies of the Weapons, I found it. The strip of leather with the small, innocuous green stone—the one that had kept me enslaved for two years—lay against the wall of a wooden house. The beryl glittered in the moonlight and I shuddered, unable to pull my eyes away from its faceted face. It called to me in a small voice that echoed in the deep chambers of my mind, begging me to pick it up, to restore it to its place. *Do not abandon me, your constant companion,* it hissed. *I am all you know. Do not leave me here.* I did not hear its words, but I felt the meanings of them in my heart.

I put my teeth through my bottom lip, urging the pain to reawaken me. Then I tore my gaze from the stone and fled.

Chapter 16

THE HAYLOFT OF THE STABLE was the one place in northern Benthol that I considered remotely safe, because the door was hidden there, lost under the strewn hay. I did not see any evidence of stablehands upon my entrance, other than that the horses seemed content and well-fed with fresh straw in the stalls. Most slept, standing with hanging heads; a few curled into rear corners. My passage did not wake them as I came in through a narrow window and went to the ladder leading to the loft.

My mind fumbled upward through the fog. The collar was gone, the chains of my slavery broken. Caspon was now just a name, no longer a terrible power over me. Or was he still in control? My gut churned with hate for him, bitter and vile as poison in my throat. I could not think through the loathing I held for him. My family dead, my home burned, and now I could make my own choices without fear of the beryl.

In the straw of the loft, I curled into a ball, scathing tears building in my eyes. Because of him, I had killed people I did not know, people who had done nothing to me or to deserve their fates. Because of him, my childhood was dead and buried and everything I loved was lost. The tears slid down my cheeks, the air burned in my lungs as I tried to hold back the wretched sobs that forced themselves from my throat.

The miserable guilt that had been building up spilled over, drowning everything inside me. All the emotions stifled by the beryl and buried deep were clawing to the surface, fighting for dominance. I wept raggedly with my face in my hands. Caspon would pay, that I vowed with my whole heart, but no one else would perish. It was the least I could do for absolution. The gods surely despised me for the atrocities I had committed in Caspon's name. I despised myself thoroughly, thinking that I could have—should have—fought more. Was there nothing I could have done

206

to end my misdeeds sooner? My mind waded through the turmoil, grasping hopelessly for an answer.

"Crying doesn't solve anything, you know," a voice said from the corner.

My head jerked up, and I struggled to see through my blurry, wet eyes and sudden vertigo. My fingers curled on the hilt of my knife, and then I saw him. In the dim light, I could just make out the rope burn on his neck.

"How did you find me?" I whispered, the knife held ready. If he moved wrong, I would gut him. Saving him meant my possible death if he brought the hounds to my doorstep.

"I hid in a barrel near the wall when the ruckus started. When things got quiet, I peeked out and saw you as you passed. I saw your ears . . . and I followed you. I had to know."

"And now you do," I replied. So many things had gone wrong.

"You must be the assassin everyone is clamoring on about," the halfblood boy whispered, eyeing me warily from his place in the hay.

I sniffled; it was not at all conducive to my terrible image, but I could not control it. "What if I am?" I answered, readying to move at the slightest hint of hostility.

"You're just not quite what I imagined, is all," the boy replied, sitting back on his heels. His face was scratched but not bleeding and there was hay sticking in his cropped hair. "I thank you for what you did. An instant later and it would have been too late."

"How do you know it was me?"

"It was simple, really. News of an assassin all over Benthol and guards lurking in every shadow, then an arrow cuts me free as I'm falling and a second arrow is aimed at Hanlon the Fool. So much screaming," he whispered, "about an assassin, a girl, a halfblood on the wall. And then you slink past with a quiver and bow and a long knife and ears that are so like mine." He sucked in a deep breath and let it out slowly. "It doesn't get any clearer than that. In addition, you're dripping blood. That alone would be a hint."

I looked down at myself, startled by his words, and saw black patches of wetness on my clothes. I had not noticed my wounds until now. "Oh, I *am* bleeding," I said in a sort of confused wonder. I was so tired, and I ached from head to heart to foot.

The boy rose to his feet and moved further back into the loft. I watched his motions with wary eyes, hesitant to trust him, and he crept back with a metal pail and a handful of cloth. "I can bring up water from the troughs," he told me quietly, "and you need to clean off that blood. I found a shirt up here, too. It's not very clean, but it will suffice for bandages." He tore the shirt into wide strips, trying not to make much noise.

"Why are you helping me?" I asked. This boy confused me. Did he not understand that I was a criminal? I was a murderer and wanted by the Weapons themselves and yet here he was, helping tend my wounds.

"You saved my life," he answered, not looking up from the shirt. "I am grateful, for what it's worth. I'm in your debt."

I said nothing more as he helped bandage me, nor when he slid down to scrub the blood from the window and ladder so my presence would not be immediately known to those hunting me. No one had ever been in debt to me before, but I knew the custom. The boy would aid me until that debt was repaid, or until I released him. Life for a life was the Caesian way. I supposed it would work for halfbloods as well.

"What is your name?" I asked, after being bandaged completely.

He looked away for a moment, dark hair like a shadow against the paleness of his skin. "Nyx Devos," he answered. "I think it is an anthela name."

Not the surname, I thought, sliding into sleep. I meant to say something before the darkness took me, but did not succeed.

I woke early, alert and feeling all the aches of the previous night rebound in full force. The linen strips wrapped about me were stiff with dried blood in some places, but the bleeding seemed to have stopped. The deeper wounds would have to be bandaged again and cleaned when I had the chance, but now was not the time and I had no supplies.

"Morning," Nyx said from above. He was sitting in the rafters two feet above the hay. "Feeling better?"

"Morning?" I repeated anxiously, my throat dry. "What time is it?" The soldiers still hunted for me and every heartbeat I stayed was dangerous.

"It's still dark out. You've slept four hours, I think, and we have a little time yet. The soldiers are circling in from the wall and this place is nearer to the center of Tanner Row."

"How do you know this?" I asked, gathering my things and readying to leave.

"The stable has a high roof. It's a nice vantage point to watch for torches. The soldiers aren't as quiet as they think, either." Nyx dropped down from the rafter and landed with a soft crunch in the straw. "There's nothing to eat but oats from the feedbags," he told me, "and a few ladles of water from the pail. A meager breakfast, to be sure, but it's all I could find."

I took the double handful of dry oats he proffered, grinding them between my teeth and washing the dust down with a swallow of tepid water. I had had worse breakfasts before, and anything was better than nothing at all. He watched me as I ate.

"It's hard to believe you're the assassin that's terrified the kingdom," he said.

"Why is that?" I replied, wanting truthfully to know.

"For one thing, you're a girl—a young *halfblood* girl. I always pictured cutthroats and nightblades to be shadowed men with evil eyes and facial hair. Also, any other assassin probably would've killed me as soon as I realized who they were. You fell asleep."

To my horror, he seemed amused. I narrowed my eyes at him. He likely thought me a fool. I did not like to be thought foolish, even if it was true.

"What is your name?" he continued. "I told you mine."

"I do not have one." I had no right to my real name, and I would never use it. That name died when Carfuinel burned.

"Everyone has a name," Nyx protested. "Is there not anything I can call you?"

I gave the mental equivalent of a shrug, resigning myself. "You may call me Nightingale. Everyone else does." My voice was flat and hollow.

"That's not a name. It's . . . it's . . . I don't like it. Haven't you anything else I can call you? At all?"

I shrugged, visibly this time. "Call me what you will. I do not care."

"How can you not care?"

"Stop asking questions," I told him, sighing in exasperation, and then took another swallow from the pail.

"You're not very conversational, are you?" Nyx asked, and I glared at him. Setting the pail down into the straw, I moved to tighten a bandage on my forearm—and my sharp ears caught the sound of voices outside. I froze, seeing Nyx flatten to the hay and stare at the front of the stable with wide and fearful eyes. Moving my hand a little, I captured his attention long enough to motion for him to keep silent. I listened intently, hoping the voices came from a few townsfolk passing by.

"General Talros wants every nook and cranny searched," a deep voice said, almost beyond the range of my hearing. "Now let's go, or are you afraid of a few horses?"

"You know it's not the horses I'm afraid of, fool," a second voice hissed, obviously terrified but trying to rein it back.

"Hurry," I whispered to Nyx, not willing to leave him to the mercies of the soldiers outside. It seemed that we did not have as much time as he thought.

"They'll find us!" he breathed in growing panic.

"I know a way out from here, so hurry!" I tugged at his shirt until he followed, and he kept so close that he nearly crushed my fingers as I slipped down the ladder. Moving past the stalls, we dashed to the last box. "Get a small bale of hay," I told Nyx as I dropped to my knees, digging for the trapdoor. I pried at it with my ragged nails, hardly able to get a grip on the iron ring set in the stone.

The barn door slid open as Nyx appeared at my side with hay in tow. He saw what I was doing and scrambled to help. Within moments, the trapdoor was ajar, but the hole was black as pitch.

"Ladder," I breathed in his ear, careful of the soldiers checking the foremost stalls. "Slick. Go slow."

"What—" he began, but I clamped a hand over his mouth to shush him.

"Go now," I hissed, and pushed him toward the door. He slipped downward into the inky blackness, his eyes huge and terrified. I grabbed a nearby shovel and shoved the handle in the gap to keep the door ajar, then broke the bale open on the hinges so that when lowered, the trapdoor would once again be hidden from view. The soldiers were fast approaching; I could almost hear

210

them breathing. I slid the door up just enough to permit me and slipped backwards into the black, but not before taking several handfuls of straw and tucking them underneath my belt.

My feet slipped on the rungs and I thought my body would explode from the burst of sudden terror. I regained my footing and held a rung in a death-grip as I lowered myself down enough so as not to crush my bow. I held the door up with my free hand to keep it from slamming down as I pushed the shovel away with a nudge of my shoulder. In seconds, the door was flush and I was lost in the perfect darkness of the sewers.

I moved down the ladder, fully expecting to either crash into Nyx or have the soldiers discover me from above. My fingers would not stop trembling and I did not think I would ever get enough air. Several times I had to stop and wrap myself around the rungs to keep myself from shaking.

Years seemed to pass before my feet touched solid ground once more. I strained in the darkness, seeking any hint of light or motion. "Nyx?" I called, hunting for any noise or smell in the alcove.

"Here," he whispered from four feet to my left. "Do you have a flint and striker? I think there's a torch here."

My fingers found my fire-making kit in the pouch at my waist and I then felt my way to the torch in Nyx's hands. I had never tried to light a flame in utter darkness before, but my hands saw what my eyes could not. The first sparks died, as did the second, but the third try caught. I breathed gently on the embers, willing them into life, and then sighed in relief when the first small flames flickered upward.

"It is spent," I told the boy. Up close, he looked around my age.

"Do you think we can find more?" he asked, peering around the alcove with wide eyes.

"No," I answered, "but the straw should help it last longer, if twisted tightly. We will have to go swiftly."

"Have you . . . been here before?" Nyx inquired in surprise, glancing at the straw under my belt as I returned my tinderbox to my leather pouch.

"Yes, and not long ago."

Nyx gave me a quizzical glance. "Just full of surprises, aren't we?" he said dryly, holding the torch aloft. I knew he saw the altar in the center, stained and intimidating. "My father mentioned a place like this," he said in awe. "There are spirits here, I think."

"Yes," I said, taking the torch from him, "and we should not linger here any longer." I urged him forward, leaving the alcove and heading back the way I had come but a day or so before.

We slunk along in silence, subdued by our situation and the pressing darkness surrounding us. There was no telling how much time passed. Twice I twisted a handful of hay into a tight knot on the torch head so the slight flame would not die. I hoped we would make it to an exit before my supply was exhausted.

I did not look at the boy who followed closely behind me, but my mind never left him. Who was he and what had he been doing in Benthol? Nyx was the only halfblood I had ever seen besides myself, and that alone made him an object of intense speculation and slight trust. He was so like me, and yet not. He spoke differently; his motions were less calculated and controlled than mine. Had he tried to pass as a *cardea*? How long had he lasted without hiding his ears? My mind would not stop but I would not ask him anything unless he volunteered an answer first.

Nyx eventually broke the silence. "My father once told me stories of places deep under the ground where the old priests sacrificed to the gods." His voice was low and soft, almost lost within the steady flow of the sewage running alongside the passageway. "The sacrifices were anthelai, he said. Living bodies offered to the deities in exchange for good harvests, healthy children or to bring rain. The priests didn't want to use people because they thought it would push them away from the gods, but anthelai were fine. They're not human, after all, and they were said to have done bad things, evil things, and so the gods wanted them dead. So many were killed that the priests couldn't find enough for the full moon rituals. No one could find them. Not the hunters with their magic and dogs, not the soldiers combing the forests, and not even the kings with their power. The people were happy that the anthelai were gone, but terrified that the priests would start taking them instead. Things started happening, though. The dark plague ravaged the cities, killing a quarter of the population. Locusts ate the crops and another quarter died. The old practice of sacrifice

212

went away as well, and people offered up coin instead of blood in the temples." Nyx took a deep breath. "My father said it was punishment." I heard him sigh. "I'm sorry for rambling, but that altar made me remember. . ."

"Remembering can be hard," I said. "Your father, he must be worried about you."

"He died when I was ten," Nyx answered. "I lived with my grandparents for five years after that, but they died two years ago of consumption."

"I am sorry for your loss." We were both silent for a time, each lost in our own thoughts. This time it was I who broke the silence. "Your mother was an anthela, then?"

"She was," the boy replied. "You know, I've never met another halfblood before. Will you tell me your story? I'll tell you mine, if you're interested."

"Please," I whispered, wanting desperately to know. "Will you tell yours first? I cannot . . . gather my thoughts." The emotions suppressed by the collar boiled within me still, two years' worth of agony suddenly unleashed. They sought every crack in my armor, striving for freedom.

Nyx took a breath and began. "My grandparents owned a large farm on the outskirts of Benthol, in a village called Oakpin Hill, and their son, my father, worked there with them, tending the stock. One winter the larders ran low and my father left to hunt, leaving my grandfather, who had earlier broken his leg, behind to look after things. Father planned for an overnight trip in the forests, hoping for elk, but got lost when a storm dropped four feet of snow over a matter of hours. Not a forester, my father, but he tried. He kept moving, trying to stay warm even as his sweat froze on his face. Eventually he spotted a fire in the distance and struggled toward it, but collapsed before reaching it. He must have made some sound, however, because the people at the fire found him and roused him back to life.

"They were anthelai, a hunting party themselves. They carried Father back to their home and tended him, for he had frostbite on his hands and feet. My mother's name was Arennile, and she was the daughter of the lord's advisor. She and my father married and lived in that anthela village for a few years. When my mother died in a hunting accident, Father took me and returned to Oakpin Hill.

213

Grandfather and Grandmother had both thought him dead, and were so overjoyed at his homecoming that they were willing to overlook my . . . differences. That's what they called it.

"After my grandparents died, I stayed in the farmhouse alone for a while until the soldiers found me. I hadn't the money for taxes and no skills for surviving in the forest. When the soldiers came to repossess the farm, they discovered me and had me taken to the gaol where I was to await my fate—the gallows. That was the first time I had seen the inside of the city walls." The air rushed out of his lungs.

So he was seventeen years old, I figured, by what he had said. I glanced over my shoulder to see the expression on his face. He seemed deflated, his shoulders drooping. I turned forward again, my feet retracing the same trail I had taken to enter northern Benthol. Halfbloods did not have easy lives, I thought, and wondered what he would think of my tale. I breathed deep. By sheer virtue of his blood, I trusted him, and I hoped it was not folly. What could he do, being a halfblood himself? He could use no knowledge against me and keep himself safe. My life now was reduced to exacting my vengeance; naught else mattered. Nothing would stop me; nothing could remove me from this path I had chosen.

I did not tell Nyx for pity's sake. As the words flowed from me, I felt somehow lighter. It felt right. I told him what my parents had told me of their first meeting, and then of the raid and subsequent burning of Carfuinel. I refused to mention my name. It was the one thing that had not been taken from me, and I would not allow it to leave the space next to my heart. Instead, I moved on to the subject of Caspon, my trainers, and the collar. Gods, the collar. I looked at Nyx's face when I spoke, trying to gauge his reaction to my revelations. At my mention of the beryl his face went pale and I saw a horrible anger wash over him, anger and terror and a deep-rooted unease. Horrible as it sounds, the sight strengthened me.

"Because of what he has done, Caspon must pay," I said, ending my tale. "I must avenge my home and my family, and myself. I have sworn it." Rage and hatred welled within me like a spring, and I shook in an effort to keep the feelings inside.

For several moments, Nyx was silent. "What will you do," he asked, "after you've had your revenge?"

"What do you mean?" I questioned, confused.

"After Caspon dies, what will you do? Where will you go?"

"I do not expect an *after*," I replied, a slender tendril of regret lacing my tone.

"You're very pessimistic," the boy said wryly, scuffing his filthy shoes along the slick stones of the aqueduct floor. "Why are you so eager to throw away your life?"

"What else is there to do with it?" I asked coldly. I was too dirtied, too tarnished for anything else. Everyone believed me a demon, and perhaps they were right.

"Why don't you start over somewhere?"

"I do not think starting over is that easy. Where would I go? There is no one who would offer me refuge."

"The anthelai might," Nyx said, to my astonishment.

Could it be possible? Anthelai generally regarded life as sacred, even that of *cardeai*—except in times of necessity and warfare. I was a murderer, and was certain that would stand as a barrier to my acceptance. But my circumstances were extraordinary, were they not? I was nobility—living Lady of a dead anthehome—for all that I slunk and fought and stayed in a state of perpetual dishevelment. Surely that meant something, anything. But my birth was no guarantee of acceptance. I spoke the language but that also might not be enough. I had killed in cold blood; I had lived among *cardeai*. Those two things were enough for ostracism.

"I think I will always be an outcast," I responded in quiet sorrow. "But you have given me cause to think."

"That's enough," Nyx said.

Perhaps it was to him, but I could not agree. There were other things to do before I could even consider life after Caspon. The possibility of my survival was abysmal, and I did not expect to trump the odds.

Chapter 17

Gₑₙₑᵣₐₗ Aₛₜᵢₙ Tₐₗᵣₒₛ, dressed in his black and silver livery, stood before the dais in silence. His tall black boots were immaculately shined, his linens starched and crisp. The graying black hair was tied back in a neat club at the base of his neck with nary a hair out of place. Clenching his hands in the small of his back, Talros took a deep breath and addressed the council of King Cosian Ilandros II, ruler of Caesia and protector of the realm. Even now his men scoured the land for the scourge of the kingdom while he counseled with the king, who had arrived in Benthol a full day and night after the halfbloods had vanished. Talros had expected a penned missive, and was unpleasantly surprised by the king's abrupt appearance.

The dining hall was packed with folk and the air was uncomfortably warm. Talros resisted the urge to loosen the throat of his black tunic, trying to formulate his thoughts in an organized manner. Evoll's banquet room had been changed into a meeting hall though the hall was devoid of food; at present, all the room contained were people sick of assassinations and plots. At the long table sat a few courtiers and ambassadors who had traveled with King Cosian. Talros glanced down the hall, seeing unfamiliar faces in every direction. He gritted his teeth.

King Cosian II, at the head of the table, leaned forward and rested his elbows on the gleaming wood. The vivid redness of his robe stood out amongst the softer blues and grays of his surroundings. The yellow hair brushed the edges of a strong jaw accentuated by a cropped beard. The glacier blue of the king's eyes rested on Talros. He was still young, Talros realized in a flash. Not yet a man of forty.

"I have heard tales of what happened here, General Talros," the king said in a flat, unyielding voice. "I would have your view of things before we take this matter further."

Any noise that had been present before silenced now. The nobles waited, intensely interested in what the general was going to say. Talros willed himself to calm, took a breath, and spoke.

"I was able to deflect an attack on Hanlon Evoll, new Guildmaster of northern Benthol. An arrow meant for him came from the top of a watchtower, through the very thatching at the apex. The assassin was pursued but managed to avoid detection in the Darklyn Forest beyond the city wall. I have men patrolling the city even as we speak, Majesty." Talros' eyes flicked over the expectant crowd, assessing their patience. He decided to make this account as swift and concise as possible. "The Nightingale reentered the area and would likely have made another attempt on Guildmaster Evoll's life. Such an opportunity did not present itself and she fled again, killing two of my men in the process."

King Cosian narrowed his eyes, tenting his grey-gloved fingers on the glass-smooth oaken table. "A female assassin, you mentioned. I have heard it told that this infamous Nightingale is nothing more than a child, General Talros. How is it that you cannot capture a *child?*"

Talros had been dreading this question. "My king, I fear that the Nightingale is something more than a mere child. I have no proof except for the words of my men, but what young girl has ever done anything like this before?" His voice was sure and even. If he showed any weakness here he would be devoured in a heartbeat's time. "Never have I seen a child as fleet or evasive as this one, or as brave."

"Brave?" the king interrupted, his eyes like chips of flint.

"She leapt from the top of the watchtower, Majesty, and then from the wall's edge to the trees. A child did this, without seemingly a second thought. Those distances would've given even the most daring soldier pause."

"Foolhardy, maybe," a baron of Lassolern drawled, "or perhaps simply careless with her life. That is *my* opinion, Your Majesty."

"Perhaps," King Cosian said. He turned his eyes away from the baron and back to Talros. His voice was hard as stone, and entirely disapproving. "Why would a child commit these crimes? There is something more here."

"I agree, Your Majesty, and I also have a theory." Talros waited a moment, until the king waved him onward. "The Nightingale killed two of my men. However, she did not leave undamaged. A strip of leather, darkened with sweat and blood, with a single small stone attached to it, was found near the site of the attack. It was severed as if by the stroke of a sword."

"You have it with you now?" the King of Caesia asked.

"I have given it to Ferril Biar, a historian in the Lenosian monastery here."

"You think this piece of dirty leather important then, General Talros?" a noble from nearby Astione asked, having finally gathered his breath and wits about him. He crossed his hands over a bent knee, tapping an elegantly booted foot above the floor.

"Yes," Talros answered.

"And why is that, General?" the king demanded, regarding the man before him with ice blue eyes.

"Because some things have distinguishing properties, Majesty," he said, turning his eyes back to the head of the table. "The archivists say that certain stones were once regarded as magical, but of course that notion is now considered heresy. That aside, once studied, the cut and clarity of the stone can reveal many things about its origin. There may be a mark, brand, or some other distinguishing feature somewhere on this article."

"An origin tells us nothing," King Cosian interjected, leaning back in his chair. "It could have originated in the isles of Alke for all we know."

"True, Your Majesty. Very true, but even so, some stones have a particular footprint, if you will. It can be traced to a buyer, then henceforth. That is not the only way an article can be traced. If you will indulge me, one instance I can recall is the case of the thief Benarnoi Ragosa sixty years ago. He had been determined uncatchable, a lost cause, until a widow stumbled upon him one night in her home. He fled and dropped a single handkerchief, a plain small square of gray cloth. From that cloth, from the thin layer of pollen and a single evergreen frond, it was determined that Ragosa had recently come from the Low Hills in Sewllyn. He was captured in his lair there a week later."

There was a long pause. "I see your point, General," the king said. The rest of the room was silent, mulling the connection between the tale and the found items. "Despite your enthusiasm for the charm and the assassin," he continued, "I have heard no evidence as to why you think she is something more than a child. I expect an explanation."

A nervous titter swept through the room as the multitude regarded Talros. There were rumors, always, and it seemed the nervous soldier's words on the wall had preceded him. There was a tension in the air, Talros thought; almost palpable.

"I believe that the Nightingale is a halfblood," he said, mindful of each word dropping from his lips like a stone into the still surface of a pond. The general paused, waiting for the commotion to die before proceeding. "My men saw evidence of this as she fled across the wall. From what I myself have seen of her abilities, I am inclined to agree."

The king pursed his lips and stared down the long table to meet Talros' eyes. "This is a heavy accusation, General Talros. There has not been a halfblood in Caesia for more than a thousand years. Perhaps not even in the whole of the world."

"That is not entirely accurate, Majesty," the Baron of Fernwallace suggested. "Had not Evoll planned an extravagance for his ascension? It is rumored that there was something there."

"The rumor is quite true," Talros answered. "Hanlon Evoll was to hang a halfblood boy on the gallows. Apparently, it had been living in a small farm beyond the borders of the city."

"Two of them?" The king's eyebrows crept upward in disbelief. "This is unprecedented. Anthelai have not been near our borders in centuries. I have forbidden raids and all type of contact, as did my father before me."

"Majesty," the general replied, "I do not think that the anthelai are brave enough to venture this far south in all but the most unusual circumstances. They are still alive in the north, though not likely in great numbers, and some regard their ears as trophies."

"I do not think where they've come from or the state of their ears matter," another noble interjected. "What matters is that they're here now. What do they want?"

"I do not think the Nightingale and the boy were together before this," Talros said cautiously. "If so, then she took an immense risk in waiting as long as she did before cutting him down. It seemed a spur of the moment decision, if I may hazard a guess.

Whatever plans they had individually have changed. They know they are being hunted, and survival is likely their main priority."

The noble of Astione spoke again. "Have you any notion as to their current whereabouts, General? Anything at all?"

"My men are scouring the city but there are no signs. I fear that they both have fled." Talros held his breath and felt his stomach clench as the table exploded into a frenzy of frantic questions and accusations, many directed at him for his apparent ineptitude. The guards in the room stood ramrod straight and silent, but their eyes darted around the room as the nobles leapt from their chairs, shouting and pointing fingers. King Cosian came to his feet, red against the otherwise drabness of the room.

"Be silent!" he cried, raising his voice to be heard over the clamor. The room withered under his glare, and the nobles subsided, sinking back into their seats with the demeanors of beaten dogs. "Now, General Talros," the king began once the room was silent. "I think we know that the creatures have blood on their hands, or at least the Nightingale does. It doesn't matter what they want, for I will not grant them anything other than a swift death. One thing matters here: *who employs her*? Or has this Nightingale gone rogue?"

"I have a theory, Your Majesty," Talros answered. How could he say that it was more feeling than proof? He would be laughed out of the dining hall or imprisoned for malicious slander, depending on the mood of the king. "I am reluctant to mention the name aloud until I have further proof."

The king made a soft noise in his throat. "Your want of privacy comes with its share of dangers, General, but I shall grant it for the time being. You have proven yourself in the past."

Talros sketched a bow. "I thank you, Your Majesty." He was using borrowed time, drawing on the trust carved free from previous assignments. The time Talros had been given was not infinite, and he could almost feel it trickling away even as he stood there in the banquet hall.

"Dismissed, all of you," King Cosian announced, rising to his feet. Around him, the nobles glanced at each other, clearly expecting more from the debriefing than what they had received.

"My king," someone asked cautiously, "what is being done to apprehend these two creatures? How long will we wait in fear?"

"General Talros is doing what he can, I assure you," the king answered, meeting Talros' gaze. There was stone in that look, and the promise of fire should he fail. "I expect this frustration will be over in no more than a month's time. Am I correct in this assumption, General Talros?"

Those icy eyes were on him, heavier than iron. To disagree would be treacherous, and Talros sincerely believed that he was close to apprehending the Nightingale. "No longer than that, Majesty." The man in black and silver placed a calloused hand on his chest and bowed, sealing his words with action.

In a month, the nightmare would end.

The spent torch had failed countless hours ago. The straw had not lasted long. I could no longer remember the concept of time. Had I grown old and died since the last light faded? It seemed so. I could not see my hand before my eyes, nor the wall I kept in constant contact. I could not see the boy that followed, silent except for the sound of his harried breath and the beating of his taxed heart. He was more anxious than I; the smell of fear rolled off his skin.

We had spoken but little since the end of my tale. There were no more words necessary for the building of our newly sprouted relationship. We were the both of us outcasts: nameless, faceless, voiceless creatures of legend and myth. There was no place for us in this world of men, and by that fact alone were we brought together.

The darkness of the aqueduct had swallowed us, and we could not stop long in the deep nothingness of its bowels. I could not be certain the hidden entrance remained unknown, or even that there was nothing lurking in the sewage waters beside us, waiting for a sign of weakness in which to strike. We had no food, no clean water, no light. Sheer force of will was all I had in reserve and I drew upon it heavily. Nyx stopped often to rest. Once, he slept. I could not bring myself to do the same.

Behind me, Nyx sucked in a breath as his foot slipped on a slick patch of something I did not care to identify. A breath of fresh stench wafted over me, and I cut my next inhalation short.

"How much longer?" Nyx asked in a quiet, wavering voice. The unexpected sound startled me. In truth, after my tale, I had not expected him to speak to me again. He had what he wanted, and the only thing more he needed was a guide from the aqueduct. Following did not require communication, not even in the dark. At the first sign of outside light, I anticipated his swift departure.

"I cannot say for certain," I answered, feeling the strange urge to whisper. The confines of the aqueduct made everything seem louder. Everything was too close overhead and panic-inducing, like a mausoleum with living corpses trapped inside. "I think, though, that we must be nearing an exit. This cannot stretch on forever."

"We've been walking forever," Nyx replied. "My legs hurt and I've never been so thirsty in my life. Are you sure the water here's that bad?"

I did not reply immediately, my mind had wandered to other things. The end of the aqueduct was a hillside just beyond the wall between northern and southern Benthol. Caspon had taken refuge somewhere not far from that area after sending me on this last mission. He had never fathomed that I might break his hold, his arcane grasp on body and mind, and that would be his downfall. I would find him—I had vowed that—and once my enslaver was dispatched, I wholly expected his guards to return the favor. They would vie for that chance, the *honor*, of killing the halfblood assassin called the Nightingale. The death of a guildmaster meant little in light of such bravery. The one who killed me would be a hero, perhaps even a saint if he played his cards right. I was ready for the danger and imminent destruction pursuing Caspon would entail, but I had no right to embroil Nyx in this dispute.

"There're no side tunnels or anything?" he asked, hoping to prod me into speaking. There was exhaustion in his voice and, I realized, for all that he was the same age as me, I was more experienced in some regards. I was weary as well, but there was always danger in letting it show and so I strove to hide it from everyone, including myself.

"I cannot remember," I answered pathetically. Remembering details was something I had staked my life on more than once. The darkness was wearing on my mind, draining me faster than I comprehended until now. I thought, though, that we had a while yet to go.

"Didn't you say you came this way before?" he sighed in angry frustration.

"I did, but that does not mean I can recall every single detail of this place," I retorted. "Do you recall every bolt in the gallows?"

"Yes," Nyx whispered behind me. "I do."

I swallowed bitterness and regret, feeling horribly sorry for my venomous tongue. It often betrayed me, though sometimes I did manage to restrain it—for a time. "Sorry," I murmured, but Nyx did not acknowledge my apology. I anticipated nothing less.

We walked in silence again after that for innumerable heartbeats, and again Nyx was the one to break it.

"You are in such a hurry to die," he said, somewhere between question and statement, and I could hear the gentle rasp of his flesh against the stone as he trailed his fingertips along the curved wall.

"And why do you think that?" I uttered, feeling my heart clench painfully and coldly in the hollow of my chest. Was it true? I could not be sure. I was not afraid of my death, but did I desire it? I searched my heart and even then I could not see the truth.

"You just seem so sad. Hopeless. Like you don't care about anything anymore."

I breathed through my nostrils, feeling the faint, hot pricks of wetness behind my eyes. Crying was weakness, submissive, fearful. My vulnerability was maddening. "Mayhap you are right." What else was there to say? He was probably correct, and I had no retort, no rejoinder, that would make any difference in his opinion.

I kept walking, creeping through the blackness with my hand against the slick stone wall. I had known this boy for—was it a few hours? A day? A week?—some amount of time and he already acted like he knew me, understood me. Was I that transparent? That shallow and dull? The thought disgusted me. I was not some lifeless, insipid creature. Or was that what the beryl had made me? It had drowned my emotions, shackled my traitorous body, stunted my growth as a person. My hatred for Caspon blossomed anew. Because of him, there was no telling what damage had been done to me. Then a thought came that chilled my blood: had the beryl made me this monster, or had I been born to it?

My throat clenched with sudden disgust and cold, pure terror. I could never know the answer now. I tried to recollect, but my mind shied away from the memories. The world had passed on, and there was no going back to before Carfuinel burned to find out. The choosing of my dagger flashed in my mind. I had picked the black one with the dark leather hilt. I had spied on training exercises when told to stay away. I had disobeyed my mother multiple times with the rebelliousness of youth. Every infraction, every little insolent or frightful thing I had done whisked across my memory. Had I been born a monster?

There were people who thought so, because I was a halfblood. There were people that thought I was a demon bound to the lowest pit of the Plains because of it. Even some anthelai agreed. The temples and priests taught that my kind, lowly and heartless, was born to evil and woe. *No,* my mind breathed. *It is not true. People can be mistaken. Doctrine can be wrong. Nyx does not seem heartless or cruel, and he is a halfblood as well. If Nyx can be good, can I not be the same?*

I sucked in a breath until my ribs threatened to crack apart. It was useless to think about things like that. I was not a philosopher or a scholar. I did not even think myself very intelligent. I was a tool, a knife with a cracked hilt turning on the hand that wielded it.

I was losing focus. With a half-swallowed growl, I wrenched my mind from its rut. "Keep walking," I hissed when Nyx touched my shoulder, hesitant to speak again in the gloom.

Minutes or hours later, something seemed unusual. The darkness had taken a different hue; the inky blackness appeared to have the faintest hint of grey. I thought I could see the outlines of the watercourse beside us, a hint of stone on the other. The air was fresher, less thick and pungent.

Following the curving pathway, eventually we discovered the source of the changes.

"Thank the gods," Nyx breathed in utter relief, seeing the tumbled stones in the dim light.

"This is new," I whispered, straining my senses for any source of life beyond us. "This was not here when I last came through."

"Good! Don't you see? We can climb those rocks. The wall's caved." He sounded exuberant.

"We do not know who did it," I answered with some concern. "Someone might have entered the aqueduct."

"Then we leave before they find us! Come on, quick," he hissed loudly, and before I could protest that someone might be waiting *outside,* Nyx had edged around me and clambered up the tumbled wall-stones.

You stupid boy! I screamed in my mind, following him with the taste of bitter anxiousness in my throat. I was not used to having someone with me, contradicting me, endangering me with thoughtless actions. I was not pleased, but I followed Nyx nonetheless. I wanted to be gone from here as much as he did.

A sharp yell sent my heart into my mouth, thick and pulsing until I nearly choked. I bolted across the stones and emerged into the late evening light. I was blind for a moment. Swiping my hands across my eyes, I struggled to clear my vision.

"Nyx!" I called, blinking feverishly. "Where are you?" My voice was anxious, and I hoped nothing had happened to the boy.

"Here," he replied happily, and I saw him lying in the thick grass to the right. There were grass stains on his face and shirt, and chaff in his hair from the tumble he had taken in his reckless emergence from the tunnel. He was grinning, limbs askew, and made no attempt to move when I came down the jumble of rock to his side.

"We need to go," I said, prodding him in the ribs with my boot.

"Right now? Can't I sleep a little? It's getting late," he protested, twisting away.

"There are signs of a fresh fire here," I told him, "and tools. We are in the wrong place at the wrong time." The break was not a welcoming place, full of crushed weeds and broken stone. The brush surrounding the makeshift campsite was tangled and sparse and full of thorns.

"What?"

"Bounty hunters. Thieves. I do not know, but we need to move before they return. Now."

He staggered to his feet, brushing the dirt from his clothes— little good it did considering the grime that coated us both. I glanced around, noticing the first spattering of stars in the bleeding-orange sky. The area seemed deserted, vacant, nothing more than grassy hillocks and a black smudge of trees against the horizon. I could smell sap and fresh water in the air. I motioned to Nyx, and together we slipped across the openness to a copse of maple and oak in the distance.

A small stream crept past the stunted trees, meandering under fallen, half-rotted logs and around large rocks to wander away down the grade, disappearing into the puddled darkness beyond. A few birds chirped overhead, intertwining their voices with those of the crickets and other night insects. I longed for the water, watching Nyx drink, but it was not with thirst that I watched.

"Should we make camp here?" Nyx asked qietly, eyeing the dark canopy over our heads.

"Yes, you start. I want a bath." Lenos only knew how long it had been since I last washed, and I wanted nothing more at that moment than to be clean. I wondered if soaproot grew around this area, but doubted it. Sand would work, not as well, but adequately. I started to slip away into the darkness.

"Wait!" Nyx called, lowering his voice when I whipped around to glare at him. "Leave me a knife or something at least. Maybe I can make a fire."

I glanced around. There was enough foliage here to make the idea viable. "Build a screen if you want a fire," I said. "I do not want the people near the duct to glimpse it."

"Right, Captain," he replied, grinning and snapping a salute in my direction. I sighed in utter annoyance, resolve wavering, and then reluctantly left him with my boot-knife. Everything else I kept with me. Of all the things I could be called, stupid enough to leave a relatively unknown boy all my weapons was not one of them. I hoped he would not be foolish enough to reveal our position, but I had done what I could to prevent it, short of tying him to a tree and gagging him. As I walked to the stream, the idea was a pleasant rumination.

As I thought, there was no soaproot. Concealed by a thick wall of brush, I set my weapons aside, doffed my clothes, removed what was left my bandages, and then scoured myself with sand in the cool water of the stream. There was horsetail growing nearby, and I plucked a few stalks, pounded them into a mash on a flat rock, and used the results to wash my hair. It cleaned the grease away better than the sand from the streambed, and washed out easier as well. Half-submerged in the stream, I eyed my filthy clothes on the bank. The last thing I wanted was to put them back on, but I could not wash them either. They were the only clothes I had, and I had no intentions of returning to camp naked or sleeping in soaked apparel. Nyx could not be left alone long, I was certain. I trusted him with my stories, but could not quite concede my life to his hands.

Thinking hard, I decided that my clothes did need cleaning—I would smell them now, and that would keep me awake—and that the night was warm enough that I would not catch a chill from the dampness. Acting quickly, I dragged my tunic and breeches into the water and scrubbed them hard with handfuls of grit and leftover horsetail strands. Most of the grime floated away, but there would always be stains on the cloth. There was not much I could do about that.

After I was satisfied that most of the muck was gone, I drank deep of the cool water and then emerged from the stream and donned my wet clothes, shaking my body like a dog to try and dry off a little. I could see the moon now, hanging like a vibrant eye over the lacework canopy of trees. It was early yet, but more stars were visible than before. I took up my effects from the bank and slipped back to camp, hoping Nyx had not endangered us overmuch. I was somewhat stunned when I noticed the small, smokeless fire half-hidden under a sweep of low-growing oak branches. It would not be visible from the *cardea* campsite near the aqueduct, but what was even more surprising was the small, skinned, nameless creature roasting on a makeshift spit over the glowing embers.

Nyx turned, glancing over his shoulder toward me, and grinned. "I'm glad you're back. You can watch this while I take my turn in the stream."

"What is this?" I asked, stunned—although in hindsight I should not have been. Of course he could do some things for himself. He had survived for a time on his own, had he not?

"Rabbit," he answered. "It dashed by as I was breaking deadfall for the fire, and I just happened to have your dagger in hand." Nyx was obviously pleased with himself, grinning like hunting a small mammal was the most awe-inspiring feat in the world.

"You know how to throw a dagger?" It was a trick that took time to learn and one that looked effortless, but precision and skill were heavily involved.

"Well, no . . . I *did* throw it, but the hilt struck and not the blade. Knocked the rabbit senseless." He scratched the back of his head, grinning sheepishly.

I raised an eyebrow at him, impressed by his honesty. "There is horsetail by the stream. It makes a decent scrub if you crush it first," I said, taking his place by the fire. He rose and stretched, then padded away, leaving me alone in the flickering light of the small fire. His coming had made things more complicated and decidedly more dangerous, but I had to admit that I was glad for his company. After years of loneliness, it was nice to have someone with whom I could talk, someone who could understand the fear in my life, and what it was like to be an outcast from humanity. I was grateful he was with me, for however long as that might be—but I was afraid, too. I did not know how to talk to him, to people in general. There had been no one in the last years of my life that I could be free and easy around, and I had forgotten how to have friends.

Absentmindedly, I twisted the makeshift spit, mouth watering at the sight and scent of the crisp brown skin and dripping juices of the rabbit. Nyx reemerged several minutes later, taking much less time to bathe than I had done. His clothes were soaked, as were mine, and his cropped hair glittered wetly in the firelight.

"Is it done yet?" he asked, hunkering down beside me. A droplet of water ran down the side of his nose, dripped off his chin, and was lost in the leaf litter under our feet.

"I think so."

"Wonderful," he answered, reaching over to twist a hind leg free. He handed it to me before taking the other for himself. The meat was crisp and hot, like I had imagined, burning the inside of my mouth. It was delicious, seasoned by hunger and nothing more.

"I see you removed your bandages," Nyx said after he had swallowed. He eyed my hairline with lowered brows, peering at a scalp wound I had obtained while fleeing to the stable in northern Benthol. "Is that wise? What about infection?"

"I have plenty of herbs with which to treat it," I answered, having seen many useful plants around the stream, "and it is no longer bleeding. I have taken care of larger wounds than this one." It was true, of course. My occupation was a dangerous one.

Nyx stripped the last of the meat from the leg and tossed the bone far into the stream where it sank below the surface with a *plonk*. On one of the flat rocks that ringed the jumping flames lay my dagger. Nyx reached for it and carved a chunk of steaming meat

228

off the spitted rabbit. As he gnawed at it, he stared into the distance at the small hillocks that rose and fell in shades of grays and blacks until they were lost in the darkness. Time passed, and the meat dwindled away to nothing but bones. Nyx still stared into the distance. I took a slip of pigweed from my pouch and nibbled the greens. I had always heard that too much meat and not enough vegetables would make one's teeth loose, so I offered some to the boy as well. He took it wordlessly, eating each stalk slowly.

"Nyx?" I asked without realizing I had spoken.

He twisted his head to look at me. "Yes?"

"You mentioned something earlier," my voice continued as my mind raced to catch up, "about the anthelai. What makes you think I could go back?"

"Why wouldn't they take you?" he asked, turning his entire body now in my direction.

"From what I can remember, they abhor the killing of anything except for need. I am . . . was . . . an assassin. If they know of me, of the things I have done, then they will refuse."

Nyx seemed to think for a moment. "If you explained what this Caspon has done to you, don't you think they might understand?"

"I cannot know that. There are any number of things they could think about me: liar, deceiver, urchin, fool." I sighed and shook my head. "It is a difficult decision."

Nyx turned his eyes back to the dark knolls beyond the grove. "You don't have any family left, maybe in another anthela city?"

"No, not one. Do you, perhaps?"

"I think I have an uncle," he answered. "Or I did, anyway. My father mentioned him once, but said that they were not overly fond of one another. I think that's also a reason why my father took me and left . . . whatever place it was where I was born. I don't even know the name of it." He sounded tired and sad, and moved his gaze from the hillocks to the flames.

I sighed again, more softly this time, disappointed in a way I could not explain. "I wish there was—" I began, then stopped short as a thought blindsided me. That room where the beryl had first captivated me, my dagger on the table, and behind, on myriad shelves. . . "Caspon has maps!" I exclaimed with brilliant understanding.

"Maps? Everyone has a map or two." Nyx leaned back on the ground and threw an arm over his eyes.

"Not one or two," I pushed. "Many. More than I could ever count."

Nyx sat up, wariness and eagerness warring in his face. "Maps made by humans, surely, with things obscured or left off completely."

"Most were made by *cardeai*, yes," I went on, feeling a tiny tendril of wonder begin to sprout within me.

I continued to speak before Nyx could open his mouth. "Other maps were made by *doshen*, known as stone-eaters or dwarves, or the sand tribes from the desert islands to the far east. Some handcrafted by anthelai, and one rumored to be drafted by a Cunning One of the mythical Crystal Vale. Caspon used to show them to me before I left on a mission so I could find a route through less-populated terrain."

"A Cunning One?" Nyx repeated in shock. "They aren't real!"

I shrugged a shoulder. "Maybe, or maybe not. But I have seen the maps." I leaned back against the bole of a slender oak. "If I could get an anthela map, then the anthehomes should be marked upon it." I frowned. Those maps had never been intended for *cardea* hands. Caspon had paid massive amounts of money for them. If I could get in that room, I would get them all. Every map he owned, I would destroy. He would never torment another people again, neither anthelai nor *doshen* nor sand tribes. I would find an anthehome that had been close to Carfuinel and hope they would accept me on my parents' behalf.

"So you want to find anthelai now?" Nyx questioned, eyeing me.

"If things go the way you wish, then I will. If they go the way *I* think they will, you will still need them. However, my business here must be attended to first. Those maps cannot be allowed to stay in *cardeai* hands. Caspon has destroyed his last anthehome, has taken his last prisoner, and he must pay his dues."

Nyx looked at me for a long moment without speaking. "So you plan to sneak back into Benthol, kill a guildmaster, steal dozens if not hundreds of maps, and then escape without being seen?"

"That is the gist of it, yes," I agreed, barring his last modifier. *He* would remain unseen, but my fate was already determined.

"General Talros, the one in northern Benthol with Hanlon Evoll, is probably hunting for you, do you realize that? I've heard he's uncanny and very knowledgeable. There is every chance this task will kill you."

"I realize that, and I am prepared to face it. I have explained this to you before. You still have a choice and I am asking you now to not come with me any further. Your debt is paid."

He shook his head. "No, I must come with you. Someone has to make sure you don't get yourself killed."

"That may not be up to you," I replied. "I meant every word I said."

"And so did I," he answered. "You can't get rid of me as easily as that. What kind of coward would I be if I left you now?"

"The intelligent kind," I retorted, my lips stiff. "Wait for me outside the walls. Do not come into Benthol with me."

"No," Nyx growled, crossing his arms over his chest. "And if you think to leave me while I sleep, I'll follow you. There's no chance you can cast me aside now. Don't you think with two people this task will be easier?"

I exhaled angrily, but the corners of my lips wanted to lift in a dangerous, treacherous smile of relief. "I wish you would reconsider, but I will not stop you, Nyx."

"Good," he replied with evident relief, again reclining on the soft, matted floor of the grove. "We can talk about this later in the morning, if you want, but right now I want to sleep." He yawned, and I heard the crackle of his jaws. He curled into a ball with his feet near the dying embers. I leaned back against the oak, twisting so that I was cradled in the raised arms of its roots, and listened to Nyx breathe as I fell asleep.

It was strange having another person around, and I found I almost enjoyed it.

"Beryls, General!"

"What of them, Historian?" Talros said from his chair by the fireplace. He had been trying to give the other man his space and time to work without undue hurry, but the decorated general was finding his patience growing thin. So far, the historian had given

231

him nothing but a spreading bruise on the top of his foot from a heavy book that had slipped through weak fingers.

"The green stone clasped to the leather is a beryl, quite a rare find in this day and age. Most have been destroyed by being ground into dust and scattered on the winds or dropped into the deepest reaches of the sea. General Talros, do you know that once the beryl was considered a form of archaic magic?"

Historian Ferril Biar was a small, slender man, bent and white-haired with a cropped beard and bushy eyebrows that jutted high over expensive spectacles. He dashed about his study, flipping through books and shuffling through the innumerable scrolls and papers that piled in corners and littered the floor and desktop, and spoke just as energetically, his words tripping over each other in an effort to be the first out of his mouth.

"That notion is heresy, Historian," Talros said, but knew he would have to follow whatever leads were offered, even those that might hold dangerous consequences if revealed. "The other priests would not like to hear your words but I give you leave to continue, provided that this conversation stays within these walls."

"Oh, they will," Biar acceded in obvious relief. "I assure you, General, nothing either of us says will leave here without your express permission."

"Good, now please continue. Time presses onward."

"Yes. As I was saying, beryls were once regarded as magical items, but only if awakened. According to the one source I could find, the beryl's awakening is not complex. Touching it can be enough in some circumstances. They seem to be drawn to certain types of users, those of great strength or speed or power. Someone with an iron will or a gift for tongues. The beryl tends to enhance these attributes, but it is also a repressor, inhibiting other qualities or inclinations. The stone could also do both, depending on those touching it at its awakening."

"Interesting," Talros murmured.

"Also," Biar continued in his rattling, rapid voice, "the leather strip was not very old. Stained with all manner of things, not limited to sweat and blood, but not old. I estimate it had not been in use for much longer than one or two years, if that. It struck me at first as a tie for either a scabbard or bow, but the wear and tear did not agree with that assessment. General Talros, I do believe it was worn

232

snugly around the neck. The knot was pulled so tightly that untying it proved impossible. Once the leather was tied, it was not meant to ever be removed."

Two or three years, Talros thought, planting his booted feet on the floor. That was almost the same length of time that the Nightingale had terrorized Caesia. She had been using the stone—that seemed obvious now—but had apparently never removed the necklace of leather. Where had she gotten the rare and forbidden object? The only explanation was Caspon.

"Have you researched the beryl's effects on species other than *us?*" Talros asked, placing his hands on his knees to steady himself. Much could be discovered here.

"I could only find information on anthelai, General," Ferril Biar explained, wandering back behind his littered desk and lifting a heavy tome from the chair. He dropped the dusty book on top of the desk with a muffled thump and opened it to a yellowed page marked with a long, ragged pheasant's feather. "Beryls are such fascinating things. I might've gone looking for this information even without your instruction. Here, we are! This entry is quite ancient, written in the middle of the First Age, I believe. There is an account of anthelai and even a small note on the halfbloods you asked about. It seems those disturbing things were more well-known in earlier times."

The wizened historian moved a finger down the page without touching the ancient parchment, not wanting the oils of his skin to damage the valuable words. He read in a strong voice, like a lecturer in an audience hall. "*Like anthelai in most aspects, the half-blooded offspring differ in four known features: firstly, they have shorter lifespans, which are equivalent to that of proper folk, though one was known to live for one-hundred and fifty years, or so the records claim; secondly, the ears of a halfblood are only slightly pointed, though still easily distinguishable from those of a pure person, whereas an anthela's ears are long like the point of a spear; thirdly, those of half-anthela blood are slenderer than normal but are of equal height, while being stockier and somewhat shorter than any anthela; fourth, and lastly, it seems halfbloods are emotional creatures. Combining attributes from a regular parent wherein emotions tend to run shallow and visible, and from an anthela parent in whom emotions are said to run deep and silent, the mixture may result in an explosive temperament with feelings that are not easily released even after weeks or years.*" Biar glanced up from the tome and cleared his throat.

"That is all it mentions on the subject, General Talros, but here. . ." This time, the man turned to the next feather-marked section.

"I'll paraphrase, if you'll allow, for this passage is quite long-winded. From the beginning: Beryls have the ability to augment or diminish chosen attributes. The stone is awakened by a desirous heart and a commanding touch, and then given guidelines. The effects are best felt when the stone is worn against the skin, wherein the magic can be absorbed directly into the body. The beryl is neither cruel nor kind, but responds to its master's desires—the one that awoke the magic—and to the wearer's mind, which in turn receives the commands. In dire situations, a beryl can wake itself and will try to draw to it the first living body it senses."

"I do not understand, Master Historian," Talros said. "The stone is alive?"

"No, General, not alive, but magic is a hungry thing. It is the nature of the occult to act as an extension of the one that uses it. I believe, however, that beryls are not conducive to kindness and charity."

Talros made a noise in his throat. He had to agree with the historian, based on the information he had heard. "You had more to mention?"

"Yes, General, a little about the effects of the beryl on full-anthela blood. I'll read, for it is a short passage." Again, Ferril Biar moved a finger downward, keeping his eyes close to the fragile, yellowed parchment. "*From the notes of King Dewylle Allern I in the First Age, who had captured six anthelai for the menagerie in his lordship's castle: Each of the six creatures were outfitted with leathern bracers on the left forearm, on each of which was set a singular stone of green called a beryl, which the magister Eos the Red had suggested. The King, wholly without fear, approached the anthelai, the creatures being tied strongly to the posts in the menagerie courtyard. My Lord King touched each beryl and spoke in a great, commanding voice: 'This anthela will not leave the menagerie nor harm any person or thing. Should the bracer be removed, or one of my commandments broken, this anthela will die an immediate and painful death.' The next day, a young male anthela did endeavor to flee the area. The groundskeeper and two laundresses claimed to see the creature drop and writhe in agony as the beryl erupted into sparks, and the anthela was burned and dead within six heartbeats.*' The text goes on to say that the other anthelai were monstrous after that, and had to be taken by the priests of Aeroyn the Darkseeker for sacrifice, and that Magister Eos fled the country before the wrath of the king."

"Interesting indeed, Historian Biar, and I thank you for the effort you took in gathering that information, but do you not have something other than magic that you can tell me?" Talros inquired, the wheels turning in his mind. "If you recall the thief Ragosa. . ."

"Of course! I do remember that, if my memory serves correctly." Biar looked at the leather and stone on his desk and fetched a shallow sigh. "I am afraid, however, that I will be of little use to you in that area, General. This adornment has seen most of the Caesian lands, due to the wear and stains. I could find no other useful elements upon it, and I do apologize for that, but I hope that some of my research has been helpful to you." The white-haired man spread his hands apart and shook his head, emphasizing his words.

"You have been a great help, Master Historian," Talros said. "In truth, I did not expect much on the origins of this necklace."

"Collar, I should say," Biar interjected.

"Collar, then," Talros allowed, and the wheels in his mind spun faster. "Your knowledge of the stone's power will be essential in the days to come. I will be certain to make note of what you told me today."

"And none of it leaves this room," Biar said, his wrinkled face serious and still—and almost sad, Talros realized after reflection. Not many outsiders from the monastery would seek out an old historian and ask him to put his many dusty tomes to use. The old man had probably relished hunting through his books.

"Yes, Historian. The other priests will not know of your knowledge." Talros stepped back and lifted a hand to his badge of office in salute. "Thank you again, and should I need anything further I will be certain to call on you." The wizened historian smiled as Talros left. The black-and-silver livery blended into the night as the General of the Weapons headed back through the narrow streets to his room at the inn. That night, he dreamed of anthelai and green stones.

Chapter 18

A LETTER WAS BROUGHT TO TALROS'S ROOM just before daybreak. It was a simple sheet of folded cream-colored vellum, stamped with the red wax seal of the king. Talros felt a chill trace down his spine looking at that waxen stamp. Something had changed since the time he had left the king and his council. Something meant for his ears alone. He rubbed a hand over his bleary eyes, straining to focus, and reached for the paper with his other hand. A quick flip of his thumb broke the seal, and Talros began to read.

"Gods damn it all," he hissed through his teeth after reading the short paragraph. He *had known* this would be the outcome, but had hoped for a little more time. The king wanted the two halfbloods dead, *that* Talros understood, but he wanted them killed without delay. No questions, no compromises, no capture. They were to be killed on sight with no mercy. The person or people responsible for the Nightingale were to be brought into immediate custody. The courtiers had begged for it, and the king had been made to see their point.

Talros had his month, if necessary, but the king had made his opinion clear. If the tasks set before him actually took a month, King Cosian would be highly displeased. The thought did not make Talros happy in the slightest.

He fought the urge to crumple the letter in his hands and instead slammed the missive down on the nightstand, causing the wood to rock under the force of his blow. He growled, exhaustion driven from his mind. There was so much he wanted to learn about the assassin first, questions only she could answer. How had she come to be here? Who found her and why was she left alive? How had she been *born*, for the Oryn's sake? Nothing about her made any sense in his mind. Halfbloods were mythical beings. So why were these two *real?*

Talros stalked across the room, smashing a fist over and over again into his palm. The king wanted him to kill these strange and mysterious creatures outright. No one understood halfbloods, so should Talros' race not try to learn everything they could while there was still time? What if another beast appeared in the future? It could be beneficial to learn how fast, strong, and agile the creatures were. Were they as intelligent as normal people? Did they sing like anthela or speak like proper folk? Talros fought a growing sickness in his mind. These thoughts had plagued him since the day before. Every waking thought was a variation of this theme; his dreams had been full of confusing, tantalizing notions. Never before had his mind juggled this rumination as frantically and desirously as it did now—when it was almost too late to entertain it.

He paused before the window, glaring down at the street below. Already the vendors were out, crying their wares as they set up shop. Several people waited impatiently in the lanes, ready to start a busy morning of bargaining and bickering. There were trussed chickens and caged geese to be bought, along with floundering ducks and wild hares, stuffed pastries, wheels of hard cheese and loaves of bread, sausages, onions, leeks, ripe fruits and green vegetables. Fish swam in barrels filled with river water. Tapped casks of wine and oil sat heavy on the backs of carts, waiting to fill clay pots and flasks.

"They can't even see," Talros muttered. The people below just a few days before had been in terror, frantic at the thought of a monster in their midst. They had called for blood, for murder, wanting to do what the assassin had done so many times before. Now, they lived their simple lives, forgetting their bloodlust until the next passing mention of the monster. Talros did not understand this wildly swinging nature of his fellows. *I must have it*, he thought. *Am I not also like them?*

He sighed and turned from the lightening sky, meaning to dress and leave before the sun rose much higher. It would be an unpleasant ride to southern Benthol and he had little time to spare.

"Wait, you have changed the rules again. Before, the scratched side won a pick."

"No, I think you're mistaken. I never said that. I said if the scratched side lands upward, you *lose* a pick. Put a pebble in the pile."

I narrowed my eyes at the boy seated across from me. Three pebbles sat next to my feet, six beside Nyx, and eleven in the pile between us. On the ground of the grove, next to the center pile of small stones, was a flat strip of bark with the paler inside surface carved with shallow chevrons. The hastily made carvings faced the newly risen sun, which I had thought was a good thing until this moment. Nyx seemed to have a great deal of trouble in remembering the rules of this game, which he called Taggle. I was not even sure whether having fewer stones was desirable. I rather thought not, at present.

I had not wanted to play this pointless game with him at first, but he pushed and coaxed until I gave in. I felt he was trying to draw me into the open, to take my mind off the tasks before me. Nyx talked more than I thought possible, as if he had vowed not to let the silence grow too deep or too long. I was grateful to him, for he beat back the depression that had steadily crept over me since the dam of the beryl had broken. However, the fact that he seemed to care was odd in and of itself. I could not understand why he bothered.

"You said to *pick* a pebble," I protested, thrusting my thoughts away. There was time yet before we had to leave the grove. Southern Benthol and Caspon's hidden den were not far. A little release might be a good thing, and why should I not have one pleasant memory to see in my last moments?

"No," Nyx griped. "I said—"

"I am picking one anyway," I interrupted, reaching out and plucking a pebble from the pile between us. A small smirk touched my lips for a moment, slipping away in the heartbeat before he glanced at my face.

"Fine," he sighed, feigning exasperation, and reached for the slip of bark. He flipped it into the air and watched as it hit the ground, bounced, and came to rest on one narrow side, leaning against a fallen limb. "Ah, see that!" Nyx crowed, grinning. "That means I win."

"What? You never mentioned that before." I frowned, cocking my head to eye him suspiciously. "I do believe you are what is commonly known as a cheater."

He clucked his tongue. "You're just mad because you lost."

"I lost because you cheated," I pressed, not caring. I argued because I wanted to, and because it seemed to be what Nyx wanted. I just enjoyed hearing another voice besides my own, and one that was not hostile at that.

"We'll play another game then, and this time I'll be sure to beat you fairly."

I glanced at the position of the sun. "We do not have time for another game. It is too dangerous to stay here longer, and we should have moved on before now." The *cardea* campsite near the aqueduct had remained empty, but there was no telling how long it would remain in that state. We had been fortunate so far, but I did not want to press our luck. A lone wolf, a sign of Lenos, had passed our campsite in the night and I did not want to think on what, if anything, that might mean.

"Spoilsport," Nyx mumbled, and then sighed. He looked up at me, his gray eyes shadowed and soft. "Talros is a crafty bastard, but can he know where you're going? You must have *some* time to relax. And Caspon can wait, can't he? Can't they both?"

I hesitated, feeling something sprout and curdle deep in my belly. A sick feeling spread over me, and I was both touched and dismayed at the tone of his voice. So ardent he was, and so desperate to keep me alive a little longer. "No, I do not think so," I answered, taking the piece of bark from our game in my hands. My thumb swept over the chevrons again and again, feeling the shallow markings under my skin. "Talros has informants, and he is canny, as you have said. He will find me, sooner rather than later. And Caspon . . . Caspon sees with more than his own eyes. He knows I survived the ascension of Evoll. He knows I failed." I took a breath, and Nyx rushed to fill the space between my words.

"But the stone, you said—the beryl—that was supposed to make you do things, right? Did Caspon tell you to return to him or to finish Evoll first?"

"In truth, I was supposed to die. Once Evoll was dead, Caspon was certain I would be as well. If I happened to survive, I was to report back. There were no provisions if I failed, other than. . ." I trailed away, thinking hard, while Nyx's earnest eyes bored holes in my skull. "Other than to try again and again until he was dead." I sucked in a breath, filled with sudden, unexpected hope. "Caspon does not know I am returning. He must think the beryl still commands me and that Evoll is still my mark."

Nyx sat back on his heels, eyes alight and gleaming. "Then there *is* hope," he whispered. "If we can avoid General Talros!"

Was I worthy of this new hope? I was not a good person and I had killed many who might have been. Nyx apparently thought I was laudable enough to survive for a time yet, and he might have need of me in the near future. Was that enough to live for? Perhaps, and perhaps not; but I would try to endure at least until I was certain Nyx could fend for himself.

"We need to stay ahead of him for as long as we can," I said, rising to my feet. I glanced at Nyx, once more thinking of asking him to wait beyond the walls, just to be safe. There had been plenty of time for him to rethink his choice and I would not blame him if he decided against coming with me. In fact, I still preferred it. Nyx caught my gaze and returned it.

"I'm not staying behind," he said, surprising me with his intuition. "But I do hope you have a plan."

My lips pursed in thought. I did have something resembling a strategy, but it was not close to polished, or safe. "It is makeshift at best," I answered, glancing through the brush toward the duct. The black hole in the side reminded me of a deep, gaping wound that would never heal, a mortal injury that bled darkness into the sunlit morning.

"That's good enough," Nyx replied, and I wanted with all my heart to agree.

Chapter 19

TALROS' LIEUTENANT AWAITED HIS ARRIVAL in a side cloister of the Temple of the Washed in southern Benthol. Talros had ridden swiftly to reach the lower city as quickly as he could, easing through crowds of market-goers, guardsmen, and priests. He had left his horse at the inn stable just outside the southern Benthol gates; it was easier and less conspicuous for a man to slip through the crowds rather than a large beast, and Talros wanted to remain unnoticed if at all possible. The Nightingale might already be in this portion of the city, and if she glimpsed him, then both she and Caspon might go to ground and be lost. Talros did not have that time to spare.

Lieutenant Vernon Majer snapped Talros a crisp salute behind the closed door of the cloister. The Weapons would have to stay out of the public eye as much as possible, for as long as possible and, just to be safe, Majer and his comrades had given up their black-and-silver livery for brown homespun and woolen tunics. It was the clothing of farmers, drovers, and dyers, and would not stand out in the crowds of southern Benthol.

"The servants of Caspon's manor have neither seen nor heard from him in two weeks, General," the lieutenant said. "We've questioned them thoroughly and none have any idea as to his current whereabouts. As for the Nightingale, only one woman in the manor, a maid, spoke of her. She said there was a young girl with blonde hair living there at one point, but she never spoke to anyone. She could not, or would not, tell us anything more."

Talros nodded, frowning. He had suspected as much. "Your disguises have been a good decision, I'll wager," he said. "The Nightingale might not yet be in town, but she will be. Keep watch for her, either alone or with the halfblood boy. They will lead us to Lorcen Caspon."

"Yes, sir," Majer replied, and handed Talros a change of clothes.

When General Talros came down the temple steps, he was dressed in rough and patched brown trousers and a gray woolen tunic. His usually immaculate black boots were scuffed and spotted with mud, and the hem of his dark cloak showed signs of wear and travel. The sheath of his sword was hidden beneath the voluminous fabric and he had wrapped a length of stained leather around the upper third closest to the hilt—the silver etchings would give him away as a Weapon should anyone see them. To this wardrobe, he had added a simple ash bow and a small quiver of pale-fletched arrows, also given to him by Majer. Talros looked for all the world like a hunter just come in from the wilderness. It was a decent disguise, and he thought it would work. He did not think the Nightingale or the boy knew his face, even if they knew his name.

The only blind spot in his plan was where Caspon would hide. Talros roamed the city, eyes and ears open for any hint of the assassin's employer. Moving unhurriedly to avoid attention, Talros strode through the back lanes and the temple district and wandered through the poorer residential area, eyeing the merchant stalls and carts that littered the alleyways. Night was falling already, and Talros hoped that the assassin had not yet made it to the city. He had given orders for his men to patrol the borders as well as the outlying lands beyond the city walls. If she came this way, they would find her. But if she did not . . . that was a situation Talros did not wish to consider. His intuition was good, and some said better than good, but he had always hated to rely upon it solely.

After some time, he began to grown angry. There was no sign of her. His feet were tired of walking and he was sure the boots had rubbed blisters on his heels. No one at the temple had seen the girl he described. No merchants remembered selling her fish or cloth or oil.

He approached a vendor hawking sweetrolls. "Have you seen a blonde girl-child in the area?"

The vendor stared. "Mister, brats swarm me night and day. How am I supposed to remember one?"

Talros sighed and moved on. Perhaps it was too late, but he could not stop. Not with the king's demands looming over him. He had to find the Nightingale or return to the king empty-handed, and the latter was not a prospect he could entertain. Not if he wanted his position—or his life.

"Yah, you looking for something?" a woman asked, leaning against a wooden post of a closed shop just outside the abandoned section of Benthol, her hips tilted seductively and her iron bangles dangling from a slender wrist. "Maybe I can help you." She smiled through dark lips stained with carmine.

Talros glanced at the woman, ready to dismiss her, but soon recognized her as one of the traveling mummers. Nomads, with their bear-baiting and coin-dances and caravans; it might be that they saw things he did not. "Have you seen a girl around here, blonde-haired and blue-eyed?"

The woman frowned. "We don't deal in children."

"No," Talros replied, discomfited by the suggestion. "She is a runaway and a thief. Perhaps you have seen her. She wears a leather strap around her throat or head."

The dark-haired woman cocked her head. "Mayhap I have seen her at our festivals. I could not say."

The look in her eyes bespoke more. General Talros reached into a hidden pocket for a coin. He passed it into the woman's hand and her fingers closed upon it. A quick test of the teeth and a heartbeat later, the coin had vanished.

"In the houses beyond the old section. There are matches there sometimes. I see this girl, and she hunts among the ruins. One house with a broken shutter near the front, many times. Our boys say she takes coin from them on occasion. We went once to check her hiding-place and found a man's footsteps in the dirt. The girl does not come anymore."

"How long ago was this?"

The hand flashed out and Talros, gritting his teeth, deposited another coin in it. "The girl has not come in months. The footsteps were fresher." She did not expound on this explanation and the general did not ask. He had the information that he deemed the most useful.

Talros thanked the woman and went on his way. Still walking leisurely, although his mind raced, Talros soon reached the abandoned rear square of town. Dilapidated houses and cottages lined the lanes, framing the large square close to the great stone wall that ringed the entirety of southern Benthol. The compacted dirt of the square, along with the rickety wooden benches, gave rise to the notion that perhaps this area was not as abandoned as previously indicated. There were signs of frequent and recent wear on the wood, and Talros thought he saw faint spatters of deep brown in the lighter ochre soil. *Mummer shows*, he thought. *Gambling and bear-baiting as he had thought, along with cutpurses.* He would have to remember to tighten patrols in this sector when this business with the assassin was over. She was not the only task he had to tackle. Mummers were illegal after all, the night-walking woman included; theirs was an unregulated business, and the king did not want a share of his taxes to slip away from his grasping fingers.

Talros plodded up the slight hill toward a row of ramshackle houses and chose the one closest to the makeshift arena. The boards were rotted and stained with moss and damp, and the rafters overheard were cracked and sighing dust, but there were no signs of squatters in this particular residence. The General of the Weapons settled in a front corner beside the partly open, damaged door and waited. Either a member of his patrol would come for him or the assassin would make an appearance, but Talros would not budge until something happened.

His uncanny instincts told him to wait, and to watch. Like a cat, he hunkered in the shadows. His prey was on the move, and he would find it.

Nearly a full day had passed since the grove. Nyx and I slunk like foxes through the undergrowth or flitted like sparrows through the treetops when the terrain allowed. The older boy had taken some coaxing to try the canopy, having surprisingly little experience with the world above the ground. He had lived among *cardeai* for longer than I, and was loath to do anything that might bring unwanted attention to himself. As it was, *cardeai* did not tend to look upward very often, anticipating opponents on ground level. Nyx and I were able to dash over the heads of several small groups of foresters—and one cluster of bandits—as they haunted the woods without any ill effects.

Even though Nyx's face was not likely known by Talros, the man had seen me; he knew how I looked. The secret of my identity—young-looking girl, slender, blonde hair and blue eyes, and softly pointed ears—was out, but with any luck had not spread, and we still needed to be cautious as we escaped. In the trees, we would mostly be hidden from view.

Soon, the stone walls of Benthol darkened my vision. Caspon was there, waiting like a spider in its web. He thought—hopefully, oh gods, hopefully—that I was still ensnared. If he knew I was free, then he might go into hiding until certain I was captured or dead. If he knew I was free, I might never have my revenge.

I stopped high in the branches of an ancient hemlock and looked out over the countryside. Nyx came to rest on the branch below me, his head at the level of my waist. There was nothing around us but forest, deep and dark and wild. Far in the distance, the wall rose above the land like an exposed spine. Caspon was there, and perhaps Talros was as well. I would have to be careful. Oh, so very careful.

I rummaged through the leather pouch that I kept tied to my belt. Cloth packets and padded vials of herbs, extra bowstrings, whetstone, striker and flint, several black feathers, and a few other items jostled against my hand as I struggled to find the one I needed. Nyx watched me with interest, cocking an eyebrow in surprise when I drew free a long strip of faded blue cloth. Working quickly, I wrapped the fabric around my forehead, hiding my telltale ears and keeping my unruly hair out of my eyes.

I glanced at Nyx, then reached once more into my pouch and extracted another strip of cloth. This one I handed to him. "You, too," I said as he took the blue cloth from my hand. He wrapped it around his head, and tucked the ends at the back so they would not dangle.

I choked back a heavy sigh, knowing what I needed next. Caspon would see, and he would know instantly if I came before him without it. Thrumming with agony, I stooped and took an extra strap from my quiver. My hands went cold and numb as I touched the leather.

"What're you doing with that?" Nyx asked.

"My collar," I answered in a voice thick with dread. The strip of leather dredged up terrifying memories, regardless of the lack of a beryl. "I will need one." My breath shuddered in my chest, burning my freezing lungs, and then soughed free.

"Think of it as a necklace," Nyx urged with no trace of mockery in his voice.

If only it were that easy.

"Do you want some help?"

I reacted negatively to his gentle tone. "I can do it," I snapped, strangling the leather in a swift, white-knuckled grip that left the impressions of my fingernails upon the strap. He backed one step away, raising his hands in a placating, defensive manner. My breath left me in a sudden, ragged sigh, and steeling myself, I knotted the collar around my neck before what little courage I had left me. I closed my eyes, waiting, but the thrumming tension in my bones did not lessen—and I did not think it would, not until the collar, fake or not, was gone forever.

"Will Caspon notice the stone is gone?" Nyx asked, not mentioning my tactless outburst only moments before.

"He should not," I answered, my voice like hollow iron. There was brittle strength in it, but press too hard and it would crumble. "As long as the leather is there, he will think the stone is as well." I moved the knot closer to the front of my throat. The beryl had often slipped around to be hidden by my hair. If all went well, Caspon would not know anything was amiss until it was too late.

We took our time navigating the forest canopy. The air was cool here, the first taste of autumn on our skin. Hemlock, red oak, and maple flourished all around us. They were huge trees, and as such we never needed to touch the ground as we made our way closer to the city walls. I estimated we would reach south Benthol by nightfall if we did not take too many breaks.

Slipping through the branches, we discussed our plans. Entering Caspon's manor and stealing the maps would be Nyx's task. There would be fewer guards there since Caspon was hidden, I surmised. The real danger would be the servants. For a few minutes, we stopped and dropped to the ground where I sketched a rough map onto a smoothed square of soil with a stick. It was a layout of the manor where I had lived, complete with the secret room where I first encountered the beryl and became a slave. The maps were located in that room, in the rear cabinets and shelves, as was my black dagger from Carfuinel. Nyx would keep my bow and quiver when he went—if he chose to do so—because in the confines of Caspon's hiding hole they would be worthless.

While Nyx dealt with the maps, I would deal with Caspon. I knew the location of his refuge and would go there alone. As expected, Nyx had protested at this part, but I refused to concede. I would not risk his life more than absolutely necessary. The maps were necessary; running headfirst and untrained into Caspon's lair was not. Nyx was to hide in the forest after destroying all the maps, save one. If I did not return by sunrise, he was to leave me and travel onward using the map he had kept. Otherwise, we would travel on together. This latter outcome was highly unlikely, I thought, but I would not tell him this again.

After erasing my hastily drawn outline, we took a short break by a nearby stream. I glanced at the boy bending to drink from the cold rush of water, thinking that he was uncharacteristically quiet. If he was lost in his thoughts, I did not want to be rude by interrupting him. He needed the little peace we had now, for in the coming night it would be gone.

I brushed through the damp rhododendron by the stream, then knelt to drink a cupped handful of water. I felt the chill of it spread through my body, and shivered.

"Bird, I was wondering something," Nyx said, raising his head from the stream. He wiped his dripping mouth with a forearm.

"Bird?" I asked, bemused. "Is that what you have decided to call me?"

"Ah, yes," he answered, and to my surprise his cheeks were tinged with red. "Is that fine?"

I lifted one shoulder in a shrug. "I do not mind it." I took another swallow of water, then rose to my feet. "You had something to ask me?"

"Oh, yes, I did. My name—do you think it's an anthela word?"

"It is," I answered, wiping my hands dry on the legs of my breeches.

He looked flustered. "Truly? Does it mean anything?"

I smiled slightly. "It means *badger.*"

"The animal or an annoyance?" he inquired, giving me a dry look.

"The animal," I replied, slipping back into the branches of a large maple. He followed me, making only slightly more noise than I did. He learned quickly, and for that I was glad.

"What about that word you used earlier? *Cardeai.*"

"It is a term the anthelai use for humans. It means "deaf ones" in Anilo, because they cannot hear the whispers of the trees."

"So you speak Anilo, I take it, the anthela language?" His voice was hopeful. "I mean, I know you were born to the anthelai, but—"

"I do." The leaves brushed against my skin, catching at my hair. The wind soughed through the limbs, making the treetops sway. It was comfortable being above the ground.

"Will you teach me, please?"

I stopped, glancing at him in disconcertion. "Why?" I did not know how to teach anyone, and the thought had never occurred to me that he might need to know another language.

He kept moving through the limbs, not looking at me. "What if the anthelai we come across don't speak Caesarn? How will I communicate? It would be good for me to know their language if you . . . aren't around to translate."

That was true. I was foolish for not thinking of it earlier, but I had not even realized that he would not know anything of the language of his mother. I had spoken Anilo less than a handful of times since I had been Caspon's slave, but I still thought in it. The tongue was special to me, a wavering link shared with my parents and the place of my birth. It would be right to share this with Nyx, for he was half an anthela, just as I was. I slipped through the branches after him.

"I will teach you what I can," I answered with sincerity, "in the time that we have. We will start now, with simple greetings. *Amún ea'desí Nyx.* That means 'My name is Nyx.'"

Nyx repeated the phrase, smiling, and that would have been reason enough to continue the lessons.

Southern Benthol was quiet and dark when we arrived at the wall. From the old, gnarled oak several yards back from the stone, I could make out the dim, dark shapes of buildings against the star-bright sky. The city was sleeping, the shops were closed, and the tavern keepers were sweeping their floors. A dog barked and was silenced, and I heard a child crying somewhere below.

The streets that I could see were empty of life, but that did not mean nothing lurked in the shadows. Thieves and guardsmen were still threats, as were drunkards and those with cruelty on their minds. There might be dogs as well, hungry mongrels that vied for scraps in the gutters. No wolves though, except for the treated skins in Lenos' temple.

"Remember the plan," I whispered to Nyx in the confines of the thick-leaved branches. "Watch for soldiers, and not just the Weapons. If things are too dangerous, leave immediately."

"They won't see me," Nyx replied in a soft voice. He had a white-knuckled grip on a slender branch and his face was pale in the moonlight that filtered through the leaves.

"Here," I said, bending to reach into one of my knee-high boots. "Take a dagger; you may have need of it."

Nyx looked at me, questions obvious in his gray eyes.

"I have my long knife and another boot-dagger. You will have my bow, but that is not much use if you are trapped in close quarters." A watery facsimile of a smile passed over my lips, but it collapsed after naught but a moment. Nyx nodded in comprehension and took the dagger, slipping it into his own shoe.

Then, shocking even myself, I reached over and took his hand, hoping to give him even the smallest bit of courage. I had not touched a person without malice in eight years, and I hurriedly dropped his hand when Nyx looked at me in puzzlement.

"For courage," I whispered, then vanished down the tree and dashed across the open ground to the wall, leaving Nyx to stare after me until it was his turn to scale the stone.

Chapter 19

A PORTION OF THE WALL overrun with tangles of sweetbriar was my path into the city limits. Sweetbriar was filled with thorns like cat claws, so the guards had not cleared it away. They assumed that very few would be fool enough to risk the razor-sharp spikes, but they had not reckoned on a vengeful halfblood with assassin's training. I slipped up the woody vines, feeling the spines touch against my skin without drawing blood. It was a tight squeeze through the iron pickets at the top of the wall, but my slender frame was not in much danger of becoming stuck as I edged through and dropped to the ground on the other side, landing on the balls of my feet. It was a long drop, but I landed like a cat on the soft ground.

I dashed into the darker shadows near the corner of a building as soon as my boots touched soil, keeping on my toes to lessen the slight sounds I made. I would have to cross through the merchant's quarter to reach the abandoned section where the mummers had once performed. My destination was there, and the end of my life.

I sucked in a breath, filling my lungs until they threatened to burst, and began my snaking trek through the darkness. I kept a hand near the hilt of my long knife, glad for the fraying fabric and stained leather that kept the blade from jingling or catching the starlight. I could not quite believe this was happening, that I was finally after Caspon with real intent and purpose. *I am doing this,* I thought in calm fear. *Finally his penance will be done.*

At that thought, my fear died down but did not vanish. I was full of something else now, something darker and hungrier. I could not deny what it was, nor did I try. It was bloodlust, pure and simple. Caspon had hurt me, had killed my family and burnt my home; there was nothing good in him, no redeeming qualities that might have stymied my thirst for a time. My fingers clenched on the hilt of my knife. I wanted nothing more than Caspon's lifeblood on my blade and my hands. These were dark thoughts, monstrous thoughts, but I did not care in the slightest. I would be a monster for now, until the deed was done. I would be the demon halfbloods were thought to be.

The dilapidated houses huddled in the darkness like splintered boulders. I was cold with fear and anticipation and could hear the blood singing in my ears. I was so close now, so close to feeling Caspon's neck under my blade. Slipping through the shadows of the mummers' circle took only heartbeats, and then the houses loomed like grasping hands overhead.

One of these houses concealed the entrance to a secret lair, Caspon's hiding place in times of unease. I smiled grimly, understanding my enslaver's paranoia. He knew I would turn on him, the first opportunity that came. Hopefully, he did not yet realize that that time had come. I wanted to savor his shock.

I went to the open window of the chosen shack, hearing nothing but my own pulsing blood. A deep feeling of unrest unfurled in the pit of my stomach as my hands touched the warped and flaking wood, and with a hiss I threw myself back as a dark figure rose up in the open portal.

I spun on my heel, fighting to flee, but the figure vaulted through the window and sprinted after me. I feinted left but the man was too quick, swifter than I expected, and I was crushed to the ground under his weight as he tackled me from behind.

I clawed and bit and struggled. I could not be stopped now, not when I was so close! But he was too heavy, my blows were ineffectual, and when my teeth clamped down on chainmail I knew I was undone. The soldier—Weapon, oh gods—trapped my wrists behind my back and put a knee on my spine, pinning me facedown into the earth.

"So," he said, breathing heavily. "I have you, assassin."

I hissed in a quick, shallow breath, feeling hot rage and deep, cold terror flood over me. My stomach churned, but I let my face betray nothing. "You are mistaken."

"I think not," said General Astin Talros. With one hand he ripped the headband from me, exposing my pointed ears to the starlight. He grabbed one, painfully. "I think not," he repeated in a voice like stone.

I made myself grin and chuckle even though my stomach threatened to spill its contents. "You are a bounty hunter, I take it," I said, wanting to offend him, to make him angry. Angry men made mistakes and generals were no exception. "This time you were lucky, but how many times has your logic been flawed?"

He made no noise, and I could not see his face. I wished that I was not belly-down in the dirt. I wanted desperately to see and gauge his reaction. "I am neither a bounty hunter nor a mercenary. I am General Astin Talros of the Royal Weapons of Caesia, and my logic is never flawed." His voice was dark but even, and I read a thin thread of anger within it. A little more. I had to push him a little more, just enough to get his weight off me.

"I do not believe I have heard of you," I lied, and although his knee dug deeper into my back he did not rise to the bait.

"Where is your friend, the boy from the gallows?"

"I am afraid I have no idea what you are talking about. I never saw him after he dropped, and I assume the crowd must have trampled him in the commotion." I snorted in the dirt, trying to make it sound like I was on the edge of laughing. I would have made an excellent mummer, I thought, with acting abilities like these.

"So you admit to being at the ascension of Hanlon Evoll?" Talros' voice bordered on disbelief.

"I can scarcely deny it, with you being so . . . certain and all," I answered wryly, slanting my gaze as far back as I could in hopes of glimpsing his face. I wanted him to see that I was not afraid and that he could not cow me. Just because I was young did not mean I was easily broken, and mere questions would not be enough. "You are so certain that I am this assassin, but what makes you think there are not other halfbloods in the kingdom?"

I heard his swift indrawn breath. The snare had been set and the rabbit was angling close. "And how many of your kind are here?" he asked, but the noose was not cinched yet, not quite.

"I am not certain," I answered, more truth than lie. "Perhaps I could think better if I were able to breathe." I wondered if I had pushed my luck when Talros did not move, but then, finally, he shifted his knee to the small of my back. I thought this an improvement until he jerked my arms up and wrapped a cord around my wrists, tying it so that the pulse began to throb in my hands. He dropped them without warning, and I took that moment to draw in a deep breath against the pain. He took the long knife from my belt and tossed it away; I heard the dull clank as it hit the dust some six feet to my right.

"How many?" Talros repeated.

I closed my eyes for three heartbeats. "Would you kill us?" I asked. "We are not all of us demons."

"The evidence I have seen goes heavily in the opposite direction."

"The Nightingale is one person. There is good and bad in every group, *cardeai*—your people—included. Cannot you agree?"

"We are not talking about me," the famed general answered. "Now, how many are you?"

"I do not know," I said. "Perhaps one, perhaps one hundred. Perhaps more. How many *cardeai* are there?"

Talros growled in the back of his throat like a dog. "I want straight answers from you, assassin—"

"I have not admitted to that," I hissed, interrupting his stern tone. "Assumptions are useless."

"The fact that you are a halfblood wearing a short sword and this leather strip," he said, twisting the leather collar around my throat, "are proof enough."

I froze. He knew about the collar? What else did he understand about it? I wondered if it might be possible to appeal to his sense of dignity and honor, should he have them. The path before me went hazy; I did not know quite what I should do. Would speaking of the beryl be even more dangerous, not only for me, but for others as well? I decided to test the waters.

"What does my necklace have to do with anything?" I asked, feeling the dry soil in my nostrils, against my lips. I wanted to breathe it deep into my lungs and choke.

"One remarkably similar to the one you are wearing was found near the body of a man killed by the Nightingale. Only that one had a stone on it, a green stone."

I closed my eyes, feeling the fear trickle back into my veins. I could feel my eloquence leaving, my words retreating back into the depths of my mind. I said the first thing that came into my head, my lips moving faster than my wits. "You want justice," I whispered, "for those killed. I think you also want answers to satisfy your curiosity. I will give you none."

His hand closed around my joined wrists and I smothered the pained whimper that rose in my throat. "You will tell me who sent you, who made you, and where you came from," he said darkly. "You will tell me about the anthelai and the Plains of Centura, and you will tell me *everything*."

"I keep my own counsel and that business is my own," I answered. "I do not pour my tale for every heavy-handed man who crosses my path."

His weight shifted and the knee lifted from my back. A quiet, unbidden sigh of relief escaped me even though I knew I would have a spreading bruise later. I waited a moment to see if the sharp knee would reappear, and when it did not I rolled onto my back and sat up, curling a leg back beneath me. Talros sat two feet away, dressed in something other than his Weapons' attire. His eyes gleamed in the starlight, with fear and hunger both. He wanted everything I could tell him; he was starving to know all that hid inside my mind. He was also frightened of me because I was different.

"You are a child," he mused. I was not truly, not at seventeen years, but my build made me look younger.

"And you are old," I hissed, but he ignored my words.

"Who is it that would make a child into an assassin? Who is it that made you a murderer?"

I said nothing, but looked at him, unblinking. Caspon was mine to kill, and if Talros knew then my vengeance might never be done. Behind me, my hands crept to my back-bent leg, searching for the blade in my boot.

"You would protect him?" Talros asked in astonishment.

"No," I said, before I could think. My fingers closed on the very end of the hilt, and carefully I began to draw it free.

A light seemed to dawn in his face. "So you would do him harm, now that the beryl is gone."

I bit my tongue to keep from speaking. The dagger was in my hands and I tensed my fingers, scraping the blade against the cord between my wrists.

"I know a fair bit about beryls," Talros continued, trying to sound like a friend instead of a soldier. "I've heard they are magic.

There is even a story that tells how the stone was once used to bind anthelai to the whims of their masters. Am I correct?"

"I would not know," I said, after several heartbeats of disbelief and agony. "I have not heard that tale." In his mind, the tale was that and nothing more. If I solidified it, made it real, then I would have made the beryl's horror true for more than me. It might be used against others if Talros knew the stories were true.

The lines of his face deepened in anger, though he tried to hide it. The cords parted and fell away as I concealed the dagger in my hands. The muscles in my legs tensed as I readied. My eyes drifted over Talros' left shoulder, and my jaw dropped in incredulity. Talros looked at me in consternation and then in sudden apprehension. He turned his head to glance over his shoulder, and I sprang.

In seconds, I was on my feet and sprinting, not even slowing to reach for my long knife below my feet. I heard Talros roar in rage and shock behind me, then the pounding of his booted feet. He was fast, but I hoped I was faster. He had surprised me at the shack, but I had gotten first-footing here.

I sprinted through the lanes made into labyrinths by the ramshackle houses, searching for refuge. This was Astin Talros after me, the revered General of the vaunted Weapons. I had to find a place to hide, and fast. I could no longer hear him behind me, but did not spare a glance to make certain. It would slow me down.

I chose a ledge and jumped, scrambled upwards onto a roof and raced down the length of the lane until a missing roof halted my progress. I spun, looked swiftly, and leapt to the nearest structure on the opposite side of the street, thanking the gods for narrow passages.

I dashed over rafters and loose roofs with heaving lungs and galloping heart until a section of rotted shingles cracked under me. I was thrown off-balance, skidded to my knees and slipped close to the edge of the pitched covering. In an instant I was up and off again, but the slip had slowed me considerably. Exposed beams like skeletal fingers stretched before me and I ran toward them.

The pain was immediate and incredible. I gasped as my shoulder erupted in agony, as I was lifted off my feet and sent spinning through the open air to land in a stunned tangle on the refuse-littered ground. I fought for breath, for sense, and came to myself just enough to notice the pale-fletched arrow protruding from the front of my right shoulder, just under the collarbone.

My trembling fingers touched it and the pain blossomed in my skull. I cried out as the redness washed over me, trying to drag me into the depths of unconsciousness.

His horrid face loomed over me, wavering in my pain-watered gaze. "Where is Guildmaster Caspon?" he rasped, grabbing me by the front of my tunic and lifting my torso off the ground. "I know he's your master, so tell me where he's hiding!"

I struggled to draw breath, to see straight. I could feel the wooden shaft against my bones, scraping against the muscles I worked to keep still. Each pulse of my heart was fire and ice, like sharp gravel in my veins. "I am. . ." I said as strongly as I could. The front of my tunic was wet with blood, sticky on my skin. "I am no one's slave." The words were more powerful than I thought they would be. I met Talros' eyes with as much dignity as I could muster.

And then I could not focus on words for my world was spinning. I screamed as the arrow shaft was snapped and my hands rebound. "You are a coward and a fool," Talros said in a flat tone, shoving my headband into my mouth to stifle the noises I must be making, and heaved me over a shoulder so that my hair hung loose around my face. I could feel trickles of my own blood creep down my neck toward my face, leaving hot trails of wet in their wake.

His arm went around my waist, holding me like a porter does a sack of flour. Each step was torture, each breath torment. Of all the arrows I had loosed, of all those aimed in my direction, not one had ever struck me. Was this what my victims had felt, this searing pain? My self-loathing redoubled. I had caused this suffering to others; it was only fair that my turn had come.

I thought suddenly of my companion. Had he made it to the manor? *Get away,* I thought. *Run from here and forget the maps.* Talros was more cunning that I had thought, to my detriment, but if I could keep him from Nyx then I would try my hardest, wounded or not. I exhaled and let my body go limp in the hopes that Talros would put me down, thinking I was unconscious or perhaps dead.

He did not fall for my ruse, and I made myself turn my head, heavy though it seemed, to gain my bearings now that we were gone from the mummers' area. The rotting shacks had vanished and the lanes were stone and soil both, giving way to cobblestone as we went onward. An upward-sloping area came up beside the lane, and I recognized it as my practice field.

The manor! *Oh gods, oh gods!* I thought wildly. *He is going to the manor. Why?* Nyx might still be in there, fool boy who had insisted on the job, and we two could not be remotely safe in the same place. I had to delay if I could to give Nyx a greater chance at escape. I was not certain how much time had passed, but it could not have been enough. Daylight could come and I would still think it had not been enough.

I twisted my body, fighting the flaring pain, and kicked outward, struggling to slip from his grasp. He grunted in surprise and hurt as the toe of my hard boot punched him in the ribs, and his arm tightened on my waist. The other wrapped around my knees in an iron grip, stopping my flailing feet almost as soon as they had started.

"Stop!" he snarled, pulling his arms tight, but I writhed like a snake and managed to contort enough to snap my teeth on the flesh right below his ear. He bellowed and heaved me from his shoulder. I landed on my side on the stone street, the wind knocked from my lungs. The hurt was incredible but I had no air to cry out. I could see my blood in the starlight, dark and gleaming like water under a full moon. I rolled my eyes to the man, seeing a black slick on the side of his neck, and bared my teeth at him.

"You are a child!" he protested in stunned fury, one hand going to the wound under his ear.

"Assumptions are worthless," I whispered, repeating earlier words.

Talros stepped closer and crouched next to my prone body, eyes glittering in the faint light. "The king wants you dead, Nightingale. I'd rather learn your secrets first, but if you push me I'll take what I can get."

"They are my secrets," I said, my shoulder throbbing. "You shall not have them while I am alive."

"Those are notable words for a girl, and dangerous ones for an assassin under arrest."

"Is that what this is?" I asked dryly, feeling a wet heat in the back of my throat. "I had no idea."

"You can make japes if you like, assassin. They simply serve to reinforce your difference."

My difference from *cardeai*, he meant, as if it were not obvious I was something else. I lay where I had fallen on my side, half-bent on the stone street. My head ached and the shaft of the arrow prodded at my bones. I would have new bruises—should I last so long—on my legs, ribs, and arms from the cobblestones to match the one from his knee on my back.

"You are cruel to a child," I countered. He hesitated, and I thought suddenly that Talros did not believe he was a vicious man. He was doing his job and it would be well enough if I looked grown. But I was small for seventeen years and gangly with the appearance of youth. Talros did not know my age but he assumed I was juvenile.

"You have murdered," he answered. "Your age is of no consequence. It is only odd that you are young still to be such a prolific killer of men."

Men, I thought. Not only men, no, but women and a child or two as well. Caspon had not been discriminatory in our targets.

"Do you not know of the northland raids committed by men?" I asked, my breath short and pained. "Think on that and mayhap it will not be so hard to consider them murderers as well."

"Anthelai are not human," Talros challenged with quiet disgust.

I made a sorrowful noise in my throat. "Perhaps not," I agreed, "but neither are you."

"What do you mean by that?" he snapped, gripping my tunic in his fist. I would not answer; my talking was done. He was caught in the snare now, finally. I hoped Nyx had done what he could and fled, for I was finished.

My breath hissed free and I could feel the darkness hovering at the edges of my vision. Caspon's manor was a dim shadow in the corner of my eye but its presence was suffocating. I slipped under, drowning in the starlight, clawed to the surface for a heartbeat, and was gone.

The world was vast and I was lost underneath it.

Chapter 20

THE ARROW BURNED LIKE FIRE, even in the depths of my unconsciousness, and I awoke with a muffled scream when Talros cut the barbs free. I was gagged and bound somewhere in the darkness, struggling against the rope and the pain. The blood poured hot and wet down the front of my body, soaking the bandeau around my burgeoning chest, and then the wound was smothered with a thick pad of cloth that my captor bound to my upper torso under my filthy tunic.

"You won't die just yet," Talros said to me, tugging the knots hard. I choked on the gag, clawing to find my voice. "I can't have you bleed out before I have my answers." He tugged my tunic down to cover his paltry bandaging. Without seeing the wound I could not tell how bad it might be. If the arrow had nicked the large vein under the collarbone, I was dead despite the bandage. I prayed that was not the case; I was not finished yet in this world.

I moved, testing my bonds. My hands were tied behind my back very tightly, my ankles trussed before me. If that was not maddening enough, the rope on my ankles was looped around an iron bar, which, on closer inspection, made up a lattice. I realized that I was inside a cell in the gaol behind Caspon's manor. My heart sank.

"You have mettle, I'll give you that," Talros said, settling a few feet away. "But mettle won't save you here, not now. The best you can do is answer my questions. Do that for me, and I will grant you what leniency I can."

My neck felt too weak to support the weight of my head. I leaned back against the bars, settling my entire side against the cold iron. The arrow wound throbbed and everything seemed to be painted in shades of red and grey. My breath whistled faintly in and out of my lungs.

Talros made an unpleasant noise in his throat and gripped my exposed ear with unkind fingers. "How similar are you to the anthelai?" he asked. "What are your differences?" He pulled and poked at my ears, pried open my eyes to gaze into them, even peered into my mouth like a horse-trader. I let him do as he would, making no move to resist. I seemed to swim inside my head, keeping my distance from what was happening around me.

"Why do you not speak?" he demanded. "You talked enough earlier." A harsh chuckle slipped free. "You can't be scared, surely. The great and terrible Nightingale, ravager of Caesia, too frightened to answer a few simple questions."

I knew his game and did not wish to play it. He would goad me into speaking, using insults so that my anger might make me careless. I had done the same to him earlier, whether he realized it or not. *You must try harder than that,* I thought with faint amusement.

"I saw you run," Talros said, taking his hands away. "How can a demon be so nimble, so swift? That is what you are, or so all the stories say. A demon and a monster. You are no person; you are less than human. You are nameless, an *it*. How does that feel, assassin, to know that you are hated and despised across the world for being born as you are?"

I said nothing. I could not even if I had wanted to, for my throat had closed on itself so nothing could pass. I did not move from my position, just stared at the bars to which I was bound. His words hurt more than he could ever know, but I would not show my sorrow, not here and certainly not to him. What I did do, however, was turn my eyes up to his face and stare. I had been told that my gaze was unpleasant, that it could make stomachs churn and blood chill, so I used that now just to see what it would do.

Talros looked at me. "Still nothing." He grimaced. "Why do you stare?"

I did not blink nor move my gaze in the slightest. I wanted him to make the first move, to show that he was weaker than a simple child. I would have that out of him before I let myself stop.

"Why do you stare and say nothing?" Talros asked again, taking a fistful of my tunic in hand and tapping my head against the bars. The pain cut across my skull like a knife, but I tried desperately to keep eye contact. My hair fell into my eyes, stinging, but I would not blink.

"Answer me, damn you!" Talros roared. "Tell me what you know. Is this some sort of invasion? Why did you say I was different?" He raised an arm to backhand me across the face and I tensed, readying for the blow.

"General Talros, sir!" a voice interrupted. Unbidden relief trickled through me. I blinked, now that Talros' attention was not focused solely on me, and looked for the speaker. A young man, streaked with sweat and soot, stood at attention. He seemed frightened, evidenced by his pallor and tense posture. I shifted, moving my wrists against the ropes so subtly that Talros did not notice.

"What is it?" General Talros barked, releasing my tunic and backing away. He rose to his feet, close enough to kick me should I move.

"Fire, sir, in the west wing of the main house. It's spreading rapidly."

"Can it be contained?" He went rigid and I felt a mixture of fear and hope. Nyx had done it, or so it seemed. I felt strangely buoyant, but the fear in my heart was an anchor. Was he safe? Had he escaped?

"I don't think so, sir. We didn't find it until it was too late. Already an entire corridor is in flames."

"The flames mustn't spread beyond the gates," Talros demanded. He knelt and checked my trusses, tightened them, then passed through the cell door and closed it behind him. "Stay with her," he told the young Weapon. "Under no circumstances are you to leave the prisoner alone or untie her. Do you understand me?"

"Yes, sir," the soldier said, saluting, but his glance flicked to me. Talros locked the door with a thick, heavy key and slid it into his shirt.

"If the fire reaches this far, the assassin burns," the general commanded. "You may save only yourself."

"I understand, sir," the soldier said, not looking at me. He put a hand on the long sword at his hip and moved to stand with his side toward me, facing down the short hallway that led to the rear courtyard. I was glad that Caspon's cells were not part of the main building, but set some ways back and on the rear quarter of his estates.

Talros' footsteps rang on the flagstones until he passed through the thick, barred door and vanished. The young guard stood rigid beside my cell, refusing to acknowledge my presence. He knew who and what I was, and I frightened him. I decided to press my luck.

"You seem young for a Weapon," I said, shifting against my ropes and completely aware of the irony of my words. He did not look at me, but his weight transferred from one foot to the other. I saw some promise in that. "Would you happen to have some willow, by chance? Some pain relief would be welcome."

His jaw clamped shut and the cords in his wrists tensed. He would snap soon, even without much prodding. There was not much fun in an easy target. "You seem tense," I said, feigning amusement. "Are you afraid?"

"Of you?" the Weapon snarled, snapping his head around to glare at me. "Never."

I snorted in feigned mirth. "You do a poor job in hiding it."

His hands gripped the iron bars, breaking off thin flakes of rust that showered the shoulders of my bloodstained tunic. "You murdered Bertrand, my cousin. It's all I can do not to kill you right here."

I raised an eyebrow, goading him without words.

"A blacksmith with dark brown hair and a burn scar in his right arm. He lived in Tennely with his wife and two children. He was cut down at his own forge early one morning. You left a black feather in his blood on the floor."

I thought if he twisted the bars any more that he might break them apart with his bare hands. There was hatred on his face, in the curl of his lips and the narrowing of his eyes. I remembered Bertrand Delanie and the thrust of the blade that took his life. I remembered the coolness of the air that morning before the sun rose, the smell of hot iron and leather, and then the smell of blood and steam.

"I am afraid I do not know what you are talking about," I said dismissively. The Weapon's face went livid and a hand flew to the sword sheathed on his hip. "Please do," I said with more calm than I felt. "I would consider it a favor."

"Killing you is kinder than you deserve," the young man spat. "General Talros will deal with you—or perhaps when the flames come I'll let you roast like a pig on a spit."

I chuckled softly, feeling sick. "Oh, I doubt I will burn," I said. "This is arson, after all. Who do you think set the fire?"

"Not you," the soldier hissed in mixed rage and doubt.

"You are correct, and you should also know what that means. I have friends here, Weapon. Do you?" I turned my fey blue eyes on him and let them work.

"The manor is filled with Weapons, assassin. Of course I have friends!"

"Ah, I said *here*—in this place. Not in the manor." I smiled. "You are alone *here*. How long would it take someone to find you should something . . . go amiss?"

The young soldier took three steps back and placed a hand on the hilt of his sword. His eyes were wide and white and I could hear the breath rushing fast through his lungs. "You have no friends here," he said, trying to sound convincing. The blade was half-drawn from the scabbard, but my gaze did not leave his.

"You would not know that until too late," I replied, not smiling. "Talros will not be back until the fire is either contained or eating everything in sight. You are utterly alone." And I shifted again against the ropes, feeling the ones around my wrists slip. My skin was slick with blood. I pulled my hands free.

"Stop moving! Stay where you are," the Weapon cried, drawing his sword.

I ignored him, instead focusing on the bindings at my ankles. Bending was extraordinarily painful and I felt fresh blood course down my chest. The ropes fell away under my attentive fingers, and I breathed in relief as the blood pulsed through my extremities once more.

"I said stop!" the soldier called again, and this time I stood to face him.

"I am still locked in this cage, Weapon, or is that not enough for you?" He could see the blood that covered me now and his eyes widened at the sight of it. "I am weaponless, defenseless, and wounded. Is that not enough? Be merciful and I will extend the same courtesy to you."

"Don't come near the bars," he said, lowering his sword.

I nodded once and took two steps back, hands raised to show I meant no harm. The soldier slid the sword home but kept a hand on the hilt. The very faint sounds of men yelling reached my ears, and then a muffled boom that even the Weapon heard. He flinched and jumped, looking a touch frantic.

"The fire has reached the lower levels of the guild barracks," I said.

"How can you know that?" He sounded breathless.

"That sound was firedust, compliments of an alchemist who once lived there. He must have left his effects behind when he moved on."

"Firedust?" The soldier was aghast. "That is an illegal substance!"

"Of course," I said matter-of-factly. Another explosion sounded, and this time the walls of my cell shook with the impact. Dust showered down from between the stones and the iron bars rattled in their sockets. "Perhaps, Weapon, now would be a perfect time for you to leave. We will not be alone for much longer."

He stared at me, but I thought he was more terrified of the fire and falling stone than of me. "I am supposed to guard you and I do not shirk my duties."

"Be that as it may, you were also told to let me burn. Being crushed is not much different in the scope of things."

"I cannot let you leave your cell!"

"It is your life, soldier. Leave while you can and enjoy it for a while longer. When the others come, they might not be so generous." I was bluffing. No one was coming for me, hopefully not even Nyx. I wanted him gone from here, as soon and as far as possible.

Another explosion rocked the gaol and it felt like the world was breaking apart. The last thing I saw before the cell vanished was the young soldier fleeing down the hallway toward the one door that led outside and into the open air. I wished him luck, and then I knew nothing. Losing consciousness was becoming an all too common occurrence.

Chapter 21

I WAS NOT OUT LONG, or so I thought. Wispy gasps of dust sifted down from the stones that creaked and groaned like old men. Blood crusted my lashes and plastered tendrils of hair to my forehead. I was on my stomach, flat and sprawling, but whole. My body ached; my muscles burned; my stomach writhed at the base of my spine. I stretched out my arms, trying to pull myself to my knees, but my joints protested at any movement.

Get up! Now, while there is a chance at escape! The door down the hall hung open and smoke drifted inside, curling along the edges of the ceiling. I could not feel the heat from the flames, not yet, but I knew it was approaching. The young soldier had left me like I had known he would. Talros had told him to let me burn, after all, and no one would risk their life for an assassin.

My head was heavy and there seemed to be a curious biting sensation at the base of my skull. I twisted my neck, trying to relieve the pain, but moving sent a swirling vertigo through my brain, making my eyes roll and my stomach protest. I groaned through gritted teeth. Talros wanted me alive, or so he had said. He wanted answers to his questions, a balm on his burning curiosity. The famed general would not have what he wanted from me.

Breathing raggedly, I slipped my hands underneath my body and shoved myself upward. A rough cry ripped from my throat as I bent, sliding my knees forward so I could kneel against the cell bars. I paused to catch my breath. Warm blood trickled down my face and the indentation of my spine. The blast had done some damage, I reckoned, but I could not know how much. There was so little time to examine the possibilities.

Nyx, why so much fire? I told you to be cautious. This was not caution. It was a mistake. I should never have let Nyx go alone. I should never have tasked him with something of that magnitude. An angry, frightened snarl curled from my lips, cutting through the fog in my mind. This was my justice, my agony. How had it come to this? I had escaped the burning of Carfuinel only to be roasted alive in the pits of a slaver's hold.

Smoke, like the haze of memory, fogged my gaze. My bloodied forehead rested against the flaking iron bars, but my mind saw the last day of Carfuinel. My mother stood tall and straight before the pyre of the dead, awaiting the moment when she would join my father somewhere inside the dancing flames. She had been proud until the last, never showing the fear that ate away inside her, but she had bought my life with hers. I could not die here without avenging her, without showing the same strength and resolve that she had shown.

I gripped the bars with trembling hands. My oath was everything. It was all that kept me from giving up and dying on this cold, filthy floor. Caspon could not die but by my hand. My hands tugged ineffectually at the padlock on the door, a dam in the river of my resolve.

"Bird?" A hissed whisper from the end of the hall.

I stopped, still gripping the iron with white fingers. My throat would not work, though my mouth moved. Everything was hazy still.

"Bird!" The voice was more urgent, coming toward me.

I blinked. "Nyx," I breathed. My throat burned, making speech painful and raspy. A blood-matted tendril of hair curled along my cheek, making the skin itch.

Nyx slipped wraithlike down the corridor, coming through the dust and smoke to my cell. His hands caught mine over the padlock, holding them to the iron. His gray eyes were wide and round as he stared at me. "Oh gods, Bird. What did he do to you?"

I did not want to answer as my knees dug into the gritty floor of the shadowy cell. I tried to rise to my feet but my deadened legs could not bear the weight. I sighed as I slumped again to my knees, feeling useless and pathetic.

"Wait, stop," Nyx protested, dropping to his own knees beyond the bars. He fumbled with one of his boots.

"Talros," I began, then paused to regain control of my muscles. "He is . . . hunting you."

"I know," Nyx answered. "I passed them outside. They're fighting the flames now, so I think we have some time." He took a dagger out of his boot and began to pick at the padlock. I dropped my hands to the crossbar, holding myself up.

"I told you . . . to be cautious. This is too much."

"It's distracting them, isn't it?" He did not pause in his work. I could hear the dagger scraping and rasping in the lock and knew that the blade would be ruined.

"Talros is cunning, Nyx. More . . . dangerous than we thought. Leave me." It was a hard thing to say, painful almost, but it needed to be heard. He needed to listen for once in his ill-gotten life. Ever minute spent in my presence was a thread added to the hangman's noose.

"I can't do that!" Nyx's stormy eyes burned with fierce intensity. "I won't do that. Don't say that again."

I was torn. *Do not stay because of me,* I wanted to cry. *I am not worthy of your loyalty.* Keeping in this vein would get Nyx killed, certain as summer, and I flinched from having more blood on my hands. My throat worked, but no words emerged. My head sank against the flaking iron bars, which warmed by the minute. I heard the halfblood boy struggle with the lock, grunting and cursing under his breath.

"If it will not open, Nyx, go." The smoke was growing thicker, the air hotter. I could no longer hear the voices of the soldiers outside. My lungs burned and Nyx coughed several times, never pausing in his work. He did not even stop long enough to reply to my comment. I had expected that of him.

Something snapped near my ear and the hinges groaned like dying men. I blinked my weariness away, tried to push my weight back onto my knees, and succeeded. "It is open?" I asked, feeling a warmth in the pit of my stomach that I had not felt in forever.

Nyx looked as surprised as I felt. He sat back on his haunches, the dagger loose in his hand. "I think so," he answered, and reached out to tug on the bars. When the bars slid forward, I dragged myself to my feet, fighting the pain and stiffness and vertigo.

I did not ask him for aid—my pride would not allow it—but I could not refuse him when he placed one of my arms across his shoulders and helped me from Caspon's gaol, bearing my weight without comment. We went out of the broken door at the end of the corridor, knocked off-hinge by the firedust blast. Nyx held the dagger loosely in his hand, and I took it from him, wanting the feel of strength and steel and death in my hand. Black smoke roiled through the doorway, thick and acrid.

We pushed into the rolling smoke and vanished. I could barely see the grass and gravel under my feet, and we were soon crawling on our bellies like snakes across the manor grounds, coughing soot from our lungs as our eyes watered and burned. I dragged my battered body as quickly as I could, but Nyx slunk faster. I kept his boots close to my grasping hands, trying not to let him get too far ahead. I wanted neither of us lost here.

I could hear the soldiers bellowing through the gloom. The sound echoed and wavered, leaving me unable to discern their positions on the manor grounds. My fingers clenched hard on the dagger, pressing knuckles into the dirt. The air was hot, filling my throat and lungs with smoke. Clenching my teeth, knowing that if the soldiers stumbled upon us or if we lingered too long near the fire then we were dead, I pushed forward, nudging Nyx's feet with my shoulder.

"Hurry," I hissed. "To the fence." I stuck the dagger in my belt, wanting both hands free to claw at the packed soil and matted grass. I could not see the stone fence near the back corner of the manor grounds, but I knew it was there. I knew these grounds like I knew the scars on my body.

"Go in front," Nyx whispered. "I can't see!"

I pushed ahead, feeling the fiery strain in each muscle, biting back screams of pain, and crawled on my belly under the smoke. Nyx touched my boots every once and again, just as I had done to him so that we could not lose each other in the chaos. Voices cried and called all around us. Somewhere there were soldiers. Somewhere there was Talros. I went faster, determined to make the fence before something untoward occurred.

By luck or by fate, we made it to the stone fence situated in the rear corner of Caspon's sprawling abode. I pressed against the stone for a moment, catching my breath and gathering strength enough to go over. Nyx came up beside me and knelt on one knee, cupping his hands before him. "I'll boost you," he said. I took his offer with a relieved, grateful sigh.

It took most of my strength to grab Nyx's forearms and help him over once my feet touched the ground outside of Caspon's manor. The smoke rolled over the city, hiding our soot-blackened skin in its writhing embrace. We ran, light and swift as shadows among the frantic citizens of the town. We melded with the panicked townsfolk fleeing with children and livestock and savings, dodging those brave enough to haul sloshing buckets of water and heavy woolen blankets and praying to smother the flames before they spread beyond the boundaries of the manor.

In the panic, it was easy to disappear. Talros, if he had survived, would be hard-pressed to find us again. Still, my mind danced two steps ahead. I grabbed Nyx's sleeve as we passed down an alleyway, pulling him into the shelter of a temple's low eaves. The priests were in the courtyard, trying to protect their well from a few men foolhardy enough to take the god's water for their own.

"Hurry," I hissed, and slipped around the corner. Nyx followed me and together we slid through the front door of Oryn Deepwater's temple and hurried across the transept to the cloisters. Nyx snagged a chalice of blessed water from the side-table as we went, only daring it because the pews were empty.

In an instant, we were situated inside the smallest of the private prayer-rooms. The floor was cold flagstone marred by a single kneeling pillow while the walls were slats of ash wood dotted with small tapestries depicting religious myths. The woven-reed ceiling was quite low. I could have touched it without standing on my toes. Nyx latched the door behind us. Now, away from the smoke and panic, I could see his face. It was streaked with grime and soot. Ashes clung to his short hair and matted the lashes of his eyes. The whiteness of his teeth stood out in stark relief, and I imagined that I did not look much different.

"Bird!" he cried, finally looking at me. "There's so much blood." He pulled at the pouch on my belt. "Get your bandages. What did he do to you?"

I reached trembling hands to the pouch and opened it, pulling handfuls of bandages and medicinal herbs to the floor. Nyx helped me remove my tunic, leaving me cold and pale in my bandeau and breeches. I pressed a thick wad of fabric to the arrow wound while I told Nyx which herbs to put on the smaller injuries.

"Marigold," I said, "the dry orange tufts. Crumble it in your hands and put it directly on the wound." I bit my lips as he pressed his fingers too hard against a bruise. "Now use comfrey, in the small blue bag. After that, we can wrap the bandanges."

I had several yards of cotton and linen bandages, a necessity in my profession. I had been hurt before but never like this. The injuries Talros had inflicted would probably take the majority of my wrappings and herbs. When a touch of anger filled me at the thought of having to replenish all my supplies, I knew I was not thinking straight.

"Yes," Nyx said, wrapping me in fabric. "That big one, though, Bird; it looks very deep."

I grunted. "We will have to wash it well and pack it before stitching."

"Stitching? Me?" Nyx gasped. "I don't know."

"Do not worry about that." I would do it if he would not. There was not time for dawdling and hesitatance.

When Nyx finished with the other wounds, he knelt before me with the chalice in hand. "Just pour?" he asked.

"Slowly," I answered, pulling the thick fabric pad away from my clavicle. "It will bleed, so beware." I bit my tongue, hoping there was nothing left of the arrowhead or shaft in the wound. Surely I would have felt it, but still, I did not want to reach dirty fingers inside my flesh to pull it out.

When the water ran down my flesh and into the gash, I flinched and closed my eyes. I could feel warm blood coming out with the water. I kept the pad pressed to my skin and leaned fornward to keep the fluids from staining my bandeau. After a moment, I looked. There was no debris coming out with the blood. It was clean and red.

"Good," I said. "Stop." Careful not not aggravate the wound, I reached down and picked a few herbs, rolled them in my palm, and hissed with pain as I pushed them into the hole made by the arrow. Nyx looked on with wide eyes and a sick grimace on his face.

I reached down again and pulled a curved needle and spool of gray thread from the pouch. After a few tries, I threaded the eye, then broke the string so that it was a few inches long. This would be hard, I thought, but certainly no harder than being shot. I set the point against my flesh, just beside the small wound, breathed deep, and pushed. I gritted my teeth and continued until I had three small stitches holding my flesh together. I knotted the ends together, set the needle down, and swallowed the gorge in my throat.

"Gods, Bird," Nyx said, face pale.

"Some water, please," I said, "then I think I might rest for a bit."

"Yes, of course," Nyx replied, hurrying to refill the chalice from the fountain beyond the door. I slept before he returned, though I feared Talros or the flames might reach us before I woke. I could not stop it. My body demanded rest and it would have it whether I wanted it or not.

I woke sometime later. Nyx sat beside me, his fingers light and careful on my hair.

"How long?" I whispered.

"An hour or two," Nyx answered, knowing what I meant. "No one has come by yet."

I struggled to sit and he helped me lean against the wall, watching my stitches to make sure they were still intact, and helped me pulled my tunic back on. I had not been able to put it on before sleep took me.

Nyx held the chalice out to me. "Feels a bit strange to drink blessed water like this," he said with the barest hint of humor in his voice.

I took the large cup and drank, feeling my throat muscles cry in pain at the movement. "If Oryn minds," I replied dryly, "he can complain to me directly." Nyx made a sound in his throat at this, but looked like he wanted to laugh. That was good. Humor was better than fear.

"Well," the boy said. "Might as well make that two of us." He drank from the chalice. A tendril of clear water dripped from the corner of his mouth, leaving a clean trail on his skin.

"Thank you," I said, surprising myself, "for setting me free of the cell. You saved my life."

Nyx set the cup on the stone floor. "I couldn't leave you there, Bird. You saved me, and it was my turn to repay the favor. Besides, you would have done the same for me, I think."

I would have. I knew it without any thought required, but I did not want Nyx dragged into my underworld. He was already stepping down to my level and I wanted him to stop, to stay where he was. "Whatever debt you had is repaid now," I said.

It was the tone of my voice that focused his attention on me, intense and wary. His face was flat and opaque. "That is what you think of me?" he asked. "After everything we've done, this is what you say?"

"I am not asking you to leave me again, Nyx," I protested, although that was exactly what I was doing. "I just . . . wanted you to know." I felt brainless and insipid, trying to explain myself without wounding him. I was still an assassin with one more mark to find. But he knew this, of course. Rehashing the same excuse was worthless, so I gave up. Instead, I sat on the pillow and leaned against the wall, taking another pull from the chalice, and let my eyes fall half-closed. I was exhausted, so tired it felt like my bones were coming apart at the seams. I leaned my head against the wall, aware that he was watching me. I could not make myself care.

"Do you know what I think of you?" Nyx asked. My eyes fluttered open, but he went on before I could speak. "I don't think you are a coward or a demon. You are someone who never runs from a situation calling for courage. You have a heart and mind that sometimes astonishes me, but never scares me. I think that you are brave and beautiful, and that you will defeat whatever is devastating you."

I could say nothing in the face of such a speech. No one had ever said such a thing to me before, brilliant and cutting as shattered glass. I could say nothing; words had abandoned me. Prickles of heat touched the backs of my eyes, the beginnings of tears that I would not allow to fall. Nyx, seeing the look on my face, inched closer and so very tentatively put his arms around me, holding me as I had not been held in years. Carefully, feeling that I might break, I lifted my arms and slid them around his waist for just a moment. After five heartbeats I moved away, uncomfortable and unused to the idea of physical contact. I could feel my cheeks burning under their layer of ash and dust. Nyx looked away, eyes falling to the silver chalice beside my knees.

"I. . ." he started, overlapping my own voice as we spoke the same word. He grinned sheepishly. For some reason, all the anxiety flowed out of me and I breathed easy. Nyx was a friend, I realized. A true friend, and I was lucky to have him.

Nyx returned to me my bow and quiver and the dagger he had used to pick the lock of my cell door. When my fingers touched the dagger, it was as if lightning struck me. This had been my blade once, the one I had chosen before my father and Rellas. The sheath was gone, but that did not matter. The flint gleamed like sunlight on water, and I held it reverently. A piece of my lost childhood had come home. Nyx must have found it in the manor, in Caspon's room. It had been under my nose all this time and I had never known. I felt strange with the dagger in my hands; it somehow felt like it did not belong there. My good memories were tainted once more by the Nightingale's touch.

"Is something wrong?" Nyx asked, lifting his eyes to mine.

"No, everything is fine." I sheathed the dagger in my boot. "Nyx, where did you get that dagger?"

A ragged breath left him. "In the map room. There was so much stuff in there but that's the only thing I had time to grab."

"Tell me."

"I went in like you said, following the back steps in the servant's quarters to the rear hallway. Every footstep I heard made me want to vomit with fear, but I kept going. When I found the map room, I was in awe. So many trinkets and baubles and chests of glittering things." His face went pale with remembrance. "I found the maps in the wardrobes on the back wall. Piles and piles of them. I pulled them all out onto the floor, digging for one with anthehomes on it. The footsteps kept passing; they sounded like Weapons' boots. They bumped the closed door once and it was enough to make my heart leap into my throat."

He paused to think. My stomach churned. They had been so close to him. If the door had not been hidden as part of the wall, he might have been found. I clenched a hand against my stomach, willing the sour fear to subside. "What then?" I prodded.

"When the Weapon bumped the door, I snatched the closest blade I could find and held it ready, just in case. But then they started talking. I heard them mention you, that you were captured and locked in Caspon's gaol. I knew I had to do something, anything, that could help you. So, I found a flint and striker on the table and set the maps on fire once the bootsteps faded."

My breath left me and I pressed a quick hand to the stiches on my chest. "How did you escape?"

"I opened the door. The fire was still small then, and I ran as fast as I could back to the stairs. By the time I reached the hedge, I could smell smoke. Everyone panicked and that gave me the opportunity to find you. It was only once I got here that I realized I still had the dagger."

I checked my bandages to allow me a moment to compose my face. He had done the impossible, without training or study. He had broken into Caspon's private room and destroyed it under the Weapons' noses. He had then escaped and broken me out of gaol. How was it possible? The thought of Lenos touched my mind, full of yellow eyes and white teeth and starlit fury, then I pushed it away.

"You did very well," I said. "Very well. And now we will need to watch for Talros and his soldiers. They may have left the fire to others." A plan was forming in my head despite the dull throb behind my eyes and the ache in my throat and lungs. I had a scratched dagger, a bow and a handful of arrows. Not exactly an arsenal, but it would have to do. I let Nyx keep the bow and quiver; as long as I had a blade I felt powerful. And I wanted to be close enough to see the fear in Caspon's eyes when I gutted him.

I looked around the small room, noting the empty chalice on its side in the corner. A few hours had passed since we had locked the door of the cloister. There were occasional voices outside, people calling for the priests and for water. The fire still burned, it seemed, but I did not think it had spread beyond the fences of the manor. I wiped a hand across my tired eyes. I did not feel quite as horrible as I had when I was locked in Caspon's cell, and most of my wounds had stopped bleeding.

"Should we wait until dark to leave?" Nyx asked.

"If possible," I said, hearing approaching footsteps. We could have left earlier, and probably should have, but we were both caught up in the cool water and relative quiet. "A worshipper?" I clenched my hands against the stone floor, ready to leap into the face of whoever approached.

Nyx raised his voice and began to pray, reciting chants that I had not heard before. The purpose of this praying was to let the approaching parishioner know that this particular cloister was occupied. I did not know *cardeai* religious rituals, and barely remembered those of the anthelai. If there was a proper way to pray, I did not know it, nor did I care to learn. If the gods wanted to speak with me, they could come down and do it themselves. I had no use for gods, not with the life they had meted for me.

The footsteps retreated and I sighed in relief. Once the worshipper left, Nyx and I resumed his Anilo lessons. He was a quick study, and in a few months he would be close to fluent. The thought saddened me. I still did not think that I would be alive a few days from now, much less months, but I did not say this aloud. The time for speaking my regrets and wishes was over. Action was once again all that counted.

We stayed there until our ears told us we were finally alone in the temple. We refilled the chalice from the small wall fountain and retreated to the cloister to drink our fill and wash what ash we could from our faces. When the day stretched into dusk, we ventured from the cloister and left the temple without incident.

There were soldiers in the lanes, but we were ready for them. I knew a variety of shortcuts and rarely used pathways through Benthol and we used them whenever possible, along with rooftops and eaves. This did not guarantee our safety, however, and our eyes and ears were on constant alert. I refused to be captured again, not with the end once more in sight.

Nyx and I made our way to the abandoned section of buildings near the rear of the city. The glow of the fire marred the horizon, turning a third of the sky gleaming orange. I could still see smoke billowing high, looking like strange storm clouds hovering above the city.

"Careful," I hissed. "Quickly now." Together we slipped through the growing darkness like wraiths, coming down the slight hill near the mummers' pit, then ducking behind the slender trees near the ringed benches. The thick dirt swallowed any sounds our feet might have made, and I was glad for the soot that covered our bodies, hiding the gleam of belt buckles and other metallic pieces of our effects. We were shadows and wind.

"Keep watch," I whispered, tapping the quiver on Nyx's belt, then knelt and took my chosen black dagger from the sheath sewn into my boot. How appropriate it had turned out to be, black, with the bird symbol on the hilt. How apt.

The soldiers' cries in the distance and the morning-bright glow of the fire on the horizon seemed like the fading of a dream upon waking. I was here, at the last, and I was ready to bury my blade in the man who had destroyed the very fabric of my life. The broken doorway gaped in the row of ramshackle, weathered buildings. Talros was not there this time to stop me, to try and thwart the yearnings of my heart and the strength of my will.

The blackness of the portal beckoned me closer. There was no turning back. This was the end for one of us, Caspon or me. One of us would die before the morrow.

A wolf howled at Caspon's door, ready to rip the flesh from his throat before a dagger buried itself between the ribs to seek his heart.

An almost insatiable urge to bellow hit Talros when he saw the ruined gaol. Instead, he gritted his teeth so hard he thought they might break. His anger began to boil under the surface of his skin, and he was already red and hot from battling the flames. Sweat dripped into his eyes and, with a hard swipe of his wrist, he wiped it away.

The Nightingale was gone and the door to her cell hung open. It was a sight Talros had not thought to see, not once he had finally captured her. The king would be furious if he knew. For years, he had tracked the assassin. For years, he had dreamed of the day when he captured the killer and brought him to justice. The fact that the assassin was a female and child did not matter. Justice mattered, appeasing the king mattered, and the work of years had just fled from under his very nose.

Talros did not often get angry, but the hot rage built under his flesh. Leaving the ruins of the gaol, he emerged back into the frantic crush of people on the grounds. Water splashed from buckets and voices echoed though the smoke but Talros was focused.

The king was correct. The assassin was too dangerous and too cunning to let live. The only way to keep her from escaping was to kill her. She had broken out from gaol, through iron bars and stone walls and fire. Surely her halfblood friend had helped, but it was the assassin who worried Talros. She had killed many times. She would do so again until she was stopped. It was a pattern Talros had seen before in his career. Certainly, the Nightingale was no exception. If she could break free of the Weapons, the king's elite force, then she was destined to die.

Talros' questions could not matter any longer. If more halfbloods were in Caesia, he would find them without the Nightingale's aid. If the anthelai planned to sweep down from their dirt-floored bowers onto the people Talros was sworn to protect, then he would fight them back without the assassin's answers.

"General! The townsfolk have come with aid," a Weapon cried, coming forward to stand at Talros' shoulder. The smoke eddied around them, acrid from burning parchment, leather, and wood in the basement of the manor.

"Good, set them to work," Talros commanded. "Form a line from the well against the rear wall."

"Yes, General," the Weapon said, snapping a salute before disappearing into the murk.

General Astin Talros could not worry about the manor. He did not fear that the flames would reach the bulk of southern Benthol. Stone roads and wide areas of soil surrounded the grounds and made an effective firebreak, or so Talros hoped. He made his way to the well along the back wall. Two Weapons stood there, passing buckets to members of the city guard.

"You two," Talros said. "Come with me." He did not want to create more panic by explaining that the Nightingale had escaped. Once free of the press of the crowd, he would tell his soldiers more. The hunt for the Nightingale had resumed, and Talros thought he knew where she was going.

Chapter 22

I WAS AFRAID. That was something I could not deny. All the years I had spent in captivity had been spent training for this moment, for this goal. I could not think of what might happen afterward, if there was an afterward. There were too many questions in the back of my mind. What would happen to me when Caspon finally died? What would happen to Nyx should I fail?

My palm was sweaty but sure on the hilt of my knife as we crept across the threshold of the dilapidated house. The glow of the fire flickered in Nyx's eyes as he glanced around the shadowed overhang of the rotten roof.

"It feels heavy here," he whispered.

"Yes," I agreed, feeling the weight of my immediate future bearing down on my thin shoulders. I took a deep breath, filling my lungs until they burned, then slowly set it free. "Come. Have the bow ready."

I crept through the flickering shadows, feeling cool air on my sweat-damp skin. Nyx was four paces behind, nearly silent, and for a moment I was proud. He had come a long way since we met, and I now thought him more cautious and careful and anthela-like. Nyx could do well in the world now without having to hide away in his deceased grandparents' farmhouse. I was glad for that.

"Won't he know you're here?" Nyx asked.

I paused at the entrance of a ruined hallway, smelling rot and dust and mildew from the decaying wood and thatch. "Probably," I answered, then turned to look at the echoes of the fire in his dark eyes. A breeze brushed my face as it swept through the ragged holes in the walls. "This entrance was designed by a spy in Caspon's employ, so I expect some impediment on the other side. Be watchful."

The wood barely creaked under the soft, worn soles of my boots. Dust and grime lay thick on the boards, cushioning our steps. Down the rotting hallway we went, disappearing into the shadows. The flicker of the flames receded until only the memory of its light remained. We went onward, moving carefully at the end of the corridor. A few broken steps led down into a cellar carved from the dark clay earth. This was where the first bead of terrible longing slipped into my veins.

I turned, no longer feeling Nyx's eyes on my back, and remembered what I had found, several years ago. *Twelve paces forward from the bottom step, eight to the left, then turn around.* I followed the instructions in my head, knelt down, and swept the cold soil from the door sunk in the earth.

"Last chance, Nyx. There is no returning from this," I whispered, peering up through the gloom to gaze upon the boy. My friend.

"I will see this through with you," he replied, though I heard the faint tremor in his voice. I did not blame him, for my heart quavered.

The door was locked, as I had known it would be, so I used a trick I had learned from my dealings with the spymaster. I took a handful of cloth from the pouch at my waist and used it to muffle the noise of the hinges as I dismantled them, pulling the long bar from the rings. The iron was rusted and brittle, showing no evidence of use. Caspon knew about this door, I was certain, but he had no reason to think I did. He would find there were many things he did not know about me.

I tossed the iron bars into the corner and Nyx and I pulled the door from the earth's grasp. Clumps of wet dirt fell into the newly made hole. This had been put in place by the original homeowners, I assumed, given that the hinges were on the outside. A cold cellar for storing food during the summer, one that Caspon had hollowed out further for his own use. I had not been any deeper into the lair than this, and wondered if this was the right way to go about things. If the tunnel beyond was impassable, my heart might burst from pure rage and frustration.

The hole was a skull's eye peering up at me. I leaned forward and listened, breathed, strained for any *cardea* sign. There was nothing but utter blackness and still silence. The air was cold as I lowered myself into the hole, and I felt flecks of dirt patter my shoulders as Nyx came down after me. There were neither ladders nor rungs to ascend. We were in the belly of the beast now.

I sucked in a deep breath through my mouth to steady my trembling nerves. Nyx stayed behind me as we crept forward, the bow ever ready. I kept my dagger in hand, ready to slash out at the first guard that sighted our presence. Caspon would not escape again. This chance could well be my last.

A cast-iron, grid-work door, much like one to a cell, halted our progress. I had half-expected such a thing, but my soft growl of consternation could not be contained. I tested it, pushing with the palms of my hands, but the door was locked.

"The spy didn't tell you of this obstacle?" Nyx breathed in my ear.

"No, he told me nothing of this place. We never went inside." I looked at the door. These hinges would not be broken, as they were on the other side of the iron and much thicker than those hidden on the previous, smaller door. "Wait. Quickly, back into the shadows!" I hissed, pushing Nyx far back into the tunnel.

A tendril of sound had touched me, quite like a voice, approaching our position. If someone found us here, all was lost. "Give me the bow," I whispered, taking the weapon from Nyx while crouching on my haunches in the dimness. I nocked an arrow to the string, pulled back slightly, and waited while my injuries screamed in protest.

The voice was soft and unsure, somewhat overshadowed by the footsteps accompanying it. "Under the latch," the man repeated to himself. "Carefully, carefully under the latch." He turned the corner and I saw him in the light of the lantern he carried. It was Bennic, Caspon's advisor. My heart seized. He had been an accomplice in my nightmare life.

My fingers twitched on the string, but I did not release. Bennic came closer, that strange mantra on his lips, watching his feet as he walked. His free hand went to his waist and came back with a ring of keys. Cold desire flowered in my chest. Those keys would be mine, as would that man's life.

I waited until he was at the door with the key in the latch before I stepped into the light of the lantern, bow raised and ready. "Dear Bennic, send a greeting to Énas for me," I said. His head jerked up, terror writ large on his face and, at the moment recognition dawned in his eyes, I set the arrow free. Caspon's advisor died with my alias quiet on his lips and blood running from his punctured throat. Wordlessly, I handed the bow back to Nyx and stepped forward to unlock the door.

"Bird," he began unsteadily.

"Silence now," I said and knelt to loot the advisor's corpse. I took his purse, feeling the heavy weight of coins, along with the small knife on his belt and the silver pin in his collar. The small waterproofed leather pouch near his belt buckle gave me pause. Was that what he had meant to place under the latch, as he said? I took the little bag and picked open the knot.

My blood went gelid at the sight of the thimbleful of gray powder. *Oh, dear gods!*. Firedust! He was trying to place firedust in the door to blow me into pieces when I came for him. I sank into the soil, unable to take my eyes from the death in my hand. I wanted to throw it away, to heave it deep into the blackness beyond the lantern light, but a forceful touch would bring the dust to life. As would a breath of flame or flick of dampness. Firedust was a tetchy, fickle thing. Slowly, I set the small pouch into a larger one situated on my belt. I could not get rid of it without anxiety, so I would keep it for now. Just in case. But I could feel it eating at me, testing my resolve and my calm. I placated myself with a simple thought: if I was killed in the attack on Caspon, the firedust might very well do my job for me. It would have done it to Nyx and me had Bennic fallen at a different angle.

I breathed deep as I gathered myself. Now was not the time for panic and Nyx could not know what had almost occurred. I was iron. I was steel. I was the fangs in the mouth of the slavering wolf. It was time to continue on. I stood, taking a steady grip on my knife, and motioned for Nyx to follow.

We slunk around the corner, leaving the lantern behind. It still cast enough reflected light for us to see shapes in the gloom. There were no guards, which made me wonder. It seemed Caspon did not trust anyone but Bennic enough to know about this place. I wondered vaguely how Nichil had found it, but then put the thought away. He had been a spy, after all.

I strained my ears and my eyes for any sign of Caspon, but there was nothing. My heart pounded in my chest. Suppose he was not here? I had never considered that before. *Stop it!* my mind cried.

He is here or he is not. This panic will change nothing. He will not escape, not even if I have to chase him to the ends of the world. Nyx touched my elbow, then, breaking my racing thoughts in twain.

"There is a light ahead. I don't think it's a lantern."

I looked harder. No, I did not think it was a lantern either. It was a light shining underneath a closed door, flickering like flames. A fireplace, my heart whispered. I tucked my back against the cold wall, rough planks reinforcing the thick dark soil behind them, and put a finger to my lips, motioning Nyx into absolute silence. Tightening my grip on the dagger, I slunk forward.

I could hear very little over the pounding of my heart. The door loomed close, overwhelming and dark, a tangible threat. Swallowing, I kept my back to the wall and reached out a hand to crack open the portal. Swiftly, I pivoted into the doorway, dagger ready to sink into the hated man's heart.

There was nothing. The room was empty. I swallowed my snarl of thwarted rage, swallowed the thunder of my heart, feeling the roaring heat sink down into the coils of my veins. Nyx pushed past me with single-minded purpose, nudging my stiff form aside. I watched with muted anxiety as he strode to the table laden with fruits, bread, and meat and began to eat.

"What are you doing?" I whispered, quickly coming into the room and closing the door behind us so we would not be seen by anyone approaching in the hall.

"Eating," he said around a mouthful of apple, bits of rind and flesh flecking from his lips. "I'm starving. Can't remember the last time I ate more than a bite." He finished the apple, turned to grab a silver pitcher from the table, and drank straight from the lip. He smacked his lips, holding the pitcher in both hands. "Good cider," he pronounced.

"We do not even know why this is here!" I hissed. "It could be a trap. Poison. Caspon could be coming even now!"

"So be it," Nyx retorted. "At least I'll die with a full belly." He did not even know that his words hurt me as he plunged back to the tables. He did not seem to trust my judgment, my superior knowledge of these things. Caspon was nothing if not devious. If he knew I was coming for him, then this spread could be poisoned. I was hungry, ravenous, but this little spark of thought kept me from partaking. I would not die writhing and vomiting on the floor. I feared for Nyx, but it was too late to do anything. If the food was poisoned, he would die. I knew some remedies, but had nothing with me. With my heart in my throat, I watched—and waited.

Eighty-seven heartbeats later, nothing had happened. I had watched Nyx devour everything he could get his hands on with no ill effects. My stomach would no longer let me stand idly. I went forward and carefully sipped from a pitcher of cool water. Nothing seemed wrong with it; there were no strange tastes. I drank enough to dull the hunger pangs. My stomach churned with too much anxiety for food.

"Come away now," I said to Nyx, taking him by the sleeve. "We cannot linger here any longer."

"I know, I know. Sorry," he said, wiping his lips with his free arm. "Can I take some with us?"

"How?" I asked, unable to hide the trace of disgust in my voice. He was insistent on endangering us. The lighter we traveled the less noise we made. Carrying food around without the guarantee of immediate survival was nothing but foolish.

With my knife, Nyx cut a large square of tablecloth and dumped an armful of fruit and bread into the middle of it, then tied the ends together to create a bundle. He attached this to his back with two more strips of cloth, carrying my bow in his hands to make room. The quiver hung from his belt.

"Drop it if it hinders you. Immediately," I told him, not taking my eyes from his.

"I will. I mean it."

I nodded and went back to the door, Nyx close behind. The water settled like a lead weight in the pit of my stomach and, combined with fear, made me nauseous. Bennic was dead. One man down. Taking a deep breath, I opened the door and stepped out into the hallway.

The sound of heavy bootsteps on flagstone came without warning, and in an instant I was sprinting down the corridor with my knife in hand. The doorknob of the next left-side door had turned; the hinges creaked as the heavy door began to swing open. Two guards in felt and chainmail stepped out, looked in the wrong direction, and died as my blade slashed twice, the first sinking into the weak bone behind the ear, the second backhand across the great veins in the throat.

I loosened my knees, absorbing the weight as my feet hit the ground, and whirled toward the open doorway. One guard was rising from his bedroll, half-tangled in the sheet. He died before he could shout, my dagger in his eye. The bloodlust was on me; I knew I was close. I did not stop to think. One closed door in the back corner, flickering lantern light below the crack. Now or never.

I pivoted to face Nyx, not caring that his face was ashen. "Stay," I hissed, stabbing a finger downward. "Remember our plan." He nodded once, jerkily, and held the bow ready. I adjusted my grip on the sweat-slick hilt of my dark dagger, and entered the unlocked door.

Caspon's back was to me; he tinkered with something on the table before him. I heard the clink of metal and stone. "Bennic, have I not made myself clear? I will eat later!" A terrible thrill shot through me. My blood bubbled with hatred but my mind was utterly clear.

"My master," I announced, holding my hand low so that the dagger was obscured by my thigh, "I have come to report."

The large man whirled with speed of which I had not thought him capable, screeching the chair against the flagstones. I caught the flash of uncertainty upon his features before he schooled them. "Have you now?" he said.

"I was not able to complete my mission. Hanlon Evoll yet lives. And General Talros has burnt your manor to the ground."

Anger flickered across his face. "I see," he said. "Find Bennic and—"

"Bennic is dead." I tried not to clench my teeth. Without taking my eyes from my enslaver, I reached behind me and latched the door. "I killed him." With my free hand, I removed the false collar and was gratified to see Caspon's eyes grow wide when I tossed the length of leather at his feet. "I am no one's slave," I snarled, taking a step forward and drawing the dagger into view. Caspon's face went pale. "Your guards are dead also," I said. "Call for them if you wish."

"This is how you repay my kindness?" Caspon asked. "With threats?"

"Kindness?" I sneered. "Threats?" I took another step forward. He took two back. "What kindness would that be? Killing my family and burning the corpses? Enslaving me to kill for you?

What a strange notion. And I do not make threats, dear master, but promises."

"It was a kindness not to kill you in the forest. My men wanted to use you for sport, to hunt you like dogs set on a hare."

I snarled, but kept my temper reined. "Why choose me when you could hire a better-trained assassin?"

"Ah," Caspon sighed. "A slave such as you would ask no questions, could grow no conscience. Utterly and completely enthralled to me and my desires. And besides, a hired man needs pay. A halfblood slave, on the other hand, is too wonderful and terrible a creature to resist. I would have the only one in the world and all I would need to invest is time! What man would not wish for that?"

"Do you not understand that I loathe you? Despise you? I dream at night of your death and the worms feasting on your bloated flesh." I was breathing heavily, enraged and somewhat confused. Caspon was not acting with the terror I had imagined.

He smiled. "And so, even without the collar, you are mine. We will always be intertwined, Nightingale. I will live in your thoughts forever."

"No!" I cried. "You will not!"

He laughed ruefully. "With your abilities, I would have ruled all the world, taking down guild after guild, king after king, until I was proven strongest. My name would have lived through the ages as a conqueror. As the god that tamed the halfblood demon!"

"No." I could not imagine the vastness of the world, nor the mind that could fathom ruling its entirety. "Now no one will remember you in a handful of years."

"They will. Not as I planned, but Talros' pursuit of you has guaranteed my legacy. My name will be connected with yours, with the power used to bind you, and with the vast records I keep. Lorcen Caspon will equal power even unto the depths of the ages." His voice was triumphant, and it was then I realized that Caspon either did not fear me or he was not afraid to die. Neither mattered; only his blood did.

"Wrong again." I advanced another step. "You will still be forgotten. I was the one in the forefront while you hid in the shadows. It seems that only Talros knows you are connected with me. If he happens to die before he speaks of you, what do you have then? Your records are burned, all of them indecipherable piles of char and soot. The beryl might be lost, but there is a chance no one has connected me to it or that it has even been found. Your precious stone could be naught but a bauble in a mummer's cart." I smirked at him. "So even you will be lost, faded into distant memory, and then gone like a wisp of smoke on a swift breeze."

"Oh, pretty words," he snarled, a pulsing vein standing out in his forehead. "Bennic pleaded with me to kill you years ago. It is to my shame that I did not. You think you are mighty now that the stone is gone? Then you are a fool." He continued onward without pause. "I do not need you any longer, Nightingale. I can find another. I could raise an army of them! Not all maps are on parchment." He tapped his forehead, glaring at me.

I hissed like a panther. "I regret all the lives I have taken, all the pain I have caused. I may never be forgiven what I have done. My heart weeps for the atrocities I have committed and I will live with that pain for the rest of my life. But you, Caspon; your death I will *savor*." I smiled, and advanced. The time for talking was over.

Caspon did not like my savage expression, it seemed, for he backed up until his rear hit the edge of the table. Though he tried for stealth, I saw one of his hands creep to the tabletop to grab the pile of steel and stone. I dodged as he whipped the bola toward me, keeping low and swift as the stone balls whisked over my head. It was fortunate for me that he had no skill in aiming.

I moved sideways, slipping toward my tormentor as the bola cracked against the wall. I heard Nyx cry out in surprise, but he did not enter the room. Caspon vaulted across the table, grabbing a length of chain from his workspace. I did not know nor care what he had been using it for; its current purpose was foremost in my mind.

I ducked under his first swing, the hissing chain missing me by several inches, and shot toward him like an arrow. He could not hit me with the chain when I was close, and he kept backing away, trying for range. But Caspon was no warrior. Others did his fighting for him. So when I pounced, driving him to the floor with my weight on his chest, he offered no skilled resistance.

He squealed with fear when my blade touched his throat. "And to think," I snarled, "that I was afraid of this. Afraid of you. Coward!" He had dropped the chain; it lay inches from his frozen fingers. I wanted desperately to drive my blade into his throat with both hands, but I would never again kill an unarmed man. "Pick it up," I hissed.

His eyes were wide, fearful, but anger still swirled in their murky depths. "I—"

"Do it!"

His fingers flicked out, touched the chain tentatively, and then slowly curled around the links. "You wouldn't dare—"

But I did. I slammed my dagger into the hollow space above the dent in his collarbone, feeling hot blood on my hands and the pain of rage and bloodlust and liberation in my heart. My enslaver's breath rushed forth, hot and moist, into my face as I plunged the dagger down again and again and again. His body twisted and writhed, shuddering into stillness. A primal howl of triumph soared from my throat. I had done it! Caspon was dead!

"Bird, let me in! Hurry!"

I leapt to my feet, whirling around with my bloody dagger still in hand. Below me, Caspon's body wept blood from dozens of wounds. His dead face was pale, terrified, defeated. I crossed to the door and unlatched it, and I looked at the boy without speaking, feeling my triumph course like fire through my veins. The door stood open, unsafe.

"I heard him. He's coming!" Nyx cried.

"Talros?" I said, feeling my victory drain away.

"Yes!"

"Gods damn him!" I cursed. I was finished here and yet I still had not found my peace. "From which direction?"

"Behind us. The gated door where we entered, I think."

"There is a second exit. Come quickly."

Without pausing to clean my former tormentor's blood from my dagger or hands, I went through the banquet room and back into the hall. Nyx was close behind me, bow in his hands and makeshift pack of supplies on his back. I turned down the opposing hallway, away from Bennic and the dead soldiers. A rabbit never had fewer than two hiding holes. Caspon was the same. However, I was unsure of where the second exit was; I did not know where to find it underground.

The muffled sound of men's voices echoed down the hallway. I recognized Talros and my skin crawled over my bones. How could he know everything? I swallowed a snarl and pushed onward. We ran, feet soft and quick on the floor, footsteps swallowed by the packed soil walls. We sprinted like the demons of Énas were after us, thirsting for blood.

I had come all this way, done all these things. Was I to die under the ground like a rat in a hole? After everything I had accomplished? My heart screamed no, but my mind whispered that perhaps this was fate. My retaliation was complete, my home and family avenged. Perhaps Lenos, in her wolfish, god-bright mind, had chosen this as my end. Perhaps the death of Caspon was the purpose for which I had been born. Even as I thought it, I disabused myself of the notion. I had been a pawn for long enough!

I turned left at a junction in the dark hallway, feeling the floor angle upwards under my pounding feet. Every third lantern was lit, shrouding parts of the walls in thick shadows. I could hear the heavier footsteps of boots behind us, and the clanking of chainmail and sword belts. We had to hurry.

I ran faster, feeling my heart thunder behind my ribs. I did not know where I was going. All I could hope for was a break in the wall, a door, a hole, anything that would help us hide or escape. Damn Talros to the Plains for his persistence! I could hear them now, closing in on us. Where was there to go? Where was that gods-damned exit?

"Assassin!" Talros bellowed, his booming voice echoing down the hall. "I can be merciful!"

He could be, I was certain, but he would not. I had escaped too many times, raised his ire once too much. The only mercy I would have would be a knife to the heart. Nyx might not be so lucky. I urged my companion onward, feeling fear well up in my throat. A knife, thrown from behind, skimmed off the edge of my belt.

"Damn!" I hissed in horror, skittering sideways across the hall. I bumped into Nyx as another blade struck sparks at his feet. He coiled away like a serpent and disappeared into a shadowed niche. Scant heartbeats later, his hand struck out and grabbed me by the wrist.

"Ladder," he whispered, tugging me into the blackness between lanterns. I followed him swiftly, spinning in the notion of gods and fate. Up we went, scarcely pausing for breath. Nyx hesitated for half a moment at the end of the new, smooth, ash wood ladder to shoulder aside a disk of ironwood barring the hole above.

I pushed him through with one hand, wrapping a leg around the bars for leverage. We emerged into a copse of trees. Through them, I could see a glimpse of meadow. We were out of Benthol, and past the meadow there were only small, scattered villages and vast, deep forest. If Nyx and I could escape the copse and make it beyond the meadow, we might have a chance at safety.

"Bird," Nyx said. "We're outside the wall." He pointed and I followed the motion. Beyond the trees loomed the great stone wall of Benthol and, rising above it, smoke and flames painted the night sky. "By all that's holy," he breathed, "you can see that for miles."

"And we should," I answered, dragging him away by a sleeve. I wanted to be gone from here, as far away as possible. This place of men held nothing but death and sorrow. I wanted my freedom, my life, and nothing but the silent whispers of the trees. That desire drove me.

We had nearly made it to the limits of the copse when a thrown dagger caught me in the arm, spinning me off balance. I struck a tree, stumbled, and instantly righted myself. One hand, still holding my dagger, clutched at my bleeding arm. Nyx twisted on his heel, planting himself in the dappled shadows several feet behind me. Even now, at the very limits of our flight, he would not leave me. I did not know whether to curse or praise this strange loyalty I somehow inspired.

I turned around and saw we were outnumbered. General Talros and two soldiers stood with us in the copse.

"Talros," I said with a calm I did not feel. "So you still come, trailing at my heels like a hound lost in scent."

"Assassin," Talros said, voice rough. Two of his soldiers flanked him. I wondered if there were more in the trees, then thought not. They could not have known about that exit. It was three grown men against two younglings. Despite my skills, I was not confident.

"Five men are dead below, assassin. You have been busy." He held his position just beyond the hole in the earth from whence we had so recently emerged. The scattered trees surrounded us, saplings and spears dotting the land between. The trees here were too narrow to hide behind, too weak to climb. All around me, the darkness of the young copse whispered in their wordless voices.

"I did what was necessary," I answered. "The guards were in my way. The others, Lorcen Caspon and Bennic Davlov, I was happy to kill and I would do so again if given the chance."

"Lorcen Caspon, Guildmaster of South Benthol," Talros said, nodding. "It was as I thought, then. He has been of special interest to me these past months. You killed him quite thoroughly."

"He can answer no questions for you now," I replied, feeling the edge of my dagger in the palm of my hand. I shifted it quickly, readying the weight in my fingers.

"He was your target?" Talros asked, taking one step forward. I matched it, moving sideways, and he instantly stilled.

"Yes," I answered. "Since the very beginning."

"Your master," he said. "I see."

"You cannot," I said roughly. "He was master to a slave, to a thing he thought beaten down and trod underneath his foot. No mind, no voice, no heart. Nothing." Ever so slightly, I turned my head and spoke in Anilo. "Nyx, take three slow steps left. Carefully."

Talros started. "What did you say?" he snapped.

Nyx, behind me and hidden in the shadow of the wood, moved thrice, lithe, just as I had taught him. The men did not even notice.

Again, I spoke to Nyx in Anilo "Move again. Four steps. Make a little noise this time."

"Bird," he answered haltingly in the language he had just recently learned. "What are you doing? Are you hurt much?"

"Later," I replied. "When I say, kill the man on the left."

"That is enough!" Talros roared. "Next time a knife will come."

Nyx moved. Twigs cracked underfoot and the soldiers' eyes all turned to him. I took the chance and sprang. I was almost too slow, for a knife skipped across the small of my back, raising a trail of fire that I had no choice but to ignore. I dipped and rolled, coming to a stop about seven feet from General Talros' right-side man. I was at an angle to the rathole of Caspon's lair. Nyx, far behind me in the depth of the copse, stood silent.

"Stop!" I cried, raising the little bag from my belt as high as I could, leaving my bleeding arm, the one the thrown dagger had stung, numb and loose. "General, do you know what this is? It is firedust, and this small pouch is enough to incinerate this entire grove."

"You dare not," the right-side soldier whispered.

"Oh, I do dare," I said, grinning ruefully. "Either you kill me here or you take me captive and I suffer a far worse fate. I have no other options. Let the boy go, and I will—"

"Bird!" Nyx cried.

"I will hand you the pouch and go with you, General, without protest."

"You lie," Talros said. "Why would you do such a thing?"

"Those reasons are mine alone. Do you accept my offer?"

Talros held my eyes with his. I could almost see the thoughts swirling behind them. I did not know what he would do. I had no plans. I was making everything up as I went along. *Gods grant me a swift mind and a swifter hand!*

"What if I said I did not believe your ruse, assassin? You offer no proof of that pouch's contents and I do not see why you would flee only to stop now, to *die* now. Come quietly, answer my questions, and I will see to it that you are granted some form of clemency."

He thought he was calling my bluff, but oh, no bluff was this. "Clemency?" I asked, my eyes trailing over each of the three men, hunting for weaknesses. The right-side man, the closest to me, shivered as I looked at him. The left's eyes would not meet mine for more than a heartbeat. Only Talros stood firm. "Your clemency would be a long rope and a sudden drop in the square, or four horses at my limbs. No, General. I will take my version of mercy to yours."

"You are old for your years, Nightingale," Talros said, "but you have much to learn." He struck, so swift for a man his size. For a *cardea*. He came at me across the copse, having to move in front of his right-hand man because of the angle I had chosen.

"Nyx!" I cried, and an arrow took the man on the left in the chest. A second followed, striking the wavering soldier at the base of his throat. He toppled like a tree.

Talros leapt toward me as I whipped my injured arm outward, sending my old dagger spinning toward the general's accomplice. It stuck in his eye like a splinter, despite the wavering in my aim. The screams were horrible, but I had no choice but to leave him for Nyx to finish.

I circled around, keeping Talros' attention on me so he would not become occupied with Nyx. "It is you who must learn," I hissed at the tall, solid man fixated on my immediate capture. "Young though I might look, I am not a child." As I snatched one of the spent throwing daggers from the dirt with one hand and clutched the pouch of firedust with the other, I crept sideways, planting my feet with careful precision.

With snakelike speed, he whipped a knife at me, scoring a line across my shoulder. I ducked, wove my way back amongst the slender trunks, and taunted him. Anger was my weapon. Caution withered before it. "I killed Caspon, Talros. I admit it. Will your king believe that a girl of seventeen is the infamous Nightingale? Doubtful."

"He knows already, assassin," Talros countered. "I am ordered to bring your corpse to Dernwellen. Your friend, on the other hand, was given no such choice. It's capture for him. And you will not be there to save him from the crowds once more."

Likely that was true, and I understood that Talros was turning my weapon against me. I vowed it would not matter what he said. I had the semblance of a plan and it was in motion. I kept moving around and amongst the slender trees, dodging Talros' swift knives. Soon he would have none, I knew. The sword would emerge once they were spent. He had not the time for his bow.

I was bleeding heavily now; the arrow wound under my collarbone ached and leaked, and scores of cuts wept crimson through my clothes.

"What will they say," I asked, "when the mighty General Talros brings back this bloody and damaged body? A vicious battle it must have been, man against girl?"

I ducked a knife; the blade cut a path through my hair, whisking across my scalp. I stepped back, feeling a rotten branch crack underfoot, and just for a moment I was off-balance. Talros leapt forward like a panther, pressing me into the dirt not five feet from the trap door. His shoulder caught me in the chest, driving the air from my lungs.

"They will say I've bested the Nightingale!" he snarled, pressing a forearm down across my windpipe. I gasped, struggling for breath, trying to stab at Talros with my knife while straining to keep the firedust from his grasp.

An arrow thudded inches from where Talros' elbow stabbed the matted floor, too close to my head. Nyx was trying to stop the general, but he was still an amateur archer. He was as likely to hit me as Talros. I sucked in a breath, the last I would draw. "Nyx!" I cried. "In the hole!"

And with a flick of my wrist, I flung the firedust high.

In an instant I was free, Talros' weight vanishing as he clambered upward to try and catch the pouch before it hit the dirt. I could hear him yelling wordlessly, arms outstretched, as I struggled to draw a breath through my bruised throat. A hard man to kill, but I had tried. He was uncanny, dangerous, but he had not won. I would not go with him alive and be paraded before the kingdom, and then die a nightmarish death. In the end, I was the one who chose my destruction. I went to my knees, feeling the pain of the fight in my battered body, and smiled.

In that final twilight, there was light and heat and pain, but I had won. Caspon had been vanquished, my home and family avenged. I had outlived my tormentor, destroyed his maps and charts that led to hidden races. I had scores of regrets, but I would meet those I had killed beyond the veil of death, and tell them of my sorrow. I hoped for some forgiveness.

Something grabbed me, tussled me from peace and acceptance. My knees dragged in the dirt. My arms screamed in their sockets as warm hands hauled on my bones with panic-driven force.

Darkness enclosed me, swallowing my screaming body, and I fell.

The black night was endless.

Chapter 23

I WOKE UP, HEAD THROBBING, and knew I was dead. It was strange, though; I had thought death would be more peaceful, quieter. The voice would not stop yammering in my ear. Rough hands would not stop tugging at my clothes.

"Wake up, please. Wake up, wake up, wake up!"

I groaned, shifting away from the noise, but that made things worse.

"Bird, you're alive!" The sound was too loud in my aching head.

Nyx, I recalled. Was he dead as well? No, it could not be! My eyes flew open and I gasped at the pain. The ground beneath me rolled as my vision blurred. "Nyx!" I groaned.

"I'm here. I'm fine," he said. "We're both alive."

Alive. I had not dared to dream it possible. "Talros?" I asked, body aching. "What of him and his men?" My head pounded, my limbs were limp and weak, and I could not see straight. How had I not died?

"They're dead. Half the grove is destroyed."

I breathed deep, relieved and free for the first time in ages. I had won. Against both Caspon and Talros, I had emerged the victor. It was heady knowledge. But we were not finished yet. "Others will come," I whispered, my throat ragged, struggling to stand. "We need to hide the evidence."

"How?" Nyx asked. In the darkness of the hole, I could not see his face. I could hear the fatigue in his voice, and felt the same in my bones.

"I will know that once we go topside," I answered, standing and wobbling toward the ladder. The hole, I realized. Nyx had hauled me into the hole to save my life. That was twice now that he had saved me.

"How did you do it?" I asked, pressing my hands against the sharp pounding in my head.

He knew what I meant. "I don't know. I pulled you into the hole before the pouch came down, before Talros could even look at me. It was fear that made me fast. Or the hands of the gods. I don't know, and I don't think it matters."

No, it did not matter. I did not care. In either case, it had been an incredible feat. Even now, I only believed I lived because I could not ignore the painful cuts and burns across my body.

The ladder sprouted splinters under my hands as I climbed. The smell of smoke and burnt hair greeted me as the wind caressed my face. The trees smoldered but there was no fire in sight. With a flash, a bang, and a burst of heat, the firedust had worked its magic. Talros and his men lay on the ground, and there was no need to check their pulses to be certain. There was nothing. They were pieces, empty broken shells of men scattered across the grove. I wanted my howl my triumph to the skies like a wolf, but refrained.

"We need to burn them," I said, crouching beside part of Talros and patting his charred pockets for coin. "Drag what you can over there beside the hole." My hands slipped under the edge of Talros' tunic and found four gold pieces and six silver.

"Burn them," Nyx repeated. "That is . . . Are you sure?"

"Yes," I replied, attaching Talros' pouch to my belt. It could be useful later. "The guards must think we are dead. They must think that these two ruined bodies are ours. We will leave Talros as he is since his insignia is recongnizable. He will be our proof." General Talros could not die without fulfilling his mission, or so the king and his Weapons would have everyone believe.

I began to gather fabric from the two soldiers who had come with General Talros. They needed to be naked, free of any identifying marks or tokens of rank or profession. Both were male, but once the fire did its job, I did not think it would matter much. As it was, there was not much left to indentify.

"I will finish this," I told Nyx, noting the green tinge of his face and the trembling of his hands. "Get some lantern oil from below. There was some in the study." He needed a respite from the horrors of the day.

Nyx swallowed and said nothing, but hurried below as my hands worked on the soldiers' clothes. It did not take him long to bring up the lantern from Caspon's study and hand it to me. I opened the base over the two corpses as Nyx watched amber oil splatter the bodies.

"You do not have to watch," I said. I retrieved a dagger and the spent arrows from one of the bodies and handed them to Nyx. When he turned his back, I could not blame him. I removed the flint and striker from my pouch, feeling the weight of them in my hands, and struck sparks onto the oil-slick skin. The flames caught immediately. I threw a few large branches onto the corpses for good measure. The bodies were already burned and broken, black and red and ruined, but I had to make sure. No one could think the halfbloods were still alive. We had to be well and truly dead.

The fire raged, licking hungrily at the lantern fuel. Black smoke curled high into the branches. I went and closed the hidden door, kicking brush and dirt over the hinges and frame. Caspon would never be found. His body would rot alone in the darkness. It was what I wished.

"Are we going to wait until the end?" Nyx whispered.

I looked at the blackened, shrinking bodies and the dancing flames. "No." I set my own dark dagger near the bodies, placing my quiver beside it. "There, some proof now." The objects were not close enough, hopefully, to burn to ash. The dagger might char, the quiver smolder, but people would see the signs of my death in that.

For all intents and purposes, the Nightingale and the halfblood boy were dead and gone, soon to be all but forgotten. That was what I wanted.

"Let us go," I said. "And hurry."

We fled to the west and hid in the deep forest until nightfall. We would travel by night and hide by day, at least until we were beyond the border of Caesia. In the limbs of an ancient oak, I plastered our new wounds with burdock and marigold, hoping to stave off pain and infection.

Nyx sighed in relief as I placed a burdock leaf on a firedust burn on his arm. "So you want to know what I did?"

"What did you do?" I asked, playing along.

"I took a map from that room before it burned."

That piqued my interest. "You got one?"

He bent and slid a folded piece of parchment from his boot. "I thought one was better than nothing. I would have told you in the temple, but you were in and out of consciousness for most of the time."

I took it from him, holding the map with careful hands. "Anthehomes," I breathed. "You *have* done it."

Nyx smiled. "Good. Are there any you know on there?"

I looked at the faded, smudged script. "Havosiherim," I said. "And Nhoternis. There are two more, but I do not recall them." Carfuinel was on there, too, the name carefully etched through with a line of ink. I folded the map and handed it back to Nyx, putting Carfuinel out of my mind. It was dead, gone. Nothing I could do would bring it back. It was time to let go.

In the morning, we scavenged for food in the woods. As the weeks passed, as we moved farther from Benthol, through thatched villages, over broken terrain, and across swampy ground, we hunted for rabbits and grouse in fields and stole young lambs and sleeping chickens from the barnyards. I kept our wounds tended with herbs, and we often climbed through the trees to avoid bandits and highwaymen and travelers. We did this for weeks and that constant running took its toll. We grew tired and, although our bruises and wounds faded and healed, our bones ached with the toil of relentless movement.

Those weeks grew into months, and in those months of constant, weary travel, the air grew colder. Autumn slipped into winter and we were still on the run through unfamiliar ground. The wide, old oaks of the south thinned into slips of birch and aspen and fir as we moved north. The hills grew stony and steep, and the wildlife grew infrequent. Roe deer, spade-footed rabbits, and sleek groundhogs, which had once been abundant, began to evade our traps and arrows. At night, our breath frosted in the air and gooseflesh rose on our skin.

I hunted and Nyx gathered, but it was not enough. Food was scarce and the branches were denuded of leaves. The brisk air chilled our skin at night; in the day, we shivered under the cloud-filmed sun. Our clothes were not meant for this weather and there had not been an opportunity to steal or buy more. Talros' coin had been spent on herbs, bandages, fruit, and tunics that had long since been eaten or worn through. Coats had been hard to find but I had managed two, and they were not heavy enough for the growing chill as we traveled north.

"We have to have clothes," I said one morning. The night had been brutal, and both of us had shivered without sleeping. The morning dawned with some warmth, and our gooseflesh had subsided. We peered from the scrub-covered rise to the farmhouse below. There were clothes on a line in the side yard.

"I know," Nyx agreed, pressing a hand to his growling belly. "We need lots of things."

"Watch me and be careful," I whispered, then slunk down the hill to the house. I stopped crouched in the lee of the barn, hidden beyond the woodpile and the edge of the rough-hewn fence. I wrapped my arms tight around my body, trying to contain the last bits of warmth my skin sustained. Beside me, Nyx shivered. We were still in Caesia, running from death and fate, and hiding like rabbits in the burrow. But we were close to the border. Then, sure freedom: if we lived that long.

Autumn was in full force, the sky full of low clouds, but no snow had fallen. A blessing, I thought. Snow might prove more powerful than Talros; it might do the job that he had not been able to accomplish. Nyx pressed against me, searching heat, and I shared what I could. My stomach protested my priorities. *Food, food, food*, it cried, and I watched the farmstead hungrily.

The farmer came out with his wife. She clutched a milk pail, he a halter for the horse in the barn. I touched Nyx's knee and motioned him for silence. The wife was talking, her lips moving swiftly, and soon her words reached my ears. At first, the husband, a dark hulk of a man, ignored her gossip. The name of Astin Talros was mentioned, and when I heard that I shrank back against the wood, wanting to slither under the pile, and listened.

Three bodies had been found in the grove several months ago, the woman said, burned beyond recognition. Talros had only been identified because of the ranking chain around his neck, under the disintegrating remains of his tunic. The two bodies with him had been roundly confirmed as the assassin and her accomplice.

The two corpses had been smashed into dust and scattered on the waters of a swift-moving river, a common ritual to prevent the resurrection of demons. There had been no identifiers on the bodies, no tell-tale remains of clothes or hair. Two things had been found at the charred site outside the walls: a dark dagger with a bird marking on the hilt and a quiver still half-full of black-fletched arrows. The Nightingale. Both were singed crisp and marred with soot. This was proof, surely, that the demons were dead. The people believed it, and sang Talros' praises that he had sacrificed himself to save the kingdom. He had been given a hero's burial, complete with a parade of weeping women and stalwart, armored men. The general's body was now interred under the foundation of the very statue that would commemorate his achievement.

Dernwellen was too far for such information to have come firsthand, I thought, though I was hoping that this tale had not been marred in the telling. I wanted it to be true; I wanted Nyx and me to be dead to the world. For in this, death was freedom. In death, we would not be hunted.

Talros had failed his mission. I was alive, as was Nyx.

But for how long?

The cold air brushed me, caressing my skin like a hand, and still I waited for something to tell me that my life was not real, that I had not truly survived. It was still a hard thing to believe.

We waited until the farmer saddled his horse and left, leaving his wife to milk the cows. She did not take long. Nyx and I slavered at the sight of the brimming pail disappearing back into the house.

"I will get the clothes," I whispered.

"I'll look in the barn for food," Nyx replied.

I ran to the line and snatched heavy shirts and socks, stuffing them into the front of my own worn tunic. The wool was damp from washing, but I clutched it to me with an arm. Glancing over, I saw Nyx rushing from the barn with a wooden pail. I caught his eye, nodded my head, and we raced back to the safety of the hill.

Once in the shadows of the brush, I dropped the load of clothes onto the dried leaves and divided them up: two pairs of woolen socks and two heavy deerskin shirts for each of us.

"Wet wool and buckskin will still hold heat," I said. "So put them on."

Nyx did not need to be told twice; he had already pulled the shirt on over his clothes and was sliding the socks on. I followed suit, feeling the toes of my boots pinch as the socks took most of the space. But I was warm, if only slightly.

"Eggs," Nyx said as I dressed, setting the bucket between us. We cracked the shells and drank them raw. It was enough to stifle the pangs in our stomachs. I would have to hunt again, and soon, but we needed to move. The farmwife would notice the missing clothes.

Snow fell after we entered a land of red stone and cliffs. At first we were grateful for the water it provided, but the severe cold tempered any thanks we had. Nyx and I were not dressed for cold such as this; I had forgotten the dark winters of my childhood in Carfuinel, having become too accustomed to the mild climate of the south, and neither of us had thought the journey would take this long. The stolen woolens worked well, but our travels soon wore them down. Nyx had the idea first, to stuff our fraying clothes with dead grasses to keep in the warmth. It worked, for a time.

One evening, we came across a cave in the red sandstone walls of a canyon.

"Smells like bear," Nyx hissed. "We should leave."

The rank, wild odor was strong. I could hear labored breathing. "It is hibernating," I whispered. "And we need food and warmth."

"Bird, no," Nyx gasped.

"Stay out here." I grasped a black-feathered arrow in one hand. There was no choice. I had to do this if we were to live. Meat and fur in one package; a fire in the cave, reflecting heat. I could not tolerate the thought of passing up this opportunity.

"Bird!" Nyx hissed in protest, but I was in the cave's mouth already.

I crept forward on silent feet, the arrow held ready. It was a small cave; I did not have to travel very far. In the back, a few feet beyond the sunlight, the bear slumbered. The small eyes were closed, the paws outstretched. I stared at the black claws and the furrows they had dug in the packed floor. I took a deep breath, held it, and lunged. The arrowhead punctured the eyelid, drove deep into the skull. The bear bellowed, flailed, claws striking at anything within range. I leapt back, pressed my back against the wall, and waited for the bear to die. It did not struggle long. The breath hissed from its nostrils as it sagged against the cave wall, then the creature slumped into a heap on the floor.

"Bird?"

"I am fine, Nyx. It is dead." I sighed in relief. I took the small knife from my boot and began to butcher the creature while Nyx gathered bits and pieces of wood and brush for a small fire. My knife was too small and it was difficult to cut through the layers of

Melissa Mickelsen

fur and skin and fat. Nyx had a small, wonderful fire burning at the mouth of the hollow before I had so much as skinned open the belly.

We pulled pieces of meat from the ribs and charred them on the coals, eating them as we worked. I cut and Nyx tugged, and eventually the skin came free. That night we slept in the safety of the stone, eating bear meat and scraping the fat off the hide.

"Do you know how to treat skins?" Nyx asked.

"No, I figured the cold would help keep it. If we wear it with the fur facing the inside, it might not be so bad," I answered, wiping my blade in the snow to rid it of clinging tissue.

"It will stink." Nyx wrinkled his nose.

"Better than freezing," I said. After cutting the heavy, grizzled pelt in half, we still had more than enough for both of us.

The morning sun eventually rose over the edges of the cliffs, painting the canyon with gold and red. Nyx and I huddled in our bearskins next to the fire and studied the map, our breath clouding in the air. We were close. So close to our destination. I was still worried, deep in my heart. Would they accept me? Had I come all this way for nothing?

Soon we left the bear carcass behind and continued our trek through the sandstone cliffs. I lost count of the days that passed. We wore the stinking skin as we plodded through the thigh-deep snows of the canyon. I was exhausted, weak from hunger. This land was too unfamiliar. I could not recognize the plants here, and had no idea what was edible and what was not. I had become violently ill the last time I attempted to forage and had not yet worked up the nerve to try again. Nyx, his hair now grown into an unruly brown mass, walked ahead of me, prodding the ground with a long stick to avoid any deep holes hidden beneath the crust of snow. He also kept talking, which annoyed me.

"Bird, where are we on the map?" He sounded breathless.

I wished he would call me something other than Bird, but I could not think of anything to suggest. "Halfway through the gorge," I answered for the fifth time that day.

"We should stop, I think."

"Probably."

But we would not, the both of us knew it. We would never get out of the canyon unless we continued on. This time, however, felt

301

different. The wind had stilled and the snow was packed more tightly underneath our feet. The ground angled upwards, and that was enough to buoy the heart. A wolf howled in the distance.

Nyx stumbled suddenly and I was too close to stop before tripping over him. I landed face-down in the snow, legs tangled and one arm twisted painfully underneath me. I was too tired to rise and Nyx seemed to be in the same predicament. How long we lay in the snow, I cannot recall, but I remember hands lifting us and voices in my ears. My first instinct was to fight, and I thrashed, clawing and biting and calling for Nyx. A hand passed over my face, pressing a scented cloth against my nostrils, and I fainted.

I awoke with a start but stayed still and quiet, taking in my surroundings. Stone overhead, reflecting firelight. Quiet voices, movement, and the overwhelming scent of meaty broth. I was wrapped in blankets on top of a woven sleeping mat. I twisted, turning my head to see what lay in other parts of the recess.

"So you are awake," a man's voice said in Anilo, which confused me. I sat up abruptly, ready to attack, but the sudden rush of blood to my head staved off my reaction. "Careful," the voice continued. "You are weak."

"Who are you?" I groaned, cracking open my eyes. I froze when I saw him.

"Lysanti Redthorn," the anthela answered, placing a hand on his heart and inclining his head toward me. It was a gesture of greeting and respect that I faintly remembered. I returned it, noticing that my hand was bandaged. "It is not frostbitten," Lysanti said, following my line of sight. "It must have been scratched when you fell."

"Where is Nyx?" I asked, not knowing if the anthela was trustworthy. So many people were not.

"Eating. Do you—"

"Where?" I interrupted, and then wished I had not. I wanted to make a decent impression on this new person and was not going about it well. "Forgive me. I forget my manners."

"Forgiven," Lysanti said gently. "Shall we join young Nyx?"

I did not want the anthela's help to rise, but found it was necessary. However, under my own power I walked carefully to the fireside where Nyx was slurping happily on a bowl of hot broth. "Bird!" he cried when he saw me. "They have excellent food here."

"So I see." I sat next to him on the padded blanket and gratefully took the proffered bowl ladled out by a woman dressed in hunting leathers. Lysanti took a seat nearby, waiting quietly as we ate. When I had finished my bowl, feeling the delicious warmth in my stomach, he spoke.

"This is a long and dangerous way for two children to come alone. Where are you from?"

I glanced at Nyx, telling him with my gaze to let me speak. "We have escaped from the *cardea* kingdom," I answered, turning my eyes back to dark-haired Lysanti. I thought of my father when I saw him. Even so, there was danger here. Nyx and I were halfbloods, undisguised and unprotected. I did not like the position I found myself in and, feeling the thrum of the blood in my veins, resolved to tread with caution in these murky waters.

"Caesia?" he repeated. "You lived amongst the *cardea*?"

"Not willingly," I replied, looking at him. "You can see what we are. Halfbloods are not tolerated there." I watched Lysanti's face as I answered, seeking disgust or curiosity or fear, but there was nothing. A blank slate, this man was, even to the depths of his eyes. I did not like that I could not read him. It made me uneasy.

"We stayed in hiding," Nyx broke in.

"How did two halfbloods come to reside in Caesia?" the older anthela asked, no trace of revulsion in his voice, as he motioned for the woman to fill our bowls again. "I can see that you are not related."

"We are not, and it is a long story," I stalled, feeling strangely lost. I did not know how to tread here. *They can do nothing but put me out*, I thought, hoping to stir up the dredges of my strength. *I can survive that, surely.*

"I have time," Lysanti answered.

I turned to Nyx and swallowed, feeling the broth curdle in my stomach. There was every chance I would be turned out into the cold again. These people would hate what I had done. They would fear me and my proclivity for death. "Nyx, tell him your story."

He nodded, perhaps sensing my fear, and cleared his throat. He introduced himself as I had taught him, so long ago. "I am Nyx

Devos," he said, placing his fist on his chest and inclining his head. And that was as far as he got, for Lysanti's eyes went wide.

"Devos, you say? Do you know your mother's name?"

"My father told me it was Arennile, before he died," Nyx answered, watching Lysanti curiously.

I thought it odd the way Lysanti phrased that last question, so I watched carefully. When Nyx spoke the name, a change came over the anthela's face. Heartache, joy, and relief warred for dominance.

"You knew her?" I asked.

"Yes. Arennile Redthorn, wife of Benjamin Devos, was my sister." Lysanti reached out and took a stunned Nyx by the hand. "You are welcome here, nephew." There were tears in his eyes. "You must tell me what happened after your father left."

The room had stilled. There was no sound. Everyone wanted to hear Nyx's story. My friend had never had such a large and attentive audience before, and although he was somewhat overwhelmed, he spoke smoothly and with charisma. I knew I was seeing something great in the making. I touched him on the knee when he finished, and he smiled when he looked at me.

"You did very well," I whispered, noting the combined brightness in his eyes of unshed tears and excitement. He squeezed my hand in return before I took it back. Taking another sip of broth, I hoped I was forgotten. I did not want to be noticed now, perhaps not ever. Though I was happy for Nyx, I was terrified for myself.

Eventually, Lysanti turned back to me and I knew my fears would be realized. "And you, now," he said, and I was terrified of the crowd that had gathered around us, drawn in and held by Nyx's tale.

I took a breath, trying to still my trembling body. "I am . . . I. . ." To speak aloud a name that had vanished was to call back ghosts. I took another breath, feeling the eyes of Lysanti and every other anthela in the cave on me, heavy as stone. Nyx touched my arm, giving me his strength. "I am Tylidae Teriel of Carfuinel, and I was the Nightingale," I said with surprising fortitude. *There. Done. Judge me as you will.*

"The stolen daughter," Lysanti breathed. "We know of you."

"Taken by *cardeai* from a place of death," the woman near the soup pot whispered.

"Slaughterer," hissed another.

"No," Lysanti said, breaking the spell. "The child cannot know what she has done."

"I am no child," I said, rising to my feet. "I have not been since Carfuinel burned. I know what I did, every instance of it, but it was against my will. The man had a green stone, and it commanded me. I will make no more excuses."

"You speak well for one so young," the woman said. "We anthela know that stone is myth. Your *cardea* master taught you our legends well."

"It is no myth," I said, hands clenching at my sides. "It was real, and it burned to the touch."

"Myths do not matter," a man said, dressed in tracker's clothes. He ignored the melting snow on his boots as he crossed the floor toward me. "You are a murderer nonetheless and we will not allow your kind here!"

There was malice in his eyes and revulsion in the set of his features. He came at me with his teeth bared and I could not stop myself. I reached for my bootknife and found it missing. My eyes searched for a dagger, an arrow, for something to defend myself. *Hurt him and any chance is gone*, my heart whispered, but I had already known that. *Kill him and more than that is forfeit.*

Now Nyx bounded to his feet. "She saved my life!" he cried, shocking the cave into silence. "They were going to hang me in the square, but Bird risked her life for me, without knowing anything about me. In a crowd of a thousand *cardeai*, Bird freed me from the gallows, nearly dying in the process." He looked at Lysanti with eyes like slate. "If you send her away, I am going, too." He raised his chin and gripped the table with white knuckles.

The angry man halted in his tracks, close enough for me to see the curl of damp hair at his temple, to see the melting snow in his eyelashes. I held the man's eyes, waiting for him to move.

Lysanti nodded, almost to himself. "You said you *were* the Nightingale, young Tylidae."

"I did," I answered, heartened by Nyx's spiel, although the last thing I wanted for him was our previous state of homelessness. "And I renounce that title."

Lysanti waved my aggressor down and the man slunk unhappily back to the fire. "My newfound nephew is more than welcome in Havosiherim, so say I, but you, young Tylidae, are a more uncertain case. Despite the situation, you have murdered in cold blood. In any other circumstance, your life would be given to Énas immediately, but you have also brought me a lost relative, and for that you deserve some thanks."

I could feel my heart sinking. Death, if not for Nyx. A sigh rose in my chest and died there; I could not allow it to escape. There could be so sign of weakness, not now. A place to stay for a time was all I asked. A place to recover and heal and rest. A place where I would not be alone. Was that so much to ask? "I do not seek to live here," I said tonelessly, feeling the throb of my fear all the way to my fingertips. "I only ask for a place to rest for a time. If . . . when . . . it is better for me to leave, I promise to do so."

I waited, feeling Nyx's anguish beside me. We had come so far, he and I, but I knew life and fate would demand that we separate. The grief already pricked at my heart, a sour, sick knot in the back of my throat.

Lysanti looked around his small cave at all the anxious faces, then turned his eyes back to mine. "For a time, you may be welcomed in Havosiherim, Tylidae Teriel, despite the pain you have caused others. I am placing my trust in you, that you will obey our laws for the duration of your stay. Should you break that trust, or should you cause grievance or injury, you must leave Havosiherim or be driven out. In this, your young age will not matter. Do you accept?"

I did not want to do it. I wanted to keep my pride and dignity intact, but Nyx was looking at me with great, soulful eyes and the cold outside seemed too harsh to survive. I would not stay long, I vowed. Only enough to learn and grow to adulthood, if possible.

To myself, in that moment, I made a promise that one day I would find my own place. I would find people who would accept me.

I would find a place where I would no longer be alone, or feared, or hated, and where I could walk with my body undisguised.

"I will accept your provisions," I said to Lysanti, and made the clenched-fist gesture of respect against my collarbone. *Live and grow and learn*, I heard whispered in the pit of my heart. It seemed like a wolf howled in my mind, all words and sound and fury.

I was Lenos' charge, the god of wolves and steel and night, and I was a hard thing to break. Caspon had not done it; Talros had not done it; Lysanti certainly would not do it. I raised my chin and looked at them all, the faces watching me with haunted, judging eyes. I would stay here until I was ready, and then I would go out into the world of my own accord.

I would live a life that was *mine*.

Acknowledgments

I would like to thank Kim Vandervort, my editor, for polishing the rough places and encouraging me to improve and expand.

Thanks to my family, even though they did not really know how much I was writing until I told them the manuscript had been accepted. Thank you for being so excited.

To my husband, Jeff, thank you for believing in me.

And to all those at Elfwood, thank you for the positive words and for helping me understand that I just might be able to do this. Special thanks go to all those who have asked me about my book, time and time again. It's finally here! If you have any more questions, visit my website http://melissamickelsen.com.

About the Author

Melissa Mickelsen, raised in Georgia, began writing in high school as a way to relieve stress. In 2003, she graduated from the University of Georgia with a bachelor's degree in Art History. Through college and various jobs, she still wrote with no real intention of publishing, although the secret dream was there. Eventually, the encouragement of others led her to submit her first manuscript for publication.

Melissa is currently working toward her master's degree in technical writing and information design. Some of her favorite things include backpacking in the mountains, drawing, reading, and strawberries. Some of her least favorite things include spiders, ice, and scary basements. She lives in Germany with her Air Force husband and two cats.

CPSIA information can be obtained at www.ICGtesting.com
Printed in the USA
LVOW111748280212

270832LV00013B/56/P